I0788581

THE
FROST
AND
THE
FLAME

Also by C. J. Brightley

A Long-Forgotten Song:
Things Unseen
The Dragon's Tongue
The Beginning of Wisdom

Erdemen Honor:
The King's Sword
A Cold Wind
Honor's Heir

Fairy King:
A Fairy King
A Fairy Promise

The Wraith:
The Wraith and the Rose
The Shield and the Thorn

Other Works:
The Lord of Dreams
Twelve Days of (Faerie) Christmas
Heroes and Other Stories

THE FROST AND THE FLAME

C. J. BRIGHTLEY

Paperback ISBN 9798363631740
Hardback ISBN 9781954768086
Ebook ISBN 9781005427788
Ebook ASIN B0B1QXCNCZ

Published in the United States of America by Spring Song Press, LLC.

www.cjbrightley.com
www.springsongpress.com

Cover design by Kerry Jesberger of Aero Gallerie.

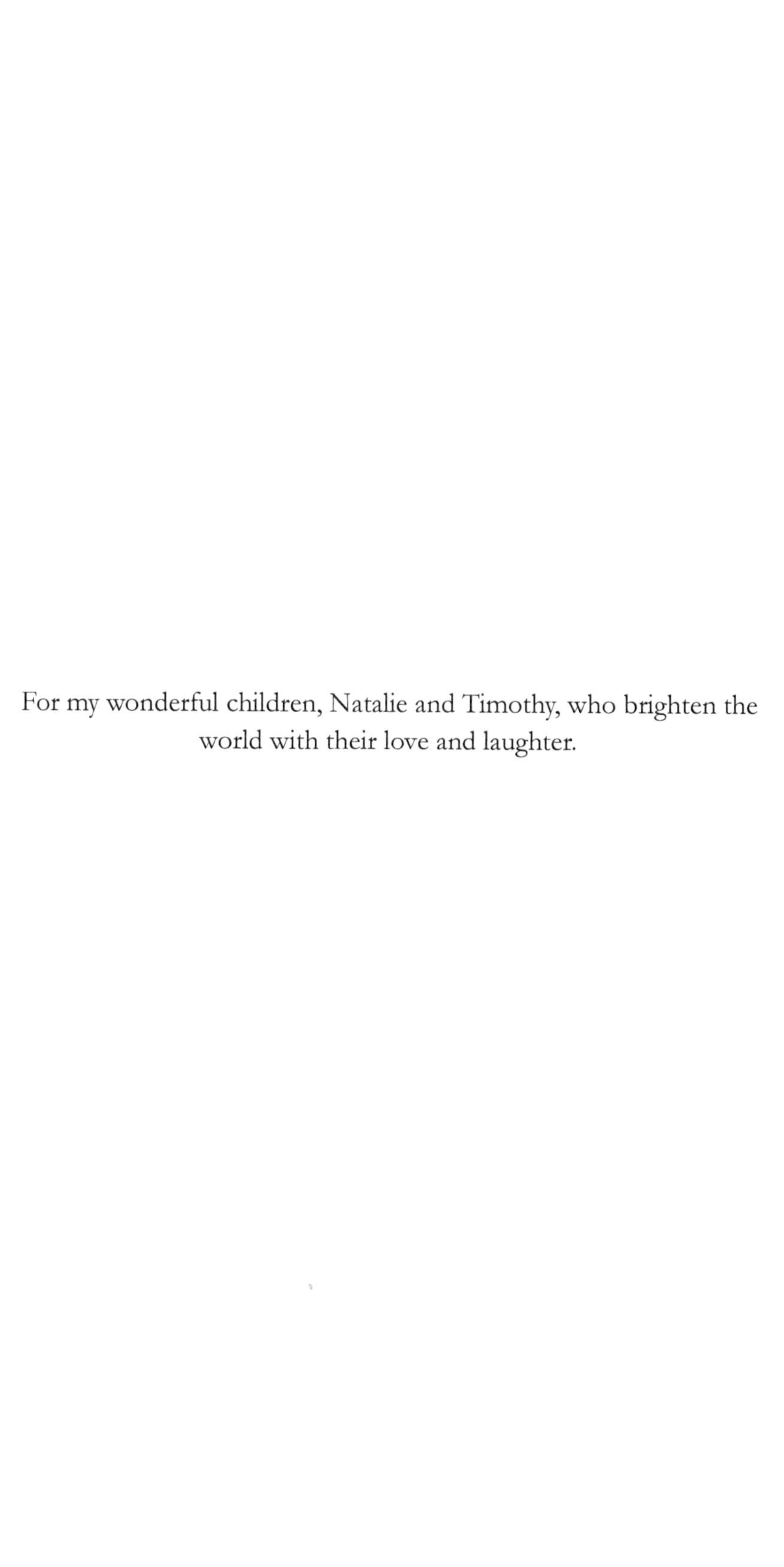

For my wonderful children, Natalie and Timothy, who brighten the world with their love and laughter.

ACKNOWLEDGMENTS

Many thanks to my wonderful friends Sarah, Suebee, Constance, and Janice, who offered encouragement, helpful feedback, and friendship throughout the writing and editing process. You are all delightful, and I am glad to have you as friends.

CHAPTER ONE
An Unwelcome Assignment

One of the servants knocked on the doorframe and said, "A note from His Majesty, my lord."

At Lord Ash Willowvale's curt nod, the servant bowed and stepped quietly into the study to proffer the paper, then retreated to the hallway.

The letter bore the seal of His Majesty Silverthorn, and the crown of silver thorns impressed into the wax glittered with magic.

Lord Willowvale snapped the seal open and read:

There has been no word from Brookbower's delegation in nearly three months. Extract them safely if you can. Leave immediately.

HRH Silverthorn

The Fair lord sighed and tapped the edge of the letter against his leg as he thought. Finally he took up the quill and wrote his reply.

Your Majesty,

My Arichtan is lamentably out of practice. Also, I promised Overton I would have tea with him tomorrow. Is there no one better suited to the task?

Willowvale

He sealed it and flicked his fingers just so, signaling the magic of the house that he wished a servant to attend him immediately.

"Yes, my lord?" The same servant, Alyssum, stood in the doorway.

"Deliver this to His Majesty."

Alyssum bowed and hurried off.

Willowvale sighed and crossed his arms. He slouched far down in his chair and leaned his head back with his eyes closed in an uncharacteristically vulnerable display of weariness. He did not want to go to Aricht. He did not, in fact, want to interact with anyone at the moment, especially not the snide Lord Brookbower, Marquess of Stormfield Heights. Certainly not the Arichtan court, which had every reason to be furious with the Fair Court, and, whether they knew it or not, with Willowvale himself.

He wanted nothing more than to stare at the glowing embers in the fireplace and eat dinner in silence and solitude.

Alyssum's knock on the doorframe came only five minutes later, when Willowvale had almost, but not quite, admitted to himself that he was looking forward to tea tomorrow with Theo Overton. The thought of a friend was not merely strange, but nearly unbelievable, and among both Fair Folk and humans, few people had more reason to dislike him than Overton did.

Nevertheless, tomorrow would be his fourth tea at the Overton manor in as many weeks, and Overton's invitation had been as sparklingly kind and inexplicably warm as ever.

At Willowvale's steady, pale gaze, Alyssum bowed and said, "He requires your presence at once, my lord."

The Fair lord hissed under his breath and stood. Two minutes later, he had buttoned a gorgeous silvery blue coat that set off his pale blue eyes and silver hair and began the short walk to the palace.

The servant who opened the door to him bowed and escorted him directly to the king's study, for Willowvale was a frequent visitor to the palace. His position at court required him to meet often with the king, and their long acquaintance, if not friendship, was the closest of which Willowvale had ever been able to boast. If they were not friends, they were at least colleagues, of a sort. Willowvale had never desired the throne itself, and his loyalty to the Fair Lands was unassailable; both these qualities had made him one of the few Fair lords the king had trusted throughout the crisis so recently brought to a close. Of course the king's word was law, and Willowvale was hardly equal to that, but he had influenced the king's decisions more than once with a quiet word or a thoughtful analysis.

With only a cursory bow, Willowvale faced his king. "Yes, Your Majesty?"

His Majesty Silverthorn gestured at the seat opposite him. "Sit." The king raised a glass of golden Fair wine, full of rich bubbling magic like the memory of sunlight. One of the servants poured Willowvale a similar glass.

The king stared at the Fair lord with narrowed eyes. "If Aricht thinks to punish Brookbower for the children, we will be forced to war again," he said at last.

Willowvale stared resentfully at the golden wine in his cup.

Silverthorn sighed and leaned forward. "There is no one else, Willowvale. I cannot trust Camphor or Aspen not to start a war while they're there, and Larch was the only other lord skilled enough with the veil to get there and back. If Brookbower is yet alive, he ought to be debriefed. It is long past time to recall him."

"As you wish, Your Majesty," Willowvale muttered.

The king's violet eyes rested on Willowvale's face with an odd intensity. "You were looking forward to tea with Overton."

Willowvale jerked one shoulder in a shrug. "He is amusing."

Silverthorn tilted his head. "Far be it from me to insist that you break a promise," he said mildly. "If you have promised him you will take tea with him, you ought to keep your word. Depart for Aricht after tea. Is it more efficient to travel to Aricht in the human world or through the veil?"

A strange sort of tension began to relax in Willowvale's shoulders. He swallowed. "The veil ought to be faster, but I doubt I have the skill to use it so. I will decide after tea. Perhaps it will be easier to tell from Overton's estate."

Silverthorn's eyes glinted with cool amusement. "He has not come to speak with me yet. Remind him of his position here, and my desire to converse with him."

Willowvale took a sip of his wine, finding it sweet and fresh, lighter than any human wine, and much preferable even to the very best he had tasted in Valestria. "I will."

Silverthorn sat back and sighed in satisfaction. "Even if there were another, I would still send you." At Willowvale's cold, steady look, the king said, "You are skilled at dealing with humans."

The Fair lord choked on his wine. He set down the cup, spilling a little, and doubled over as he coughed. Finally, flushed and breathless, he straightened to stare at the king.

Silverthorn blinked once and said, "Do you not agree?"

"I think you overestimate my competence in this matter, Your Majesty."

The king smiled slowly, sharp white teeth glinting, and said, "I hope not, Willowvale."

Snow drifted lazily down from the iron gray sky as Willowvale stalked back to his manor. It crunched beneath his boots and glinted upon his white curls. When he stepped inside, he let Alyssum take his coat and brushed the snow irritably from his hair.

"Pack me a bag for tomorrow. I'll be in the human world for a week or more."

"Yes, my lord. Who will attend you?"

"I'll go alone." It would be irritating to procure his own meals and lodging in Aricht, but the solitude would make the trouble worthwhile. Besides, it would be easier to extract Brookbower and the rest of his delegation by force, if necessary, without the additional logistical concerns of servants.

In the kitchen, Alyssum and Hemlock prepared a week's worth of food and drink, enchanting each meal so that it would be hot and fresh when Willowvale activated the magic. Tansy packed a week of clothes, which would be easily extended to last months, given the Fair lord's facility with both glamour, to change the appearance of the clothes, and the minor magic of freshening cloth without need of washing.

Willowvale sat before the fire with a cup of steaming butterscotch and vanilla tea, a gift from Theo Overton, and examined the record of Lord Linden Brookbower's diplomatic dispatches to the Fair throne. The last note had come by way of the Marquess Camphor, who had personally obtained the last two children from Aricht before… well, before that effort had been brought to a dramatic close by Theo Overton's confrontation with His Majesty Oak Silverthorn.

Anti-Fair sentiment grows by the day, and I fear we will be forced to war again, if some solution other than that currently being pursued cannot be devised. If the children's dancing is not effective, shall I pursue another option here? I await your direction.

With all due respect,
Linden Brookbower, Marquess in the Fair Lands

The delegation consisted of Brookbower himself, one personal servant named Cyprus Hawksbane, two administrative assistants named Cricket Fallingwater and Bramble Tarragon, and the security and intelligence specialist, Astrantia Berrydell.

Willowvale wrinkled his nose in disgust. Berrydell must be related to his aunt, Lady Orchid Berrydell, a most detestable Fair lady. She was even richer than Willowvale himself, though her connection to the king was only distant, and she would not dare approach the king to give her opinion as Willowvale did. Lady Orchid had assumed some five years before that, since Willowvale was yet unmarried, he must by all logic be waiting for her daughter Miss Dewdrop Berrydell to come of age.

If Willowvale had intended to marry, he could certainly have done worse than Miss Berrydell, for the young lady was beautiful and accomplished, as young Fair maidens of her status were expected to be. However, she had long since learned the subtle art of making snide insults with a straight face and wide, innocent eyes. How could she not learn this, after spending time with Lady Orchid?

Anyway, Willowvale had never intended to marry Miss Berrydell or anyone else. He was by nature solitary, and though he would not have admitted it, he had long known himself to be bitter and cold. Yet he was not so entirely remorseless that he wished to inflict his bitterness upon some otherwise happy maiden, to thereby ruin her life as well.

Miss Berrydell's assumption of her right to his name and money, bolstered by her mother's assumption of the same, had soured him not only on the idea of marriage to her, but any remaining hopes of marriage at all.

Still, this Miss Berrydell was not that Miss Berrydell. He felt a faint twinge of interest in Miss Astrantia Berrydell, for what sort of Berrydell would lower herself to work in the diplomatic delegation staff? Only the Ambassador himself held a position of respect within the Fair Court; the staff was only one step above the servants. Still, she must be competent, for Brookbower's security detail was an assignment of some responsibility. It was not so long since Aricht and the Fair Court had been at war.

Willowvale spread the map of the human world across the table and frowned. Ardmond, the Valestrian capital, was just over two hundred fifty miles from the Arichtan capital, Idosa. It would take well over a week to get there by land. Overton's manor was several miles outside of Ardmond in the opposite direction. Perhaps it would be easier to find the way through the veil after all.

He hated the veil. In recent weeks, when he had traveled to and from the Overton manor for tea, it had not made any serious attempts to kill him, and that was both reassuring and slightly terrifying, because the veil seemed to particularly enjoy catching him by surprise. This relatively peaceful interlude seemed likely to merely presage a more frightening, more painful, and possibly successful attempt when he had been lulled into complacency.

He flicked his fingers to call Alyssum, and when the servant appeared in the doorway a moment later, he said, "Make it two weeks of food."

"Yes, my lord."

He spent the rest of the afternoon and evening reading the accumulated dispatches from Brookbower describing the politics of the Arichtan court and the profiles of the Arichtan royalty and courtiers. Over dinner, which he took in the Iris Room, resplendent with irises of all shades and boasting a little pond with brilliant gold and indigo fish, he formulated his plan for his discussion with the Arichtan throne.

A Fair presence in Aricht was, of course, non-negotiable; after the war, surely Aricht would understand that, even if they did not like it. However, if Brookbower and his delegation had lost what little trust they might have once had, Silverthorn had given Willowvale leave to agree to instate a new ambassador with new staff. He had also authorized Willowvale to offer some explanation, albeit perfunctory, of the Fair throne's previous distress and the solution, which ought to reassure the Arichtan king, Valor Elmerick.

The Fair lord pushed his plate away and sat back, stretching his long, lean body before shoving his chair back and resting his elbows on his knees. He stared at the floor. With a little tickle of magic, he grew a vine, then another, which coiled around his legs.

He lifted the tip of one vine and twined it around one finger. With an experimental twist of magic, he made the vines grow thorns, which slid through the fine fabric of his trousers and deep into his skin. He hissed in pain and hesitated, then drove the thorns a little deeper.

He studied the magic in the vines, how it recoiled from the pain it produced. It did not recoil as strongly as it had when he had tormented Overton, but it did not enjoy causing pain, even to him. His nostrils flared with the effort of keeping his breath steady. The pain was actually quite remarkable, and the thorns were scarcely half as long as they had been by the time Overton had escaped him.

The Fair lord loosened his grip on the magic and let the vines slip away. Once the wounds were open, they bled freely, leaving damp stains upon his trousers. Willowvale stood, sucking in a sharp breath through his nose; he had known that the movement would hurt, but still, the sudden pain was startling in its intensity.

He hissed through his teeth. Was this regret? Was this what guilt felt like?

Could guilt and regret so easily be wiped away, by the administration of a little pain? He let out a bitter little chuckle. What a foolish idea! He wondered that it had tempted him. Not that he regretted the pain; it was fitting, after all.

With a flick of a finger, he indicated to the house that he was finished with dinner and that one of the servants should come fetch the dishes. He strode upstairs to his study. When he changed into his evening clothes, he flung his trousers into the bin to be repaired and bathed the pale blood from his calves with fresh spring water that flowed from the installation in the wall. The wounds were, truly, quite trivial compared to those which he had inflicted upon Overton.

Humans could be made of stern stuff indeed. Yet it was not only Overton's courage that had so shamed Willowvale, that had made his heart feel as if it were being turned inside out. It was the bright, pure, passionate love that met pain with anger but not hatred, and showed, with words and actions, that love was stronger than death.

Pale blue blood streaked his snowy white skin. He sat with his feet in the basin and watched the blue disappear into the water.

It would be some time before he could again enjoy the comforts of his beautiful home, a refuge in the political mach-inations of the Fair Court. To be sure, he was immune to much of the maneuvering and intrigue; his position was relatively secure. Still, Aricht would feel much like the vines, sharp irritations sliding through his skin to prick the tender, hidden parts, the little pieces of himself that he had never acknowledged or admitted existed.

He sighed and swished the water up onto his legs a final time, washing away the blood again. He blotted away the last of the blue and pulled on the soft, silken trousers in which he slept.

Like many fairies, he preferred to sleep in an elevated bed. His was a particularly luxurious example of the type, a wooden platform with a soft mattress and layers of silk blankets hanging from the crystalline ceiling and edged in fuchsia blooms that cascaded merrily down from all four corners to sway softly as the bed moved. With a flick of his fingers, the Fair lord lowered the lighting in the room.

Yet he did not sleep until nearly dawn, for a thousand unident-ifiable emotions kept him staring at the ceiling, which to his sharp sight glittered with the starlight reflected off the snow outside. The room was warm enough, but he felt cold inside. Cold and broken.

But there was something like the scent of spring in his heart even now, in the dead of winter.

It was so unfamiliar that he could not at first imagine what it might be, and it was only when he thought again of the warm butter-scotch and vanilla scent of Overton's tea that he realized what it was.

Hope.

CHAPTER TWO
An Unexpected Invitation

T he Fair sky gleamed gold and pink in the sunrise when Lord Willowvale opened a door to the veil the following morning. With one foot in the veil and one foot in the thin layer of snow atop the grass of his garden, he looked over his shoulder, drinking in the familiar resplendent beauty.

Then he stepped into the darkness of the veil and let the door close behind him.

He had to stand in the cool, dank tunnel for a minute to orient himself. Overton's sense of direction in the veil was uncanny; Willowvale was more gifted than most in the veil, and it still baffled and terrified him in equal measure. Not that he would admit to the terror.

There it was, the sense of the human world to the left and a little upward. The tunnels were unsteady, and Fair understanding was that they were actually passages in concept more than structure. They formed and reformed as the traveler moved, allowing or hindering his progress according to unknown and unknowable whims.

The veil had a personality, of sorts, though no one had been able to ascertain if it had a consciousness. It *liked* Overton, for lack of a better word; though it was still perilous for any human or fairy, it hindered his passage less and helped him more than anyone else ever known. The veil did not like Willowvale, and the feeling was entirely mutual.

So the Fair lord strode cautiously through the dark, always listening, for there were many dangerous creatures that lived in the tunnels. The ground suddenly shivered beneath him, and he nearly lost his footing. The motion ceased as abruptly as it had begun. Willowvale stepped softly forward. Was it his imagination, or was the veil amused by his fear?

He snarled inaudibly to himself and walked a little faster.

Between one moment and the next, the ground disappeared beneath his feet. For two heart-stopping seconds, he plummeted into nothingness, and then the floor met him with stunning force.

With a muttered oath, he flicked light to his fingertips for a moment. When no terrible creatures lunged at him, he let the light fade and clambered to his feet, bruised, shaken, and irritated. In the ominous silence, he could hear nothing but his own slightly tremulous breathing.

An hour later, he had climbed to the top of the steep slope before him to reach the path, which had changed course in the time he had been climbing. Breathless and furious at the veil and its many idiosyncrasies, he almost fell into another hole as soon as he started forward again. He hissed in frustration and turned into a nearby passageway.

It took four hours to get close to the human world, and another hour to reach the portion of the veil that would let him reach Ardmond. At long last, hungry and annoyed, he stepped out of the veil into the middle of one of the main thoroughfares of the Valestrian capital. A horse pulling a light carriage just to his left startled, and the coachman shouted in surprise. Willowvale snapped a sharp retort as he stepped aside, narrowly avoiding another carriage before he reached the side of the road.

The Fair lord had already glamoured his dirtied clothes to hide the evidence of his fall, and he had chosen human attire for the day.

He had not otherwise glamoured himself, and his cold, pale features and willowy stature marked him as a fairy, so he received more than a few unfriendly looks as he walked to the inn he knew best. There he hired a horse for the day, a high-stepping chestnut that tossed its head proudly.

He spent some minutes letting the animal become familiar with him before he mounted. Then it was off to the Overton estate with the winter wind in his face. Frost glittered on the grass at the edges of the road, and the patches of shade beneath the distant trees had remnants of snow from several days before.

Willowvale took a deep, bracing breath of the icy air.

What a pity that his visit to the Overton manor would be so short. He approached the drive with something like dread, for if he arrived, he would of necessity have to depart not much later, and the anticipation of tea with a friend—a friend!—would no longer give this unfamiliar light of hope to his day.

Still, he would enjoy the brief interlude fully, and he would admit to himself that he enjoyed it, for this one last time.

He was nearly late, for Overton had specified that he might arrive in time for lunch, if he were so inclined. He had been so inclined, and the veil had delayed him even longer than usual. The bare branches of the trees lining the drive to the Overton manor cast only the most delicate of shadows that danced in the breeze, and the brilliant sunshine glittered cheerfully upon the packed earth. He trotted up the drive, for it would not do to seem too hurried.

One of the grooms met him near the front door and took the reins of his horse. The Fair lord nodded to him and strode up the steps to the door.

The door opened immediately to his knock, and Anselm, the Overton butler and Theo Overton's manservant, welcomed him politely.

"He is waiting for you, my lord." Anselm led the fairy through the marble-floored entry hall and then through a hall to a bright, intimate dining room papered in an elegant, foliage-inspired print.

Willowvale was startled to see that Lord Fenton Selby and Miss Crocus Firethorn were present, along with Theo Overton and his wife,

Mrs. Lilybeth Overton. He hadn't seen Selby since the strange event just over a month ago in which Selby and Overton had nearly died, or should have died but wouldn't, for Overton's fierce, steadfast love of his friend had prevented it.

"Welcome, Lord Willowvale!" Theo sparkled at him in a way that had been utterly infuriating for most of their acquaintance. What *right* did a human have to smile at him so, as if he were a friend of humanity, and as if the world and everyone and everything in it were delightful?

And yet Willowvale felt the faint ghost of a smile cross his lips as he bowed to them each in turn. Not deeply, but still… the gesture had a sincerity it had not had when he had first come to the human world.

"Did you have any trouble getting here?" Theo asked, with every indication that the question was genuine.

"None worth mentioning." The fairy's cold, pale eyes flicked from Theo to broad-shouldered Fenton Selby, noting the easy strength in his erect posture and the warmth in his dark eyes. "You're well, I see." It was a statement, but there was the slightest hint of relief in the words, for Selby had been decidedly peaky when Willowvale had last seen him.

Selby's kind smile widened, and he said, "Yes, I am. Thank you."

Miss Firethorn bowed in the way of the Fair Folk, her blue eyes wide and cautious.

Mrs. Overton curtsied to him. She was remarkably lovely for a human woman, though he doubted most other Fair Folk would have agreed. Her beauty was quiet and steady, not striking. Her hair was medium brown, lustrous but not as rich as Selby's dark waves, and her blue-gray eyes were soft and gentle. Her figure was pleasing, but that was hardly remarkable; most women could achieve that with a well-fitted dress and a little glamour.

Still, she seemed to fit Theo. That fact had enraged Willowvale when he had first seen them together; now it sent a strange, melancholic pang of wistfulness through him. She had, after all, spoken kindly to him, though she neither liked nor trusted him, and he had used that to cause her beloved husband pain.

Theo, ever the delighted and gracious host, welcomed him to the table.

The food was delicious; humans as a species had a gift with food that the Fair Folk had always appreciated. Fairies had their own culinary delights, of course, and they took inspiration from human recipes at times, too. But the Fair Lands had fewer edible herbs and vegetables than the human world did. A great many plants were dangerous either by virtue of being toxic to the body or by flowing with magic which would dampen or otherwise disrupt a fairy's magic, and no fairy would be willing to sacrifice his magic for the sake of a particular flavor in a meal. Also, humans had what the Fair Folk described as a chaotic way of thinking, and this creative anarchy had resulted in a great many flavor combinations utterly incomprehensible to fairies. No fairy would ever have thought of covering pork with an orange glaze; when the dish had been put before Willowvale at a party the previous summer, he had been appalled and then shocked at how delicious the combination was.

Lunch was relatively simple. Tender herbed chicken breast stuffed with a creamy cheese sat beside roasted winter vegetables. On another little plate there was a flaky, buttery pastry of a kind Willowvale had not seen before. There were hothouse tomatoes tossed with fresh basil and a soft, mild cheese quite different than the other. Then there was a smooth, sweet custard topped with a crust of caramelized sugar.

Forgetting himself for a moment, Willowvale closed his eyes to savor the exotic luxury.

"Do you like it?" Theo's voice startled him.

The young man's smile was so bright and warm that the Fair lord's reflexive frown softened a little, even if no one could tell. Willowvale swallowed and gave a curt nod. "I do." The admission felt like weakness.

Selby smiled across the table at him. He pulled an envelope from his jacket pocket and slid it across the table. "You know Miss Firethorn and I are betrothed. The wedding is in two months, and we would be honored if you would attend."

Nothing, not even the gut-wrenching shock of seeing the apparently empty-headed Theo Overton caught in the vine trap laid for the Wraith, had ever bewildered Lord Ash Willowvale as much as this invitation.

The Fair lord stared at the envelope, then looked back up at Selby. The young man's dark eyes were alight with joy and an entirely unjustified warmth.

The fairy picked up the envelope between thumb and forefinger, as if it were something vile, or something dangerous. His name was written on the front, *Ash Willowvale, Marquess of Sparrowdell and the Willow River Valley*. "How did you know my title?" His voice sounded sharp and angry, for this felt like another vulnerability exposed. In actuality, there was little reason to fear that a human could use his title against him as a fairy could use his full name, for even then, the magic was not so easily manipulated that one's full name alone was dangerous. It took deeper knowledge and magic humans did not possess.

"Theo told me." Selby's smile did not waver at the Fair lord's tone.

Willowvale's gaze flicked to the smiling host for a split second. Curiouser and curiouser. The Wraith, for all his personal lack of magic, had several Fair allies; surely one of them might have been capable of using Willowvale's name against him, if Theo had asked it. The guilt that already weighed upon him seemed to twist in Willowvale's guts, tight and hard.

His fingers were pale as alabaster against the blue linen paper, as fine and lovely as its equivalent in the Fair lands, for all it lacked the magical seals that an invitation to a Fair wedding would have. No. He narrowed his eyes at the invitation. Selby's signature at the bottom had no magic, but Miss Firethorn's glittered with her personal magic, just enough to indicate her Fair lineage.

He swallowed, his face devoid of any expression other than his customary chilly unfriendliness. "Thank you for the invitation," he said stiffly. "I cannot say whether I will be able to attend."

Selby frowned and said, "I would be grieved if you could not attend. May I ask what might keep you away?"

"Why should you want me there?" Willowvale snapped. "My presence cannot but bring a cloud of unpleasant memories to an otherwise happy day. I offer my congratulations now." He stood and bowed sharply. "Good day."

The others stood in turn, and Selby said, "Wait, please, Willowvale. Have I offended you in some way? I did not intend to."

The fairy's jaw tensed, and he turned away, then hesitated. Selby did deserve an answer, however uncomfortable it was to voice. He swallowed again, considering his words. "I have been given a new assignment," he said at last. "I intend to complete it, but I doubt very much if I will be both free and alive when it is finished."

The words brought a sudden, shocked silence to the room, and the humans stared at him with suddenly grave expressions.

He huffed out a soft, furious breath and turned away again. "Never mind. I am glad for you. You deserve your happiness." He strode quickly from the room, his long legs carrying him down the hall and to the front door in moments.

"Wait!" the humans called out behind him, and he quickened his steps. He had not intended to reveal this to them, and he regretted it already.

Theo called out again, "Lord Willowvale, please wait!"

The fairy flung the door open and discovered with dismay that the groom, assuming the Fair lord would stay longer, had taken his horse to the stable to be given a little hay and water. The animal was not waiting for him as he had expected.

Theo reached him and caught his arm, and the fairy whirled to snap at him, "I don't want your compassion, Overton!"

The young man's eyes widened, and he said, with a hint of laughter in his voice, "What do you want then?"

Willowvale's chest heaved, and he snarled, "I don't know!"

"Come, my lord." Theo slung an arm around the fairy's lean, hard shoulders, as if they had been friends for years. "Let us walk in the garden. It is winter and the trees and bushes are bare and grim. Perhaps it will fit your mood and you will allow me to be the friend I thought I already was."

Willowvale found himself trembling, just a little, deep down inside, though he doubted the human could perceive it. He had, indeed, claimed Theo as a friend, and he had meant it at the time. Still, there was little for Theo to do in this situation, and the friendliest, kindest thing Willowvale might do for this human friend he did not deserve was to go away.

The door stood open behind them. Someone handed Theo a thick cloak, which he wrapped around Willowvale's stiff shoulders, and a second cloak, which he shrugged easily around his own shoulders.

The fairy let himself be shepherded down the wide marble steps and across the drive into the friendly little maze of hedges and topiaries closest to the house. He shrugged his shoulders irritably, and Theo let his arm fall away, though he otherwise stayed close. Physical contact was a strange feeling for the Fair lord, for there had been little of it of any sort throughout his life, and certainly none had ever been affectionate. Still, the cold that then seeped through the fabric into his skin felt more desolate after that brief touch of Theo's arm. Willowvale had witnessed Theo and Fenton helping each other in turns when they had been so terribly wounded in the Fair Lands, and Oliver and Cedar helping Theo before that, and though there was a pragmatic utility in their movements, there was also affection and compassion.

But affection and compassion were almost as alien to Willowvale as friendship itself, and it would have been easier to accept Theo's compassion if his wounds had been physical. He rolled his shoulders and scowled at the frost-covered pebbles of the path on which they walked.

Without speaking, Theo led him through the maze to a little sheltered enclave surrounded by rhododendrons that looked over a pond. He sat upon a white-painted wooden bench, and, with only a little hesitation, Willowvale threw himself onto the other end of the bench.

The silence drew out for several moments, until finally Theo said, "You seem troubled, my lord."

Willowvale gave a bitter little chuckle. "I suppose I am." He stretched his long legs out and slouched into the corner of the bench, feeling the bite of the cold wood through the seat of his trousers and the fabric of his jacket and the borrowed cloak. He sighed and stared at the water. By every measure, the Fair Lands were fairer and more beautiful than the human world. The Fair Folk were exquisitely lovely in every respect. Why then, did this view send a pang of something like longing through him?

The magic in the ground shifted uneasily beneath him, and he pressed back against it, feeling it recoil. Even the natural magic of the human world disliked him.

Could he blame it? If it loved Theo, as everyone did, it *ought* to hate him.

"Is there anything I can do, my friend?" Theo's voice was so kind that Willowvale closed his eyes and swallowed.

"I wouldn't want you to," he said quietly. "You've done more than enough, and at every turn have met my cruelty with kindness. I cannot ask anything more."

"May I ask what your assignment is? I cannot imagine what is so dangerous, now that your land is stable and the war is long over." Theo tilted his head, his bright eyes warm and curious.

The Fair lord let the silence draw out, pondering the question and what might happen if he answered. Finally he said, "The ambassador to Aricht, Lord Linden Brookbower, and his delegation have not reported to His Majesty Silverthorn in months. His Majesty suspects they have either been executed for their presumed role in the kidnappings of the Arichtan children, or perhaps they are merely being held captive. I am to ascertain what has happened to them and extract them if possible."

Theo raised his eyebrows. "That is a tall order."

Willowvale gave a faint huff. "I wish I had your skill with the veil. Your talent is uncanny."

The young man grinned. "Thank you, my lord. I can boast a little talent, but it would be dishonest not to admit that I have practiced a great deal."

"That is true." Willowvale couldn't help a melancholy chuckle. "Still, it is admirable."

Theo sat back and stretched out his legs in a pose similar to that of his companion. "My friend, much as my talent with the veil vexed you, I doubt it is what is troubling you so deeply now."

The fairy sighed, keeping his eyes on the water, but said nothing for several minutes. Finally he said, "It can do you no good for me to give you any detail. Let me be a friend for once, in the only way I know how, and keep you from charging into danger like the heroic idiot you are."

Theo blinked and turned a little toward him. "How will you get to Idosa? It is quite a long way from here."

The faint line between Willowvale's snowy brows deepened. "I will ask your advice on that," he conceded. "I doubt I can find the way in the veil, but the map I have of your world is sorely lacking in such details as roads passable over the mountains at this time of year. If I might purchase a map from you, I would be well pleased."

Theo studied the fairy's pale face for a moment. "I am grateful for your concern," he said at last, "though I wish it were not motivated by guilt. However, it is little hardship to escort you through the veil to Idosa, and it would be an honor to so help a friend. It would save you weeks of freezing travel. The mountains are difficult and dangerous at this time of year."

Willowvale said more testily, "I can hardly ask you to escort me through the veil."

Theo gave him a sparkling smile. "You didn't! I would be ashamed, though, if I had the ability to save you weeks of miserably cold travel and didn't offer, with great stubbornness, to so assist you."

The Fair lord sucked in a quick, irritated breath through his nose. "I don't *need* your help," he protested.

"I never said you did!" said Theo cheerfully. "I merely thought to save you some time and effort in the travel, so that you might be at your best when you go save your people."

Willowvale gave him a sharp look. "Don't paint me as a hero," he muttered. "You have no reason to think well of me."

Theo said, "My lord, you are in a wretched mood indeed. Perhaps the winter garden is not as beneficial as I had hoped, and quiet tea by the fire would suit you better."

The fairy laughed, soft and despairing. "I looked forward to coming," he admitted almost inaudibly. "Friendship is a balm to my soul I never thought to enjoy, and now I find that the thought of leaving makes me bitter, as if I would have been happier going to my death if I had never enjoyed friendship at all, for at least then I would not grieve what I had lost." He stood and turned his back to Theo to look back at the house. "Thank you, Overton. I have been sour indeed, and I did not intend to ruin your afternoon."

He pulled the cloak from his shoulders and held it out toward his host. The clear winter sunlight glinted on Theo's copper hair as he stood in turn.

"I'll manage on my own," the fairy said.

Theo shook his head, his hazel eyes as warm and kind as ever. "Please, Lord Willowvale, if you consider me a friend, let me help." He stepped forward and put a hand on the Fair lord's shoulder, as if they really were friends, and gave him a gentle shove toward the manor. "Come. Have some tea. We'll leave this evening or tomorrow morning, as it suits you."

"But…" Willowvale gave a shuddering sigh, saddened and relieved and furious and grateful in equal measure. "It cannot benefit you."

"It would grieve me deeply if I could not help a friend," said Theo.

"And we are friends," said Willowvale with a sense of finality and inevitability.

"We are!" Theo sparkled at him, as if their friendship brought him joy rather than grief.

The fairy laughed, low and quiet. "We are friends," he murmured to himself.

Without further protest, he walked with Theo back to the manor and through the halls to a casual, comfortable sitting room, where Mrs. Overton and the other guests were already enjoying tea and pastries. Selby and the young fairy Juniper Morel were engaged in a chess game with steaming tea cups near to hand, while Mrs. Overton and Miss Firethorn spoke quietly by the fire, books nearby but apparently having been set aside for the conversation.

Selby looked up first and stood politely. "Come join us, Willowvale," he said with a smile. The others stood and greeted him cautiously.

The Fair lord sat in a nearby chair to observe the game, his pale eyes sharp and his mouth tight. Juniper watched him warily from the corner of his eye.

"Tea?" Theo offered solicitously.

Willowvale blinked, then nodded. "Please," he said almost inaudibly.

Juniper stood, and Theo waved him away. "I'll do it." He poured steaming water over the tea, then said apologetically, "I must speak with my wife a moment. Please, make yourself comfortable."

With that, he strode to Lily where she sat upon the couch near the fire. She looked up at him, her eyes alight with love.

"My darling, might I speak with you a moment privately? Excuse me, Miss Firethorn, I will not keep her long."

Lily rose and followed him out to the hallway, where he wrapped his arms around her and rested his cheek against her hair.

"What's wrong, my love?"

He sighed softly. "Willowvale must go to Aricht to extract the Fair delegation, which has not reported to Silverthorn in months. That's assuming they're still alive. Travel through the mountains is slow and perilous at this time of year. It's rather a long way to Idosa through the veil, too, and besides, he doesn't know the way. I can feel it out from the magic, and if I take him, the veil will be more agreeable."

She shifted to look up at him, frowning just a little. "You're going to Idosa? When? How long will you be away?"

"Only a few days, I would hope. Maybe a week? We'll leave tomorrow, if I can convince him to stay the night. Otherwise we'll leave this evening."

She glanced at the doorway, though Willowvale could not be seen from where they stood, and then looked back up at Theo trustingly.

He kissed her forehead. "You are marvelous, my darling, to accept this so gracefully. I will miss you every moment I am away."

With a soft smile, she stretched up to kiss his cheek. "I will miss you, and I wish you weren't leaving," she admitted. "But it would be foolish to grieve the fact that you're being exactly who I fell in love with."

He blinked.

"You're generous and kind. Of course you want to help your friend, even though it inconveniences you." Their hands were entwined, and she brought his hand to her face and pressed her cheek against it. "The wonder is that you're so generous to Willowvale, of all people, but I ought not be surprised by that anymore."

His huff of laughter was so quiet she felt it more than heard it. "He's not hopeless you know, even if he feels he is."

"No one really is hopeless, are they?" She tightened her arms around him. "I love you, Theo. Be careful." Her throat tightened with emotion, and she said again, "Be careful, my love."

"Always!" He gave her a sparkling smile, his eyes bright and warm.

Her brows lowered and she said gently, "*Please*, Theo."

"I will!" He stopped her protest with a kiss, and then murmured into her ear, "I will only be foolish when absolutely necessary, and I will hurry back to kiss you a thousand times over. I promise." He added, "And I will be back in time for Oliver's wedding."

Several minutes later, after more murmured endearments, they rejoined the group in the sitting room. Theo asked his manservant Anselm to pack him a bag with a week of clothes, and excused himself again to go speak to his parents, who lived in the other side of the manor.

The afternoon passed in agreeable calm. Fenton advised Juniper so well that the young fairy managed to claim the victory, which he did with flushed cheeks and a small, proud smile. "You let me win," he said.

"Only a little." Fenton grinned. "Would you like to play, Willowvale?"

The fairy blinked. "I don't know the rules." His tone was mild, and that pleased him. The tea and quiet of the afternoon had soothed his agitation a little. For a time he had regretted letting Theo badger him into accepting help, because it stung his pride to need it. Still, the mission took precedence over his pride, and he could finally admit, if only to himself, that Theo's assistance would be useful and his company amiable.

"I'll be happy to teach you."

Juniper hesitated, then ventured, "He is an excellent tutor, my lord."

Willowvale's cold eyes flicked to the young fairy, who swallowed nervously. "It appears you have learned well," Willowvale said. "I had thought to depart this evening, though, and it would be discourteous to leave the game unfinished."

With a kind smile, Fenton said, "I will not take it as a discourtesy, though I do hope you can stay for dinner."

Willowvale nodded once. He was naturally competitive, and this had served him well much of his life. Games of strategy were a particular favorite of his, and he had already deduced the permitted moves of most of the chess pieces. Thus the reluctance he felt to take Fenton's first pawn was particularly odd, and he examined the feeling with consternation.

The light of the setting sun gilded the rich colors of the room. When Theo returned, he surveyed the game with a smile and said, "Might I convince you to stay the night here? I believe it will be quite a long walk even through the veil, and I confess I would find it considerably more pleasant to begin well-rested than to walk through the night."

The fair lord hesitated. "You need not go at all, Overton. It is hardly incumbent upon you to assist Brookbower."

"No, but I have promised to help you, my friend. Is it so urgent that you must depart tonight, or might we wait until tomorrow morning? We can breakfast early and depart at first light, or even before, if you feel it necessary."

One more night was unlikely to make a difference to Brookbower or his delegation. "I suppose dawn is early enough."

Theo beamed at him. "I am delighted to hear it." He glanced at Anselm, who was waiting in the doorway. The footman nodded and disappeared.

After a delicious dinner, dessert, and poetry and tea by the fire, Theo showed Willowvale to a guest suite on the first floor. The suite was, of course, decorated in the human style, devoid of soft moss upon the floor and flowers cascading down the walls. The bed and its richly carved wooden frame were, lamentably, upon the floor rather than suspended from the ceiling. Still, the room was luxurious; Theo offered him every possible courtesy, from a soft silk dressing gown in the wardrobe to the steaming water with which he might wash. The rug upon the wooden floor was woven of fine wool in an elegant, understated pattern of blue and green.

"Good night, Lord Willowvale. Please do not hesitate to call if you need anything before morning." Theo smiled warmly as he bowed.

"Thank you." Willowvale returned the bow.

When he was alone, Willowvale surveyed the room again, appreciating the elegance of the wooden bed frame and the detail in the painting of a vase of gladiolus spikes upon the wall.

There was a vase of hothouse blooms atop the wooden chest of drawers, and the fairy examined them in fascination. They were quite fresh, having been cut no more than an hour ago, and the colors were as vibrant as any in the Fair lands. Deep red ranunculus blooms contrasted vividly with white calla lilies and dusty miller, all set off by green juniper branches. It was not exactly the sort of arrangement Willowvale might have devised himself, but it was beautiful, and the thoughtfulness of the gesture felt like a knife twisting inside him.

Curiously, he tried on the dressing gown and, finding it fully as comfortable as his own at home, wore it as he washed his face and refreshed himself before turning to the bed.

He slept well, despite his tumultuous thoughts, for he was fatigued and the bed was surpassingly comfortable.

Still, he woke just before first light, dressed quickly, and strode to the breakfast room where Theo had said he would meet his guest.

The young man was already there, dressed in elegant traveling clothes of thick green wool that set off his bright copper hair. A leather satchel sat already packed by the door. Theo looked up when the Fair lord entered.

"Good morning!" Theo said, with a sparkling smile. "I hope you were comfortable last night."

Willowvale nodded curtly. "I was." At Theo's invitation, he sat at the little breakfast table. Anselm served a satisfying breakfast of eggs, sausage, steaming flaky biscuits with butter and jam, and both tea and coffee, as well as a little cup of exotic orange juice.

The Fair lord nearly flinched when he took the first sip of the chilled juice; the unfamiliar flavor was so fresh and sharp that it felt like an assault upon his senses.

"Do you like it?"

The liquid left a strange taste in his mouth, and he washed it away with another sip of tea. "I do not know," Willowvale admitted.

Theo shrugged cheerfully. "Perhaps it is an acquired taste."

The hint of early morning light barely brightened the garden outside the window, and the light of the lamp upon the table was much brighter and more cheerful. Every inch of the room radiated cozy, luxurious comfort.

Willowvale's pale, sharp features softened a little, though he did not realize it. Perhaps this was what it was like to have a friend, a little bright enclave of safety in the frigid world.

Soon they finished eating. Having already said his farewells to Lily, his parents, Anselm, and Juniper, Theo slung his bag over his shoulder and opened a door to the veil right there in the breakfast room.

The Fair lord eyed him. "Your skill is quite remarkable."

"Thank you!" Theo beamed at him. "It took quite a bit of practice, I'll have you know. I've gotten lost in the veil, and come out in the wrong place on both the Fair side and the human side, more times than I can count." The young man stepped into the veil first and stood aside, as if to shield Willowvale from any danger within the dark recesses.

Before he let the door close, Theo added, "My lord, perhaps you might grip the strap of my bag."

"All right."

With no more delay, Theo led him into the unfathomable darkness.

28

CHAPTER THREE
A Long, Dark Walk

T he Fair lord and the young man walked in silence for over an hour before Theo paused. Willowvale listened but heard nothing, and he was fairly confident his hearing was better than Theo's. Fair Folk had sharper senses than most humans.

"What is it?" he asked quietly.

"Something in the magic." Theo set off again, trailing his left hand along the wall.

Willowvale shivered. The wall of the veil was always coated in unexpected textures, slimy, mossy, crumbling stone, rough brick, even once a silky-smooth surface like the finest cloth. Beneath the texture was the restless, writhing magic, unpredictable and treacherous, liable to throw one down a bottomless shaft or conjure a venomous lizard made of shadow and lichen.

After another hour in silence, the magic of the veil felt like an itchy weight upon Willowvale's mind. The vague sentience of it, if it could even be described as sentience, felt hostile and irritated. The Fair lord focused upon the dank air of the tunnel, the chilly, forbidding damp, and the echoing whisper of things skittering in the distance. He reviewed his plan for negotiating with the Arichtan king for the release of Brookbower and his delegation, presuming that Brookbower was actually captive and had not departed from Aricht months earlier and died in the veil.

There was no guarantee that Brookbower was still in Aricht. He might have been dead months ago, and the Arichtan court blissfully unaware of his failure to return to the Fair Lands and report to Silverthorn.

One could only hope.

Willowvale felt a pang of guilt at the thought, for though he bore no love for Brookbower, his staff probably did not deserve to die miserably in the dark of the veil.

The magic of the veil brushed against his mind, cold and slithery and alien.

He said abruptly, "I confess I did not know it was possible for you to remain so reticent, Overton. I thought you talked all the time."

Theo laughed lightly, ignoring the harsh edge in the fairy's voice, for he heard it as the desperation it was. "I am actually capable of keeping my mouth shut occasionally. Would you rather I irritate you with my silence or my words?"

The question startled Willowvale, and he gave a soft snort of amusement. "Must you irritate me at all?" There was little acrimony in this reply, though.

"I don't know if I'm talented enough to avoid irritating you, my lord, but let me say that I will not do so intentionally for the present." Theo's smile was evident in his voice, and he added, "What shall we talk about?"

Willowvale gave a sharp bark of laughter. "You ask me that as if I were skilled at conversation. What do people talk about with their friends?"

"Have you any family? Will you tell me of them?"

"Very little. A disagreeable aunt and her spoiled, snide daughter. A distant cousin I haven't spoken to in fifteen years."

With a sudden jerk, Theo pulled back, and only by dint of his excellent reflexes did Willowvale avoid running into him. The young man backed up another step, then pressed his hands to the wall.

"That's all?" he said, as if the conversation were more interesting than his ability to get the veil to cooperate with him.

"Yes. What are you doing?" Willowvale flicked a little light to his fingers for a moment, just enough to see Theo's eyes closed against the light and his eyebrows slightly drawn together in concentration. He had stopped just before stepping into a yawning abyss, and in doing so had pushed Willowvale back from it as well.

The fairy let the light fade.

"It's teasing me," Theo muttered. "There's a shortcut here, but it made that hole just to see if we'd fall in it." His long fingers pressed against the damp lichen on the wall, and he added, "Let me see if I can convince it to stop harassing us."

Willowvale put his own hand against the wall, hoping to discover what Theo was doing with his magic, but was unable to decipher anything from the swirl of power beneath the lichen and stone.

"How do you manipulate the magic?" he asked in fascination.

"I haven't a clue!" Theo said cheerfully. "I tell it what I want, and I ask it to help, or at least not to hinder me, and sometimes it cooperates a little. Sometimes it doesn't. Over the years it has gotten a little more agreeable." He let out a heavy breath, pressing more magic into the veil. A sudden wave of fatigue shook him, and he leaned his head against the wall for a moment, grimacing at the unpleasant feel of the damp lichen against his forehead. "I think it likes to be asked and treated respectfully."

In the pitch black darkness, even a fairy could not see his companion, but Willowvale heard the faint strain in Theo's voice. "Your skill is commendable. Perhaps it dislikes me for the same reason others do."

With a smile in his voice, Theo said, "Ah, well, perhaps it will learn your worth eventually, as others will."

Willowvale blinked. "Why should you assume that?"

Theo started off through a tunnel that had not existed a few seconds earlier. "Well, I did."

After a shocked silence, Willowvale laughed quietly to himself. "You're hardly ordinary, Overton," he muttered. "I don't expect others to do the same."

"Is that a compliment?" Theo said in delight. "No, don't answer! Let me believe that it is, because it means so much coming from you."

Willowvale laughed again, a bright, surprised little chuckle. In the silence that followed, he wondered whether the veil was actually a little more friendly, or it was only that he felt more cheerful in the same darkness that had been so oppressive before. The air was just as frigid and damp, and the vague sense of danger lurking in the unseen recesses of the veil had not lifted. Nevertheless, he felt a smile upon his lips.

"I wonder that your king did not object to your generous offer of assistance," he said after several moments of a companionable silence. "Surely he bears me, and the Fair throne, no good will."

"His Majesty Alberdale trusts me a great deal," Theo replied. "He has given me a considerable amount of freedom, especially since I actually have no official authority or position at all."

"Has he given you any indication what might have happened to Brookbower?" Willowvale asked shrewdly. Of course Overton would have communicated with his king before leaving for Aricht.

"He has not." Theo trailed his left hand along the wall of the veil, which now felt like long-dried moss upon crumbling bricks. "I doubt he knows. Valestria and Aricht are not close allies, although we did send troops in support of Aricht in the war."

"I remember."

"Did Brookbower see combat?" Theo asked curiously.

"No. One of Aricht's conditions for accepting any Fair ambassador was that he must not have fought directly against Aricht. Brookbower was, however, part of the faction in court that advocated for the war." Months earlier, even this small disclosure would have felt like disloyalty to the Fair Court; the Fair Folk preferred to share as little information as possible with humans, for humans feared what they did not understand, and fear was always a useful tool.

Yet Willowvale found that no pang of guilt assailed him when he said this. No harm would come to the Fair Lands from this revelation, and perhaps it might be of some assistance to Theo.

Theo made a thoughtful sort of sound. "Might I ask when he last reported to your king?"

"Nearly three months ago."

"That long? Hm." After a moment, Theo said, "Surely it was not the Ambassador stealing the children from Aricht."

"No."

"Might I ask whom it was?"

Willowvale hesitated. This was, perhaps, more chancy than the earlier revelation, but he had a strange sense of comfort. After walking for hours upon hours in the frigid darkness, with Theo's kindness as a strange solace against the guilt that weighed upon him, he could find no reason not to answer. Had not Theo already proven his friendship toward the Fair Lands?

"Lords Camphor and Aspen," the fairy said. "Silverthorn did not think he could trust them not to start another war with Aricht."

Theo considered this in silence. "So he sent you," he murmured thoughtfully.

"Indeed." Dark amusement colored Willowvale's voice. "Apparently I am the most personable of the Fair lords he trusts."

Theo's huff of laughter was almost lost in the sudden shriek of some unseen creature not nearly distant enough for comfort.

"What say we stop for lunch?" Theo said.

"Where are we?" Willowvale gripped his sword hilt.

"Does it matter?" Theo opened a door into the human world and stumbled back at the gust of icy wind that roared into the veil. Then he stepped forward, pulling Willowvale after him and shutting the door hurriedly against a rush of dark mist that snapped at their heels.

They stood upon a narrow plateau between the side of a mountain and a steep, crumbling slope of pebbles and rock out-croppings. The sky overhead was iron gray, as cold as the wind which whipped through their hair and cut through their jackets.

Willowvale looked around, and, noting no potential shelters nearby, said, "Wait a moment." He let out a breath, pushing his magic into the earth. The human world did not respond as easily as the Fair Lands did to his magic, but even here the vines responded. There was nearly always some seed, or the memory of a seed, from which the magic could snap into reality.

Within a matter of a few minutes, he had a grown a thick dome of interwoven vines covered in wide green leaves as big as a man's hand. He made no door, because the vines would obey him when he wanted out. A door would only let in the cold. He and Theo stood in the relatively peaceful shelter as the wind howled around them.

"What a remarkable skill," Theo said quietly.

The Fair lord glanced at him. In the leaf-tinged shadows, Theo's fair skin looked a little green. "Thank you," he said. He slung the bag off his shoulder and added, "The vines will keep the wind off while we eat."

As if Theo Overton, the Rose, would be intimidated by vines. The man was utterly terrifying in his audacity, and of course it was foolish to imagine that he was nervous now, surrounded by Willowvale's vines, just because they had nearly killed him quite painfully only a few months ago. The very idea was ridiculous.

Willowvale gave a soft *pfft* at his own thought. Still, it had felt vaguely discourteous not to offer some reassurance, however unnecessary. In another few minutes, he had grown two chairs and a little table between them, adequate but not particularly luxurious.

"Thank you." Theo smiled and sat down in the chair nearest him. He opened his bag. "I have a few days of provisions for us. Fresh bread, several kinds of cheese, summer sausage, roast chicken, tomatoes, grapes, and blueberries."

Willowvale frowned at the spread. "How much longer until we arrive in Aricht?"

"It will be a long day, but I hope to get there by late tonight."

"I brought my own meals." The fairy opened his bag and pulled out one of the spelled bundles. When he unwrapped it, the fresh, spicy scent of the Fair bread and meat filled the air. "You've brought less than I have, and it will not keep as long. I ought not eat your provisions since I cannot reciprocate by sharing mine."

Theo grinned. "I can restock in Idosa, but your thoughtfulness is much appreciated. I had planned to share. Please, feel free to enjoy what you like."

The wind screamed outside, though little of the wind made it through the tiny, unseen gaps in the leaves. Though the air inside their little shelter was mostly still, it was frigid.

Theo offered Willowvale a canteen of water, which the fairy refused, and drank from another. "What a wind!" he murmured, eyeing the layers of leaves and interwoven vines opposite him. "I am glad not to be out in that gale."

Other than this comment, they ate in silence and were finished in only a few minutes. Then Willowvale let the magic of the vines recede. The hut vanished, and they set off into the veil again.

Seven hours later, they stepped out of the veil again to eat dinner on a snowy hillside beneath the brilliant light of the setting sun.

"Your skill in navigating in the tunnels is beyond compare." Willowvale turned in a slow circle as he surveyed the land below, which was dotted with expansive stone farmhouses and crisscrossed by stone walls separating one pasture from another. "Where are we?"

"The foothills of eastern Aricht. I believe we should reach the capital in a few more hours, though our progress will be slower. I'm not familiar with the magic here, so I have to feel it as I go."

They ate in a tired silence and, being reassured by their proximity to Idosa, Willowvale did accept a few grapes and slices of cheese before they packed their supplies again and stepped back into the veil.

After another three hours walking, Theo sighed and said, "This is as good a place as any." He opened a door into the human world and stepped out.

Moonlight spilled across the wide avenue in shades of gray and silver, highlighting the facades of the buildings marching away to their left and right and casting inky shadows beneath the trees lining the street. There was little traffic at this late hour, but a man far down the street stopped and stared at them.

Willowvale stepped out of the veil behind him, and Theo let the doorway close.

"Do you know where we are?" the fairy asked in a low voice.

Theo looked up and down the street, then stepped into the street to get a better view of the building behind him. "Not precisely. We ought to be able to find an inn for the night and visit the palace tomorrow."

The Fair lord nodded. Little good would come from beating on the doors of the palace at midnight. Besides, if there was any hope of a positive resolution, he must be at his best when he negotiated with the Arichtan king.

He would not have admitted it unless forced to, but he was thoroughly fatigued and chilled to his bones, and had been so for hours. The only outward sign was that his skin was even paler than usual, and who could see that in the silvery moonlight? Still, his steps were long and swift as he followed Theo down the broad thoroughfare. He let Theo lead, for this was the human world, and the young man must be at least as exhausted as he was. The walk had been long and frigid, and humans were, as a species, more susceptible to cold than the Fair Folk.

Not that Theo showed any obvious signs of fatigue. Willowvale snorted softly to himself. Of course not.

"Is something wrong, my lord?" Theo asked, with a curious glance.

"Not at all."

Theo stopped at a door beneath a sign which read *The Woodlark*. "I might suggest a glamour, Lord Willowvale, at least until we have spoken with His Majesty Elmerick."

The fairy nodded, and in the blink of an eye, donned a glamour utterly convincing to human eyes. He kept his lofty height, but his shoulders now looked a little broader, more befitting a human man of his age. His skin looked darker and warmer, the tone appropriate to a human rather than the icy white of his Fair coloring. His hair appeared a rich brown which set off his now-dark eyes. However, his face had kept its harsh lines, and his mouth still looked pinched with irritation. He had chosen human clothes to travel in that morning, so these the glamour did not change.

At this late hour, the door was locked. Theo knocked briskly, and then knocked again after they received no answer. Finally there was a clattering of multiple latches on the other side of the door.

"What do you want?" The deep voice was husky with sleep. The owner of the voice had opened the door only a crack, and the room behind him was dark, so Theo could see little of him aside from a flash of pale shirt below his shadowed face.

"My friend and I would like lodging for the night. Two rooms, and breakfast in the morning, if you offer it."

"Ten pounds extra per room for checking in after ten o'clock."

Even Willowvale knew this was exorbitant.

Theo sighed. "All right."

They followed the innkeeper through a spacious common room to two small rooms at the end of the corridor. The man opened them each with a key and said, "The linens are clean. Breakfast is at seven. Pay in advance."

Theo dug some money from the inside pocket of his jacket and handed it to the man. "Thank you. Good night." Willowvale belatedly produced his own money, and Theo waved it away.

The man nodded and shuffled back down the hall.

"Good night, my lord," Theo said to Willowvale.

With that, they shut their doors and readied themselves for sleep. Theo resolutely ignored the lumpiness of the mattress and quickly fell into the peaceful sleep of the innocent, his mind filled with thoughts of his beloved wife and the delight that awaited him when he returned home.

The Fair lord across the hall, equally fatigued, did not sleep nearly as well.

For one thing, the mattress on which he was attempting to sleep was not only lumpy, but gave off a strong and lingering fragrance of old sweat which he found particularly objectionable. Also, his thoughts were filled with the negotiations that would consume the following days and the unpleasant necessity of humbling himself to the Arichtan throne on behalf of the Fair Folk.

Brookbower did not deserve Willowvale's efforts.

Still, Silverthorn had asked.

Besides, had Willowvale not himself received undeserved grace?

Lord Ash Willowvale, irritable, aching with fatigue, and dreading the following day, fell asleep scarcely an hour before a clamor of male voices and heavy footsteps hurrying down the hall woke him at dawn.

Changing into the formal attire he had chosen for his audience with the king was a matter of only a few minutes. By the time he stepped out into the hallway with travel bag in hand, he wore a glamour of simple human clothes over the severe silver and white. Theo's door was closed.

Willowvale listened for a moment, and, unable to discern any hint of movement within, knocked sharply. Silence.

The Fair lord scowled as he strode swiftly to the common room. Theo was already seated at one end of a long table, dressed in a traveling suite of the latest style. His immaculate jacket and trousers were clearly of far better cut and fabric than the clothes of the other men seated in the room, and he looked altogether too handsome and happy to be tolerated.

Willowvale sat across from Theo.

"I've already ordered breakfast. It should be here shortly." Theo smiled so warmly that Willowvale almost forgot, for a moment, that he was as clever as he was.

It was strange indeed for someone so cunning to be so cheerful and kind, for did not cleverness inevitably lead to a grim mood? If one thought about the world, and oneself, honestly, without shrinking from the truth of one's detestable nature, a surly temper seemed entirely warranted.

He looked down at the many layers of stains on the worn table. "Thank you for coming, Overton."

"You're welcome."

At this moment a young woman put plates of eggs, ham, and cream-filled pastries in front of them, along with steaming mugs of tea. Willowvale waited until she moved on to the next table before he spoke again.

"When you return, give my regards to Mrs. Overton, Lord Selby, and Miss Firethorn."

"Of course I will. But I hope you don't mind if I accompany you to the palace. His Majesty Alberdale gave me a letter of introduction, and I thought I might speak on your behalf, however briefly."

Willowvale's brows drew together. "The Fair Lands are already in your debt, Overton, to say nothing of my own obligation to you."

Theo blinked. "I am not seeking to put you further into my debt, my friend. You know I am a friend of the Fair Lands; surely you cannot begrudge me the opportunity to improve relations between the Fair Lands and a country with which my own is allied." He took a sip of tea and gave a faint, aggrieved grimace. "Besides, my family has investments here. Since it is such an inconvenient journey, I might as well drop in and visit some associates while I'm here."

The Fair lord's frown deepened. "If Elmerick's anger cannot be appeased, your name and business will be tarnished by your association with my people."

The young man gave a careless shrug. "I'll risk it."

CHAPTER FOUR
An Audience

Seated across from each other in the jostling, dusty interior of the hired coach, they looked out their respective windows. Beneath his glamour, the Fair lord was even paler than usual, his mouth pinched with fatigue and a sense of inevitable failure.

The easy smile that flickered over Theo's lips as he watched the buildings pass by seemed not only foolish, but actively designed to aggravate him.

Willowvale curled his lip in irritation and focused again on the Arichtan neighborhood through which they now traveled. Theo was not actually trying to annoy him now; he knew this. Still, the lack of sleep that made his eyes gritty and the disquiet in his gut seemed to transform every little bump of the coach and every expression on a human face into a personal affront.

His heart and soul were raw, and this vulnerability seemed to have come upon him at the most inconvenient time.

The coach wound through the city, up long curving avenues and wide straight boulevards. Willowvale found the presence of so many people in one place appalling. The Fair Folk had cities, certainly, and even large ones, but even the relatively densely populated capital of Dewspring-in-the-Wood contained large green spaces and tracts of forest. These stone and wood houses all side by side made him feel twitchy and claustrophobic.

They drew to a halt in front of an ostentatiously ornate wrought iron gate wide enough for four carriages abreast. The gate was closed.

Willowvale reached for the door first and stepped out into the late morning light. Moments later, bags in hand, they stood before the great gate.

The gate guard said nothing until Theo approached the left side of the gate, where the man sat inside a tiny, many-windowed shed.

"Good morning! My friend and I request entrance," Theo said cheerfully.

"What is your business in the palace?"

Theo glanced at Willowvale, as if allowing him to speak first, if he wanted.

"I am Lord Ash Willowvale, Special Envoy of the Fair Court, and His Majesty Silverthorn sent me to ascertain the whereabouts of our Fair Ambassador, Lord Linden Brookbower, and his delegation." Willowvale said this with all the cold, acerbic condescension with which he had first addressed Theo.

The guard's eyes narrowed, but he nodded once. "And you?" The lack of a *sir* seemed a deliberate insult, which Theo ignored.

"I am Theodore Overton, IV, of Valestria, and His Majesty Alberdale gave me a letter of introduction to His Majesty Elmerick."

The guard frowned but, casting his eyes over them again, said, "You may enter." He clanked a latch hidden behind the wall, then stepped forward to open the gate.

Once inside the gate, they were greeted by another guard and escorted down the long, tree-lined drive toward the palace.

The only sound from their little party was the crunch of the gravel beneath their boots. The murmur of carriages and voices in the street faded in the distance as they approached the palace, replaced by the soft rustle of the icy breeze through the evergreen branches above them and the muffled activity in a distant courtyard.

At last they reached the wide marble steps of the front entrance of the palace. The guard led them up to the enormous doors. The dark wood was inlaid with brightly polished gold in a geometric pattern which seemed to Willowvale's Fair tastes to be particularly unpleasant in its linear harshness. The Fair Lands were unparalleled in their beauty, and his loyalty to them was only reinforced by this graceless human attempt at loveliness. Only a human would think such lines, with nary a flower or leaf to be seen, were appropriate for an entrance to a building, much less a palace meant to exemplify the honor and dignity of the nation.

Willowvale snorted softly, his lips bearing an unconscious sneer.

The guard gave him a sharp look, but said nothing. When the door opened, he gave them into the guidance of another man, tall and dark-eyed, with a severe frown.

Several minutes later, after their new guard had conferred in a low voice with a servant wearing a different uniform, they were brought to a spacious, elegant sitting room.

"Wait here," said their guide, before stepping into the hallway.

Willowvale crossed his arms and looked around the room, noting the quality of the paintings upon the walls and the luxurious upholstery of the chairs and sofas. There was not a bit of moss or natural greenery to be seen, much less a flower. No, that was not true; there was an excellent painting of an arrangement of white peonies upon the near wall. But a painting, however beautiful, was not alive.

He curled his lip and turned away, looking out the window to see a paved courtyard in which several well-dressed men were talking in a little knot, their breaths fogging in the frigid air.

"His Majesty will see you now." The guard sounded almost surprised by this.

"Thank you!" said Theo with a smile.

The guard escorted them not to the throne room but to a larger and more ostentatious sitting room. The king sat at a heavy desk, and a guard stood nearby.

"Lord Ash Willowvale of the Seelie Fair Court and Mr. Theodore Overton, IV, of Valestria."

The king looked up as they were announced. His dark eyes were shrewd beneath heavy brows, and he studied them a moment before nodding.

"Lord Willowvale, is it? Is that your true face?"

Willowvale dropped his glamour and bowed stiffly. "This is my face, Your Majesty. May I approach?"

The king's eyes flicked over him, then to Theo. He nodded. "Why are you here, and why have you come together?"

Willowvale stepped forward and presented a sealed letter from the inside of his jacket. "His Majesty Silverthorn sent me to ascertain the whereabouts of Ambassador Linden Brookbower and his staff. I am authorized to negotiate terms for their release, if they are captive."

His Majesty Elmerick examined the seal, which glittered with Silverthorn's personal magic. Then he broke the seal, read the letter, nodded, and put the paper to one side.

He looked toward Theo, his expression giving away nothing.

"I have a letter of introduction, Your Majesty." Theo bowed and offered it with a smile.

The king examined this seal with equal interest, then opened the letter and began to read. He blinked and looked up at Theo, then continued reading.

Finally he said, "Do you know what is written in this?"

"His Majesty Alberdale told me the general outline of it, but I did not read it myself. I was with him when he wrote it."

"Does he know?" The king flicked a cold glance at Willowvale.

"That I am the Wraith? Yes, Your Majesty. He was the one who caught me, more or less." Theo smiled.

Elmerick's impassive expression flickered for a moment. "What could you possibly say on his behalf that would incline me to look kindly on any interest of the Fair Court?"

Theo beamed at him. "Well, for one thing, His Majesty Silverthorn has already sworn to never take or harm humans again, directly or indirectly, and has asked specifically for my guidance and advice in his continued reign. Not to mention that my friend Lord Willowvale has demonstrated great honor in his friendship to me."

The king glanced Willowvale with a faint frown that deepened as he looked back at Theo. "What interest do you have in Brookbower's delegation? Your friendship to the Fair Lands cannot extend so far, can it?"

"I have no personal interest in Ambassador Brookbower's delegation, Your Majesty. My involvement is only because I perceived that it would be so difficult for Lord Willowvale to reach you, and since I can travel through the veil more easily than most, I offered to travel with him here. Since I am here, I thought I might visit some business associates here in Idosa and in Skystead."

"Do you have anything to add, Envoy of the Fair Court?" The king's voice was still smooth, but there was a hint of icy anger in it.

With extraordinary effort, Willowvale kept a sneer off his face. Instead, he said, "Mr. Overton's friendship has wrought marvelous changes in the Fair Court, in His Majesty Silverthorn, and in me. I also have no personal love of Lord Brookbower, but honor compels me to obey my king in this. I find it difficult to believe you would prefer his continued presence in your nation over the appointment of a more pleasant appointee, and I should hope that you would allow His Majesty Silverthorn to appoint a new ambassador more acceptable to you."

Elmerick said, "Mr. Overton, I would like to speak with you this evening privately. Allow me to offer you the hospitality of the palace. Martin will escort you to a guest suite."

The invitation seemed not so much a question as a demand, and Willowvale bristled on Theo's behalf. Still, Theo gave the king a sparkling smile and bowed deeply. "As you wish, Your Majesty. I am delighted to be of service."

Theo bowed again and retreated cheerfully into the hall, where the grave-faced servant took his bag. "This way, sir."

The study seemed colder and emptier in Theo's absence, and Willowvale's misgivings about the whole mission grew deeper. Still, he said nothing. He resisted the urge to clasp his hands behind his back and throw back his shoulders; this king was far too canny to be convinced by such an obvious display of confidence. Instead, he relaxed his shoulders and shifted his long, lean body as if he were bored but too polite to want to show it.

"Your Majesty," he said at last, when the king showed no sign of initiating any further conversation. "Where is Ambassador Brookbower?"

"He is awaiting trial." Elmerick's voice was thick with fury.

"On what charges?"

"Aiding and abetting the kidnapping and abduction of minors, forced labor, child endangerment, coercion and threat of coercion… the list is quite long."

"I suppose there is no chance of him claiming diplomatic immunity."

The king gave a short, hard huff. "Oh, he tried that already. Diplomatic immunity is extended for offenses such as littering in the streets and cheating our merchants, not for exploiting our children. We have no diplomatic presence in your capital, Willowvale, so we had no reason to grant even what license we have. We have already been more than generous, and your people have abused what little trust we had in you."

The hatred in the king's voice would have given anyone pause.

Willowvale's pale lips twisted, and he snapped, "I have enough guilt of my own; I will not claim Brookbower's guilt as well. Can you not see the utility in accepting Silverthorn's offer to appoint a new ambassador more to your liking?"

"It is not a matter of my liking as a matter of national interest. I am not sure that peace is preferable to war if it comes at the expense of our children, our integrity, and our humanity. Much of my court agrees."

"Have I not already told you that Silverthorn has forsworn all future such actions?" Willowvale snarled. "Do you think he lies? Or that I do? We do not lie, unlike you humans! How can I be sure Brookbower is alive at all?"

"He'll rot in prison until we have finished compiling the evidence against him, and then we'll try him, fairly and publicly, and then he will be executed for his crimes, for we all know he is guilty." The king stood, his motion slow and deliberate, hands clenched as if he were restraining himself from throttling Willowvale only by the barest thread of self-control. "You're very close to joining him, Willowvale, for you've as much as admitted you participated in the atrocities committed against Arichtan children."

"I stole no children from Arichtan homes." Willowvale kept his hands at his sides, deliberately loose. Silverthorn had entrusted this negotiation to him. "Your Majesty, I request proof that Brookbower's delegation is alive. What shall I offer in exchange?"

His Majesty Valor Elmerick, veteran of the war with the Fair Folk, for he had taken the field himself, albeit briefly, stared at the lean, elegant Fair lord before him. The fairy was as slim and bright as a sword, dressed in silver and white that matched his snowy hair and icy white skin. His blue eyes were so pale they were nearly silver too, and there was a hard anger lurking in them that Elmerick did not trust.

Still, Elmerick was not quite ready to declare war. It was tempting, but he owed it to his people to at least try to find some peaceable resolution if it were possible.

He thumped one clenched fist upon the desk as he thought. "What exactly did your king promise to Mr. Overton?"

"His Majesty Silverthorn promised never to take or harm humans again, directly or indirectly." Willowvale tried to keep the sneer out of his voice, but did not entirely manage it. "The effort involving the children was borne of desperation and was a last resort, and while I know it is abhorrent to you, it was not undertaken lightly."

"It was not only abhorrent, but I presume intended as a punitive measure for our successful resistance in the war," Elmerick snapped.

Willowvale clenched his teeth so tightly his jaws ached. Finally he said, "What shall I offer in return for your proof that Brookbower and his staff are still alive?"

The king pressed his lips together. "Stay in the palace under guard tonight and we will speak again tomorrow at nine in the morning. Overton will be free to visit you, but you will stay in the suite you are assigned aside from our meeting. Proof will be provided to you at lunch today, which will be brought to your suite. Any attempt to leave without permission will be considered a deliberate act of aggression and dealt with accordingly."

Willowvale bowed stiffly. "Thank you, Your Majesty. I do hope that this visit will lead to improved relations between our peoples." This was not *exactly* a lie. Willowvale did hope this, however unlikely it seemed.

"As do I." The growl in the king's low voice made this agreement sound like a threat.

The Fair lord bowed again even more shallowly, imbuing the motion with a hint of mockery, not because he intended to, but because in his frustration and anger he could not help it. He picked up his bag and followed the guard into the hall.

The guard strode briskly through the marble-floored corridors, his steps echoing hollowly as they passed through various larger rooms. The guard went up three flights of stairs and turned to the left down another long hall. Willowvale's long legs allowed him to keep up easily, and he looked about surreptitiously, for it would not do to seem too awed by the palace.

The building was grand in every sense of the word. Every floor was the finest white marble, and many of the rooms were accented with inlays of pink or gray marble in intricate woven patterns. Every ceiling was painted with delicate frescos depicting the creation of the world and historical scenes of splendor and triumph. The walls were adorned with paintings and tapestries, all old and ornate.

Even for a fairy, it was fascinating. Willowvale's gaze darted from one painting to another, drinking in the loving detail in the painting of a rose and noting the precision in the light that played upon a horse's muscles. Humans were, if not in tune with the natural world as fairies were, at least sometimes capable of creating beauty.

He scowled. His respect, even awe, for Overton seemed to be softening him toward other humans, and it remained to be seen whether these Arichtans deserved his regard.

This was hardly the time to grow soft. Silverthorn had entrusted the negotiations to him because he would not be swayed by petty anger, but surely the Fair monarch had not intended for him to be swayed by an antique painting in the Arichtan palace either.

"Here you are, sir." The guard opened a door for him and stood aside. "As the king commanded, you are not to leave the suite, but if you need anything, the guard posted at your door will likely be able to accommodate you. I have the first shift."

Willowvale muttered, "Thank you." He closed the door behind him, consciously keeping himself from slamming it. Slamming the door would be petty, and pettiness was weakness. Then he opened it again. "When Overton is free, I should like to speak with him."

"Yes, sir. I will let him know."

Willowvale nodded and closed the door again.

He set his bag down and sighed.

The room was elegant and clean, if not excessively luxurious. Apparently Elmerick did not intend to throw him into prison quite yet. Through the door to his left, he could see that the bed linens were fresh and white, and the coverlet was embroidered in gold in an angular pattern similar to that which had adorned the front door. Willowvale rubbed a hand over his face. There was not a speck of greenery to be seen.

This would not do.

He stalked about the sitting room, examining the art upon the walls and inspecting the spotless little water closet. The curtains at the window, for he did have a window that looked out upon the courtyard, were of fine fabric, with a light and airy silk layer that let in the bright sunlight even when drawn. It would be inconvenient to climb out from this height, but certainly not impossible, even without his vines. He glanced around the room again.

A little table by the window seemed as good a place as any.

He sat in the chair, noting with some surprise that it was a relief to get off his feet. He spread his hands upon the polished wooden table surface and called upon his magic.

The wood of the table had been dead for so long that it was difficult to remind it what it felt like to be alive, to breathe and grow and shift, but wood *wanted* to grow, and if the magic would not last forever, it was at least a good reminder of the fact that Willowvale would also not live forever. He coaxed it gently, soothing the wood with a tender understanding of the ache of change, the pain of bending when one was accustomed to being rigid. Within a few minutes, a miniature azalea bloomed upon the top of the table, bright pink double blooms in exuberant contrast with the dark green leaves.

He turned his attention to the floor beneath the table. In less than an hour, he had carpeted half the floor in vibrant moss, the fresh green accented by mounds of tiny blue and white flowers.

The Fair lord took off his boots and set them aside, then took off his jacket. He lay upon the moss with one arm over his eyes and tried to forget the fatigue and frustration of the preceding days. The moss cushioning his head tickled his neck, and he sighed deeply.

If he could not sleep in an elevated bed, the moss might be preferable to the bed with its aggressively angular embroidery. He scowled with his eyes closed. What a horrible place.

Perhaps he dozed briefly, for when the knock sounded upon the door, it startled him into sharp alertness. He yanked his jacket on and straightened it hurriedly before he opened the door, already glowering.

"What?" he snarled into Theo Overton's face.

Theo blinked. "I take it your meeting with His Majesty Elmerick didn't go especially well."

The guard at Theo's shoulder snickered, and Willowvale gave him a black look.

"Come in if you want," he muttered. He strode across the room to the armchair near the fireplace and flung himself into it.

Without another word, Theo stepped inside and closed the door gently. He glanced about the room for a moment, noting the azalea and moss without comment, then strode quietly to the chair opposite Willowvale and sat.

"It's rather chilly in here. Shall I start the fire?" he asked.

"I don't care," Willowvale grumbled.

Theo busied himself with that task for several minutes, conscious of the fairy watching him work. Finally he said, "This isn't the dungeon, so I suppose it could have gone worse."

"Do you ever tire of looking at the bright side?" Willowvale said, as if astonished. "Those around you surely tire of hearing about it."

Theo laughed aloud. "All right, Willowvale, I can take a hint occasionally! I'll sit here in obnoxious silence until you get so annoyed at me that you tell me what's really bothering you."

"Spare me." Willowvale rubbed both hands over his face and leaned forward to rest his elbows on his knees, face still hidden. "I asked for proof that Brookbower and his staff are still alive and asked what Elmerick wanted in return. He said proof would be brought to my suite at lunch, and I am effectively detained in this suite until further notice. He hasn't told me what he demands in return for this proof yet, either."

The fairy's long, lean body nearly trembled with irritation and frustration. He shoved his hands through his snow-white curls and leaned back in the chair again, stretching his sock-covered feet toward the tiny, crackling fire. He crossed his arms over his chest.

Theo eyed Willowvale's silver socks with a smile and sat back on his heels. "May I stay for lunch?"

Willowvale huffed softly. "I had hoped you would," he admitted.

The young man raised his eyebrows and said, "That's almost friendly, my lord."

The Fair lord's lips curled in a tiny, reluctant smile. "I imagine I might appreciate your advice upon the arrival of the proof." His white eyebrows drew downward.

"Ah, I understand." Theo smiled warmly, with a twinkle in his eyes. "It is only practicality. You need only my advice, not my company."

"I will not implore you to keep me company in this horrible place!" Willowvale snapped.

Theo laughed. "Peace, Willowvale! I was teasing, not mocking. There's a difference, you know."

"Is there?"

"Indeed. There's no disdain behind teasing, at least not as I was employing it." Theo poked the fire again and then sat in the chair, relaxed and smiling. "A man might tease his friends, but he ought never to mock them."

"You mocked me before," Willowvale muttered, but there was no heat in his voice this time.

"You weren't my friend before," Theo protested. "Besides, I had to keep your attention off those more easily intimidated."

Willowvale laughed, low and quiet. "All right, Overton. I concede that point."

They sat in silence for some time, listening to the fire crackle. Finally Willowvale said, "I'd offer you tea, but I don't have any."

"I brought some." Theo pulled a packet out of his jacket, and the fairy stared at him.

"Do you always bring tea wherever you go?"

Theo chuckled. "No, but last time I was in Aricht, years ago, I was subjected to some deeply disappointing tea, so I thought I might bring a little to save you the same fate."

Willowvale blinked, then blinked again. "You brought it for me?"

"Well, I did expect you to share. I brought enough for us both." Theo grinned.

The fairy's insides twisted, and he caught a sudden breath, as if he wanted to sob, but he wasn't sure exactly why. Why should tea bring sudden dampness to his eyes, as if the mere thought of a steaming black brew could undo him? He rubbed his hands over his face and pinched the bridge of his nose.

"I don't have a tea pot," he said.

Theo rose and strode to the door. He requested a tea pot with hot water and a set of cups from the guard, who informed him that lunch would be arriving soon.

The silence that followed was broken only by Theo's quiet observation that the azalea was lovely, at which Willowvale nodded without a word.

CHAPTER FIVE
The Security Specialist

A knock upon the door sounded nearly twenty minutes later. Willowvale pulled on his boots and straightened his jacket again before crossing the room to open it.

Three guards flanked a striking Fair lady, and behind their little group, His Majesty Elmerick stood with another three guards. The king watched Willowvale's reaction with sharp attention.

One of the guards, said, "Lord Willowvale, this is Miss Astrantia Berrydell. Miss Berrydell, Lord Ash Willowvale." The man's voice was carefully neutral.

Willowvale's cool eyes flicked over Astrantia for a moment before he gave her a stiff, shallow bow. "Miss Berrydell."

Her hair was a shocking magenta, and it was cropped quite short for a Fair maiden, so that it scarcely reached her jaw. Her skin was nearly as pale as that of Willowvale himself, though it had a slightly warmer tone, like milk rather than ice. Her delicate features were surpassingly lovely, even by Fair standards, but her pink lips were pressed together tightly as if she were furious.

"Lord Willowvale." She bowed politely in the Fair custom.

"Is Miss Berrydell to join me for lunch?" Willowvale addressed this question to the guard, who looked back at his king.

Elmerick nodded. "That is acceptable. Miss Berrydell, you will keep your word."

"I will." The Fair maiden pressed her pink lips together.

With little further commotion, the guards stepped aside as Willowvale led her into the room. The king watched through the open door as Willowvale performed the introductions. His eyes widened as he caught sight of the miniature azalea blooming upon the table by the window.

"Mr. Overton, Miss Astrantia Berrydell, security specialist for Ambassador Linden Brookbower. Miss Berrydell, this is Mr. Theodore Overton, IV, of Valestria. A friend."

Theo bowed to Astrantia, who returned the courtesy with a curious glint in her eye.

Willowvale said, "When you bring lunch, bring another chair. Please."

The nearest servant bowed in acknowledgment, and then Willowvale closed the door, shutting out the inquisitive gazes of everyone in the corridor.

"So His Majesty sent someone at last," Astrantia said.

Willowvale inclined his head. "Indeed. My assignment is to extract Ambassador Brookbower and the delegation safely. His Majesty Silverthorn has offered to assign an ambassador more acceptable to His Majesty Elmerick. Elmerick said the delegation was all alive and relatively unharmed. Is that true?"

"It is." Astrantia's pink eyes glittered.

Willowvale's gaze swept over her again, taking in the dust on the hem of her simple dress.

"Where is Brookbower now?"

"In prison, where we have all been for the past three months," she said, her voice soft and cold.

"Were you not able to escape?" Willowvale frowned thoughtfully.

Her jaw tightened, and she said, "Yes, I could, but for what purpose? Only Brookbower can open the veil, and we have all vowed not to escape."

"Why would you do something so idiotic?" he muttered.

Astrantia snapped, "My lord, with all due respect, which isn't much, *you weren't there*. We were drugged, and upon awaking, we were restrained by iron manacles within the iron-barred cells. With an iron blade to Brookbower's throat, I felt I had little choice but to accept their terms."

The Fair lord's frown deepened.

"Moreover, I cannot say I disagree with the Arichtans, my lord." Astrantia's voice had sharpened, though it remained low. "I believed, when I vowed to protect Brookbower, that he was worthy of my respect. Upon our imprisonment, I learned that not only was he aware of the plan to steal human children for the benefit of our lands, he actively participated by hiding the activities of Lords Camphor and Aspen."

Willowvale said, "You are angry." It was an inane comment, but he was not sure exactly what sort of reaction she expected, and, to his own surprise, he did not want her to be angry. She had a face that looked like it ought to smile easily, and the cold fury radiating from her seemed not only wrong, but deeply wounding to her very essence. He was cold, but she was not so by nature.

"Of course I'm angry!" she snapped. "My most honorable impulses, my character, my skills, and my magical talents were used to support an effort I find utterly abhorrent and reprehensible. Can you countenance it? To punish children for the failings of our own king?"

The Fair lord glanced at Theo for a split second. "Then you will be glad to know that a new solution to the plight of the Fair Lands has been found, and His Majesty Silverthorn has vowed never to take or harm humans again."

Theo said gently, "Lord Willowvale, Miss Berrydell, shall I leave you?"

"No!" Willowvale answered abruptly. "Please stay."

Theo blinked. "As you wish," he murmured. "Miss Berrydell, perhaps you would like to sit by the fire? I imagine that wherever you were held was not warm."

She gave him an evaluating look. "And why are you here, Mr. Overton?"

Theo gave her a warm, sparkling smile. "I helped Lord Willowvale reach the city, and I spoke on behalf of Lord Willowvale to His Majesty Elmerick."

"What would a Valestrian say to the Arichtan king that would be of any use at all?" Astrantia's brilliant eyes flicked up and down his figure in fascination.

Theo was, of course, dressed with immaculate perfection in the latest style, in green silk that set off his coppery hair and made his hazel eyes look especially bright. He was the very picture of lean, relaxed elegance and sophistication.

Willowvale sighed softly.

Theo grinned. "Miss Berrydell, suffice it to say that I have a unique perspective on events in the Fair Court. That's really how Lord Willowvale and I became acquainted, you see." He gestured at the chair he had occupied only a few minutes earlier. "Please, make yourself comfortable."

The Fair lord blinked, for he realized just then that Miss Berrydell did indeed look chilled. "Do they not provide you with enough blankets?" he asked.

"I gave mine to Brookbower months ago." Her mouth was set in a grim expression. She moved to stand close by the fire, holding her skirt away from the flames. Her bare ankles were visible in this position, but this was not as scandalous among Fair Folk as among humans, so Willowvale scarcely noticed, and Theo resolutely ignored it.

Willowvale stared at her. "Did he not have one of his own?"

"He did. He was chilled, and I offered mine. He accepted." She stared at the moss upon the floor in the bedroom, which was more visible from where she now stood.

"Is he ill?"

Astrantia's gaze flicked to Theo, and with a sardonic twist of her lips, she said, "Not as far as I am aware. He likes to be comfortable."

Theo's frown deepened. "Not much of a gentleman, is he, to leave you with no blanket while he has more than his share."

The fairy maiden twitched one shoulder. "I vowed to protect him, and I believe I am fulfilling that duty by protecting him from the chill."

Willowvale growled, "I wonder that Silverthorn wants him back at all."

Miss Berrydell blinked. "I do not mind the blanket so much," she said with precision. "What infuriates me is that anyone in the Fair Lands stooped to such a horrific scheme in the first place, and that somehow my desire to serve the Fair Lands, which I had thought noble, was twisted into utility for such a despicable purpose."

She leaned her shoulders against the brick above the fireplace, apparently soaking in every bit of heat she could.

At this moment, there was a knock on the door. Willowvale opened it.

Servants brought in three trays generously laden with food which filled the air with tantalizing scents. Herbed roast chicken, new potatoes generously slathered in butter, field greens with a tangy dressing, baked pears in a sweet sauce, and other delicacies were artfully displayed. Another servant brought a large teapot and three porcelain teacups adorned with the crest of the Elmerick family upon one side and the Arichtan throne upon the other. The servants placed the trays upon the table around the little azalea, eyeing it curiously.

Willowvale nodded to the servants, and Theo said, "Thank you, Martin, everyone."

The Fair maiden echoed his thanks almost inaudibly, and she watched them as they stepped quietly from the room.

"Have you been mistreated by the Arichtans other than the fact of your detainment itself?" asked Willowvale.

"Not in any way that merits complaint," the Fair maiden said. She stepped to the table. "If you will forgive me, I am rather hungry. May we eat while we discuss matters further?"

"Of course."

Theo, having already been standing closer to the table, obligingly held her chair for her. With quiet efficiency, he filled each tea strainer with tea from his bag, put the tea strainers in the cups, and poured steaming water into each cup.

"Thank you," said Willowvale, with a glance at Theo.

They ate in near silence, aside from a few polite inquiries as to whether she would like more tea and when Willowvale passed her the butter for her roll. When Astrantia had finished, she said quietly, "I would like to sit by the fire, if I may. I imagine the guards will want to take me back to my cell soon, so I would like to enjoy every minute of this relative freedom and comfort."

"Please do." Willowvale's sharp, pale eyes caught the faint tremor in her hand as she stood. "Are you well, Miss Berrydell?"

"I am fine, Lord Willowvale." She looked at him in confusion. "Why do you ask?"

"Your hands are trembling." It was merely a statement of fact, with no obvious warmth in it, but she blinked.

"I'm fine," she repeated. "I was thinking of… well, I was wondering what I would do once you succeed in obtaining Lord Brookbower's release."

She moved to stand upon the stone hearth, and the Fair lord moved aside while she arranged her skirt so that it stayed safely away from the flames as she leaned closer to the fire, soaking in the heat.

"I would presume you would desire to return to the Fair Lands," he said, with a cold sort of curiosity.

She gave him a flat look, then looked at Theo.

"I can step outside, if you would prefer to speak in confidence," Theo said.

Astrantia pressed her lips together, and then murmured, "Well, I suppose it doesn't matter." She swallowed, her striking magenta eyes searching Theo's face for a moment, then Willowvale's face with similar intensity. "If it were up to me, I'm not sure I would return to the Fair Court at all. How can I serve a king who would resort to such measures, even in desperation? I cannot betray my vow to protect

Brookbower with my life, but once he is safe?" She gazed bleakly at them each in turn. "I have half a mind to ask Elmerick if he'll let me live quietly here in the human world. Surely there is something I can do to help make amends for what our people have done."

Willowvale stared at her. "I thought you loved the Fair Lands," he breathed.

"I do." She swallowed, and there was a faint gleam of unshed tears in her eyes. "But perhaps my best service to them is to show the human world that not all Fair Folk are so selfish as to sacrifice innocent children to save themselves. Even if it is like exile, there is honor to be found in such a life."

The Fair lord clasped his hands together behind his back. "That is quite sacrificial of you," he murmured. "I assume you have not told Brookbower?"

"Of course not." She smiled, pale and proud, with her chin high. "Might I ask how the negotiations are going?"

Willowvale huffed softly and turned away. He paced once around the room, but found the furniture arranged in such a way as to make his first course about the space irritatingly irregular. He came to a stop near her again. "I suppose it will take some time to convince him," he said at last. "Silverthorn has already agreed to appoint a different ambassador and an entirely new delegation, if Elmerick desires, so unless Elmerick plans to go to war again, he'll agree eventually."

He glanced at Theo. "You're speaking with him later, I believe."

"I am." Theo smiled.

"How much longer are you staying in Idosa?"

"Unless His Majesty Elmerick requests my presence longer, I thought I might depart tomorrow. I have some associates I'd like to visit here in Idosa, and some in Skystead." Theo said this for Astrantia's benefit, since Willowvale had heard it earlier. "Then I thought I would go home. If you like, I can come back in a few weeks, if you think the negotiations will last that long."

At this moment there was a sharp knocking upon the door.

Willowvale's snowy brows drew downward in a fierce scowl. Theo murmured, "I'll get it," and strode to the door.

"Miss Berrydell," the guard said tersely.

She bowed politely to Willowvale and Theo, then strode toward the door, her face carefully serene and her chin high.

Theo stepped closer to Willowvale and murmured, "A blanket for her," into the fairy's ear.

The Fair lord started and, turning away, said brusquely, "Wait a moment." He crossed into the bedroom and returned a moment later with the fine wool blanket from the end of his own bed, still neatly folded. "There is another one. Would you like it too?"

Astrantia stared at him. "That is kind of you, Lord Willowvale. Thank you."

"You're welcome." Perhaps a faint hint of a smile flickered over his lips, but it passed so quickly that the Fair maiden later thought she'd imagined it. He didn't look happy; in fact, he looked simultaneously annoyed and mortified, his narrow features sharp and his mouth pinched as he glared at the guards.

The guard said to Theo, "His Majesty is ready for you now. I'll take you to him while the others take Miss Berrydell to her accommodations."

Theo bowed deeply to Astrantia. "I am honored and delighted to know you, Miss Berrydell," he said, his voice warm and kind. "I look forward to our next conversation."

Willowvale bowed to her gracefully, but he had no pretty words.

CHAPTER SIX
The Fair Ambassador

The cell block beneath the palace seemed especially dark and cold after the bright luxury of Willowvale's suite and the warmth of the fire. Still, Astrantia carried the blanket folded in her arms, and it felt like a gift.

She laughed to herself. Lord Willowvale had not been so thoughtful; she had not missed the fact that Mr. Overton had prompted him to offer the blanket to her. Humans could be charming indeed, despite her present captivity.

The guard did not take the blanket from her, as she had half-expected. He merely nodded his head to her as he locked her back in the cell.

From the cell to her left, Lord Brookbower barked, "Well?" His voice echoed in the stone cell block.

It was not exactly a dungeon, though it had certainly felt like one at times. The walls were solid stone, but smoothly sanded and mortared together, neither rough nor damp. Still, with winter well underway, the air was frigid. The lack of sunlight was a constant, gnawing ache, but every other day the guards took the Fair Folk in pairs up to exercise in the courtyard for an hour, and despite the chill, the sunlight and scent of distant trees during these excursions were delightful.

"His Majesty Silverthorn sent Lord Ash Willowvale to negotiate for our release. There was a human there with him, Mr. Theodore Overton, IV, of Valestria."

"A human? Why?"

"Apparently they are friends." Astrantia wrapped the blanket around her shoulders and sat upon her cot.

Brookbower paced in his cell, his boots making the familiar clicking which had filled much of the preceding three months. "Willowvale has a human friend? I cannot believe it of him; he's far too proud for that."

Astrantia did not bother to argue. She put her face in her hands and inhaled the faint, lingering scent of the smoke from the fire which had warmed her so recently.

The Fair ambassador continued pacing. Across from Astrantia, Brookbower's personal servant Cyprus Hawksbane sighed heavily and lay back on his cot. Astrantia quirked an eyebrow at him, and he lifted his gaze to the ceiling in a rare gesture of frustration. Hawksbane was the most reserved of the Fair delegation and even in the enforced equality of captivity had said little. He spoke when necessary, but revealed little of his own thoughts or feelings. The two administrative assistants, Cricket Fallingwater and Bramble Tarragon, were not much more talkative. Still, all of them except Brookbower would take a turn singing in the nightly routine they had established. Fallingwater had a bright, clear voice as pure as his name, while Tarragon's voice was a little deeper and richer. Hawksbane had the deepest—and to Astrantia's ears most pleasing—voice of them all. Astrantia's own voice was high and lovely, and formed a particularly beautiful counterpart to Hawksbane's.

Brookbower permitted the singing only because he was seething with boredom; three months in the relatively featureless cells had nearly driven them all to madness. None of them possessed plant magic strong enough to grow moss or anything else beneath the ground and surrounded by stone as they were; perhaps Willowvale might have been able to do it, but it would challenge even him. Brookbower's ability with the veil was slight, at best, and of course he had vowed not to make any escape attempts, so even if he could have opened a door here, he could not have escaped. Moreover, the humans, not entirely trusting the word of the Fair Folk, had bolted iron grating to every wall, floor, and ceiling of the cells. The floor had then been covered in a thin carpet, for the iron was not intended to torture the fairies but rather to prevent them from opening a door into the surface.

Astrantia had been darkly amused that the humans knew even less about how the veil worked than Brookbower did. Everyone knew it made little sense to open a door into the veil in the floor, for it would be beyond dangerous to drop into the veil without knowing where one would land, and the veil was hardly likely to reveal that until one was entirely inside it. Still, Brookbower had been infuriated enough that had he not been prevented both by his word and by the iron, he might have been willing to risk it. He would undoubtedly prefer to die in the veil than wait in the human world for His Majesty Elmerick to try, convict, and condemn him.

"Why do you think Willowvale and the human are friends? What led you to that conclusion?" said Brookbower, skepticism filling his voice.

"Willowvale introduced Overton as such."

Brookbower stopped pacing, and Astrantia imagined him staring at the wall that separated them in bafflement. "Willowvale said it?"

"Yes."

"What a bizarre turn of events!" The Fair lord resumed pacing more slowly. "When did he arrive? Did he tell you anything about how negotiations were proceeding?"

"Only this morning, and that they were not going well, though he hopes to be successful in time."

The ambassador made a noise low in his throat. "I should hope so."

Hawksbane, who was directly across from Astrantia, caught her gaze, and in a rare display of emotion, raised one eyebrow in wry amusement. "Would it be so bad if a fairy made a human friend?" he said thoughtfully.

Brookbower laughed. "It would be disgraceful! I find it difficult to believe of Willowvale. Perhaps his words were not as clear as what you conveyed to me. I imagine he plays some game on our behalf."

Astrantia pressed the heels of her hands against her eyes and took several slow, deep breaths. "He was quite unambiguous, Ambassador," she said finally, and if there was an edge of offended fury in her voice at being doubted, everyone but Brookbower felt it justified.

CHAPTER SEVEN
Counsel to a King

"His Majesty will see you now, Mr. Overton."

"Thank you!" Theo beamed at the servant.

Their steps echoed coldly upon the marble floors as they walked through the palace. At last the servant knocked upon a heavy wooden door and, hearing a greeting from within, entered and bowed.

"Mr. Overton, Your Majesty."

"Send him in."

A moment later, Theo was standing in front of His Majesty Valor Elmerick in a darkly elegant sitting room. The walls were painted a rich burgundy, which looked even deeper beside the ridiculous ornate gilded frames of the many paintings upon the walls. Most of the paintings seemed to be of buildings, which Theo supposed were probably historically important, since the paintings looked antique.

Theo bowed deeply. "Your Majesty."

"Mr. Overton." The king studied him a moment and then gestured to a chair across from him. "You may sit. The letter of introduction from your king was *fascinating*."

The young man's cheeks flushed.

"In fact, I would very much like to hear the whole story, from the beginning, if you will tell me." The king glanced at the servant near the door and said, "Tea."

So Theo spent the next hour telling the Arichtan monarch about his talent with the veil, his months as the Wraith, his love for the Fair Folk and their dangerous, beautiful, alien land, and his friendship with the irascible Lord Willowvale. He told of Silverthorn's abdication, his own refusal of the offered crown, and, finally, the influence he had been invited to wield in the Fair Court in the future.

Through the whole quiet recitation, Elmerick had listened in rapt attention, his fingers interlaced in his lap. His cup of tea grew cold beside him.

At last, he said, "How extraordinary."

"Thank you, Your Majesty." Theo smiled modestly.

"Will you show me the veil? I've never actually seen it."

Theo stood and the king rose with him. With a twist and a pull of magic, Theo opened a door a few feet away, so that the clear afternoon light from the window fell onto the brick floor of the veil, illuminating the dusty passage.

The king stepped closer, peering cautiously into the silent tunnel. He let out a soft breath. "Can you open a door anywhere?"

"More or less, though it has taken a great deal of practice. I have very little precision when attempting to open a door from the veil into a place I've never been; yesterday Lord Willowvale and I entered Idosa by way of the southern quarter. I haven't been in the city for years, and I never spent enough time here to know my way well."

Elmerick glanced at him. "Your Arichtan is excellent. I would have thought you'd grown up here."

"We spent some time here when I was young, and I enjoy languages."

"Now that you have been here, can you now open a door from the veil directly into my palace?" The question was not exactly hostile, but there was an edge of concern in it.

"Yes, Your Majesty." Theo met the king's gaze steadily.

The king made a thoughtful sound in his throat and then gestured at the door. "How does it close?"

Theo let it close and said, "It prefers to close. I was keeping it open."

"Can anything from the veil enter the human world?"

"I've never heard of that happening, and I've escaped creatures of the veil several times by stepping into the human world and closing the door in their faces."

With a deep sigh, Elmerick turned to face him and crossed his arms. "Am I to understand from your story that you support Lord Willowvale's task here?"

"I do."

"Brookbower is hardly innocent, you know. Not only was he aware of the kidnappings, the fairies who were actually abducting the poor children asked him for advice and succor at times. He supported their efforts both morally and materially."

"I don't doubt it," Theo agreed. "Still, he is a legally appointed delegate of a foreign power, and you're treating him like a criminal without a formal declaration of war. Do you intend to make such a declaration?"

The king stared at him, his jaw tight. "I'm very close to doing so."

"Would that serve your people best, Your Majesty?" Theo asked gently.

Elmerick sighed. "Probably not. Still, how can you, or anyone, contend that there ought to be no repercussions for what they have done?" He frowned. "Well, not all of them. Miss Berrydell is innocent of any crime, and the staff... we have less evidence of their support."

Theo let this admission settle in the room, quiet and serious. When Elmerick looked away again, the young man said, "Does it not seem wise to let His Majesty Silverthorn's change of heart affect the Fair Court before provoking them into another war?"

"It would hardly be provoking them; it would be a well-considered response to an unforgivable offense. Anyway, what interest do you have in this? You did not suffer in the war." The king studied him, brows lowered. "Is it concern for the Fair Court or humanity that motivates your advice?"

"Both, Your Majesty. I love the Fair Lands, and I have friends there. But I am human, and my heart is in the human world as much as it is in the Fair Lands. It would be tragic to let this opportunity to improve relations between the Fair Folk and humans to pass by."

The Arichtan monarch made a soft *hm* sound.

Theo sighed and said, "I am not a diplomat, and I am sure you have many concerns and considerations of which I am unaware. Nevertheless, I implore you to choose mercy and wisdom over your very justified anger."

"What will the Fair Court do if I declare war?"

"Undoubtedly they would return hostility for hostility. But Silverthorn does not desire a war, Your Majesty. He apparently chose to send Willowvale because he believed Willowvale the least likely to offend you, of those capable of traversing the veil at all. Willowvale was chosen for his amiable personality." Theo said this with an amused little quirk of his lips.

"You cannot expect me to believe that." Elmerick's eyebrows drew downward in sudden anger. "He's insufferable."

"As preposterous as it sounds, it is absolutely true." Theo pressed his lips together and looked down, considering his words. "I misjudged him at first as well, Your Majesty. It is easy to see what someone shows you in their words and actions, and he certainly showed me the worst of himself. Still, shall we all judge each other by our most desperate, shameful actions, as if that is all we are? Wouldn't it be better to look for the best in each other, even when it is deeply hidden?"

Elmerick paced across the room, frowning at the floor. "I suppose your own king takes your counsel, does he?" he said suddenly.

Theo blinked. "Rather often, I suppose, all things considered. He does listen when I speak of the Fair Court. But I'm hardly his most important advisor in other matters."

The king gave a soft *hmph*. "Thank you for your insight, Mr. Overton. I will give Willowvale a chance to convince me. You are free to go about your business in Idosa, and you are welcome to stay in the palace."

"Thank you, Your Majesty." Theo bowed deeply. "I thank you for your consideration, and I hope I have been of some assistance."

CHAPTER EIGHT
A Series of Frustrating Conversations

The moss under the table tickled Lord Ash Willowvale's bare toes as he ate supper alone in his room. The fuzzy fronds were cooler than he preferred, but the texture soothed him, and he relished this little scrap of solitude. The Arichtan king already hated him, Overton was undoubtedly going to leave the following morning, and his doomed mission was likely to end in execution sooner rather than later.

He sipped his tea and stared out the window at the darkening sky. The sunset had been rather lackluster, for there were no clouds to catch the brilliant light and turn it to gold, orange, coral, and magenta. As he watched, the last of the glow faded, leaving a soft blue gray.

The night sky in the human world was never graced with pink or cerulean streaks, and Willowvale thought morosely that he was unlikely to ever see those beloved colors above him again.

Tomorrow morning he would demand to visit Brookbower and his staff in the prison to get a full report. His snowy brow drew fiercely down at the thought of Brookbower. If he had disliked the ambassador before, he hated him now. To accept Miss Berrydell's blanket for his own comfort, while the Fair maiden went without?

It was unconscionable.

His anger needed an outlet, but it would not serve him well to produce a tangle of thorny vines that ruined the walls and paintings. The Fair lord snorted in derision as he imagined Elmerick's anger at the destruction he might cause. Instead, Willowvale yanked off his jacket and paced, scowling ferociously, for nearly an hour, while his tea grew cold.

At last, frustrated by his swirling thoughts, he threw himself into a chair again and poked at the dying embers of the fire.

The following morning, Willowvale woke to the first hint of soft gray in the sky. He had slept in the bed, for the room was too cold to sleep well upon the moss, but as soon as he awoke, he stepped his bare feet onto the thick carpet of moss beside the bed. Then, with a sigh, he dressed in the nicest suit he had brought and pulled on his low boots.

He opened the door to see a guard stationed in the hallway. The man looked at him with hard, wary eyes.

"When can I have breakfast?" Willowvale asked, his voice sharp.

"I'll send for it now."

Willowvale closed the door and crossed the room to look out at what he could see of the courtyard from his vantage point.

Several minutes later, a knock heralded the arrival of breakfast. Willowvale accepted the tray with a muttered, "thank you" and a nod. It took effort to be so friendly, especially to someone whose last name wasn't Overton, but the mission was already difficult enough. Rather than indulge his irritation and pessimism, he would put on the most agreeable facade he could in hopes of freeing Miss Berrydell and Brookbower.

Brookbower. Brookbower was the mission. Miss Berrydell was merely collateral.

He stared at his plate. Of course Brookbower was the mission. He had only thought of Miss Berrydell first because her face came to mind so easily, with her lovely pink eyes and magenta hair, and that faint delicate blush across her cheeks.

Willowvale blew out a soft *pfft* at his own thoughts. What a ridiculous distraction! He was nearly ashamed of how her soft smile lingered in his mind. What business did he have thinking of a Fair maiden, as if she would have any interest in him, even if she were free? She would not, she ought not, think of him at all.

He found that he wasn't hungry after all, but he ate anyway, because it would be foolish to face the day's challenges with anything less than all his wits.

Just after he finished eating and was morosely contemplating the prospect of speaking with Elmerick again, another knock sounded on the door. He sighed.

He jerked the door open and barked, "What?"

"Good morning to you, too, my friend!" Theo's eyes danced with mirth.

Willowvale's scowl deepened, but he held the door open wider. "Is it?" he muttered.

"It is." Theo swept in, full of cheerful energy. "May I sit down?"

"Make yourself comfortable." Willowvale nodded the servant in to take his breakfast tray, and the servant did so, eyeing Theo and the Fair lord curiously as he passed by.

Theo studied the fairy, his sparkling good humor undimmed by Willowvale's pale glower. "I have a little good news, and some advice, if you'll allow me to be so bold," he said finally.

The Fair lord's pinched lips softened, just a little, and he sighed again. "I have need of good news," he admitted. He sank into the chair by the fire and stared at Theo. "Though what reason you have to offer it is beyond me. What magic have you wrought now?"

The young man raised his eyebrows. "Lord Willowvale, do not tell me you have despaired already! You've barely begun negotiations!"

The fairy blew out a soft breath and looked at the glowing coals in the fireplace. Overton's bright, friendly face was like salt in the wound of his coming failure. He shrugged one shoulder.

Theo leaned forward to prod at the fire, as if he thought Willowvale were chilled. "Well, first the good news, I suppose. I spoke with His Majesty Elmerick on your behalf yesterday, after your audience with him. I believe he is nearly ready to agree to a new Fair ambassador more to his liking than Brookbower. He doesn't want war much more than Silverthorn does, but I am sure you can understand how deeply he is offended and horrified by what was done to the children." He held Willowvale's pale gaze.

The fairy swallowed and his eyes slid to the fire. "I understand," he said in a low voice.

"So I thought I might visit my business associates this afternoon, while you're speaking with His Majesty, and leave tomorrow morning for Skystead."

Willowvale glanced at him. "You said you had advice."

Theo made a thoughtful sort of *hm* sound. "When a man is nearly ready to agree to something, but he is reluctant, it will do no good to push him. Let him see reason in his own time. Show yourself to be reasonable and trustworthy."

The fairy looked down at the subtle pattern in the silken fabric of his trousers, and then at the toes of his boots. He sighed.

"What troubles you?" Theo asked.

"Do you want a comprehensive list?" Willowvale said, almost inaudibly.

"All right," said Theo, with a hint of laughter in his warm, kind voice.

This startled Willowvale into a melancholy chuckle. "It galls me that you think me reasonable and trustworthy, when you've so little reason to think well of me at all," he said. "But that is beside the point." He sighed and muttered, "If Silverthorn had been in Elmerick's place, so righteously offended by a human ambassador to our lands, he would have executed the ambassador months ago. I do not understand why Elmerick hasn't, and I fear that somehow I will further offend him and cost the delegation their lives."

Theo frowned. "I did not realize your ill temper troubled you as much as it does those around you."

Willowvale stared at him. "Do you think I enjoy being intolerable? It is long habit and despair that make me so now." He could not hold Theo's gaze, and he looked down again. "Besides, I suppose there is always the last option. You would approve of it."

"And what is that?" Theo asked gently.

Willowvale managed a thin smile. "If Elmerick won't let Brookbower go, I will offer myself in his place. If Elmerick must execute a Fair lord for crimes against Arichtan children, mine merit death just as much as Brookbower's do."

Theo blinked. "My lord, I really don't think that will be required," he said at last.

Willowvale shrugged. "Not all humans are as eager to forgive as you are, Overton."

"Not all humans are as unforgiving as you seem to think, either. I sincerely doubt His Majesty Elmerick would accept such a sacrifice, even if you offered it, my friend."

The fairy blinked and then laughed under his breath. "You persist in calling me a friend, when I do not deserve it. I am more deeply in your debt by the hour." His lips twisted in a bitter smile, and he added, "I fear I will not able to repay you appropriately before the end."

Theo gave a soft, theatrical groan. "I wish you would trust me, Lord Willowvale!"

This response startled the fairy even further, and he stared at Theo. "I do," he said in surprise. "I didn't realize it, but I do. You've wrought yet more magic when I wasn't looking."

Theo's warm eyes sparkled, and he said gently, "Then trust me in this, please. Be patient with His Majesty Elmerick. Don't lose your temper while you wait for him to see reason. You know the Fair Court; tell him all about every possible replacement ambassador. Be open with him, and through you, he will see that the Fair throne has changed."

Willowvale swallowed grief and regret, fury and despair, and he had no words for several minutes. He stared at the fire, acutely aware of Theo's quiet, compassionate regard. Finally, he said, as though it pained him, "Thank you, Overton."

Theo inclined his head. "You're welcome. Shall I come back in a week or two to escort you triumphantly home to the Fair Lands?"

Willowvale rubbed one hand over his eyes. "Well, I certainly can't stop you," he muttered.

Theo laughed. "Don't be sour about it!" He stood and put a hand on Willowvale's shoulder, warm and strong and reassuring. "Trust me."

The fairy huffed something almost like a laugh. "All right, Overton. I'll try."

"Good. I'll see you again in two weeks, then." Theo bowed with a sparkling smile, and added, "Don't despair."

Shortly after Theo left, Willowvale had resolved to petition Elmerick to allow him to visit Brookbower in the prison. He straightened his vest and jacket, ran his fingers through his snowy curls, and took a deep breath. He stepped out into the hallway.

"I want an audience with His Majesty Elmerick." Willowvale's voice was not exactly warm, but he thought he did a commendable job of sounding politely neutral. Then, with Theo's patience and kindness fresh on his mind, he added curtly, "Please."

"He will summon you when he is ready to see you."

"Oh." Willowvale resisted a very strong urge to snarl an insult at the man. "In that case, I want to visit Lord Brookbower's delegation wherever they are held."

Much to the fairy's surprise, the guard said, "Follow me."

Blinking at this unexpected success, the Fair lord followed the guard through the expansive corridors. At the end of a long hallway, they exited the building and crossed the courtyard to the far side, whereupon they entered another door and continued through more marble-floored passages.

Although this corridor was floored in marble, it had a slightly less ostentatious air. The walls had high wainscotting of dark oak, and the upper portions were painted a rich burgundy. Only a few large, gilt-framed paintings adorned the walls at long intervals between heavy wooden doors. Some distance from the end of the hall, the guard stopped at one such door with a sign on it that said, "Security Staff Only."

He turned to face Willowvale. "His Majesty requires that you swear not to break them out of prison, nor help them escape captivity. You are to be allowed to visit them, and they will be freed only when His Majesty permits it."

"I so swear."

The guard nodded sharply. He pulled a key from his jacket and unlocked the door.

When he pushed it aside, the room revealed behind it was mostly empty. A young guard stood behind a worn desk, and he nodded respectfully to Willowvale's escort. His wide, curious eyes followed the Fair lord as he crossed the room.

The guard used a different key to unlock another heavy door on the far side of the room. Behind it, a stone staircase descended into darkness. The guard behind them pulled an oil lamp from behind the desk.

Willowvale flicked light to his fingertips and then let the fairy light drift toward the ceiling, where it spread like glowing mist against the stone.

The elder guard said, "I'll take the lamp."

Willowvale resisted the urge to roll his eyes. He let the guard go before him down the stairs.

The lamplight danced upon the stone walls, the yellow tones muted in the bright, cool fairy light.

At the bottom of the stairs, the guard turned left and unlocked another door with the same key.

He pulled the door open and paused, frowning, and the Fair lord looked over his shoulder.

A bright, cheerful light shone upon the stone walls and floor of the little cell block, apparently emanating from a tree growing in the middle of the common area between the cells. Each cell was fronted by a door of iron grating, which would provide no privacy during the necessaries or when it was time to sleep. The space was nearly ten feet across, with a ceiling at least ten feet high, if not twelve; the space felt cavernous and cold rather than small and cramped.

The tree was thick and squat, its branches spreading nearly into the cells on either side. The leaves rustled softly in a wind they could not feel, casting glittering pink and golden light across the stone floor and upon the iron doors.

"What is that?" the guard growled.

"Just a glamour." Astrantia's clear voice came from one of the near cells. "Surely you do not begrudge us a little harmless entertainment."

"Will it hurt humans? Will it help you escape?"

"We have already sworn we will not escape," a male voice said acidly. He did not address the question of harm.

"I've brought Lord Ash Willowvale," the guard said without stepping forward. "Will your magic harm me?"

"No, idiot!" the same male voice snarled. "It's a glamour."

Willowvale did roll his eyes at this. A human could hardly be expected to understand the various sorts of magic. He stepped forward, not bothering to duck as he passed through the ethereal tree limbs and fuschia leaves. "Brookbower, I see you are as pleasant as ever." He smiled sardonically at the other Fair lord's glower.

"Willowvale." Brookbower approached the door to his cell but did not touch it. "I understand you're here to negotiate on our behalf." He was as tall as Willowvale and a little broader of shoulder, though still quite lean. His hair was a rich olive green, and his eyes gleamed yellow in the golden light from the glamoured tree. His skin was a walnut tone, a color more familiar to human eyes, though not common in this part of the world.

"I am." Willowvale looked through the glamour at the true form of the cells; this was not a strong glamour, however impressed the guard might be.

The captive Fair Folk stood when he stepped forward to look more closely into each cell, noting the rough provisions for the necessaries, the unpadded cots, and the lack of windows. The fairies bowed in turn to him, and he returned the courtesy.

The Fair Folk had glamoured their cells to appear more pleasant, though Willowvale was skilled enough that he could see through most of them. Hawksbane was apparently the most gifted in glamour; Willowvale couldn't see through the glamour in his cell at all, though he could guess where the cot was because the fairy had been sitting on it when he'd first seen him. Hawksbane's cell was covered in a profusion of pale pink anemone flowers, with the illusion of an expansive view from a high window over a lush valley where the far wall stood.

Miss Berrydell had given her cell the glamour of a rough crystalline ceiling that glinted in a hundred shades of pink. The floor had the appearance of a forest floor covered in thick moss, with bright red toadstools in one corner and a cascade of pink and purple blooms falling down one wall. The other two walls had the illusion of a lovely view much like that of Hawksbane, though she looked out upon a valley in the first blush of early spring rather than Hawksbane's mid-summer.

Brookbower's cell was adorned with blue and deep purple irises, with white jasmine upon the walls and clear quartz glittering upon the ceiling. Fallingwater had enlivened his cell with a thousand shades of green leaves, with only a few delicate red and white shelf funguses creeping up the wall in one corner. Tarragon's cell looked like the walls had been made of pale wood, and the windows he had glamoured in the solid walls had views of a forest of silvery beeches.

The guard could not see through the glamours, and he stood where Willowvale had left him. The younger guard had followed them down the stairs, and he stepped closer to mutter into the man's ear.

Willowvale said, "I assume you were informed that the Fair Lands are no longer fading. The solution is not entirely permanent, but it is secure for the foreseeable future, and a more permanent solution is in progress."

Brookbower blinked and narrowed his eyes. "Explain."

"Silverthorn will make everything clear at your debriefing." Willowvale had no inclination to tell the entire story here, not only because Brookbower's supercilious scowl made him want to annoy the ambassador in every way, but because revealing how the Fair Lands had been saved would also reveal the weakness that had made such salvation necessary.

The ambassador muttered something savage under his breath. "When will we be free?"

"I don't know yet." Willowvale's cold gaze flicked to the others in the cells. "I'd like to speak with everyone individually."

"Why?" Brookbower snapped. "I hold all authority over our delegation."

"I'm not actually asking," said Willowvale caustically.

"You presume too much, Willowvale," snarled the ambassador. "Do you aspire to my position?"

Willowvale gave a sharp bark of laughter. "Your months in prison haven't injured your pride at all, have they?"

Brookbower nearly bared his teeth. "You don't deny it."

"No, I don't want your position." Willowvale studied the ambassador, eyes narrowed. "It would be much easier to convince them to let you live if you could pretend to be a little less offensively arrogant."

With biting sarcasm, Brookbower said, "Oh, that's *rich*, Willowvale! I shall take you as my model of humility and gracious condescension."

Willowvale snarled, "If it were up to me, I would have left you here to rot."

"Fortunately it isn't, then." Brookbower gave him a toothy grin. "Still, I wonder if you're capable of fulfilling the king's decree."

"Just because you are incapable does not mean I am as well."

From Astrantia's cell, a slight sound caught Willowvale's attention, and he glanced at her. She was sitting on her cot with her knees pulled up in front of her and her skirts demurely folded around her feet, so that only the tips of her low boots peeked out. She looked away, her lips twitching.

Pale cheeks flushing with humiliation and fury, Willowvale ground his teeth together and turned away. He glowered at Hawksbane and said, "Who are you, then? Hawksbane, Fallingwater, or Tarragon?"

"Hawksbane." The fairy smiled thinly at him. "Why should you want to talk to me, my lord?"

"What did you know of your master's part in the kidnappings?" Willowvale growled.

"I was aware that Lords Aspen and Camphor visited at odd hours, but the ambassador did not take me into his confidence in that matter."

"But you were aware of it," Willowvale pressed.

"I am very good at my job, and part of my job is to know my lord's business. Of course I knew of it."

This was the first time Astrantia had ever heard that edge of irritation and scorn in Hawksbane's voice, and she looked at him in surprise. Then she let out a soft breath of betrayal, for even Hawksbane had known what she had not, at least at first.

"You approved of it?" she said softly, and he glanced at her, then away.

There was a tense silence, and finally Hawksbane muttered, "I saw no alternative." His yellow eyes glittered.

Willowvale felt a twinge of unwelcome sympathy. "If you had been aware of an alternative, would you have advocated for it?"

"Of course," Hawksbane replied.

Brookbower interjected, "You presume the alternative would work. I would not be willing to risk the Fair Lands on anything less than certainty."

Willowvale raised his eyebrows and glanced at him. "I wasn't speaking to you, Brookbower," he said witheringly.

The ambassador snarled something under his breath, and then said more clearly, "After I've spoken with Silverthorn, I'd like to run you through."

"The feeling is entirely mutual," Willovwale muttered. He turned his attention to the fairy in the next cell, whose pale blue hair stuck up like dandelion fluff. "What about you? Who are you, and did you know about the effort involving Arichtan children?"

"I am Cricket Fallingwater." His violet brows drew down in a scowl. "I found out shortly before we were detained."

Tarragon, in the cell beside him, nodded once but said nothing. A faint flush lit his orange cheeks.

Willowvale turned to look at Brookbower again, his gaze flicking over the other fairy's rumpled but still elegant attire. He inclined his head in a bow so shallow as to be an obvious insult, and said, "Brookbower." Then, with a deeper bow, "Miss Berrydell." He nodded to the others, feeling himself to be graciously condescending in doing so, for they were scarcely higher than servants, and in the Fair Lands, servants were considered nearly invisible.

Hawksbane snorted softly, his lips wrinkling in wry amusement.

The ambassador's shoulders twitched, and he paced around the cell again, restless and annoyed.

Astrantia inclined her head to Willowvale gracefully, but he could not read the expression in her lovely pink eyes.

He strode past the guards and up the stairs.

When he returned to his room, Willowvale was surprised to discover that Theo had left his pack of tea on the little table beside the azalea, along with a sealed note.

Lord Willowvale, I have not forgotten my promise to visit your king, and so, while I must depart upon my own business, I wish to assure you that I will fulfill this promise before I return in two weeks to escort you and the Fair delegation home.

Let it also be made clear that the tea confers no obligation upon you and is a gift in the human tradition.

Sincerely,

Theo

The Fair lord's request for an audience that evening with the Arichtan king was denied, and Willowvale was left to his own devices in comfortable confinement for the next three days.

He rationed the tea carefully, for it seemed an oddly precious gift of peace and friendship in the sharp Arichtan palace. He made one cup of tea in the morning, which he drank sitting at the table with his bare toes deep in the thriving moss. Each evening he drank a second cup, savoring the rich vanilla and butterscotch scent by the fire.

Since he was alone, he indulged in minor comforts that would not have occurred to him at all if anyone were there to see the indignity. He took off his jacket and sat upon the hearth with his back to the flames. The dry heat through his shirt made his skin prickle, and his pale cheeks gained a flush of pink across his cheekbones. He closed his eyes and thought of the bargain he would make with Elmerick, if no other solution could be found.

Overton's optimism seemed baseless, given Willowvale's current inability even to gain an audience with the king. It would certainly be possible to fight his way out of the room; the guards were no match for him with his sword, much less with his magic. He could probably break into the prison, and with his magic, might even be able to rip the iron bars right out of the walls. Brookbower's water magic was not even close to Willowvale's magical gifts in either strength or utility in this case, for Brookbower could only use what little water was available to him. Besides, Brookbower and his delegation had promised not to try to escape.

Even if Willowvale did rip the doors off the cells, Brookbower's delegation would likely be unwilling, or unable, to escape. The vow had been explicit, and they had vowed to make no attempt, or effort that the magic might construe as an attempt, to escape. Even the slight motion of stepping over the threshold of their cells before they were released would violate that vow. The Arichtans were being unnecessarily cautious in their attempts to contain the fairies, with their stone cells and their iron bars. A cleverly worded vow such as they had already obtained was quite sufficient.

The third morning of his solitary confinement, the tension and boredom of this enforced inactivity drove Willowvale nearly to distraction. His room was as lush a paradise as he felt practical within the palace without actively offending the human king, and there was little other outlet for his offended pride and agitation within his room.

If the king intended to execute Brookbower, he would likely have done so already.

Unless he intended to make a public spectacle of the Fair ambassador in front of Willowvale.

The thought of such a scene slithered into his mind in quiet horror. Humans lied. Perhaps Elmerick was merely assembling the human spectators for the execution.

With this awful prospect in mind, unlikely though it might be, he felt the delay as an abrasive reminder of how powerless the human monarch apparently thought him. If he ought not rip the doors off the cells and extract the delegation by force, at least he ought to be prepared for a hurried escape into the veil.

So Willowvale attempted to open a door into the veil from his room. He pressed his magic into the air, tentatively at first but with increasing frustration as the veil stubbornly resisted him. Perhaps it was not the veil's stubbornness; perhaps it was merely his own lack of talent and skill in this area.

He pushed, twisting the power tighter and squeezing it into what felt like a crack in reality, until he felt his own magic writhing in protest. Sparkles appeared before his eyes, and he pushed more desperately.

The Fair lord collapsed to hands and knees, gasping and furious. The black spots in his vision grew, and he lay face down upon the moss with his eyes closed. His heart raced, and his hands tingled as if from a great distance.

If he fainted, he wouldn't have to think about his failure for a few minutes. It would be cowardly, to be sure, but the thought tempted him.

At this moment, there was a brisk knock on the door.

He struggled to his hands and knees, and then had to pause, for the black spots nearly overcame him. After a few steadying breaths, he made it to his feet. He yanked on his jacket and buttoned it as the knock sounded again.

At last, embarrassed, annoyed, and more than a little dizzy, he jerked the door open. "What is it?"

"His Majesty will see you now." The guard seemed to smirk at the Fair lord's annoyance.

Willowvale stepped out of his room and followed the guard without another word.

The hallways seemed particularly long and unfriendly as the fairy stalked behind his human guide. Perhaps it was the fact that the spots kept dancing in front of his eyes, and he felt he would actually die of humiliation if he were forced to stop and put his head between his knees while the guard waited. Perhaps it was the elegant Arichtan decor, all intricate patterns of harsh angles which grated upon his sensibilities like the high-pitched whine of a hundred angry wasps.

Still, he kept his feet steady, his posture straight and proud, and his lips firmly pinched together during the long walk to the king's study.

"Here you are, sir." The guard knocked upon the door, and then opened it and stepped aside.

Willowvale bowed as he entered, and as he straightened, the dizziness rushed upon him, so that he swayed and caught himself.

His Majesty Elmerick did not, at first, stand to greet him, but at this unusual movement, he half-rose, his brows lowering. Then he sat again, his gaze sharp upon Willowvale's face. "If I agree to release Brookbower alive, who might be appointed in his place?" he asked.

The Fair lord forced his mind to the task. "There are several lords His Majesty Silverthorn suggested who meet your qualifications, Your Majesty. Lord Cedar Mosswing might be most acceptable to you; he advocated against the war with your people, he saw no combat, and he was an integral part of the Wraith's operations in the Fair Lands. He and Mr. Overton are close friends."

Elmerick nodded and glanced at the man standing just to one side and a little behind him with a paper and a thin board to keep it steady. He appeared to be a scribe or assistant, and Willowvale mentally dismissed him.

"Any others?"

"Lord Agapanthus Birchbark is another possibility. He also advocated against the war and is said to have refused a direct order to fight from His Majesty Alder Silverthorn, the current king's father. He was not charged with treason, for the reported refusal occurred only a day or two before the king died."

"I have heard rumors that the king died under suspicious circumstances; is it possible Lord Birchbark was involved in his assassination?" the king asked.

Willowvale's frown deepened. "I have no personal knowledge of the assassination, Your Majesty, so I cannot say with certainty, but I would venture that it would be out of character for Birchbark. He is widely known to be of a peaceable temperament."

"Was he ever questioned about it?"

"Not to my knowledge." Willowvale's stomach churned. If Mosswing and Birchbark were not acceptable to Elmerick, there was no hope at all.

The king nodded thoughtfully. "Any others?"

The Fair lord sighed, trying to will the lingering shadows from his vision. He felt weak and light-headed from the effort with the veil. His timing was lamentable, for he felt sure he ought to be completely alert for this conversation.

"There is Lord Laurel Bayberry, but I think both he and you would be deeply displeased by his appointment."

"Why?"

Willowvale blinked, feeling himself suddenly on dangerous ground. He had already revealed more about the Fair Court than was customary, and openness had never come naturally to him. Still, Overton had advised him to be open, and Overton was unquestionably more skilled than he was at convincing people, and fairies, to see things his way.

So the Fair lord smiled wryly. "He prefers hunting with his wolves to asserting his influence in the Fair Court, and he is not fond of humans in general. Or fairies, for that matter."

The king nodded. "What others?"

"Lord Aster Bloodroot. Lord Bitternut Sassafras. Lord Cosmosia Moonflower. None of these, to my knowledge, speak Arichtan at all. Mosswing and Birchbark might speak a little. I doubt Bayberry does. Mosswing speaks Valestrian fluently. There are others acceptable to His Majesty Silverthorn, but they served in the Fair forces against your people, so I imagine you would not accept them." Willowvale took a steadying breath. The spots had nearly faded from his vision, but he felt as weak as a fading peony petal after a heavy rain.

The language barrier did not, of course, preclude Mosswing or any of the others from being assigned, but it would make the assignment more challenging on both the Fair and Arichtan sides.

"Are you eligible for the appointment?" Elmerick's voice was cold.

Willowvale blinked and narrowed his eyes, trying to see the trick in this question. Theo's admonition to be patient felt oddly easy to carry out; in his magical exhaustion, he could not muster the energy to be as irritable as usual. "If you insisted upon it, I expect Silverthorn would agree, but I did fight briefly in the war, so I would not expect to be selected."

The very idea of being assigned to Aricht was horrifying.

Elmerick studied his face. "I never told you what I wanted in return for the proof you demanded."

"You did not." Willowvale's skin felt suddenly cold. This was when Elmerick would demand something impossible, something terrible, that would jeopardize the Fair Lands again.

The Arichtan king crossed his arms, pulling his jacket tight across his broad shoulders and let the uncomfortable silence lengthen.

Willowvale pressed his lips together and said nothing. He could be as taciturn as any human, and the thought of the king attempting to wait him out, to frighten him with silence and cold looks, gave him a twinge of bitter amusement. He gave the faintest chilly smile and met the king's gaze.

"I haven't decided yet," the king said at last. "However, I will grant you this. Brookbower is the only one of the delegation who actively participated in the kidnappings, or even knew of them for any real length of time. Thus, he is the only one who will remain detained in the prison while we decide what to do. The others will be moved to accommodations along the hall in which you are staying, and you may speak freely with them. You may visit each other at will, but neither you nor they may leave the hall."

The Fair lord blinked. Then, with a stiff bow, he murmured, "Thank you, Your Majesty."

Elmerick nodded, and the audience was over.

CHAPTER NINE

A Gift of Moss

T rue to Elmerick's word, the Fair delegation, save Brookbower himself, was installed in the guest rooms along the hall in which Willowvale was staying later that afternoon.

When he heard movement in the hall, he opened his door to see Hawksbane entering the room across from him. Miss Berrydell, Fallingwater, and Tarragon were escorted a little farther down the hall, where Miss Berrydell was given the suite beside Hawksbane and Fallingwater the suite beside Willowvale. Tarragon was given the suite on the other side of Miss Berrydell.

He stood in the doorway to his rooms with his arms crossed, watching with sharp eyes as the guards then stationed themselves at each end of the hallway.

He retreated into his suite again, feeling a twinge of pleasure that he could not identify at first. It was not a result of his successful negotiations thus far, for he felt he could take no credit for this pleasant development.

Several hours later, there was a knock at his door, and he opened it to find a servant with his dinner tray.

"Thank you."

He waited until the servant had exited the room before he stepped out into the hallway. The guard at the end watched him warily, and he ignored the scrutiny as he walked to Miss Berrydell's door.

He knocked on it.

She opened it and stared at him. "Lord Willowvale?" Her voice was even lovelier speaking the Fair language than Arichtan, and he found himself smiling a little, without even meaning to.

"Miss Berrydell, I wonder if you might find it pleasant to eat with different company than you have had for the past several months."

She blinked, her delicate eyebrows drawn down. "Are you asking me to eat dinner with you?" she said carefully.

"I am." There. That was a sufficiently dignified way of addressing the issue.

The Fair maiden swallowed. "Just a moment," she said. She turned away and strode across the room to retrieve her own dinner tray, which she had just received. Laden with a plate of roasted chicken, turnips, carrots, greens, steaming bread, and a custard, not to mention a tall glass of water, it was rather heavy.

Astrantia sighed inwardly as she picked it up. She had dearly hoped to spend the evening alone for the first time in months, to weep quietly for the bone-shaking disappointment and disillusionment that so deeply grieved her.

The delegation had devised some conventions for privacy. They were all capable of devising a relatively strong glamour for at least a few moments, certainly long enough to hide the entire cell while they took care of any physical necessaries. Also, they were all courteous enough to look away when any of the others used such a glamour, for although they might have been able to see through it if they devoted their entire focus to the task, such a glamour in this situation indicated a desire for privacy. All Fair Folk trended toward reticence in comparison to many humans, and such a desire for privacy would generally be honored, and all the more so in their difficult situation.

Still, it would not do to be impolite, especially to Lord Willowvale, who had apparently already worked some improbable feat of diplomacy on their behalf.

The Fair lord stood aside while she stepped out of the door. "I'll take that," he muttered, and he swept the tray out of her hands.

She blinked at him, but said nothing. He stalked down the hall back to his own room, the door of which was standing open.

Within a few moments, she was sitting across from him at the little table with the exuberant little azalea between them. The pink blossoms were several shades lighter than Miss Berrydell's hair, and the contrast seemed to make her hair and eyes particularly vibrant.

Or perhaps it was merely that she was rather pale.

"Are you well, Miss Berrydell?" he asked abruptly, in the Fair language.

Her pink eyelashes fluttered, and she replied in Arichtan, "I am, Lord Willowvale. Why do you ask?"

He seemed to take no notice of her change of language. Perhaps it did not occur to him that the Arichtans were listening, or perhaps he felt that there was nothing to hide in whatever conversation he hoped to have with her.

"You look rather peaked, I think. It must be the deprivations of captivity."

She stared at him. "Do you always assess a maiden's looks so bluntly? My face is not, and has never been, relevant to my competence in my position."

Willowvale pressed his lips together. "I never said it was. Your face is perfectly nice. I only thought you looked pale. I assume captivity would produce an unpleasant pallor in anyone."

"Unpleasant pallor?" She smiled prettily, though there was a sharp gleam in her eye. "I suppose you would be a qualified judge of that."

He opened his mouth, and then closed it again without a word. Finally he said, "I was expressing a concern for your health, not disparaging your face. I thought my comment phrased rather well, ascribing any unusual pallor to your difficult situation without any intention of insult."

The humility in this half-apology did not come easily to him; he had bitten back half a dozen insults before he had come to this statement. Yet he did not *want* to insult her; the bitter words that came so easily were merely borne of long habit rather than intention.

His cold blue eyes took in every nuance of her expression, the way she pressed her pink lips together into a pale line and the delicate furrow between her magenta brows. She was quite lovely, and her pink eyes sparkled with quick intelligence. He could not abide a dull intellect.

Moreover, she had given every indication of being morally admirable, with her sympathy for the human children and her stated intention of carrying out her assignment to protect Brookbower at whatever cost to herself. As much as he despised Brookbower, Willowvale would have been shocked and horrified to his very soul if Miss Berrydell had given any indication of a desire to shirk her duty toward the ambassador. She had vowed to do it, therefore she would, as a Fair maiden; to do otherwise was not only unconscionable but nearly unthinkable.

"Have you had a chance to settle in to your room?" he said into the uncomfortable silence. He spoke in Arichtan, having taken her cue without apparently having realized her purpose.

"There was little to settle. Most of our effects are still in the house Lord Brookbower had rented." Her voice was politely neutral. She focused on her plate, as if she did not want to look at him.

"Shall I have them brought to the palace?" He had no idea whether Elmerick would allow this, but it seemed worth the attempt.

She glanced up at him through her pink lashes. "You may certainly try." She dabbed daintily at her mouth. "Might I ask how the negotiations are going?"

Willowvale stabbed a turnip with entirely unnecessary force. "Better than I had expected," he said cautiously. The less detail he gave on this matter, the better, as far as he was concerned.

Miss Berrydell took a deep breath and said, "Well, I thank you for the change in our circumstances. The rooms are more comfortable than the cells. I will return the blanket when we are finished with dinner."

Willowvale swallowed. "Thank you. You may keep it as long as you like." Then, with a grumpy twist to his lips, he added, "I would like to claim the credit for your change in accommodations, but I cannot in good conscience. His Majesty Elmerick informed me this morning of his decision in that regard."

Astrantia paused. "Did he say what prompted it?"

"He said that Brookbower was the only member of the delegation who even knew of the kidnappings for any real length of time, and several days ago he acknowledged that you personally were innocent of any crimes against the Arichtan children."

The Fair maiden's pink eyes narrowed in thought. Finally she said, "Hm," in a thoughtful sort of way.

"What do you think?" Willowvale asked.

"Oh, I certainly don't know." She smiled to herself and focused on her meal in a determined silence.

Willowvale sighed.

Astrantia had already deduced that the Arichtan king had his intelligence officers listen in on most of the Fair delegation's conversations in the prison. While very few of the humans spoke the Fair language with any fluency, those few had undoubtedly been tasked with nearly continuous covert surveillance of their cells in case the Fair delegation revealed anything. Still, their conversations had revealed little in the months of their imprisonment.

Upon the arrival of Lord Willowvale and his Valestrian friend Mr. Theodore Overton, IV, their first conversation had been conducted in this very room in Arichtan, for Mr. Overton spoke Arichtan like a native and Willowvale's Arichtan was passable, though accented. Miss Berrydell spoke almost no Valestrian at all.

If Mr. Overton had not been there, they would have conversed in the Fair language. But since Willowvale's human friend was present, they kept their conversation in Arichtan, and thus the intelligence officers no doubt hidden in the walls had heard every word of her grief-filled lament about her disappointment in her own king and her desire to make amends to Aricht on behalf of her people.

So it was with the Arichtan king in mind that she said, "Well, that was generous of him."

Willowvale swallowed. "Yes, it was."

"I suppose they're still assembling the case against Brookbower?" she asked.

"That is what I understand."

Miss Berrydell frowned gently. "I cannot say I disagree with his anger, but I do hope he will relent, if only out of consideration for the pain war would bring to his people."

Willowvale grimaced. "I must agree, though I confess my concern is more for our people than for the humans. As yours should be, Miss Berrydell." There was a slight edge of remonstration in this.

She raised an eyebrow at him and said, "I thought you said the fading of the lands was already solved."

"I was speaking of the pain and loss of war." The Fair lord gazed at her, noting the delicate flush upon her cheeks and the brightness of her raspberry pink eyes. The flutter of her magenta eyelashes was enchantingly winsome, all the more so because she seemed to have no intentions of gaining his admiration at all.

"The humans suffered every bit as much as our people did in the war, my lord, and they did not initiate it." She smiled primly at him, as if this point mattered.

Well. Perhaps it did. Willowvale frowned as he took a last bite of custard. "Tea?" he asked abruptly.

She blinked and hesitated. "Thank you," she said, with a hint of reluctance in her voice.

Willowvale rose and stepped to the door, where he told the guard that he would like hot water for tea.

He knelt by the hearth and stirred the fire. In the silence, Miss Berrydell rose and smoothed her hands over the tabletop gently. She reached forward to touch the azalea leaves, her lips curving in a soft smile. After admiring the blooms, she knelt to sink her hands into the thick, soft moss near the wall.

"Do you like it?" the Fair lord said.

"It is lovely. I have little talent with plants, and I am out of practice."

"I'll grow some moss in your suite, if you like." Willowvale was simultaneously pleased with himself for thinking of this and slightly horrified that he had made the offer so impulsively.

The hot water arrived only a few minutes later, and it was a welcome distraction from the silence that Willowvale felt had grown increasingly uncomfortable. He spooned a little tea into each strainer, then poured steaming water over each cup.

"Thank you," said Miss Berrydell with a polite smile.

The Fair lord nodded sharply.

They sipped their tea in silence. At last Miss Berrydell rose and said, "Thank you, Lord Willowvale." She bowed gracefully, and her host returned this courtesy.

He walked her back to her room, feeling both confused and elated.

She let him in and stood by the door, as if she wanted to ask him to leave but was too polite.

"Where would you like the moss?" He turned to look at her.

"I had not anticipated any at all, so I am sure that wherever you put it will suffice." She smiled.

The Fair lord crossed the room to the window. He knelt and pressed his hands to the floor where the blue and gold rug did not cover the stone. He coaxed the magic, reminding it how moss liked to be draped over stone, lending soft, living green to hard-edged rock. The moss grew over the floor, adorned with tiny pink flowers along the edge of the wall and beneath the table. Vines grew up the wall in the corner farthest from the fire, sprouting fuchsia blooms shaped like stars, and a cascade of white jasmine grew from the windowsill and spread down the wall and to the left, creeping to the very edge of the nearest painting. A group of brilliant pink lilies edged in white grew beside the table, bowing their heads gracefully toward the wide-eyed Fair maiden. Soon the carpet of moss covered half the floor, soft and green and far friendlier than the cold Arichtan decor.

"This is extravagant, my lord."

Willowvale stood and shrugged, vaguely disquieted by this statement. "The colors suited," he muttered. "Good night, Miss Berrydell."

"Good night."

Before he returned to his room, Willowvale stopped to speak with the guard at the end of the hall. "The delegation's effects ought to be brought to them."

"They have no effects."

"Certainly they did." Willowvale blinked in consternation. "They had clothes and personal items when they arrived. Miss Berrydell informed me that their possessions had not been returned to them."

The guard shrugged. "I don't know. They might have been confiscated, or still part of the investigation."

Willowvale clenched his teeth so tightly his jaw ached. *They have no effects* and *I don't know* were two entirely different things, and the discrepancy felt like an unmitigated lie, which grated upon his Fair sensibilities like iron in a wound. "Those are not the same answer," he snarled.

The guard shrugged again. "How should I know what they had at their residence? They had no effects when they were brought to the prison."

"I would presume their effects were left at the residence!" the Fair lord snapped. "Bring them now!"

"With all due respect, my lord, I do not work for you and do not answer to you."

"Does your king intend to further punish those he has already judged innocent of wrongdoing?" Willowvale's voice was tight. "I was led to think better of your people than that."

Of course, this was not true of what Silverthorn or other Fair Folk had said, but Theo had certainly implied such, so it was not exactly a lie.

"I will inquire." The guard scowled but said nothing else.

Willowvale stalked back to his room without another word. He threw himself into the chair before the fire, then stood again to poke the fire viciously. He poured himself another cup of tea using the same leaves and let it steep while he readied himself for bed.

Then the Fair lord sat on the hearth, letting the heat make his pale skin prickle, sipping the tea from his friend, and trying not to think of the beautiful Fair maiden just down the hall.

CHAPTER TEN
The Inconvenience of Drowning

The next four days followed much the same pattern for the Fair delegation. Each was provided breakfast, which they ate alone in their rooms. Willowvale requested an audience with the king each morning, which was promptly denied.

He spent each morning pacing in the suite and adding vines to the greenery which had nearly overtaken the bedroom. The exterior wall was now entirely covered in ivy and morning glory vines, and the floor was more moss than oak or rug. There was a dogwood sapling in the corner, spreading its white-blossomed branches over the bed. The blankets themselves were unchanged, but the posts of the bed frame were now adorned with soft cascades of white jasmine which gave off their distinctive sweet scent.

The verdant exuberance of the suite, so fresh and clean and relaxing, so home-like, soothed Willowvale's tension, but not as much as he had hoped.

When the lunch tray was delivered each day, he stalked down the hall to knock upon Miss Berrydell's door. "Will you take lunch with me?"

"As you wish," she said politely.

He carried her tray to his suite, for it would be impolite to invite himself into her suite. He wanted her company, but he did not wish to offend her.

The meals were, if not exactly full of sparkling delight, at least punctuated by pleasant conversational salvos. "How long have you worked for Lord Brookbower?" Willowvale asked the second day.

"Three years. I came with him when he was first assigned to Idosa."

"How did you come to be the security specialist? It is not a position commonly assigned to the lovelier sex."

She blinked at him and tilted her head to the side, as if debating whether to be offended by the question. "My magic lends itself to defense," she said at last. "Moreover, I enjoy training with blades of all types, and my enjoyment of such has understandably led to some skill, which His Majesty thought to be useful."

"Have you been content in your position, aside from this issue with the children?"

Her pink eyes flashed. "I suppose you could say that I have been, in the same way that one might agree that one is content to live underwater, aside from the little inconvenience of drowning. My disappointment and fury at what was done to the children casts a great cloud over all my experiences here."

Willowvale took a sip of tea, admiring the Fair maiden over the rim of his cup. She was quite striking, with her eyes flashing that way, and her pink lips contrasting against her white teeth. Her cheeks had gained a little color in the past few days of freedom. The sunlight through her windows and the warmth of a fire and a bed had undoubtedly made the most difference, but perhaps his flowers and moss had comforted her a little.

"Have you been forced to use your magic here to defend the ambassador?" he asked curiously.

She shook her head, her short magenta hair catching the light most becomingly. "No, my lord. The only time it might have been even slightly necessary was when we were captured, and I judged it safer for the ambassador to comply." There was an edge in her voice at this, and at Willowvale's inquiring look, she added, "Besides, I have no wish to kill humans, especially not when I agree with them. Their complaint against Brookbower is just."

"Do you trust their legal system? Are you not concerned that you will all be executed together for a crime only he and Lords Camphor and Aspen committed?"

Astrantia sighed and looked down at the table. She caught her lower lip between her teeth as she considered her words. "I hope your diplomatic efforts are successful," she said at last.

This wasn't much of an answer, but Willowvale felt it was likely to be all she would say on the matter.

"Let us speak of more pleasant topics, then." He smiled, and the expression felt strange upon his face. He was not accustomed to smiling, and the effort felt awkward and unconvincing, even to him. "What about Aricht has won you over?"

She raised an eyebrow. "I would hardly say I've been won over, because I was never on the side of those abhorrent Fair Folk who thought us superior to humans in the first place. But if you must know, I felt that we were treated fairly, albeit with a great deal of caution, from the time we arrived. Veiled hostility, snide remarks, unfriendly looks… I felt it all quite justified, when considered from a human point of view. Our court was the aggressor in the war, after all.

"Still, I felt that for the most part we were treated as individuals, as well as representatives of our court, and with a little courtesy to smooth the way, we had achieved a peaceable relationship with the humans.

"I believed in our mission, Lord Willowvale. I still believe in it. Our people *ought* to be able to live at peace with humans, and the fact that we have not is an indictment of our own leadership, not theirs. What right have we to consider ourselves superior? Is an adult, in full strength and full control of his or her magic, of more value than a child, who is both weak and unskilled? Surely not. Thus how can we contend that we, with greater strength and power, are of more value, and are more worthy of land, wealth, and safety, than humans, who have little magic to use at all?"

Willowvale bowed his head just slightly. "I concur," he said quietly. "Your passion is admirable."

He ignored the guilt that twisted in his guts, for he had been one of those she called abhorrent, who believed themselves superior. He was still half-inclined to think Fair Folk superior to humans, but now it felt more like a reflex than a true belief. Still, he would hardly reveal this to the lovely Fair maiden, whose opinion of him seemed more important with every passing day.

His concurrence with her statement was not a lie; in fact, it was an honest admission of what he had hardly even thought to himself previously. Overton had been the catalyst, to be sure, but humans had surprised him so many times by now that he could not honestly argue that Fair Folk were superior.

"Shouldn't one be passionate about the truth? About goodness? And it is good to see the worth in the weak and defenseless, even if one's so-called superiors do not." Miss Berrydell said this with quiet conviction.

"You call humans weak and defenseless?" Willowvale's lip curled in amusement.

Miss Berrydell shrugged one shoulder gracefully. "I do not, not as a species, but certainly that has been the Fair attitude toward them, I believe. Even if it were a true understanding of their abilities, upholding their worth would be more honorable than seeking to take advantage of their weakness."

The Fair lord poured more tea for them both. "As you say," he murmured.

In the following days, the Fair lord mostly avoided such topics, though Miss Berrydell's flashing eyes were quite lovely when she spoke with passion about the equality of humans and Fair Folk.

Instead, he asked about Aricht itself, where and how the delegation had lived before they had been apprehended, more detail about how they had been detained, and about Miss Berrydell's family and home in the Fair Lands.

"I do not have much family, my lord," she said. "My father is a sword maker, and my brother followed him in the art. My mother died many years ago."

"Who is your father?"

"Sedum Berrydell, and my brother is Agaricus. Do you know them?" She looked at him expectantly.

He blinked in surprise. "Sedum and Agaricus? I did not realize they were Berrydells." The sword makers' shop had been well-respected, but he recalled some controversy about it during the war. He had not even heard of the shop in years. "Did they make weapons for the war?"

She stiffened slightly and raised her chin. "My father refused to make weapons for those who said they meant to make war upon humans. They suffered much for their principles."

Willowvale digested this in silence. "I did not know they were still in business," he said at last.

The Fair maiden gave a tight smile. "It would be a stretch to say that they are still in business. The shop is open, but they have had three commissions in the last four years."

"Perhaps I am not the only one who believed them to have quit the business."

Miss Berrydell raised one eyebrow. "I am sure that, were you aware, you would have patronized the shop and lent your good name to their reputation. I would like to think others so generously inclined, but I think it is obvious they were deliberately frozen out. The shop was vandalized more than once, and His Majesty's officers of the law never seemed inclined to do much about it."

Willowvale swallowed. A year ago, he would have sneered at her naive assumption of his support. "I can inquire, if and when I return to the Fair Court," he said quietly.

"I would very much appreciate it," she said, with sudden warmth. "That is kind of you, Lord Willowvale."

He shrugged one shoulder, feeling suddenly out of sorts. "It is no hardship to ask the question," he muttered. Then he forced something like a smile, though it looked as thin and awkward as it felt. "Have you any other family?"

"Not that I am close to."

"I have an aunt with the Berrydell name. I was curious."

She blinked. "Lady Orchid Berrydell?"

"Yes."

"Oh dear." Her magenta eyebrows drew downward, and she gave him a sympathetic look. "I hope you don't think I bear too much similarity to her."

Willowvale was startled into a soft chuckle. "None at all, save your Fair lineage and sex. How are you related to her?"

"My father's father and her husband's father were brothers. My grandfather was the younger of the brothers, and received little inheritance and no title. Lady Orchid brought her own fortune to the marriage."

This Willowvale had known, but he had not known that the Berrydell clan had other branches.

"How are you related to her, my lord?" Astrantia gazed at him curiously.

"Her younger sister was my mother." His own mother had hardly been much more pleasant than Lady Orchid, and had brought a similar, though slightly smaller, fortune to her marriage to Willowvale's father, the even wealthier Betula Willowvale.

If there was one topic Willowvale wished to avoid even more than the kidnappings of the children, it was his thoroughly unpleasant childhood. He said abruptly, "Are you and Miss Dewdrop Berrydell close?" It was not, perhaps, a good question, but it served its purpose.

Astrantia laughed, light and amused. "I imagine she would be mortified that you even asked the question! No. She is very much the accomplished young lady of leisure, and I work for my dinner. In the human world, no less! I'm practically a servant."

The Fair lord gazed at her, at the sparkling amusement in her eyes, the curve of her lips, the pale smooth curve of her cheek.

"You are astonishingly lovely when you smile, Miss Berrydell," he said, quite by accident.

She blinked once, and then again. "Pardon me?"

Willowvale swallowed. "I said, 'you are astonishingly lovely when you smile, Miss Berrydell.'"

Astrantia stood and bowed politely to him. "Thank you, Lord Willowvale. That is kind of you to say. I shall retire to my own room. Good afternoon."

Willowvale stood and bowed. "Good afternoon, Miss Berrydell."

CHAPTER ELEVEN
A Pleasant Hope

The Fair maiden sat her room, sipping the hot water she had requested on the way back from Lord Willowvale's room. She had not asked him for tea to enjoy alone in her room.

He probably would have given it to her, she reflected. He seemed to have decided to be agreeable to her, and perhaps only to her, which had seemed merely a harmless idiosyncrasy until he'd offered that startling compliment.

She had eaten with him in his room only as a matter of diplomacy. The humans were no doubt scandalized by the idea of a lord hosting a maiden in his suite alone, but the Fair Folk were not quite as excruciatingly strict in such matters of propriety as humans were. There was nothing scandalous in a quiet meal and respectful conversation. Lunch with him was awkward and unpleasant only because Willowvale himself was awkward and unpleasant.

Oh, not to her, aside from his comment on her pallor that once. But his lips seemed stuck in a permanent sneer, his eyes bright with annoyance and scorn.

Still, he had, albeit unconsciously, offered her the valuable opportunity to plead the case of the Fair Folk to the Arichtan intelligence officers and thus His Majesty Elmerick himself. She had kept their conversations in Arichtan, and Willowvale had not questioned this, at least aloud.

Had he realized she intended the Arichtans to hear her? She doubted it, though it was certainly possible. He seemed capable of dissembling, at least a little, and he seemed amused and fascinated by her regard for the Arichtans rather than horrified. Still, he had not shown any real indication of a similar respect for the humans.

No, he could not be considered an ally as she reevaluated her life. He was too much like Brookbower; he listened to her because he was bored and annoyed at their interminable confinement, not because he cared about anything but his own pride in a job well done.

She rolled her eyes and swallowed the last of the water.

The Fair Lands were stable, at least for now, and that news had soothed the gnawing guilt and fear within her heart. Astrantia narrowed her eyes as she pondered how such a feat might have been accomplished.

She poked at the fire, then sat back and stretched her bare toes toward the heat and closed her eyes. The warmth of the coals, and the comfort of the chair in which she sat, so much softer than the cot of her cell, brought a gratitude to her heart that softened her toward the ill-tempered Willowvale. At least he had made this much progress. Perhaps he would get Brookbower free as well, and they could all go home.

As much as she wanted to stay, she would have to accompany them back to the Fair Lands. She wanted to see her father and brother again, and she had sworn to see Brookbower safely home, if she could. But she could request that Silverthorn assign her to the new ambassador's delegation, and he would likely grant the request, because not many Fair Folk spoke Arichtan, and after three years here, everyone in their delegation was more fluent than anyone who might replace them. Except Tarragon, who barely spoke at all in either the Fair language or Arichtan.

With the pleasant hope of her return to Aricht in her heart, she dozed in her chair by the fire.

CHAPTER TWELVE
An Onerous Demand

T he next morning, Willowvale said to the guard at the end of the hall, "I want an audience with His Majesty Elmerick."

To the fairy's surprise, the guard gave the slightest smirk and said, "He will see you after lunch."

"Oh." Willowvale frowned. This somehow seemed an ominous development, but he forced himself to nod as politely as he could.

He went back to his suite and paced as his thoughts whirled. Finally he stepped out into the hallway and said, "I want to visit Lord Brookbower."

"That is permitted."

Willowvale stalked through the corridors behind the guard. Their footsteps echoed on the marble floors.

The air in the courtyard was cold but still, and where the bright sun hit the packed earth, the frost had melted. Willowvale felt the stillness as the calm before a coming storm.

When the guard opened the door to the stairway down into the prison, or dungeon, the Fair lord brushed past him, not waiting for the lantern.

He flicked fairy light to his fingertips and let it dance along the stone ceiling ahead of him.

At the bottom he stepped forward so the ambassador could see him. He bowed slightly, in respect of Brookbower's position if not Brookbower himself.

"Willowvale." The ambassador returned the bow stiffly.

"Brookbower." Willowvale's silvery blue eyes flicked up and down the prisoner's form. "I assume you are well."

"As well as can be expected, given this ridiculous confinement." With a wave of his hand, he made the glamour upon his cell and person vanish, revealing the smooth stone walls of his cell and the wooden cot in the corner with a mound of blankets at the end. All fairies had the ability to freshen clothes, so although Brookbower's shirt, jacket, and trousers were slightly rumpled, they were clean. "How go the negotiations?" There was a sneer in Brookbower's voice as he asked this, as if he expected Willowvale to have to admit to failure.

"I have a meeting with Elmerick this afternoon." Willowvale added, "The others of your delegation are already nearly exonerated, and I doubt Elmerick has any desire to execute innocent prisoners, especially not when it might provoke war. You, on the other hand…"

"Spare me the lecture, Willowvale," Brookbower snapped. "We all worked for the good of the Fair Lands. My position here was more perilous than yours in Valestria; you can hardly hold your success over me as proof of your superiority."

"The Fair Lands are safe, for now, and that is what matters," said Willowvale sharply. "Believe it or not, I didn't come down here to antagonize you, much as I enjoy it. My intention was merely to ascertain if there were anything you could say in your own defense."

Brookbower said with a sneer, "I have no desire to defend myself to humans, as if they deserve some explanation of my actions. I did what I had to do, for the good of our people. Just as you did."

Willowvale gritted his teeth. "You make it difficult to help you. His Majesty Silverthorn swore to never take or harm humans again, directly or indirectly. Will you take such an oath?"

The ambassador's eyes widened. "What induced him to do *that*?"

"Shock. Awe. Guilt. Terror of what might result if he didn't agree. It was an unprecedented situation. But I do not believe he has had any cause to regret it. Much to the contrary; the Fair Lands are more stable than they have been in many years." Willowvale's pale eyes held Brookbower's green gaze. "Will you take such a vow?"

Brookbower let out a soft breath and pressed his lips together. "If His Majesty Silverthorn himself required it of me, I would do so," he said at last. "Not with any lesser inducement. My preference would be to keep myself free to do whatever I judge necessary for the Fair Lands. If humans must be sacrificed, so be it. But I will obey my king."

Willowvale inclined his head. "Understood."

"Did you make a similar vow?" Brookbower asked.

"I was not asked to." Willowvale smiled thinly.

"Why not?" The ambassador said sharply.

The thought of baring his shame and grief to Brookbower was not to be borne. "You'll hear it from Silverthorn in due time, if I can get you free," said Willowvale at last.

"You must have succeeded in your mission, if you're here," said Brookbower with a frown.

"In a manner of speaking." Willowvale's stomach churned, and he bowed abruptly. "Good afternoon."

Brookbower bowed in return, scowling.

CHAPTER THIRTEEN
Returning Home

While Willowvale was confined to one small section of the Arichtan palace, Theo met with the Valestrian ambassador to Aricht, who listened to Theo's explanation of his activities, and what he was doing in Idosa, with astonishment. His Majesty Alberdale's letter to the ambassador contained assurances about Theo's trustworthiness and an admonition to support Theo as the young man requested, so the ambassador asked what assistance Theo required.

"Nothing at all, my lord," Theo said cheerfully. "I'll drop in my father's business associates this afternoon and then depart for Skystead this evening, if I can."

The ambassador directed him to a reputable stable where he could hire a carriage, and Theo thanked him.

He crossed town to his father's representative in Idosa. That obligation took one very long afternoon, and he departed late the same day over land for Skystead.

Perhaps he might have been able to find the town from the veil, but by the time he departed Idosa, the hour was late. It seemed easier to simply travel the usual way. Besides, he could sleep in a carriage.

Rather than hiring a carriage of his own, he found several carriages departing together from the livery stable that was leaving for Sharnwick that very evening. Sharnwick was not too far off from the direct route to Skystead, and it was apparently large enough to have a sizable inn.

He paid the fare, handed his small luggage to the driver, and clambered in to the shadowed carriage.

The passengers appeared to be a prosperous father, his lovely wife, and their daughter, who appeared to be in her late teens.

"Good evening," Theo said politely. "I apologize for having troubled you; I'm sure it would have been nicer to have the carriage to yourselves."

"It's no trouble at all," said the man. "Where are you going?"

"Skystead. You, sir?"

The *sir* was a guess; the man didn't look like a lord, but he might easily have been prosperous enough to be a baronet or even a knight.

"It's only mister, my lord. Mr. Henry Chilvers."

"Mr. Theo Overton, IV. It's a pleasure."

"This is my wife, Mr. Overton, Mrs. Irena Chilvers, and our daughter Miss Blanche Chilvers. We are also going to Skystead."

Theo murmured polite greetings to each of them.

In a few minutes, they had settled into a comfortable silence. Theo found himself drowsing at intervals, his head nodding slightly as the carriage jostled.

At Sharnwick they disembarked in the courtyard of a prosperous inn, where everyone from the three carriages took rooms for the night. Theo was pleased to note that the room was much cleaner than the ones in which he and Lord Willowvale had stayed in Idosa.

In the morning, the passengers ate together in the inn's common room, and he got a better look at his traveling companions. Mr. Chilvers appeared successful, if not exceedingly wealthy, and his wife and daughter were attired in the current fashions, if not the very latest and most elegant versions of those fashions. His eyes were kind in his homely face, and he smiled when he looked at his family.

Theo thought of his beloved wife, and their future children, unknown and yet already cherished, and he felt a flush of heat upon his cheeks.

"Good morning!" he said to the Chilvers family.

"Good morning." The older man's eyes swept over Theo's green jacket and trousers, taking in the embroidery upon the collar and the rich fabric so elegantly fitted to Theo's lean form. A spark of interest lit his eyes. "Are you Valestrian, by chance?"

"I am." Theo's smile sparkled.

"Please, sit with us, Mr. Overton." Mr. Chilvers stood politely to welcome Theo to the table.

"Thank you!" Theo slid into a seat across the table.

"It is rumored that the Wraith was Valestrian," Mr. Chilvers said.

"Is it?" Theo focused on the steaming biscuit and sausage gravy which a serving boy slid in front of him without a word. "Thank you."

"So I've heard."

His wife added, "We have a personal debt to the Wraith, if ever we should meet him. One of our nieces was stolen by the fairies, and the Wraith rescued her. She was brought back to Aricht in the autumn, before the snow made the passes so dangerous."

Theo met her gaze and asked kindly, "And how is she now?"

"Quite well, considering what she must have suffered." The lady smiled slightly. "She hates dancing, but otherwise seems to have put it behind her, as well as anyone could be expected to put captivity behind them."

Mr. Chilvers added, "I don't suppose you know the Wraith personally?"

"I have it on good authority that the Wraith is delighted with the thought of the children being safely home and cherished, and he would feel quite awkward about having too much made of his part in returning them to their rightful place." Theo smiled, his eyes gleaming with warmth and kindness. "I'm sure you can understand."

Mr. Chilvers's gaze sharpened, and he said "I'm sure you can understand our desire to express our deep gratitude to the man personally. He needn't feel awkward, or even say anything at all. I would be delighted if he would merely accept our gratitude, if you would convey it to him. If you know him, or have any way of conveying the message, of course."

Theo beamed at them. "I will convey the message, and if I might speak on his behalf, I'm sure he would say something about how he was delighted to hear that the child was recovering well."

"I'm sure." Mr. Chilvers looked at him steadily. "You speak Arichtan remarkably well, Mr. Overton."

"My father has business connections here, and I spent a good deal of time here when I was young." Theo smiled again with disarming sweetness. "That's why I'm on my way to Skystead."

"I see." The man's eyes sparkled with a friendly, warm amusement. "I understand from my niece that the Wraith spoke Arichtan so well she thought him a native, and only heard rumors later that he was likely Valestrian."

Theo's eyes widened. "Isn't that interesting!"

Mr. Chilvers chuckled softly. "Well, I do hope you will convey my thanks, if you have the opportunity to let him know."

"I shall do my best to pass the message along."

The carriage ride was mostly quiet, punctuated by polite inquiries about innocuous topics.

The convoy stopped for lunch at a little town with well-provisioned inn, which offered decent food and tea which made Theo sigh in disappointment at his first sip.

"Not to your liking?" said Mr. Chilvers.

"It isn't my preference," said Theo diplomatically.

The man laughed under his breath. "I have some better at home in Skystead. I'd be honored if you would be our guest as long as you stay in town."

"That is very kind of you," Theo answered. "I'd be delighted to, although I can't stay long."

Soon the convoy was on the road again. Theo spent much of the day looking out the window thoughtfully, surreptitiously feeling for the magic. It would be convenient to have a shorter route to Skystead in the future.

Skystead was a bustling town known for its silk weaving and embroidery. The Chilvers family had a spacious row house near the center of town, and when they arrived late that evening, Theo complimented them on the front garden and the spare, elegant entry. A servant escorted him to a guest room on the third floor.

Theo slept well, though he missed his beloved wife. The following two days were taken up with conversations with the heads of the various weaving and embroidery workshops, as well as the artisans themselves. Sir Theodore had always impressed upon Theo, when he was younger, the importance of treating everyone, of every station, with respect and kindness. Thus this sudden trip to Aricht had seemed like an excellent opportunity to inspect the workshops unannounced to ensure that the workers were treated as well as Sir Theodore required of the managers. Theo was pleased to discover that everything was as he had hoped.

In the evenings, he enjoyed dinner with the Chilvers family, who proved to be gracious hosts. The evening of the second day, Theo said, "I thank you for your hospitality. I have one more person I'd like to see tomorrow, and I'll head directly home from there. So I will bid you farewell at breakfast. If you are ever in Valestria, I would very much like to reciprocate the kindness you have shown me."

The journey back through the veil was a little shorter than the journey to Aricht with Willowvale had been, for Theo knew the feel of the magic better now. Still, it was arduous, and the young man was exhausted and relieved when he finally stepped out of the veil onto the far edge of the Overton front lawn.

He let himself in and strode up the stairs to the suite he shared with Lily. She was asleep, but she woke at the soft rustle of his satchel as he put it upon the floor.

"I didn't mean to wake you, my love," he whispered. "I'm going to bathe and eat something before I join you."

Lily wrapped her dressing gown around herself and stood. She crossed to him and embraced him, noting a scuffed area on the fabric of his jacket and a warm, sticky dampness on the back of one shoulder. "Are you hurt?" she said in alarm.

"Just bruised and tired." Theo's voice was reassuring. "The veil was annoyed, I think, and it made the journey a little more troublesome than it might have been."

"Is this blood?" she said more precisely, setting her hand on the outside of his shoulder, near the damp area but not touching it.

"I don't think so!" He chuckled. "There was a gelatinous sort of creature in the veil that got a little too close. I'm fine, really, my love. You might want to wash your hands, though."

Lily pulled away, but then leaned up to kiss him, which sent a thrill of delight through them both. "I missed you."

While Theo and Willowvale had been gone, preparations had begun at the Overton estate for the wedding of Lady Araminta Poole and Oliver Hathaway, Lily's brother. Months earlier, Theo had offered to host the reception at Overton manor, since the townhouse of Brock Poole, Duke of Bricklewyte, Araminta's father, was certainly luxurious but not quite large enough for the many guests required by the duke's status, and of course the Hathaways were not able to host such a gathering. Theo had returned three days before the wedding, in case he needed to assist with anything, but of course Anselm and the duke's servants had everything well in hand.

The ceremony was every bit as lovely as Araminta had dreamed since she was a little girl. Lily brushed happy tears from her eyes at the sight of her best friend united with her beloved brother.

Theo and Lily danced for hours, interrupting this entertainment only for refreshments and friendly conversation with the many guests. When Araminta and Oliver finally departed in a whirlwind of congratulations, Lily was able to embrace them each in turn, her heart full of joy.

"Thank you for everything, Theo," said Oliver, his cheeks flushed. "I don't think I'd be here, and certainly not so happy, if not for you."

"Don't mention it," said Theo, with a sparkling smile. "You deserve every happiness! I am delighted for you both."

CHAPTER FOURTEEN
A Promise Fulfilled

After a delightful day of rest after the wedding with his beloved wife, Theo said over dinner, "I promised I would visit Silverthorn soon. I think I shall do that tomorrow morning."

Fenton, seated across the table, said, "Not that you need assistance, but I should like to help you, if I can."

Theo smiled affectionately at him. "I hate to drag you through the veil, Fen, but I do believe the king admires you a great deal, as well he should. I expect he would be delighted to receive you on my next visit. Still, I should not like to overstep this time."

The young nobleman frowned thoughtfully. "Certainly not. Still, is there anything I can do from here?"

Theo almost demurred, but then said, "Perhaps if you would give him a packet of very nice tea. I'll do the same." With a warm sort of amusement in his eyes, he said, "Tea is quite a delicacy in the Fair Lands, and though it will hardly change the course of history, I would enjoy presenting the king with a token of our friendship."

Accordingly, the next morning Theo stopped by the Selby manor to pick up a beribboned packet of Fenton's preferred breakfast tea, topped with a note.

Your Majesty, please enjoy this tea as a token of my gratitude and regard. It is a gift in the human tradition.

Sincerely,

Fenton Selby, Marquess of Ambervale

Theo had packaged his own gift similarly, though his packet required no note. He placed Fenton's package in his other jacket pocket and stepped into the darkness of the veil between worlds.

The veil had a strange scent of iron and jasmine and fresh grass, and Theo considered this as he walked toward the Fair Lands. The trip was remarkably free of sudden dangers, and when he reached the Fair palace garden, he pressed his gratitude for the easy trip into the moss-covered wall before he stepped out into the bright golden morning.

Without hesitation, he strode through the garden and up to the palace door.

He knocked.

The servant who opened the door actually smiled when he saw Theo.

"Mr. Overton," he said, bowing in the Fair style.

"Good morning!" Theo said. "I'm sorry, I don't recall your name."

"You never heard it," the fairy said, his smile deepening. "I'm Caraway, my lord."

"Oh, I'm not a lord," Theo protested. "My father is a baronet; I don't even have a courtesy title, and I hope to not bear my father's title for another fifty years, at least."

Caraway gave him an odd look. "How long do humans live?"

The young man laughed a little. "Well, my father is exceptional, and though humans do not often reach one hundred years, I have every reason to hope he does. I came to see His Majesty, if he will receive me. If it isn't a good time, I can come back another day."

"I am confident he will make himself available for you, Mr. Overton." He led Theo to an unfamiliar sitting room and excused himself.

Within a few minutes, the servant returned and said, "He will see you now, Mr. Overton. Please follow me."

The servant led him through mirrored and tapestried hallways floored in crystal and jade and redolent with scents of petrichor and jasmine, moss and gold. At last they reached an opening covered only by dangling strands of some sort of vine covered in tiny purple hairs and iridescent blue flowers. "In here, sir," said the servant.

"Thank you." Theo brushed the vines aside and stepped into a crystalline wonderland.

"Mr. Overton." His Majesty Silverthorn stood, and Theo recognized this as the honor it was. "Thank you for coming."

"Thank you for receiving me, Your Majesty." Theo beamed at him. "Lord Selby and I thought you might enjoy some tea." He pulled out the packages of tea from his pockets. "Please accept these as gifts in the human tradition."

"The human tradition," Silverthorn said doubtfully, eying the packages. "These confer no obligation? No debt? No expectation of reciprocation?"

"None at all," Theo confirmed.

"Under those conditions I accept your gifts," said the Fair king.

He offered Theo human wine and said, "So, Mr. Overton, how goes Lord Willowvale's mission in Aricht?"

"It is a difficult assignment," Theo allowed. "But I am confident of his eventual success."

"How, and why, did you come to befriend my closest advisor? I would accuse you of coopting my most trusted confidant, but you do not use your power over him, or me, as I would have expected." The Fair monarch's violet eyes were sharp upon Theo's face, but his gaze was more puzzled and wary than hostile.

Theo smiled. "I doubt you are much more surprised than I am, Your Majesty." So he began, still standing, for Silverthorn did not indicate to him that he might sit, and the Fair king listened in fascination.

CHAPTER FIFTEEN
The Fury of a King

When Willowvale returned from visiting Brookbower's cell, he knocked at Astrantia's door.

She opened it and said, "Yes, my lord?" she said, her pink eyes wide and curious.

"I have a meeting with Elmerick this afternoon. I doubt it will go well, so it would be wise if you were near to Brookbower in case he needs you." He did not know the extent of her magic, but Silverthorn was not likely to have assigned someone incompetent.

The Fair maiden nodded. "Thank you."

"There is no need to go to him yet, I think. I will knock when I am on my way."

"Thank you, my lord."

Willowvale bowed and then strode to his own suite and closed the door.

He asked for a pot of hot water, and when it came, he brewed tea.

Inhaling the scent, he thought of friendship, trust, and his inevitable bloody end after this final meeting with Elmerick.

He sipped the tea meditatively. The coals in the grate were low, and he stirred them but didn't add another log.

The servants brought a thick beef stew for lunch, with a fluffy roll topped with cheese steaming beside it. It was a uniquely human meal, rich and comforting. The Fair lord tried to enjoy it, despite his dark mood.

When he finished, he set the bowl and bread plate aside and wrote a letter to Theo, which he folded and sealed, then propped against the little azalea.

Mr. Overton,

Although I am sure you understand already, I ought to say how grateful I am for the grace you have shown me personally, and for what you did for the Fair Lands. Your friendship was a light in an otherwise joyless life.

Please convey my best regards to Lord Selby and your other friends and family.

Sincerely,

Ash Willowvale

He sealed this note and wrote *Mr. Theodore Overton, IV,* across the front, then set his pen to another blank page.

Your Majesty,

You commanded me to extract Brookbower safely if I could. I believe Elmerick intends for someone to die for the Fair crimes against Arichtan children, and though he has been patient, I doubt we have much longer. I cannot free Brookbower from his current imprisonment without sacrificing the safety of the others in the delegation, which I am loath to do.

Therefore, this afternoon I intend to buy his life with mine. You've debriefed me thoroughly, and though I had hoped to be of further service to the Fair Lands, this sacrifice will have to suffice.

The details will be a bit thorny; I am not sure whether even my most solemn vow to return for execution will allow Elmerick to let me take Brookbower and his staff back to the Fair Lands, or whether I will have to bargain for their further confinement until Mr. Overton returns in a little less than a week, as he promised.

In either event, I doubt I shall see you again. It was an honor to serve you and the Fair Lands, and I entreat you to follow the example of Mr. Overton, as I do in this last act of devotion to the lands we both love.

Sincerely,

Ash Willowvale

He stared at the letter a moment longer, wondering if there was anything left to say, and decided that there was not. So he sealed it and wrote *His Majesty Oak Silverthorn* across the front.

He knelt and put his hands deep in the moss, caressing the magic. He unbound it gently, setting the moss and vines free to recede into the stone when they wanted to. The moss would last longest; it was never quick to respond to a release of magic. The jasmine folded its flowers up softly and quietly.

Within an hour the jasmine would be gone. The dogwood in the corner would be merely a sprout by nightfall and vanish by midnight. The azalea would last perhaps a day, and the moss perhaps half a day beyond that.

Willowvale stood and glanced around the suite, noting each little bit of green that his magic had brought to life.

As much as the fairy loved the green moss and leaves and flowers his magic had produced, he imagined that the humans would see the changes he had wrought in the suite as both an insult and an injury to the honor of Aricht itself. To modify the rooms so dramatically, covering the marble floor and wool rug with plants, which humans seemed so determined to keep outside, would not incline Elmerick to kindness toward any future Fair delegation.

When Elmerick killed him, as was likely, it would serve the Fair Lands better to leave the suite as he had found it, cold and angular and unfriendly, though elegant.

He flung himself into the couch and stared at the glowing embers as the room began to return to its original state around him. He sighed and pressed his magic into the ground, searching out the plants in Miss Berrydell's room down the hall. Reluctantly, he unbound them as well.

Miss Berrydell,

With regret, I must inform you that, given the likelihood of my death in a few hours, I have released the magic binding the plants to your room. This will, I hope, incline His Majesty Elmerick more kindly to any future diplomatic missions from the Fair Court.

With respect,
Ash Willowvale, Marquess in the Fair Lands

He did not exactly mind Miss Berrydell knowing his title; she was too honorable to use it against him. Still, it seemed unwise to have it written here in Aricht for anyone to read, if anyone here could read the Fair language.

Just as he wrote *Miss Astrantia Berrydell* across the front of this note, a knock sounded upon his door.

"Yes?"

"His Majesty Elmerick will see you now."

The Fair lord stepped out into the corridor and strode down the hall, where he knocked briskly upon Astrantia's door.

She opened it immediately, stepped into the hallway, and closed the door behind herself. "May your meeting go well, my lord." Astrantia bowed, deep and graceful and elegant, and Willowvale returned this courtesy gravely.

"Farewell," he muttered. He handed her the folded note and turned away.

The Fair lord stalked after the guard through corridor after corridor. The inlay in the marble floor, like the embroidery upon the blanket in his room, seemed to be aggressively angular, as if intended to cause anxiety and offense in its very human style. Willowvale pushed the feelings down, bottled them up tightly and shoved the bottle far, far down deep in his mind, focusing only on the conversation that was to come.

He would be controlled and courtly, not petulant and irritable. He would show the human king the dignity and honor of the Fair Court.

He would not threaten war unless absolutely necessary.

Lord Ash Willowvale, bitter and cold and proud, held this determination tightly in his heart, for if there was one thing he loved above his own pride, it was the Fair Lands themselves. He would *not* jeopardize them with some impatient little fit of pique.

The Fair lord's scowl deepened as they walked through the palace. His stomach churned.

His Majesty Valor Elmerick looked up at his entrance. The guard stepped back to stand by the door, but he kept his hand on his sword, as if he expected to have the opportunity to run Willowvale through at any moment.

"Your Majesty," Willowvale said, and he bowed with exquisite correctness.

The king steepled his hands and studied the fairy. Willowvale was dressed in his most formal human attire, to which he had applied the very lightest of glamours. The deep charcoal gray of his jacket was unchanged, but the fairy had glamoured his waistcoat to be navy blue rather than burgundy and changed the subtle vine pattern woven into the fabric to that of roses. It seemed a fitting tribute to Theo's efforts on his behalf, and, if Elmerick were going to execute him, Willowvale felt he ought to honor his only friend.

Elmerick let the silence draw out, his eyes hard, and Willowvale stood unflinching, pale and lean and straight as a sword.

"I do not want war with your people," Elmerick said at last. "I never wanted war. I didn't start the last war, and I won't start the next, if your king will honor the accord I will present to you on his behalf. Do you have that authority?"

"I do."

"I want a new ambassador, one with the highest authority in your court, who did not fight against my people. I want a promise from your king that he will not take or harm Arichtan citizens ever again, nor will he countenance any such acts by any of the Fair Folk. I want every fairy to set foot in my lands bound by the same vow of non-aggression toward my people.

"If you can ensure all of those points, I will release Brookbower and all his delegation unharmed."

Willowvale raised an eyebrow. "I have already told you His Majesty Silverthorn made such a vow not to take or harm humans ever again." His voice tightened. "Mr. Overton was quite persuasive, and he did not limit His Majesty Silverthorn's vow to Valestrian citizens.

Silverthorn has already made such a promise, and he will hold to his word."

"Do you swear it?"

Willowvale blinked and narrowed his eyes. "Perhaps it is not well known in Aricht, Your Majesty, but when a fairy makes a promise, we will keep it unto death. It is well-nigh impossible for us not to keep our word, and we value it higher than life itself. Only you humans lie with frequency and ease."

Elmerick stood in anger. "I wonder that you have the temerity to cast aspersions on the honor of humans, when *you* stole children from their very place of refuge." He lowered his voice ominously. "If you want this peace, Willowvale, you will hold your tongue."

A vice-like pressure started in Willowvale's chest, a deep, icy fury that squeezed his heart and made his fingers twitch, the magic of the vines beneath the marble floors ready to answer him.

"If you want peace, Your Majesty," he said through gritted teeth, "you will rely upon the promise my king has already made. He holds Mr. Overton in unprecedented respect and honor. If my king were to break his word, *which he will not,* he would break his word to you sooner than he would to Overton."

Elmerick blinked. "Is that so?"

"It is." Willowvale's voice was cold.

"And you swear that you and all other Fair Folk to set foot in my lands will be bound by the same oath?"

"I will so bind myself, and I will attest that my king has already sworn not to take or harm humans, directly or indirectly, regardless of what nation they call their own. I will vow that I will convey your demand to my king, and I can speak on his behalf to assure you that he will likely accept it." Willowvale tried to keep his temper. He added, "I will endeavor to ensure that all Fair Folk who come to Aricht take the vow you require, but I can only do what I can."

Elmerick smiled tightly. "You will." There was the slightest question in this, and a satisfied gleam in his eye.

"I will." A muscle in Willowvale's jaw twitched. "Your Majesty, I have been given authority to negotiate on behalf of my king and the

Fair Lands. I do not have unlimited power in the Fair Lands, and I would not like to mislead you as to what I can promise."

"Your people have misled us before about your intentions." Elmerick said this with a sharp edge in his voice. "Brookbower was treated with courtesy while he was working against us."

The Fair lord swallowed his fury. "Yet do you not wish to forge a better path?" he asked.

The king clenched his hands, as if he wished to punch the supercilious smile off Willowvale's face. Finally he said, "I will release your ambassador and all his staff home alive and unharmed. In return, Brookbower will swear today never to return or his life is forfeit. The others will take the same vow you and your king do.

"I wish to interview the lords you offered as possible replacements for Brookbower, Mosswing and Birchbark, before I accept one. Bring them back, after they swear no harm to Arichtans, after you take Brookbower and his delegation home."

The fairy nearly vibrated with the effort of keeping his anger under control. To be spoken to by a human, as if he were under a human king's command, felt like a deep and deliberate insult. Still, he had not expected such a positive outcome, so he bit back his affronted fury and said, with admirable steadiness, "You have made a wise decision, Your Majesty."

"I would have you all out of my lands this evening, but Mr. Overton implied that the journey was difficult and dangerous. I will allow you stay one more night in Aricht and depart in the morning."

Willowvale swallowed his pride yet again and said, "Thank you, Your Majesty." He bowed, and if the bow was slight and mocking and sharp with wounded pride, Elmerick pretended not to notice.

"You will all attend dinner this evening with my diplomatic staff. Brookbower will make his vow then. I cannot say the event will be a celebration, but the agreement ought to be marked by both the Fair Folk and my own nobility."

Willowvale nodded but said nothing. The Arichtan court was known for its tendency to mark any diplomatic event with a formal gathering. To the Fair Folk, this had always seemed a bit silly; the Fair

Court had its own formalities, but diplomacy with humans was not one of the areas where protocol was especially strict. After all, humans were not historically accorded enough honor to merit a great deal of Fair effort.

The king added suddenly, "Miss Berrydell may be assigned to the replacement ambassador, if that is acceptable to Silverthorn. I have no quarrel with her, and she has shown herself to be admirable in every way."

The Fair lord blinked. "I will convey such to my king," he said. "Thank you, Your Majesty." He bowed again.

The walk back to his suite felt surreal to the Fair lord. His head and heart buzzed with a strange expectancy. Even Brookbower's obstinate pride and undeniable crimes against the Arichtans were not enough for Elmerick to lose all sense of reason.

This doomed mission was actually going to end well after all.

Lord Willowvale had kept his own pride in check, albeit only by remembering Theo's good advice, and now, in the sudden shock of realizing both he and Brookbower's delegation would live to return to the Fair Lands, he felt something like the effervescent joy that seemed to always suffuse his friend. Never before had he understood why Theo seemed to be smiling all the time.

But why not smile?

A faint, pleased little quirk tugged at the Fair lord's lips as he stepped into his suite.

CHAPTER SIXTEEN
A Horrifying Revelation

While Lord Willowvale had been meeting with the Arichtan monarch, Astrantia asked the guards to take her to the prison to see Brookbower for the first time since she had been moved to the guest suite. A twinge of guilt assailed her; she ought to have gone to see him earlier, out of kindness if not out of mistrust of the Arichtans.

Elmerick had been fair, more than fair, to their delegation, and the fact that he had delayed Brookbower's trial so long hinted that perhaps he did not actually wish to execute the Fair ambassador at all. Certainly he wanted to kill Brookbower; the king's righteous fury was easy to see. Still, the king could have expedited the process considerably, and instead had let his investigators spend a great deal of time compiling evidence and writing reports.

It seemed clear to Astrantia that the king did not desire another war with the Fair Lands, no matter how much he personally wished to string up Brookbower by his neck in front of the palace.

With this in the back of her mind, Astrantia had relished the comfort and solitude of her suite these past few days, secure in the knowledge that Brookbower was not actually in any more danger than he had been in the previous months.

Nevertheless, she ought to have checked on him. He would be arrogant and snide, and she would know that she had done right by him, regardless of how much she disliked him.

She doubted her protection would be necessary, but it was certainly better to be prepared for the worst than to be unprepared in case of attack.

Astrantia followed the guard, her long, smooth strides easily keeping up with his.

He opened the door to the prison steps. "I'll bring the lamp."

"Thank you." Astrantia waited for him, not because she needed the light but because it cost nothing but a few seconds to let him be courteous.

She let him lead the way, lamp held high. The light of Brookbower's glamoured cell and the tree in the center of the cell block made the lamp unnecessary once they reached the bottom of the steps.

"Good afternoon, Lord Brookbower," she said with a bow.

Brookbower stood and approached the iron-barred door, though he did not touch it. He rolled his eyes, as if annoyed by her presence. "Is it?"

"It is a polite greeting, my lord, as you well know." She tried to keep the edge of frustration out of her voice. "I'm sure the afternoon is well for someone, even if it is not to be us."

"How is Willowvale getting on?" The ambassador rolled his shoulders. "He said he was going to meet with Elmerick this afternoon. Is he there now?"

"He was on his way when I left my room."

Astrantia crossed her arms and leaned back against the stone across from Brookbower's cell, where she could see both the Fair ambassador and the entrance to the cell block, where the guard stood with the lantern. The guard looked bored, and she couldn't blame him; she imagined that she might be down here for hours.

Brookbower sighed and threw himself onto the uncomfortable cot. He waved his hand in the general direction of the cup of water sitting on the stone floor nearby, and the water spiraled upward, forming intricate loops and braids and little flower shapes as it rose. He scowled and set the water back into the cup again.

If he had not sworn not to try to escape and not to harm his captors, he could have sent the water up and out through the iron bars, across the cell block, and up the guard's nose and down into his lungs to drown him. But aside from his vow, such an act of aggression would not actually open the cell door, and would only ensure his immediate execution.

Still, it had been tempting.

Astrantia looked at him, knowing exactly what he'd been thinking. "I wish you wouldn't toy with the idea. It would be murder," she said in the Fair language.

"I won't do it," he growled. "I'm just as tired of this pathetic little human world as everyone else."

"I don't despise it, my lord." Astrantia's voice was soft.

Brookbower rolled his eyes. "You're soft."

"I don't think being soft-hearted is the insult you think it is, my lord." She smiled, but it was melancholy.

The Fair lord crossed his long legs and looked up at the stone ceiling with a derisive smile. "Anyway, I doubt we will have to be here much longer. I'm sure Willowvale will bring Elmerick to his senses soon enough."

"You think so?" She looked at him with interest. "I was not under the impression you thought him capable."

"Oh, I dislike him thoroughly. He's arrogant and obnoxious and richer than I am. The king listens to him, too, and we've stood on opposite sides of more than one argument in court." Brookbower's lips curled in something that was more of a grimace than a smile. "Still, Willowvale is brilliant. We've never gotten on well, but far be it from me to say he's incompetent." Brookbower stood again and paced, as if this admission agitated him.

"What was his job before he came here?" Astrantia asked with interest.

He glanced at her. "Oh, he was in Valestria, hunting the Rose."

Astrantia felt a strange, sick feeling in her stomach, something between dread and horror. "He came with a Valestrian friend," she said quietly.

Brookbower looked at her with sudden, sharp interest. "I was thinking about that, and I realized he must have found a traitor in the Valestrian court. How delightful!" His eyes gleamed. "That must have taken skill indeed, for I've heard the Rose was quite popular in his own country, despite his anonymity."

The bodyguard frowned. "Do you think Willowvale manipulated the human?"

"Undoubtedly. Willowvale is far too proud to call a human a friend, but he is not above letting the human believe them friends, if it served the Fair Lands." Brookbower paced restlessly. "Still, I would not have thought he would unbend enough to take that tack deliberately. I wish I knew that story."

The Fair maiden's frown deepened. "It was Lord Willowvale who described the human as a friend, not the other way around."

He shrugged one shoulder. "Perhaps he meant only that the human shares his disdain for the Valestrian court."

Astrantia pressed her lips together, remembering Mr. Overton's bright, warm smile and his explanation of how and why he had come with Willowvale.

When the ambassador continued pacing, she said, "Willowvale suggested that I come down to protect you, since his meeting was likely to go badly."

Brookbower huffed under his breath. "Always dutiful. I doubt his pessimism will be borne out, though. He is quite good at his job, and I am sure he will be able to manipulate Elmerick just as he manipulated that Valestrian."

"What happened to the Rose?" Astrantia asked quietly.

"I imagine Willowvale killed him," said Brookbower with satisfaction.

The little curl of horror and fury that had been slowly growing in Astrantia's heart caught fire, and it was all she could do to keep her voice steady. "Was that his mission? I thought he was merely to gather information."

The Fair ambassador scoffed. "Even now, you are so naive? Of course he was to kill the Rose! What other purpose would Willowvale have in Valestria?" He crossed his arms and faced her, his eyes glittering with admiration and triumph. "I wish I'd been there to see it! A proud Fair lord finally bringing that tricky little human chameleon to his knees! Willowvale made us all proud." His smile sharpened. "I do wonder what solution Silverthorn found to the fading of the land."

"What a horrible way to save our lands!" Astrantia breathed.

Brookbower shrugged carelessly. "What is the suffering of a few humans in comparison with the danger to the Fair Lands? Don't be ridiculous, Miss Berrydell. It is unbecoming."

She shot him a dark glance, her eyes shimmering with outraged tears. "My lord Brookbower, it is unbecoming of a member of the Fair Folk to put so little importance on justice and mercy to those of lesser power."

"You forget your place!" Brookbower snapped.

Astrantia gritted her teeth. He knew, and she knew, that she would hold to her vow to protect him regardless of what horrible thing he said.

She took a tremulous breath. "So the Rose is dead, and somehow the lands are saved, and Silverthorn vowed never to take or harm humans again through some sudden softening of his heart? Is that what I am to believe?"

"I don't care what you believe, imbecile," Brookbower snarled. "The Rose is almost certainly dead, or Willowvale would not be here in triumph to negotiate for our release. I do not know what he and Silverthorn did to stabilize the lands, but I am sure it was clever.

"As for why Silverthorn made that vow? I cannot possibly imagine what would have induced him to do such a thing. But I suppose if the land is stable, there is little harm in it for the moment." His lips curled in scorn. "Shame, perhaps, but no harm."

"And Willowvale's part in it was to catch and kill the Rose?" Astrantia said again, her voice tight.

"Have I not said as much?" Brookbower laughed, hard and proud and cold. "It must trouble your human-loving heart to think of it. If your magic were not so strong, I would petition to have you recalled, Miss Berrydell. You're too soft for your position."

"I will do my job, Lord Brookbower," Astrantia said with bitter frustration.

Brookbower paced in impotent annoyance for some time without speaking. Astrantia crossed her arms and looked away.

In this tense silence, they passed nearly an hour. Astrantia read Willowvale's note, her heart burning within her.

At last another guard came down and conferred briefly with the one at the bottom of the stairs.

"Lord Willowvale is back in his suite. Lord Brookbower, you are to be transferred to the suite across from Miss Berrydell's."

Brookbower finally stopped his pacing and looked toward Astrantia. "I told you so."

Astrantia resisted the urge to roll her eyes. It seemed such a light-hearted response to his pettiness, and she did not feel light-hearted at all. Instead, the first fury of her understanding of Willowvale's part had deepened and grown, until it now felt like a coal smoldering deep in her chest.

CHAPTER SEVENTEEN
Guilt and Shame

Willowvale stood inside his suite for several minutes, breathing deeply and wondering at the bizarre success he had met.

Still, his triumph was not entirely assured. Brookbower must be convinced to make the vow Elmerick required.

Willowvale opened his door again. "I need to see Lord Brookbower," he said to the guard.

"He will be here soon," replied the guard.

"Oh. Thank you." The Fair lord frowned thoughtfully. Perhaps Brookbower was to be moved to a guest suite for his last night in Idosa.

Willowvale had not properly addressed the issue of their departure. Theo had promised to return to Idosa precisely because Willowvale would have trouble getting the company safely back to the Fair Lands. Now, upon contemplation, he thought he might be able to find the Overton manor again, with a great deal of luck, but opening the door into the veil from the palace itself was still nearly impossible.

He paced in the hallway. Theo's promised return was in only three more days. Once Brookbower made the vow, it would be much easier to convince Elmerick to let them stay these few extra days.

Brookbower would be the challenge, not Elmerick.

At the sound of steps in the corridor, he stopped pacing and stood straight, hands clasped behind him.

The little group came into view around the corner.

Brookbower grinned, his white teeth sharp and his eyes bright. "Excellent work, Willowvale!" he said in the Fair language, sincerity making his usually-snide voice unexpectedly warm. "You always were good at dealing with humans."

Willowvale said, "There is the little matter of the vow Elmerick requires of you."

"Not to harm or take humans, yes." Brookbower's lips twisted in dismay and annoyance. "I will do it if Silverthorn requires it of me."

"More than that." Willowvale felt Astrantia's eyes on him with unexpected weight, and he glanced at her for a split second. Why should she look so brittle and pale?

He pushed the thought aside and said to Brookbower, "His Majesty Elmerick requires that you vow never to return to Aricht, or your life is forfeit."

Brookbower blinked and stared at him. "I cannot make such a vow without Silverthorn's sanction and direction. It is unreasonable of Elmerick to ask it of me."

"You certainly can, and my sanction will have to suffice," Willowvale said. "Silverthorn gave me authority to negotiate on his behalf. That is what Elmerick requires of us, of you, in order to keep your life, and by the authority invested in me by Silverthorn, I hereby order you to comply."

Brookbower recoiled as if Willowvale had struck him across the face. His eyes wide, he opened his mouth, then closed it again without a word. Finally, he said, "You would do such a thing? You would order me to betray our lands that way?"

Willowvale said sharply, "I do no injury to the Fair Lands by such an order! You are and have always been a faithful servant of the

Fair Lands, and I aim to preserve your life. There is yet much good you can do alive, but I wish for you to see the changes in the Fair Lands before you throw your life away to preserve your pride."

Brookbower blinked, his hands clenching and unclenching at his sides. "I find it difficult to believe you would so easily agree to bind me, knowing as you do my long and faithful service," he said at last, his voice thick with grief. "I trusted you to serve the lands I love, Willowvale."

"I am doing so," Willowvale said quietly. "You will understand better when we return home and hear the reasons from Silverthorn himself." He swallowed and added, "The vow is to be taken tonight, at the dinner Elmerick insisted upon to mark the occasion of our accord."

Brookbower grimaced, but said nothing else.

"You will do it," Willowvale said even more softly.

"If I must," muttered the ambassador. In Arichtan, he said, "Which is to be my room?"

The guard gestured toward the open door to his left, and Brookbower stalked into the suite and shut the door firmly behind him.

Willowvale let out a soft sigh.

Astrantia said, "Until tonight, my lord." She bowed gracefully to him.

Her magenta hair just brushed her delicate cheekbones as she turned away, and he said impulsively, "Miss Berrydell, I would be much obliged if you would take tea with me this afternoon."

She looked back at him. "Lord Willowvale, while I ought to congratulate you upon your diplomatic success, I am not in the most celebratory of moods at the moment. I would rather be alone."

Willowvale blinked, then narrowed his eyes. "I don't need your congratulations, Miss Berrydell, but I would like to know why you seem so grieved by my success." He felt his lips curling into a sneer, and with great control, smoothed his expression into something more dignified. "I believe that my success saved you some trouble keeping the ambassador safe. You ought to thank me, indeed."

"Thank you, my lord, for that excellent explanation of my job and my debt to you." There was an edge of cold fury in Astrantia's lovely voice, and this coldness shocked Willowvale more deeply than he could have expressed. Astrantia bowed again, every line of her form elegant but tight with unvoiced anger.

The Fair lord swallowed. "It seems you are angry with me, and I confess I do not understand why you should be."

Astrantia's eyes blazed. "Oh? I think you know. Brookbower informed me of your position and mission in Valestria. You let me believe that you understood and agreed with my respect and compassion for humans, while all the time you must have been looking down upon them, and me, as beneath you!"

Willowvale flinched, though it was hardly visible to Astrantia, distracted as she was by her own anger.

"Moreover, to think that I took tea with the murderer of the Wraith! I am disgusted with you, and with myself for believing you to be merely awkward and unpleasant, and not a reprehensible, remorseless villain!"

"The Wraith isn't dead," Willowvale snapped.

Astrantia looked up at him, her eyes shining with tears. "He isn't?"

"No, he isn't!" snarled Willowvale. "You didn't think to ask *me*, when you knew Brookbower had no firsthand knowledge?"

"Well, I'm asking now!" she cried. "You hid your position from me for selfish reasons, because you wanted me to think you agreed with my own sympathies toward the humans. Is it not true that you were sent to identify and kill the Wraith?"

"Of course it is true!" snapped the Fair lord. "Yet he is still alive, and the Fair Lands are more stable than they have been in years."

"Why were you sent here if you failed your mission in Valestria?" Astrantia said, her intelligent eyes bright upon his face. "Your Valestrian is quite a bit better than your Arichtan."

"I didn't want to be sent here," said Willowvale sharply. "I obeyed His Majesty Silverthorn in this, as I did in my mission in Valestria." He rolled his shoulders, for they felt tight with anger, humiliation, and shame. "If your good opinion of me depends upon hearing the whole story, I will tell you every horrible detail." This offer cost him more than Astrantia could have guessed.

"You don't answer to me, my lord," she said with precision. "If you can stand here without shame and admit to having attempted to kill the hero who rescued the helpless children our king ordered stolen, and in so doing accuse *me* of injustice toward you… well, I have no polite words for you."

"And that is your opinion of me?" Willowvale breathed, trembling from head to foot with outrage and indignation. To think he was *proud* of what he had done to Theo?

"It is, my lord." She straightened, her pink lips pressed together. She nodded to him, apparently unwilling to bow to him again, and stepped into her suite without another word.

The door clicked shut.

Willowvale stalked to his suite and almost slammed the door. What an arrogant, disagreeable maiden!

What lovely eyes she had, blazing with righteous fury!

He leaned against the wall and let his head bump back against the plaster.

He slid to the floor and sat with his arms resting on his bent knees, suddenly weary to his very soul.

The guilt he could not forget, could not wash from his soul, welled up like poison in his heart, until he wished to crawl out of his skin.

Miss Berrydell wasn't disagreeable. Not really. She was merely horrified by what she imagined he had done. Willowvale ran his long fingers through his white curls and clasped his hands behind his neck. If she knew the truth of it, the way he'd used his vines, full of vibrant life, to bring Theo nearly to death before he even faced Silverthorn, she would hate him even more.

The Fair lord sat with his head hanging down, letting the weight of what he had done settle into his heart again.

Still.

Theo had forgiven him.

He straightened and, without rising to his feet, began to push his magic into the space in front of him, trying to open a door into the veil.

The veil seemed slippery, sliding past him and resisting his attempt. Finally, breathing heavily, he managed to find a crack, the barest hint of an opening, and he shoved his magic into it with all his might. Sparkles danced before his eyes, and still he could not open the veil more than the width of his hand.

He let the magic go and leaned back against the wall, gasping and dizzy. His head felt like it would float away, and his hands and feet felt distant and hollow.

The blood thundered in his ears, and he considered being sick on the floor beside where he sat. Or perhaps fainting would be easier.

There was no chance of getting them all into the veil tonight. They would have to wait for Theo to return, however angry Elmerick might be.

Willowvale shoved himself up the wall, then leaned against it for a moment as the world spun giddily around him. He closed his eyes and took several deep breaths to push down the nausea. The Arichtan palace must have been built in a location unfriendly to Fair magic, just as the Valestrian palace had been. It was little wonder that Brookbower had never been able to step into the veil; if Willowvale himself could barely open the smallest door, Brookbower's minuscule talent with the veil would never be able to achieve even that.

The Fair lord wondered if even Theo would be able to do it.

No matter. When Theo returned, he would either take them directly home or be able to find a place more agreeable to entering the veil.

Willowvale staggered to the nearest chair and fell into it. He rested his head on his fist and closed his eyes.

Miss Berrydell was right, after all. He knew himself to be awkward, disagreeable, and cold. Though he had believed his own words when he told Theo it was not guilt that assailed him, he now recognized it for what it was: guilt and shame, layered with a dark, hopeless conviction that even Theo's forgiveness would not be enough to wipe his soul clean.

Still, as the dizziness and nausea receded, he focused on what he knew to be true. There was beauty and grace in the world, whether he felt it at this particular moment or not, and it was worth fighting for. If Theo could befriend his bitter enemy, Willowvale could set his mind on beauty and truth, just as he had advised Silverthorn to do.

Between one breath and the next, he fell into the soft, welcoming darkness.

In her suite, Astrantia wiped angry tears from her eyes. How *dare* that arrogant lord accuse her of being unjust to him! *She* had not attempted to murder a hero! *She* had not presented a facade of morality while secretly looking down upon both humans and Fair Folk alike.

She felt wholly justified in her view of him, but her conviction on this point did not lessen the turmoil in her heart.

CHAPTER EIGHTEEN
Collateral Damage

A loud, insistent pounding brought Willowvale slowly back to consciousness. He staggered to his feet, disoriented and feeling oddly hollow and shaky, and straightened his jacket. The pounding sounded as though it came from a fist upon his door. He shook his head to clear it before opening the door.

"What?"

"You're to meet His Majesty and sign the agreement tonight, or have you forgotten?" the guard said. "The others are waiting for you."

Willowvale blinked to see that Brookbower, Miss Berrydell, Hawksbane, Tarragon, and Fallingwater were already in the hall. Everyone's eyes were upon him.

In the Fair tongue, Brookbower said acidly, "I suppose you thought it amusing to make us wait."

Willowvale's nostrils flared as he took a deep, steadying breath and strode out to lead the little group through the hall after the guard. "I had no such intention," he replied.

"You must have been occupied with something more important, then?" the ambassador pressed, his voice sharp.

"I was occupied, yes." The floor seemed to rise before him, so fatigued was he, and Willowvale said nothing for several moments, fully focused on staying upright. Then, with a strange urge to justify himself, he added, "If you must know, I was attempting to open a doorway into the veil."

"Did it work?" Brookbower asked.

"Better than last week, but hardly enough to get us free. I will have to negotiate with Elmerick to let us stay a little longer." Willowvale blinked spots from his eyes and clamped his mouth shut.

"Until what?" the ambassador muttered bitterly. "So we've moved from captivity in the dungeon to captivity in a suite. It is an improvement, to be sure, but hardly the success you presented to me, Willowvale!"

"Can you *please* be silent?" Willowvale snarled. "Let me think!"

From the rear of their little group, Tarragon muttered to Fallingwater, "Two of a kind, those lords are."

Stung, Willowvale gritted his teeth and focused his gaze upon the heels of the guard leading them through the corridor. He was *not* like Brookbower, not any more.

Three more days. He could keep his temper for three more days until Theo came.

Late afternoon sunlight slanted through the tall windows to their left, making the gold veins in the white marble floors shine. The almost inaudible swish of the clothing of the Fair Folk was entirely drowned out in the sharp sounds of their human escorts, so loud in the echoing halls.

Astrantia, as always, was conscious of their surroundings and alert for any threat from the humans. Still, the human servants they passed and the guards who escorted them presented no indication of any hostile intention. Indeed, the guard behind her seemed to look at her with a little too much admiration in his gaze. She was reasonably sure that looking at him and smiling would be misinterpreted, so she pretended she did not notice his attention.

They were ushered in to a relatively modest dining room already occupied by the king and seven noblemen Willowvale had not previously met, though Brookbower obviously recognized them.

"I suppose I must introduce you," muttered Brookbower in the Fair language.

"Yes." Willowvale, for all his customary arrogance, did not take much pleasure in this rare opportunity to assert his temporary authority over Brookbower.

With an almost inaudible growl deep in his throat, Brookbower straightened even more rigidly. Then, with anger in every line of his body, he bowed toward the human king and each of the nobles in turn.

"Lord Ash Willowvale, I present to you His Majesty Valor Elmerick, king of the human nation of Aricht. Your Majesty Elmerick, Lord Willowvale, Marquess in the Fair Lands."

Willowvale shot Brookbower an appreciative glance, amused and slightly surprised that Brookbower had not revealed his title to the human king. It seemed the sort of vindictive act that Brookbower might relish. Still, he had not chosen to do so, apparently counting his loyalty to the Fair Lands still greater than his resentment of Willowvale himself.

Moreover, he had insulted the Arichtan king by introducing him to Willowvale, rather than by first introducing the lower-ranked Willowvale to him.

Elmerick was certainly astute enough to have noticed this slight, but he gave no outward sign of his irritation other than a narrowing of his eyes.

"We've met," he said curtly.

Brookbower bowed again, far too shallowly, and turned to the nearest nobleman. "Lord Ash Willowvale, this is Lord Christopher Nott, Duke of Waeldestone. Lord Nott, Lord Willowvale." Then, "Lord Charles Hollowway, Duke of Mournfield Glen. Lord Hollowway, Lord

Willowvale." The humans bowed to Willowvale in turn, and he returned the courtesy with as much grace as he could muster.

He still felt vaguely light-headed, and irritated about it, not to mention that his stomach churned with nerves. Servants were bringing in steaming dishes of quail, roast pork, and vegetables, which they arranged upon a table. The spread was, if not exactly lavish in celebration, at least sumptuous enough to not be openly insulting to the Fair Court.

"My lord," someone murmured politely, and Willowvale turned to see a servant offering a tray of wine glasses to him. The Fair lord accepted one but did not drink it. Arichtan wine was even less satisfactory than Valestrian, and even Overton's excellent vintages could not equal those of the Fair Court. Save the tea, of course; tea tasted like comfort and unexpected grace.

The servant offered the tray to Brookbower, who reluctantly took a delicate crystal glass. Then the servant turned away without offering the tray to Miss Berrydell, Hawksbane, Tarragon, or Fallingwater.

Hawksbane muttered something under his breath in the Fair language but did not otherwise protest.

Willowvale said sharply, "I thought you human men prided yourself on your courtesy to the lovelier sex, and yet you did not offer Miss Berrydell refreshment. Do you mean to deliberately insult her?"

The servant blinked and stared at him with what Willowvale took to be feigned innocence. "I was informed that the lady was to be offered drinks from another tray," he said with a polite inclination of his head.

"Why?" Willowvale snapped. "There is no reason for your court to discriminate against her merely because she is of lower status in our court. You will accord her all rights and privileges you accord Lord Brookbower and me."

Beside him, Brookbower let out a disgusted sigh. In the Fair language, he said, "Willowvale, come to your senses! What purpose does this serve?"

Willowvale snarled, "It isn't about purpose, but about the principle of it! If you committed the crime, there was no reason for them to imprison her at all. Certainly there is no reason for petty slights against her now."

Astrantia said to the servant in Arichtan, "I have taken no offense. It is customary to serve those of higher rank first, and I had no expectation that you would break protocol for me." She smiled politely at him, and he ducked his head again.

Then he slipped away, still without offering the tray to Astrantia or the other Fair Folk.

"This is ridiculous," Willowvale said in bitter irritation. He handed his glass to Astrantia and inclined his head. "Miss Berrydell." He did not expect this to change her opinion of him, and so he was not surprised when she did not smile as she accepted the glass.

Still, she did accept it, her eyes wide and serious. "This is unnecessary, my lord," she murmured.

"It is entirely necessary," he grumbled, and he meant that it was necessary for him to do it. It served no diplomatic purpose, and he knew it, and that irritated him too.

His Majesty Elmerick said, in a voice that carried across the room, "Let's get on with it. Lord Linden Brookbower, I have been assured that you will swear never to return to Aricht, as well as swear never to take or harm humans again, just as your king swore."

Willowvale said, "Your Majesty, there is one little matter I would like to clarify before Brookbower takes such an oath."

Elmerick's eyes narrowed. "What is it?" he growled.

"I tried to open a door into the veil this afternoon." Willowvale's voice was tight with anger and frustration at his failure and at the necessity of admitting it in front of all these humans. Not to mention the Fair Folk behind and beside him. Especially Miss Berrydell.

"I was able to reach the veil with my magic, but not to open a doorway sufficiently large to let us pass into the veil. I must reluctantly ask your forbearance for a little longer until we can depart."

Brookbower turned to glance up and down Willowvale, as if he had not already heard this in the hallway. "Your Majesty," he said, in a voice with thick with scorn toward the human king, "it is a rare talent indeed that can open a way into the veil at all, much less here in the Arichtan palace. It is extraordinary that Willowvale could do it at all." He gestured gracefully with his still-untouched glass of wine. "I am confident you will not hold against my staff what you ought to hold only against me."

The king smiled tightly. "So you admit your crimes against the children?"

With a dangerous glint in his eye, Brookbower said, "Are we to have the trial now, after all? I thought we were to make oaths."

Astrantia said quietly, in the Fair language, "My lord Brookbower, please do not antagonize him now. I should like very much not to have to kill anyone after we have made it this long in peace."

The ambassador turned and looked at her, his eyebrows raised. "Miss Berrydell, what a soft heart you have!" he replied in the Fair language, his voice sharp with derision. "I am not provoking them, as you can clearly ascertain. I am merely reminding them of our purpose here. If they wish to kill us, I am more than willing to return the favor."

Astrantia sighed. "Yet is it not Lord Willowvale's prerogative to direct the conversation?" She did not look at Willowvale, though she was acutely aware of the fact that his pale, silvery eyes were upon her face.

She was still holding the glass he had given her, and to distract herself from his unpleasant scrutiny, she took a sip.

It was not the best wine she had tasted in the human world, and human wines were as a rule disappointing in comparison to those of the Fair Lands. Still, with the human king's eyes suddenly on her face as well, she felt obliged to take another, slightly larger swallow, to show that not all Fair Folk utterly despised humans.

She swallowed and barely suppressed a grimace. The wine had an odd aftertaste, even more unpleasant than most of the varieties the Fair delegation had tasted during their years in Aricht. In the Fair language, she said quietly, "Lord Willowvale, your insistence upon courtesy was noted, but the wine is not worth drinking. Lord Brookbower, I wouldn't bother if I were you."

Brookbower snorted softly in derision. "Thank you for your sacrifice, Miss Berrydell."

One of the humans, James Copley, Marquess of Taedmorden, said sharply, "What are you saying? We can't understand you."

The ambassador said smoothly, "Only a little comment on the wine, Copley. If you were meant to understand it, we would have spoken in Arichtan."

The marquess gritted his teeth but said nothing else.

"What do you want, then, Willowvale?" the king said curtly.

"Merely your leave to stay, here or in town, it matters not, until Mr. Overton returns. Failing that, I want your permission and safe passage through your lands to Valestria."

"When is Overton returning?" the king asked.

"In three days."

A sudden, sharp inhalation caught Willowvale's attention, and he turned to see Astrantia looking rather strained.

"What is it?" he asked.

The king frowned, and one of the human noblemen shifted, although Willowvale didn't really pay attention to who it was.

Brookbower looked at Astrantia with one eyebrow raised, his golden eyes curious.

The Fair maiden tensed, half doubled over, and breathed, "Don't drink the wine."

Brookbower held the glass up to the light from the windows and frowned at it. "Poison?" His voice had a hard edge. "Is this the hospitality of a human king?"

"It is not!" The king's voice rang out. "Who has done this?"

Astrantia held up a hand, and a faint shimmer in the air gave the first hint of the power of her magic.

Then there was a commotion behind them, and Willowvale whirled to see a cluster of guards spreading out behind them.

"Stand down!" shouted the king.

The guards appeared ready to obey him, so Willowvale turned his attention to Astrantia, who had one arm curled about her stomach and was retching.

Brookbower brought his slight water magic to his fingertips, pulling the wine from every glass at once. The wine gathered in a swirling ball which caught the light like a brilliant gem.

Astrantia said roughly, "Brookbower, let me handle this! If you kill them you'll never get free."

The ambassador curled his fingers into his palms, his golden eyes flicking from human face to human face. "I'm sorely tempted to kill them all right now, Berrydell. A little wine down their throats and into their lungs. It wouldn't take long. You won't even have to do it yourself."

Willowvale snarled, "I forbid it, Brookbower! Make the vow you promised you would!"

Brookbower shifted from foot to foot. He glanced at Astrantia again, who still had her hand raised. The air between the humans and Fair Folk shimmered as if the light danced.

"*You* could kill them, Berrydell. You're not bound by the vow." Then with a glittering smile, he said, "Who has done this, humans? Shall we kill you all or merely the guilty party?"

Then Astrantia's magic collapsed in a rush of power that made everyone, human and fairy, stagger. Astrantia herself shook like a leaf, retching and gasping.

In the disorientation that followed, in which the entire world seemed to be rippling, one of the noblemen managed to get within arm's reach of Brookbower before any of the fairies noticed. The Fair ambassador had turned his attention for a moment to the guards behind them, apparently fearing some attack, and Willowvale had focused upon Astrantia.

The human, Sir Roger Buckley, pulled a dagger from inside his coat and attempted to plunge it into Brookbower's stomach.

Astrantia gave a pained little gasp of effort and flung up her hand; her magic tossed the attacker aside as if he were a child. She collapsed to her knees and vomited.

Willowvale spared a glance for the humans, and then, with a sudden effort that left dark spots dancing in his vision, managed to open a door into the veil.

It was barely the width of his shoulders, but it would have to do.

Then there was a screaming agony in his side, and the face of an angry Arichtan lord only inches from his.

"Die, fairy," he hissed.

And the knife twisted, and Willowvale sucked in a breath of air that felt like fire.

He clasped his hand over the man's hand on the hilt of the knife and drew it out, then with his other hand pulled his vines from the magic of the air and pressed them into the wound, deep and rough, enough to stanch the bleeding for a little while. All the while he kept his eyes on the human's, taking in the grief and fury that ruled him.

He shoved the man back with Fair strength, sending him reeling, knife still in hand.

Hawksbane and the two Fair servants stood with Brookbower a little distance away, and the king seemed to be shouting something, but Willowvale could not make out what it was.

The pain was so distracting, he almost didn't notice when the lord lunged at him again.

He twisted away and reached for Astrantia as he ripped at the veil.

CHAPTER NINETEEN
A Desperate Flight

With a grunt of effort, Willowvale shoved Astrantia into the veil and jerked the door closed behind him just in time to avoid being stabbed again. He stumbled into her as she doubled over, retching helplessly.

The darkness pressed upon him, filled with whispering hints of distant predators drawing closer. The air of the veil was frigid and damp, as if they stood in a cave deep beneath the earth rather than a passage between worlds.

Feeling a more than a little unsteady, Willowvale leaned against the wall. "I'm sorry I don't have any water," he said.

"Just go," Astrantia snarled.

"I will not leave you here in the dark," Willowvale snapped. "I'll come back for Brookbower once I get you to safety."

She retched again. "Brookbower is the priority!"

"He's your priority, not mine!" Willowvale pressed his hand against the wound in his side and let out a hiss of pain. "You are far more honorable than Brookbower, and if he wants to fight the Arichtans, he will do it alone. He has no support from the crown in that endeavor."

Astrantia sighed heavily and said, "Then let His Majesty discipline him."

There was a rustle, and a low groan, and then silence broken only by the sound of her labored breathing.

"Why are you doing this? I should be there to defend him." After a fraught moment, she added, "Why do you care what happens to me?"

"Because despite my best efforts, you have captured far more than just my respect," the Fair lord growled.

She let out a soft, pained breath.

Blood slicked Willowvale's fingers, and the magic of the veil pressed against his mind, heavy and hostile.

"Can you walk?" he breathed.

She didn't answer.

"Miss Berrydell, can you walk?" he said more sharply.

When she still did not answer, he flicked a little light to his fingertips. She had shifted to lean against the wall, on her knees and doubled over, so that her forehead was upon the moss-slimed floor. He could not see her face through her mane of raspberry-pink hair. He knelt beside her and put a hand on her shoulder.

"Miss Berrydell?"

She groaned softly.

"Let me help you up." He shifted to get a better angle on her shoulders and hauled her upright, ignoring the searing pain in his side. Her head lolled against his shoulder, and she would have fallen, but he swept her up in his arms.

Then he had to lean his left shoulder against the wall, for the pain made everything waver for a moment, even with the light from his fingertips giving form and shape to the tunnel.

She was entirely unconscious, her pink lips unnaturally pale and her bright hair stark against her pallor. He let the light fade and closed his eyes, feeling for the magic.

The Fair Lands were much too far to walk, even if she had been able to stay on her feet. He imagined it would take days to reach anywhere familiar in the Fair Lands, and she did not have that much time.

Ardmond it must be, however shifting and unpleasant the way, for Ardmond was not so far from the Overton manor, and Overton knew how to contact Mosswing. Mosswing could save Astrantia, if she could be saved at all.

The magic writhed against his consciousness, unwilling to be helpful, and he leaned more heavily against the wall. He let his head rest against the damp stone and pressed his own magic firmly into the veil, trying to convey his determination without words.

He had the distinct sense that the veil was laughing at him, and he snarled to himself in frustration. With a huff of pained effort, he shoved away from the wall and set off in the direction he believed Overton's manor to be.

A sense of foreboding slowed his steps, and just in time, too, for the ground suddenly sank beneath his feet, and within moments he was stuck up to his ankles. A clicking sound came from the hall behind him, and he struggled forward. Nothing that made a clicking sound as it ran was pleasant.

He hissed as the movement sent tongues of fire through his side, making his breath come too fast and tight. He risked the light again for a split second, just long enough to see the floor of the tunnel turn to stone again some ten feet ahead and to glance behind him. The creature pursuing them was distant enough that he got only an impression of horns and shadow before he let the light fade and struggled on. The mire beneath him was not quite quicksand, for it was not grainy, but rather had a gel-like texture, smooth and slick and slippery, and it sucked at his feet as if it would pull him completely under it.

Now he was up to his knees, and his chest was heaving, and the blood thundered in his ears.

With the next step he fell upon the stone, and the Fair maiden in his arms tumbled bruisingly to the floor as he lost his footing in the slime. If Astrantia had been awake to hear it, he would have been ashamed of the agonized breath he let out when he regained his feet and lifted her again. The creature struggled in the slime behind him, and Willowvale hurried onward, heart racing.

He took a turn that did not lead toward the Overton manor, but rather up a steep incline, and at the top the passage suddenly became so narrow that he sidled through, Astrantia's limp body pressed tightly against his. Her hip dug into his wound, and for a moment he had to stop and remind himself to breathe, for the pain stole the air from his lungs and rational thought from his mind.

Still, he pressed on. The creature he had seen was far too large to easily pass through this cramped hole, and when the passage widened after some fifteen feet, he stopped and leaned against the wall. The breath trembled in his lungs, and his muscles burned.

Astrantia groaned weakly.

"Miss Berrydell?" He slid down the wall to sit against it, supporting her with aching arms.

She mumbled something indistinct and turned her head.

He flicked a little light to his fingertips and she flinched, as if the light hurt her eyes. He let it fade.

"I'm taking you to a friend." He laughed under his breath at the word 'friend' and added, "He'll be able to contact someone with healing magic. I don't know if I can claim *him* as a friend, but he will help you if he can."

The Fair maiden moved her head, as if to pull away, and he steadied her with careful hands. He realized with dismay that his hands were shaking. How mortifying! He clenched his hands into fists and then spread his fingers wide, trying to still their trembling. It didn't work.

"You were part of it," she whispered. "You stole the children!"

"Only once," Willowvale said sharply. "My assignment was to catch the Rose."

"You think that's somehow more honorable, to catch the hero who rescued the helpless children rather than stealing them yourself? If anyone in the Fair court with any power at all had a shred of decency, we would never have been at war at all, much less stealing children!" She said venomously, "I *despise* you, Lord Willowvale!"

"So do I!" he snarled.

There was a shocked silence, and they heard the beast which had been pursuing them scrabbling at the passage through which they had come. Then the sound quieted as the creature padded away.

Finally Astrantia said, with cold precision, "What are you going to do with me, then? I can hardly believe you have a friend at all, much less one who would help me."

"You think me a liar?" Willowvale said with equal coldness. "Like all our kind, I like to think I have a facility with words, but I have no more outright lied than has His Majesty himself, or anyone else you care to respect."

She blew out a dismissive *pfft* and said, "Silverthorn devised the scheme to steal children. He's hardly worthy of respect." Then her whole body convulsed and she sucked in an agonized breath.

"Miss Berrydell?" He was a little surprised at how steady his voice was; he did not feel steady.

"Go away," she breathed. "I'd rather die in the veil than accept your help."

Willowvale closed his eyes, though the veil was so dark it made little difference, and rested his head against the wall of the tunnel. The little shred of hope in his heart died, quietly and without protest.

He sighed. "Still."

She made no answer, and her breathing sounded more labored. He flicked the light to his fingertips again, and she did not flinch away. She had not managed to sit up after all; she was lying more or less face up, though curled slightly to one side, and one graceful hand lay palm upward in front of her face.

The poison had stolen what little color had remained in her cheeks and lips and given her skin an unhealthy blue tint. Her lips were pressed together, and Willowvale imagined she might have let out some indication of her pain, if he had been someone else. Someone she liked and trusted.

Then he let the light play over the wound in his side, but he could see little other than the dampness of the pale blood that now soaked his shirt, vest, and jacket, and down his trousers. Even the color was barely discernible against the pattern of the fabric.

"Miss Berrydell," he said again. "I'm going to help you up." He said this as if he hoped she would hear him, but he did not expect her to answer.

With a hiss of pain, he shifted closer and got his feet under him, and then he lifted her again and staggered onward.

The tunnel twisted and turned, leading him up and down, but there were few turns, and when he was forced to choose a direction, he felt the veil was not pressing upon him quite so ominously. Once he strode through thigh-deep water, cold as ice and full of slithering things he did not want to see.

Nothing bit him, and he considered that a mercy. He kept Astrantia mostly out the water, though one of her hands trailed limply through the frigid liquid before he managed to rearrange her arm so that it lay upon her stomach instead. She did not react either to the chill or to his muttered apology.

The pain in his gut was an ever-present fire. At times, he almost managed to ignore it, as if it were merely a fact of being in the veil, but then it flared with some twist or strain as he struggled onward, and it was all he could do to keep breathing.

His head throbbed with the magic that weighed upon him, and he could no longer suppress his shivering. If he put Astrantia down to rest a little, he would not be able to rise again. His muscles shook with strain, and he had to stop and lean against the wall at intervals, because sometimes the pitch black tunnel swam before him, as if the darkness had form and shape that did not match the passage they traversed.

"I hope you will forgive me," he finally said, more to say it aloud than from any hope that she would hear him. "You said you didn't want my help, but I've failed too many times to give up now, when I might actually do a little good." His voice was a harsh rasp, for he was breathing too hard to give the words their customary smooth polish.

"You are wrong, though. I do have one friend. I cannot say why, or how, or even how long it will last, and I do not deserve him, but I have a friend. You met him, but I don't think you realized how much you would like him. He saved the children. I might even claim to have a second friend. I think if a man invites one to his wedding, he might be a friend, however unlikely it seems." His chest heaved with effort, and he staggered drunkenly onward.

"Frost on a bud gleams in moonlight, the promise of a bloom locked inside, waiting. Waiting. Should spring sunlight ever fall upon it, perhaps it might show its lovely face, but winter… ah, but winter is harsh. Not all hope is fulfilled." The poem was old, and though Willowvale did not often read poetry, that one had stuck with him.

He walked without speaking for another hour, feeling with increasing desperation the magic of the veil squeezing and pressing and writhing against his consciousness. "Mosswing's magic is quite strong," he gasped, as if Astrantia could hear him. "I'll leave you there. You don't have to ever see my face again. Overton will let you stay as long as necessary." He fell against the wall, no longer caring that each breath sounded like a groan. His arms shook, and his legs trembled, and the wound in his side made him want to whimper like a wounded animal, helpless and agonized and despairing.

Yet he shoved himself away from the wall again with a huff of effort. He had no more breath for words, nor could he think of anything reassuring to say, for his mind was filled with blood and pain and a terrible, hopeless determination not to weep like a coward as his strength failed.

Then at last there was the feel of the magic of Ardmond, which he barely recognized through the haze of exhaustion. With a gasp, he opened the veil and stepped out into the twilight of the human world.

For a moment he feared he would not be able to figure out where he was at all. Then he saw the road some distance away, the same road he had ridden several times between Ardmond and the Overton estate. He shifted the Fair maiden in his arms and set off down the road toward the manor.

A mile and a half later, he staggered up the steps to the front door of the Overton manor and kicked at the door. His arms had long since cramped, and if he had attempted to shift Astrantia against him, he would have dropped her.

He kicked again, swaying and half-delirious.

When Anselm opened the door, the fairy stumbled forward. The servant, startled, helped catch Astrantia and took her weight as the Fair lord fell to his knees.

"Lord Willowvale!" Anselm looked down at the Fair maiden now in his arms. "What's wrong with her?"

"Poison. Call Mosswing!" Willowvale gasped.

Anselm nodded and hurried away. "Mr. Overton!" he called down the hall, his voice sharp with urgency.

Theo met him in the hallway, and the two men put the Fair maiden into a guest room with swift competence. There was the sound of fabric, and then Theo hurried down the hall to the garden, from which the bird to Mosswing would be dispatched.

Willowvale remained on his knees on the marble floor. The sweat on his body felt icy within his coat. His trousers were still damp and his feet were frigid within his soaked boots. He could not stop shivering, and each tremor sent screaming anguish from his side up through his chest and down through his belly. He thought he might be sick upon the floor, but swallowed and closed his eyes, forcing down the feeling. The blood rushed in his ears.

After several minutes, in which he heard Theo's voice in the hallway again, he managed to shove himself to his feet. The shivers grew worse. His knees nearly buckled, but he turned to the door.

"Where are you going?" Theo said from behind him. "Surely you don't intend to leave now!"

Willowvale closed his eyes, faint and dizzy with pain.

Theo's voice sharpened. "My lord, is that blood upon your jacket?"

The fairy sighed. He was too tired to be clever or bitter or even properly grateful, though he was glad they had sent for Mosswing. "It doesn't matter," he muttered.

Without further warning, Theo somehow slipped under Willowvale's arm and wrapped his own arm around the fairy's body, and then he began hurrying him down the hall with surprising alacrity and strength.

Willowvale groaned under his breath.

"Where are you hurt?" Theo asked.

Willowvale realized with dismay that the young man was unbuttoning his jacket with clever fingers, though he fumbled a bit with the buttons going the direction opposite that to which he was accustomed.

"Lord Mosswing will help when he gets here, but until then we can at least slow the bleeding with a good bandage. Let me see it."

There was no arguing and little use in being embarrassed or ashamed. Willowvale closed his eyes and stopped paying attention, because the roar of his pulse in his ears was too loud to hear Theo's sympathetic words.

He didn't really care if he lived anyway.

CHAPTER TWENTY
Much-Needed Help

The veil had helped Willowvale more than he realized at the time, distracted as he was by pain, fatigue, and fear. With Theo at his side, the walk from the Overton estate to Idosa had taken nearly eighteen hours, including their stop for lunch. The veil had allowed Willowvale, carrying Astrantia, to reach Ardmond in only twenty-three hours, an extraordinary act of kindness, considering how much it usually opposed him.

The Fair lord was by now unconscious on a guest bed in the Overton manor. Theo and his father examined and dressed the fairy's wound, and the afternoon light streamed in, making the room feel warmer than it was. Anselm started the fire.

"The poor wretch walked all the way here from Idosa in the veil?" Sir Theodore marveled. "He must have been in agony."

"He's a stubborn, disagreeable scoundrel," agreed Anselm.

Theo shot his servant a quelling look. "I'd say resolute and courageous, Anselm. He did it for Miss Berrydell, not for himself."

Anselm shrugged. "Call it what you like."

Theo frowned.

Astrantia was also unconscious in the neighboring room. Her cheeks were nearly as pale as Willowvale's, and it looked even more alarming on her. The fire in the grate had already been started, and Theo stirred it again, though it didn't need it yet. Her breathing had an alarming rasp in it, and the sound felt like fear in the air.

Theo paced in the hallway and finally said, "Perhaps I ought to go fetch Cedar myself."

By this time Lily, Theo's mother Lady Overton, and Juniper had joined them in the hallway. Juniper peeked in to each room from the doorway.

Lily said, "Should I sit with Miss Berrydell? I think someone ought to be there if she wakes up."

Theo smiled at his lovely young wife. "I think that would be kind, yes. Thank you, my darling." Then, to Anselm, he said, "I'll leave Willowvale a note. I doubt he'll awake before I return, but if he does, I imagine he would prefer to be alone."

With affectionate farewells to everyone, and sweet kisses for his wife, Theo set off through the veil to fetch Cedar.

He was disappointed, but not entirely surprised, to find that when he entered the veil, he felt no indication of any Fair presence within the veil at all. It was certainly possible that Cedar had perished in the veil, but the veil liked Cedar nearly as much as it liked Theo himself. Theo thought it more likely that the veil had merely eaten his messenger bird.

An hour later, Theo stepped out of the veil in front of Cedar's house. He bounded up the steps and knocked upon the door.

The veil did not oppose them, and indeed seemed to speed their passage more than usual. Theo apprised Cedar of what he knew of the situation as they hurried through the darkness. They reached the Overton estate only an hour after leaving the Fair Lands.

CHAPTER TWENTY-ONE
Compassion and Courage

Lord Cedar Mosswing tested the very limits of his healing magic on Miss Astrantia Berrydell.

He poured golden magic into her for hours, and if he had been any less gifted than he was, he would have made no headway against the vicious poison.

"What is it?" Theo asked, when his friend sank to his knees on the floor beside the Fair maiden's bed.

"Faebane," Cedar gasped. The Fair lord had one hand upon Astrantia's wrist, and he sucked in a deep breath, steadying himself.

"What can I do to help?" Theo said.

"I don't know."

After three hours of wordless, desperate strain, Cedar slumped forward to rest his head against the edge of the bed. His chest heaved.

Theo put a bracing hand on his shoulder.

"She's stable enough for now," Cedar mumbled. "Help me up and I'll look at Willowvale."

Theo hauled Cedar to his feet and helped him into a chair.

"Willowvale will be stable for a little longer," Theo said. "How can I help?"

Cedar swallowed and stared at the Fair maiden motionless on the bed. "I should probably eat something," he admitted. "I feel dizzy and hollow and I don't think I'll be much use for a few minutes."

Anselm, who had been waiting to hear something like this, hurried away.

When he returned a short time later, he bore a tray with a generous bowl of rich chicken and rice soup, hot and filling, and a full pot of what he knew to be Cedar's current favorite tea, the same butterscotch vanilla black tea that Willowvale had enjoyed some weeks previously. Juniper trailed in his wake, quietly helpful and polite.

"Thank you, Anselm," Cedar said, his deep voice warm with appreciation.

He ate with slow, steady determination, and sat back with a satisfied sigh at the end. "Anselm, you're incredible," he murmured, eyes closed. "If Willowvale can hold out a little longer, I think I'll just… faint for a minute."

Theo chuckled. "He's far too stubborn to die now. Rest a little."

Cedar grunted but couldn't manage anything more.

For the next half hour, the room was nearly silent. Astrantia's breathing was not easy, but it was steadier than it had been, and it did not seem to be worsening. Her eyes had dark blue shadows beneath them, and her lips had a blue cast. Still, she seemed to be stable for the moment.

At last Cedar took a deep breath and shifted. "I'm all right," he said a little hoarsely. "Let me see Willowvale."

Soon, Theo and Cedar stood at Willowvale's bedside. Sir Theodore, Anselm, and Theo had bandaged the wound earlier, and so he lay beneath the covers, silent and still. His brow was pinched with pain and fatigue, but otherwise he looked more relaxed than Cedar or Theo had ever seen him.

Cedar did not need to see the wound to use his healing magic, so he merely placed a hand on Willowvale's shoulder, mostly covered by the blanket, and let his magic seep in gently.

He frowned. "There's something in the wound." He tilted his head, letting the magic swirl and rush and recede, feeling the ripples and unpleasant little interactions between his own magic and Willowvale's plant magic.

"He walked a very long way," Theo said. "If I were him, wounded that badly, I would have tried to stop the bleeding with vines or leaves or whatever I could conjure up in the moment."

"I think you're right," Cedar said. "Well, it will have to come out, but not yet. His magic doesn't receive mine well, so it will take a few days for this to really heal. When he wakes, let him know he should remove it and you and Anselm can bind it up again."

"All right."

Cedar straightened. "That should do it for now." He looked down at Lord Ash Willowvale. "What a strange turn of events."

He took a deep breath.

"And how are you, my friend?" Theo looked at him with concern. "I've never seen you so pale."

"I'm all right," Cedar said stoutly, but he put a hand on Theo's shoulder to steady himself as they crossed the room. "Faebane is… well, it's an extraordinarily potent poison to the Fair, and it is resistant to Fair magic of all sorts."

They reentered Miss Berrydell's room, where she still lay motionless and deathly pale. The bright raspberry-pink of her hair stood out against the sheets.

Cedar moved the chair closer so he could reach the Fair maiden's hand when he sprawled in it. He put his fingertips on her wrist, the touch light and gentle, and looked up at Theo.

"I wouldn't mind some more tea," he said, with an apologetic smile.

"Of course." Theo poured him another cup and handed it to him, for it became apparent that Cedar intended to maintain contact between himself and Miss Berrydell.

Cedar drained the cup of tea without pausing, and then breathed, "Thank you." He closed his eyes. "I think, if I can hold on a few more hours, she can fight the faebane herself. She's remarkably strong, you know."

"Is she?" Theo felt a strange urge to keep Cedar talking. The Fair lord's brilliant turquoise eyes, usually so alert, seemed oddly dazed, as if the magic he had expended so generously had left him disoriented.

Juniper appeared in the doorway. "My lord, is there anything I can do to help?"

Cedar blinked blearily and poured more golden magic into Astrantia. "I don't know," he mumbled.

The young fairy stepped closer. His eyes widened. "Lord Mosswing, let me help you!"

Cedar's eyelids fluttered, and he made some inarticulate sound, perhaps of protest. Juniper put his hand on the older fairy's shoulder, and Cedar sucked in a sharp breath.

Juniper retreated, his eyes wide, and sat down suddenly on the floor near the door. He leaned his head back against the wall.

Theo knelt beside him. "What did you do?"

The young fairy smiled faintly. "Lord Mosswing was draining himself dry, metaphorically, fighting that faebane. He's strong, but so is faebane. I bound his life to mine, so he can draw on me if he needs to."

With that, Juniper curled up on the floor as if he intended to sleep there.

"Bind his life to mine as well. Surely we two can keep him alive better than one."

Juniper blinked. "You don't have enough magic, Mr. Overton."

Theo swallowed and glanced at Cedar, who was slumped motionless in the chair, eyes closed. "How much more does he need?"

"I think he'll be all right now." Juniper smiled, his narrow face hopeful. "He's very strong! He probably doesn't need me at all. I'll remove the binding when he asks me to."

"I'm all right," Cedar said almost inaudibly. Still, the ghost of a smile flickered across his lips, and he added, "Thank you, Juniper."

Theo helped Juniper up and to a comfortable couch in one corner. "I wish I could help."

"I'm all right," Cedar said again.

For another hour, the room was silent but for the sound of their breathing.

Astrantia's breathing strengthened and steadied, and some time later she turned her head.

Half-conscious, she jerked her hand away from Cedar and flung it toward him, palm open.

The Fair lord was startled out of his exhausted daze by the immense power that flung him across the room and slammed him into the opposite wall hard enough to shake most of the house.

Cedar crumpled to the floor, struggling to breathe, for the air had been knocked out of him.

"Wait, please, Miss Berrydell!" cried Theo. "Wait! You're safe here!"

Astrantia's pink eyes were wide and wild. "Where is this?" She struggled to sit up, and then looked down at the covers and back up at Theo. "Mr. Overton?" Her voice squeaked with surprise and dismay.

"Yes," Theo said. "Let me help my friend up, please."

Cedar had managed to get to hands and knees, and he stayed in that position, head hanging down, chest heaving. "I'm all right."

"*Lord Mosswing?*" Astrantia's voice rose in shock.

Cedar nodded, still dazed and breathless. He let Theo help him back to his chair and fell into it. His attempt at a smile looked more like a grimace, and his hands shook with fatigue and shock.

Astrantia looked around again, taking in the distinctly human style of the decor in the room. "Where is this?" she said again. She pushed herself up to sit against the headboard of the bed and laid her hands in her lap, as if she wanted to be ready to defend herself at any moment.

"This is my house in Ardmond, in Valestria," Theo said. "Lord Willowvale brought you here because he knew I could contact Lord Mosswing, and Lord Mosswing is a gifted healer. He has spent much of the day, and a great deal of effort, saving your life."

The fairy swallowed and looked at Cedar. "Thank you," she said quietly. "I'm sorry I…"

Cedar gave a soft huff, and then winced. "It's all right," he said gently. "I know you were just startled. It must be disorienting to wake up in a place you've never been before."

Astrantia nodded wordlessly. "Why would… why would he bring me here to you, though? I told him to leave me in the veil."

"I assume he wanted to save your life as well," Theo said.

The Fair maiden frowned and studied his face. "Lord Brookbower told me that Willowvale had told him he had killed the Rose. Well…" She frowned. "No, he said he imagined Willowvale had killed the Rose. Certainly he had succeeded in solving the problem of the fading of the lands. When I confronted Lord Willowvale about his murder of the Rose, he said the Rose was still alive." Her frown deepened. "Am I to understand that you are a traitor to your own lands, as Brookbower suggested?"

Cedar gave a shocked huff of laughter. "No, Miss Berrydell! Not at all. Mr. Overton is the furthest thing from a traitor you can imagine."

Astrantia's pink eyebrows drew together. "Then how could he possibly be friends with Lord Willowvale, whose express purpose was to identify and murder the Rose?"

"Well, we weren't friends at first," said Theo, with a sparkling smile. "He nearly killed me more than once, and when I stopped the fading of the Fair Lands, it appalled him that a human did what Fair efforts had been unable to achieve. So our friendship took a little work on my part, and some bending on his. But I think we've both found it worth the effort."

She blinked and stared at him. "Are you meaning to imply that you are the Rose?"

"I am." His smile was so warm and genuine, so kind, that she wanted to believe him.

But every fairy knew the dangers of humans, who could lie without effort and even without malice. She looked back at Lord Mosswing. "Will you vouch for him?" Her voice shook. "How can that be true?"

"It is true, and as for how, well… I don't really know how he made that prickly lord change his heart, but I know better than to underestimate humans by now." Cedar smiled tiredly. "Perhaps I could tell you the story as I know it, and it will help you fill in what gaps you might have in your knowledge."

Astrantia swallowed and studied the Fair lord's face. She knew of him, though she had not previously spoken with him personally; everyone knew that in the Fair Court, in which all fairies told the truth, the Mosswing family was one of uncommon honor and kindness.

Glancing past Cedar's shoulder, she saw Juniper's narrow face and his shock of dark purple curls. "Thank you, my lord," she said. "And who is the young fairy there?"

"I'm Juniper Morel, miss." Juniper smiled sweetly. "I was honored to help Mr. Overton, the Rose, in the Fair Lands, until I was discovered. Lord Mosswing helped me escape into the veil, and when my route was accidentally confused, Mr. Overton came to rescue me. I've been here ever since." His gemlike eyes shone. "I have found extraordinary kindness here, miss."

Astrantia glanced at the others again, and her gaze settled upon Cedar. "I would very much appreciate an explanation, Lord Mosswing."

Theo bowed and said, "I ought to check on my other guest, Miss Berrydell. Please let me know if I can do anything to make you more comfortable."

Cedar chuckled under his breath as he watched his friend leave.

"What is funny?" Astrantia asked cautiously.

The Fair lord's smile lingered. "That man will face Silverthorn himself with nothing but a smile and his own brilliant mind, but just hint that I'll tell someone about his heroism and he runs. He is ridiculous."

"He really is the Rose?" she asked.

"Indeed."

"How did it begin?"

Theo fled to the library, where he found his beloved wife Lily enjoying tea and a book. Across from her, Miss Crocus Firethorn, the beautiful Fair maiden who was to marry Lord Fenton Selby in a little over a month, was enjoying a similarly quiet afternoon, although the book she was reading was in the Fair language.

"Good afternoon," he said cheerfully.

The ladies stood to greet him. "How are our guests?" Lily asked.

"Lord Willowvale hasn't woken yet. Miss Berrydell is awake, and Lord Mosswing is apprising her of the situation. He was beginning to endanger himself, and of course Juniper stepped in to lend him a little magic." At their concerned expressions, he added, "He will be all right with a little rest."

He took Lily's hand and kissed it, smiling into her eyes with his usual warmth and sweetness, then turned to Miss Firethorn. "Is Lord Selby coming for supper?"

"I believe he planned to." Crocus couldn't help smiling at Theo. The past few weeks had been remarkably refreshing and peaceful, a welcome solace to her heart after the terror of that day in which Theo and Fenton had freed her from Silverthorn's power. The cost of that freedom had weighed upon her, but Fenton's quiet, steady kindness and shy determination to see her smile, coupled with the Overtons' easy hospitality and warmth, had somehow transformed that first appalled grief and guilt into gratitude and trust.

Theo strode to the window, for from this vantage point, if he stood just so, he might be able to see Fenton riding over the hill that separated their estates. His friend was not visible, however, so he said, "I do hope to see him." He added thoughtfully, "I imagine I shall be heading to Aricht tomorrow."

CHAPTER TWENTY-TWO
A Fair Lord Undone

A thunderous crash against the nearest wall woke Lord Ash Willowvale into shocked awareness. He started to sit up, but then gasped at the sudden pain in his gut and let his head fall back onto the pillow.

There was no second crash or other sound of violence, and Willowvale took stock of his surroundings.

He had only a vague memory of Theo hauling him down the corridor, and none at all of the room in which he had been deposited. Still, it had every indication of being one of the Overtons' many luxurious guest rooms. He lay beneath soft white sheets and several layers of warm blankets. The tall posts of the bed were delicately carved, and a pair of similarly elegant little tables sat on either side of the bed. The table to his right had a glass of water, a bell, a little plate covered by a cloth, and a folded piece of paper.

Willowvale moved to lift the cloth and winced. The plate held slices of cheese and three little pastries apparently filled with some sort of fruit preserves.

The Fair lord smiled faintly. No doubt there would be tea, if he rang the bell.

He let out a soft, pained breath as he twisted farther to reach the note.

My dear Lord Willowvale,

Thank you for coming, for trusting me in your distress. As you no doubt expected, I sent for Lord Mosswing immediately. However, when he did not arrive within a few hours, I went myself to ask him to come. My message had not reached him, but he came as soon as he heard.

As I am sure you intended, Lord Mosswing saw to Miss Berrydell first, and then to you. Miss Berrydell's condition is quite chancy, but I assure you we are doing everything possible for her.

Ring the bell when you wake, and Anselm will bring you some hot tea and a more substantial meal. The biscuits and cheese are to hold you while you wait.

Sincerely,

Theo

P.S. - I do expect you will be polite to Anselm. He is a servant, but he is also a dear friend, and I should not be pleased to find that one of my friends has been discourteous to another.

The Fair lord let his eyes close. It seemed too much work to reach for the little biscuits. His stomach twisted in hunger, and he sighed.

The sound of voices in the hallway woke him again a few hours later.

He felt fuzzy and warm, oddly disconnected from the lingering pain in his side, which seemed to belong to someone else. He stared at the ceiling, which had soft shadows slanting across it from the fading sunlight.

It must be almost evening. He pressed a hand against the wound and sat up, slowly and painfully. The letter from Theo crinkled, and he set it aside, for he had fallen asleep with it still in his hand.

His bare skin prickled in the cool air, white as marble. The wound was neatly bandaged with white cotton, and though he wanted to examine the injury, he didn't want to have to bandage it again. Mosswing's magic was obviously working, though, because he felt markedly better than when he had stumbled into Overton's house.

He stood, swaying, and stepped to the nearest window. The sun was low, and there had been the faintest dusting of snow that day, for he didn't remember snow upon the ground when he'd walked up the Overton drive. The light was odd, more like morning than evening, and he leaned against the wall for a moment, considering this with a vague sense of misgiving. Surely he could not have slept all afternoon and evening and through the night.

He looked around for his shirt.

There, folded and clean at the end of the bed. He put it on, noting with dismay that his hands were still trembling. Perhaps it was only the chill.

There was no slit in the fabric where he had been stabbed, and this puzzled him, in his fuzzy-minded fatigue, until he remembered that young Juniper Morel was likely still living in the Overton manor. Morel was extraordinarily talented with binding magic, and while such a small fabric repair would be possible for most fairies, only those with binding magic could achieve such an invisible repair.

His belly was hollow and his head felt light and strange.

He pulled on his vest and jacket, hissing as the movement made his side flare into sudden fiery pain. Then he opened the door and looked out into the hallway.

Anselm was walking toward him. "Lord Willowvale!" he said, surprised. "You're up."

"Yes." The fairy swallowed. "How is Miss Berrydell?" He looked down the hall, wondering which door hid the Fair maiden's room.

The servant said gently, "Lord Mosswing is with her. Perhaps you ought to sit down."

Willowvale leaned against the doorframe. "I don't need to sit down. How is she?"

"She is alive. Let me help you to a chair, my lord." Anselm stepped closer.

"I don't need to sit down!" Willowvale said again. "Is Mr. Overton available? I'd like to talk to him."

"Sit down and I'll ask him to come." Anselm frowned at him.

"Fine." Willowvale scowled and turned away. He stumbled on the way to the chair and fell into it, biting back a grunt of pain. Perhaps sitting down was not entirely foolish after all.

Theo swept into the room only a moment later, bright and brisk and cheerful. "Anselm, would you bring Lord Willowvale some dinner, please? And tea? Thank you!"

He sat in the other chair, all graceful elegance, and smiled reassuringly at the fairy. "My lord Willowvale, I am delighted to see you, of course, but I did not expect to see you in these circumstances. Will you tell me what happened?"

"How is Miss Berrydell?"

"She has made it through the worst, I think. Lord Mosswing has done what ought to have been impossible." Theo met Willowvale's eyes gravely. "What happened?"

"She will live?" Willowvale pressed. His chest felt tight, and his heartbeat thudded in his ears.

"Yes, I believe so." Theo's eyes were so warm and kind, and his voice so sympathetic, that Willowvale had an unexpected urge to weep.

He buried his face in his hands and breathed through his nose, slowly, focusing on the rhythm. When his breaths were steady, he ran his fingers through his disheveled white curls.

"Thank you." His voice shook, and his hands would not stop trembling, and he felt hot and cold in succession. He put his hands over his face again.

Theo stood up and got a blanket from a chest, then stepped closer to wrap it around the fairy's shoulders. "If it is too difficult to speak about now, perhaps you could tell me after you've had dinner?"

Willowvale nodded once, not trusting his voice. He watched as Theo stirred the coals and added a log to the fire.

The young man stepped to the door, where he conferred briefly with Anselm. Then there was a tray of human food, the scent rich and comforting, and a pot of steaming water and a pair of porcelain teacups.

It was all so generous and sincere, so compassionate. Willowvale closed his eyes and let his head rest against the back of the chair.

"You might feel a little better if you ate something," Theo said gently.

"I don't know if I can stomach anything," Willowvale muttered.

At Theo's steady gaze, he started upon the chicken and rice soup. He found it as flavorful and strengthening as any human food ever had been, for he had not often been so hungry or worn out at all, and certainly not in the human world.

Theo settled back in the opposite chair, apparently content with his own thoughts. He did not stare at Willowvale, and the fairy felt this as a gift, for he did not want to be examined and found wanting in his weakness and distress. When Theo did glance at the fairy, his expression seemed reassuring and warm, full of a solicitous concern for his guest's comfort without any attempt to pry too deeply.

When Willowvale had finished the meal and Theo had poured him a second cup of tea, the Fair lord sat back with a faint sigh and said, "Thank you, Overton."

"You're welcome."

Willowvale swallowed and said, "Not just for dinner. For contacting Mosswing. For… I knew I could come here, and whatever you might hold against me, I knew you would not hold it against Miss Berrydell, and I knew you would do the right thing. The generous thing. No matter how impossible it would be to repay you."

Theo blinked. "We're friends. I forgave you months ago. My lord, don't let the past weigh upon you any more, please."

"I wish you'd call me Ash," said the fairy, with a catch in his voice. "I heard friends do that, and I do not… I do not like to think of you calling me 'my lord' as if I'm greater than you are. Not because I'm Fair, or because I'm a marquess, or for any reason at all." He took a trembling breath and flinched as bright pain flared through his gut.

"If you will call me Theo." Theo said, his hazel eyes sparkling with warmth and kindness.

Willowvale nodded once. He took a sip of tea, mostly to gain time to steady his voice, and said, "Thank you."

Then he stared at the fire, gathering his thoughts, for the pain was distracting, and Lord Mosswing's healing magic was a faint golden fog upon his mind, and he wasn't entirely sure what day it was anymore.

At last, he took another sip of tea and began, as clearly and concisely as he could, for it took a great deal of effort to keep his voice mostly steady and his thoughts coherent.

When he had recounted everything, he felt wrung out like a rag, and he rested one elbow on the arm of the chair and put his head on his fist.

"Either Brookbower is dead, or he has started the war again," he said bleakly.

At this moment, a knock sounded upon the door, and Theo said, "Let me answer that."

Anselm said, "Might I have your assistance, sir?"

"Excuse me," Theo said to Willowvale, who nodded.

The last golden light of sunset through the windows faded. The Fair lord stared blearily at the softly glowing coals until he fell asleep with his head still on his fist.

CHAPTER TWENTY-THREE
A House of Respite

Theo followed Anselm down the hall to Astrantia's room and knocked perfunctorily on the open door as he stepped inside. "Yes?" he said with a bright, warm smile.

Miss Berrydell had her head against the headboard of the bed, her eyes half-closed. She blinked at Theo as if she were half asleep, then looked at Cedar.

Theo's gaze followed hers, but he couldn't see Cedar's face until he stepped farther into the room.

The Fair lord's dark skin was distinctly gray, and his eyes were closed.

"Is he all right?" said Astrantia in alarm. She moved quickly to get out of bed, then paused, suddenly dizzy and nauseated.

"He'll be fine after a little rest," said Theo reassuringly, though his tender heart twisted within him. "How do you feel?"

"Quite a bit better than dead in the veil," she said, which was not exactly a whole-hearted statement of vigor.

"Lord Mosswing, I think you've done enough for now," said Theo gently. "Come on." He and Anselm helped Cedar up, and though the Fair lord got his feet under him, he didn't respond with much coherence to Theo's inquiries.

"Let's take him to the green guest room," Theo said to Anselm. Then, "Miss Berrydell, someone will bring you supper shortly. Just pull the ribbon on the wall if you need anything."

"Thank you," she murmured, watching with concern as the two humans half-carried the Fair lord into the hall.

When Cedar was bundled into bed, Anselm stepped back and said, "This has become a house of respite for injured Fair Folk, Theo. How many more can we expect?"

Theo frowned. Cedar's dark, rich complexion had never looked so ashen, and a little tendril of fear rose in his heart. "I can't think of any others." He looked around to see that Juniper had followed them. "How are you feeling, Juniper?"

The young fairy was rather pale, but he said, "I'm fine, sir, just a little tired. Lord Mosswing didn't want to draw on my magic, even though I offered."

Anselm said, "I'll check on him every hour, if not more."

CHAPTER TWENTY-FOUR
The Beginning of a Plan

Willowvale awoke shortly after the sun went down to a quiet voice that said, "How are you feeling, Ash?"

He blinked at the fire, which was burning merrily and throwing light and warmth into the room. Theo put a lamp on a nearby table and said, "Would you like to eat something before I help you into bed? Anselm made a tray for you." He put a tray on the table between their two chairs.

The Fair lord looked at him without speaking for a moment, until Theo said again, "How are you feeling?"

Willowvale swallowed. "Better." He pressed his pale lips together and then said, "I told Miss Berrydell that I would go back to retrieve Brookbower once she was safely here. I've rested in comfort long enough." He stood, one hand on the arm of the chair to steady himself.

"Either Brookbower is already dead, or he's already well contained," said Theo. "But if you really think it necessary, I'll depart for Aricht tonight."

The fairy stared at him. "You've already done far more for me, for the Fair Lands, than anyone had any right to imagine, much less ask. I cannot possibly expect you to go on my behalf." He leaned harder on the chair, a little dizzy with the effort of speaking so much.

"Sit down and eat," suggested Theo. "And we'll make a plan." He smiled reassuringly and sat across from the fairy. "I already ate, so don't mind me."

Willowvale frowned more deeply. "How is Miss Berrydell? "

Theo said, "She is feeling much better, though not entirely well yet. Lord Mosswing spent a great deal of magic on her behalf, and he's… shattered, honestly. He'll need some rest before he gives her any more healing magic. He also said there was something in your wound. Can you get it out?"

The fairy pressed a hand to his side. "It will bleed."

"Lord Mosswing's magic should be able to help you heal more once it is out."

The Fair lord gave a soft, pained breath, and his fingers tightened on the arm of the chair. He let the magic holding the little knot of vines and leaves dissolve, and the disappearance of the makeshift packing in the wound produced an odd disturbance in the golden healing magic that lingered in his body. Lord Mosswing's magic flowed differently now that it didn't have to fight the vines.

"Sit down, Ash," Theo said gently.

"I told Miss Berrydell I would retrieve Brookbower." The fairy shook his head, for there were strange shadows dancing in his vision, and he felt dizzy and sick. Every muscle in his body ached.

Seeing that Willowvale did not intend to sit down, or was too dazed to even realize he ought to, Theo stood and stepped closer. "Shall I shove you into the chair before you fall?"

Willowvale blinked several times, focusing on the burning pain in his side to push aside the odd sensation that his head was floating away. He sank into the chair. "I must go to Idosa," he said.

"All right," Theo agreed. "When Lord Mosswing can give you a little more magic, we'll go. I imagine that will be tomorrow morning. In the meantime, eat and rest and heal."

The room danced and spun, and Willowvale closed his eyes. "Tomorrow," he mumbled.

After some time, it became clear to Theo that Willowvale was not going to wake up again that night. His exhaustion was greater than his hunger. So Theo stirred the fire, put a blanket over him, and let him sleep.

Lord Fenton Selby listened to the story with surprise and concern over dinner, which he ate with Theo, Lily, Crocus, Sir Theodore, Lady Overton, and his own mother, Lady Selby, as had become their custom.

After dinner, Theo stepped through the veil for a conversation with the Valestrian king to apprise him of the situation in the Arichtan capital. When he returned, he spoke with Anselm about his many guests and was assured that, as far as could be ascertained, none were in immediate danger. He packed a bag for the next morning on the off chance that Willowvale would somehow wake from his exhausted, feverish sleep and want to leave by dawn.

Lily assured him that she was ready to host their various guests and make them as comfortable as the Overton wealth and hospitality could, and Sir Theodore and Lady Overton voiced their concern and support as well.

"Be careful," said Sir Theodore. "You could be walking into a war."

Theo nodded seriously. "I will." He bade his parents good night and walked back through the halls with his wife's hand on his arm. "I am sorry to leave earlier than expected, but…"

"Of course you must," Lily said. She stretched up to kiss him, and he smiled down at her. "I will worry, of course, but I have faith in you."

His smile widened. "Thank you, my love."

CHAPTER TWENTY-FIVE
An Early Departure

Before the sky had begun to turn gray, Willowvale woke to the burning pain in his side, which combined with the aches in his arms, back, and legs, and the lesser, though still quite noticeable, discomforts of sleeping slouched in such an uncomfortable position for quite a few hours.

He groaned as he shifted, then staggered to his feet, light-headed and annoyed by his own unsteadiness. He leaned on the chair until the room stopped spinning and then made his way carefully to the window.

This guest room looked north, and from this vantage point on the lower floor, he could not see far across the countryside. The tall evergreens that provided winter color to the Overton garden stood in shadow, but the thin carpet of snow made most of the rest of the garden unexpectedly bright under the light of the waning moon.

Even at the height of his arrogance, he would not have thought himself capable of facing the veil in his current state. But what filled his heart now was not arrogance but a mortifying conviction that he had already failed to carry out his promise to Miss Berrydell.

Somehow, in all the chaos of the escape from Aricht, he had arrived at the Overton manor with his sword still belted to his hip. When he looked around the room, he found his sword leaning against the wall near the bed. He belted it back on with a sense of doomed finality.

He really ought not leave without telling Theo; he owed his host, his friend, the courtesy of an explanation and a farewell. He looked around for a quill and paper but was disappointed to find only a few sheets of paper in the desk in the corner.

Lord Ash Willowvale opened the door and looked out into the hallway. It was empty.

He leaned on the doorframe, because it seemed too much work to stand up straight while he thought. And while no one was watching.

He glanced at the window again, noting that the sky had grown lighter in the past few minutes while he had been debating what to do. At least one of the servants ought to be awake by now. He would go to the kitchen, where one of them ought to be able to procure paper, ink, and a quill for him to leave Theo a note.

The fairy strode slowly down the hall, noting the unpleasant lightness in his arms and legs, and the odd sense of walking uphill, although he was reasonably confident the floor was actually level.

At the end of the corridor, he found himself at a spacious atrium which he had seen before. A number of hallways left it, and there was a wide set of glassed double doors, with beveled glass above them, that led out to an enormous brick patio with tables and chairs arranged for conversation and entertaining in the warmer months.

"It's rather early for you to be up, my lord," said a voice from behind him.

Willowvale turned to see Anselm, looking rather worn, eyeing him with caution.

"I would be glad to escort you back to your room," the servant added.

"I was intending to leave for Aricht as soon as I can leave Mr. Overton a note," said Willowvale.

"He'd like to talk to you himself. I believe he's planning to accompany you."

The fairy said, "I can't ask him to do that. May I have paper and a quill? Please?" He put a hand against the wall, feeling rather put upon. Why couldn't this insolent servant just offer the paper and quill that Willowvale had already indicated he wanted?

"Do you need help back to your room? I'll wake Mr. Overton; he's already packed." Anselm stepped closer and, with a feeling of magnanimity, offered the fairy a steadying arm.

"Oh, don't help me," muttered Willowvale in bitter annoyance. "I don't deserve it, and I don't want it, and I'm quite sure you don't want to offer it to me."

Anselm huffed a quiet laugh and stood there, his arm out in the most convenient way.

"You're almost as intolerable as Overton," Willowvale muttered. He walked past Anselm, keeping steady on his feet only by force of will. Then, guiltily, he muttered, "Thank you anyway."

Anselm chuckled under his breath and followed. At the fairy's room, he said, "I'll fetch Mr. Overton."

Willowvale sat by the fire to wait.

Less than ten minutes later, Theo knocked at his open door, dressed for travel and carrying a small satchel. "I did not expect you to be ready to travel yet," he said.

Willowvale sighed. "I ought to have left last night."

"I think I ought to let Lord Mosswing rest, but I feel it would be wiser to get a little more healing magic in you before we set out for Aricht." Theo sat across from the fairy and studied his face.

The Fair lord was always pale, but now his ashen face had dark circles under his eyes, and there was a grim despair in the set of his lips. "I would rather not wait. I told Miss Berrydell I would return for Brookbower once she was safe."

"Just a moment." Theo started toward the door.

The fairy stood too and cleared his throat. "I'd like to leave a letter for Miss Berrydell, if I may."

"All right." Theo strode out of the room, and returned just a few moments later with a few pieces of paper and a quill, inkwell, and blotting paper.

Willowvale murmured his thanks and sat at the desk. Behind him, Theo settled into a chair, as if he had all the time in the world. His eyelids drifted closed, for it was indeed quite early and he had not slept much.

The fairy wrote for some minutes in silence, and then he closed his eyes and thought. The fire crackled softly behind him, and he glanced back to see Theo sitting with his arms crossed and his eyes closed.

Willowvale took a deep breath and winced, and then focused again on what he wanted to say. It was not an apology, exactly, nor was it a plea. But it was the truth.

The Fair lord sealed the letter and stood, feeling drained by the effort of admitting what he had admitted only piecemeal in his own heart, now fully in a letter, to be read by someone whose good opinion he desired and would now never have.

The wound in his side was painful enough to scramble his thoughts. He leaned on the back of the chair for a moment, jaw clenched, and took several deep breaths, feeling how the pain changed as the muscles moved.

His young host had apparently dozed off by the fire, his eyes closed and his breaths slow and steady.

"Mr. Overton," Willowvale said quietly. "Theo."

Theo twitched. "I'm sorry. What did you say?" He ran a hand over his face.

"I am ready to leave." He indicated the letter sitting on the desk. "That is for Miss Berrydell."

"Just a moment. Why don't you sit down until I come back?" Theo stood and strode out, quick and energetic.

Willowvale sank into the chair by the window and waited. The silence was almost peaceful; it would have been peaceful, if his heart had been less troubled.

He stared morosely out at the gray dawn, as bleak and chilly as his mood.

He was startled when Theo returned followed by Lord Mosswing. The dark Fair lord was wrapped in a sumptuous dressing gown, bleary-eyed and markedly pale. Still, he met Willowvale's gaze with a wry smile.

Willowvale stood and bowed slightly. He and Lord Mosswing were of the same rank, and Willowvale was several years older, yet he had a sudden urge to bow lower than usual. He could not have said whether it was gratitude, respect, awe, or something else entirely, but the unexpected emotion made his voice rough when he said, "You didn't have to come."

"I know." Cedar smiled, his white teeth bright against his dark skin. "After I give you what I can, I'll check on Miss Berrydell, and if all is well, I'll go back to bed."

"You don't have to," said Willowvale again, helplessly.

Cedar stepped forward and put a hand on the other fairy's thin shoulder. "I choose to."

The bright golden magic poured in like liquid light, illuminating Willowvale's bones in sparkling life. He shuddered, and the ever-present agony of the stab wound in his side felt like the fading sting of a bee.

"Thank you." Willowvale's silver blue eyes met Cedar's turquoise gaze, and he bowed again.

"You're welcome." Cedar braced his feet a little farther apart, for he felt a little dizzy himself now.

A moment later, Theo had opened a door into the veil right in the wall of his own house.

"Be careful, Theo," Anselm said with quiet intensity.

"I will." Theo smiled brightly. "Thank you, Cedar, Anselm. I'll return as soon as I can." He bowed, and then led Willowvale into the darkness.

CHAPTER TWENTY-SIX
Making an Entrance

The Fair lord held the strap of Theo's satchel in one hand as they walked, for it was always safer to maintain physical contact in the veil. Willowvale felt light-headed with Cedar's golden healing magic flowing in his veins, and though the pain in his side lingered, it seemed to be lessening with every minute that passed.

They walked in silence for nearly half an hour before Theo said, "How are you feeling?"

"Lord Mosswing's magic is quite strong," Willowvale said, with sincere admiration. "I feel… odd. I can walk."

Theo chuckled softly. "He is incredible. I had no idea how strong he was until you caught me in your vines, or I might have done a few things differently."

The fairy swallowed. Guilt pressed upon him, and the magic of the veil, heavy and dark and unfriendly, writhed against his consciousness.

He started, "I wish…" and the apology choked him. "I wish I'd done things differently," he managed, and while it was true, it was only the smallest part of the truth.

"I wish you wouldn't torment yourself about it," Theo said flatly. "When I apologized to Lord Selby for not warning him about what Lord Larch was likely to do, and persisted in my guilt after he forgave me, he told me it was nigh on insulting to presume that his forgiveness was so weak and small. Shall I present the issue to you the same way?"

Willowvale considered this in silence. "It isn't that I doubt you," he said at last. "But I think it is well-established that your capacity to forgive is greater than my own. My guilt weighs upon me, not only for what I did to you, but for my part in what happened to the children."

A sudden whiff of air was the only hint that something darted at Theo's face. He jerked back so suddenly that the Fair lord behind him bumped into his back. The shadow's sharp edge cut a stinging line from Theo's left eyebrow back across his temple, and he sucked in a surprised breath.

Then he ripped the shadow from the wall and threw it into the darkness ahead of them. He flicked a bit of light to his fingertips for a moment, assuring himself that it was gone. The passage through the veil now appeared to be a tunnel dug through the dirt, with little oddly-proportioned nooks at long intervals. To their left was a tunnel that curved downward, the bottom of which they could not see, and some way ahead the light glinted upon water.

Theo let the light fade. "None of us can change the past," he said. "But I dare say you have changed, and the world is a better place for it."

"There is no way to make amends," Willowvale said, his voice thick with grief.

They set off again in the darkness.

"Oh, drat," Theo said suddenly. "Just a moment."

"What is it?"

"I need my handkerchief." He dug in his inside jacket pocket, pulled out the cloth, and pressed it to his forehead.

"Why?" Willowvale flicked a much brighter light to his own fingertips and looked around before looking at his companion. "You're bleeding!"

"It's all right." It looked gruesome, because the blood had dripped down Theo's cheek and onto his collar before he'd gotten the handkerchief on it. "It barely hurts."

"You're lying to me." Willowvale blinked, looking startled.

"I'm really not," Theo said cheerfully. "It's a clean cut. It only stings a little." He waved a hand dismissively. "Let's go before something with teeth finds us."

The fairy let the light fade and gripped the strap of Theo's satchel again. They walked in silence for several minutes before Theo said, "I don't know what sort of amends are to be made to the children. I've done what I can to help them heal, but I think it will take time, and love from others, and a great deal of strength and determination from the children themselves. All things considered, though, I think most of them are recovering well."

Willowvale murmured, "I am glad to hear it." Then, abruptly, he said, "If Elmerick is intent on war, I would very much appreciate it if you would leave immediately."

"Noted," Theo said, with a smile in his voice.

The fairy frowned into the darkness. "I don't want more of your blood on my hands," he growled.

For another hour they walked without incident.

"Oh look!" Theo said in delight. "A shortcut!"

He turned to his left, then continued so that it seemed to the Fair lord that he was doubling back, albeit in a new tunnel. Then he turned to his left again and almost spun in place, as if he walked into the very space Willowvale occupied.

The fairy followed so closely he stepped on Theo's heels more than once.

"Here!" Theo said, stopping suddenly. He seemed to be assessing his surroundings, though he did not conjure any light by which to see. After a moment, he started forward again. "We're almost there."

Willowvale followed without a word.

After another ten minutes of walking in silence, Theo said, "Are you ready? I think it might be good to make an entrance. How do you feel about stepping directly into the Arichtan throne room?"

The Fair lord sucked in a breath. "I suppose that would get Elmerick's attention," he said. "Is that what you did when you stepped into Silverthorn's throne room to confront him about Miss Firethorn?"

"That was mostly pragmatism, though I will not deny that it crossed my mind that it would get Silverthorn's attention." Theo's grin made his voice warm and bright. "I doubt they will attack immediately, but it would be wise to be prepared."

"I am ready."

Theo opened the door and they stepped out into the glittering Arichtan throne room.

CHAPTER TWENTY-SEVEN
More Uncomfortable Conversations

The marble floor gleamed with intricate angular gold inlay, and there was not a hint of leaf or vine or floral decor to be seen. The windows were leaded in a similarly angular pattern, and they cast sharp shapes of golden light across the marble.

His Majesty Elmerick was not seated upon his throne, but rather standing in front of it in a heated conversation what appeared to be a small group of advisors. They were all richly dressed in the current fashions of Aricht, their clothes glittering with gold embroidery upon burgundy silk and satin.

One of them cried out in surprise at the sudden appearance of a human and a fairy nearly in their midst. Magic flared, but it was weak human magic. Even Theo, with his limited magical senses, could tell it posed little threat to him, to say nothing of Willowvale.

Lord Ash Willowvale stepped forward, his empty hands spread wide, well clear of his sword hilt. "Your Majesty, I require an audience to discuss the attack so recently perpetrated against the legally appointed Fair ambassador, his delegation, and me, His Majesty Silverthorn's representative to your court in the matter of our ambassador's detention."

The king stepped forward, his heavy eyebrows drawn downward fiercely. "You're alive."

"I am." Willowvale smiled, fierce and dangerous. "Miss Berrydell is too, and you should be glad of it, because I only hold attempted murder against you, rather than the successful assassination of an innocent, honorable member of the Fair Court."

Elmerick took a slow, deep breath, his dark eyes sharp on Willowvale's face.

"Where are Brookbower and the rest of his delegation?" Willowvale's voice rang out.

"In guest suites." The king raised his chin. "The assassins are in prison."

Willowvale blinked. He had thought of any number of possible challenges, but he had not considered this possibility.

"Has Silverthorn already declared war?" asked Elmerick.

"I haven't been back to the Fair Lands yet," Willowvale said.

Elmerick's eyebrows twitched almost imperceptibly, but he said, "Then there is hope of preventing war yet. Come, let me offer you hospitality and rest while we parley." He looked toward one of the advisors, who bowed and strode away.

The king looked at Theo. "What happened?"

"Just a little bit of shadow in the veil. They have sharp edges." The wound had stopped bleeding, and Theo held the thoroughly bloodied handkerchief in one hand.

Elmerick nodded, looking vaguely confused by this answer, and eyed them both. "Are you planning to declare war?" he said softly. "Is there any way to prevent it?"

The Fair lord tilted his head. "You didn't order the assassination attempt?" he said.

"Of course not!" Elmerick exclaimed. "I wanted peace! I have always wanted peace! I wanted your promise that we could have it without sacrificing our children and our honor."

"You caught all the assassins?"

"I am reasonably sure, yes." Elmerick stood tensely, as if he expected Willowvale to erupt into murderous Fair anger and magic at any moment.

Willowvale glanced at Theo for a split second, then at the advisors who seemed to be waiting for some sort of outburst. "I will speak with Brookbower then," he said at last.

The king let out a slow breath, as if he were relieved. "I will take you to him myself," he said. "Mr. Overton, my physician would be honored to see to your wound."

"Thank you, but I would like to accompany my friend, if he doesn't mind, and I do not want to delay him." Theo glanced at the fairy.

"Brookbower and his staff can wait five more minutes," said Willowvale, his eyes sharp on Elmerick's face. "I am confident you will not harm them, knowing how it would further endanger your nation."

"They will not be harmed. Come with me." Elmerick led them the length of the throne room. Their steps echoed in the vast space.

When they exited the throne room into a spacious hallway, several servants were waiting. "Have Mr. McCallum meet me in the west atrium at the entrance to the hall where our Fair guests are staying," said the king.

The guards surrounded them as they followed the king and his advisors through the vast palace.

When they reached the hall where the Fair delegation was being held, there were five guards at the end of the hall, who bowed deeply to the Arichtan king as he approached.

"Hello," Theo murmured with a smile, as he saw the guard with whom he had spoken on his first visit.

The guard nodded but said nothing, eyeing Theo's bloodied collar and the dark blood smears upon his cheek.

A moment later, a man dressed in a long, dark jacket with gold embroidery upon the collar and cuffs hurried up. "Your Majesty," he said, looking first at Elmerick, then at Willowvale and Theo.

"See to Mr. Overton," said Elmerick without preamble.

Theo was a bit taller than the physician, so he bent obligingly to let the physician examine his cut from a better angle. The older man darted wary glances at Willowvale, then focused on his task. He cleaned the wound with a damp cloth and wiped the crusted blood from Theo's cheek and neck.

"What did this?" he asked.

"A very sharp shadow," Theo said, his eyes amused at the man's confused look. "In the veil between the Fair Lands and here."

The man's confusion increased, but he said only, "It's a clean cut, nearly sealed up already. Just leave it alone and it ought to heal nicely."

"Thank you."

His Majesty Elmerick said to the guards, "Let them in to see Brookbower and his staff. Bring them to the golden room when they're finished."

The guards stepped aside.

Willowvale knocked on the door on the left which the guard had indicated.

A moment later, Brookbower jerked it open. "What?" he barked, then his eyes widened. "Come in." Then his eyes narrowed at Theo as the young man started after Willowvale. "Not you, human."

Willowvale said, in the Fair language, "He is my friend, and you *will* respect him, Brookbower."

The ambassador looked at him, shocked. "Your *friend?* I thought Berrydell had misinterpreted something. How did that come to be?"

"Let us in and I'll tell you," retorted Willowvale. "But first you must tell us what happened after Miss Berrydell and I escaped."

Brookbower frowned. With a grimace of distaste, he stepped back and let Willowvale and Theo into his suite.

The sitting room was fully as luxurious as Willowvale's had been, and Theo's too, on their previous visit, though since Brookbower did not have Willowvale's gift with plant magic, there was no refreshing moss or jasmine scenting the air.

"Sit," Brookbower said. He added a log to the fire already burning in the grate, and then turned to look at them, his arms crossed fiercely. "Who is he and why is he here?" he asked Willowvale, still in the Fair language.

With sudden caution, Willowvale said, not looking at Theo, "I'm not sure whether he would prefer to be known, especially by you. He saved the Fair Lands when all our Fair efforts had failed, and extended astonishing kindness to me, when he had every reason to treat me as an enemy. Now tell me what happened here, Brookbower."

The ambassador was clearly unsatisfied by this, and he gave Theo a sidelong look. Theo smiled innocently at him. Knowing that hardly any humans spoke the Fair language at all, and influenced by his own arrogant prejudices against humans in general, Brookbower took this to mean that Theo had not understood Willowvale's words, exactly as Theo had intended to imply.

So Brookbower did not guard his words quite as closely as he might have if he had realized Theo understood him.

"I could have killed them all, Willowvale. You know that." Brookbower said, with a hint of defensiveness in his voice.

"But you didn't."

Brookbower gritted his teeth. "You said His Majesty Silverthorn did not want a war. I sacrificed my pride and freedom to honor that."

"That is commendable." Willowvale nodded. His pale eyes flicked up and down Brookbower's tense posture. "You saved the lives of your assistants, I imagine."

Brookbower shrugged one shoulder, as if this fact were irrelevant. "They are skilled. I assume Silverthorn would prefer not lose them and train others to fill their positions."

"Undoubtedly. How did you deescalate the situation?"

The ambassador blew out a disgusted *pfft*. "Ugh, it hardly bears repeating. I am *mortified*, Willowvale," he muttered. "No Fair lord should have to do what I did."

"I will not repeat it. I must know, though, before I speak with Elmerick again."

Brookbower shot a glance at Theo, who merely smiled. "I said I would swear never to return to Aricht, as they required, and swear never to take or harm humans again, on the strength of your word that

Silverthorn had sworn such an oath, if they would swear that the attack on our party was not instigated by the crown, that Elmerick still desired peace, and that they would detain the attackers themselves. For if I did it, it would lead to war."

"Did you make the vows, or merely promise that you would?" Willowvale asked.

"I did it, then and there, though the words stuck like gall in my throat." Brookbower shoved another piece of wood into the fire with unnecessary force, sending sparks flying up the chimney. "The Arichtan guards subdued the two noblemen who seemed to be in on the plot, as well as two of their fellows who aided them, and I have been informed that only one of the servants was involved in the poison aspect of the plot. He has also been apprehended."

"It was aimed at us, I presume," Willowvale said.

"Of course it was. Miss Berrydell was affected only because of your stupid insistence upon unnecessary courtesy to our staff." Brookbower raised an eyebrow at Willowvale's pale glower. "Oh, don't pretend it isn't true."

"I am not." Willowvale swallowed and smoothed his expression a little. "It did not cross my mind that the Arichtans would stoop to such underhanded vengeance, but it grieves me that Miss Berrydell suffered for it."

Brookbower eyed him. "I assume she is still alive."

"She was when I left her."

"What did Silverthorn say about the attack?"

"I have not been back to the Fair Lands yet."

The ambassador blinked. "How are you walking?" he asked in surprise. "I thought you wounded nearly to death, and Berrydell certainly was. Surely you required healing magic, and there is none to be found here."

Willowvale let out a thoughtful sigh and glanced toward Theo for just a moment.

"Don't tell me your human friend has healing magic!" Brookbower said with a sneer. "It is rare enough among our kind; I have never heard of it among humans."

Theo said in the Fair tongue, "No, Lord Brookbower, I don't have healing magic. However, I do have a friend gifted with such magic, and I was able to contact him in time for him to save Miss Berrydell's life, and likely Lord Willowvale's life as well."

The ambassador stared at him in horror. "You understood all of that," he breathed. "Are you Fair, wearing a human glamour? No, it cannot be. Who are you?"

Theo smiled. "Theodore Overton, IV. It is an honor to meet you, my lord."

"You're human!" Brookbower's expression was caught somewhere between humiliation and rage. "How *dare* you speak our Fair language! How did you learn it?"

"From a dear friend." Theo's eyes sparkled, enjoying Brookbower's discomfiture. "And I'm glad of it, because if I'd had a Valestrian accent by the time the Rose began rescuing children, I doubt I would have been so successful."

Brookbower's eyed widened; he would have been less surprised if Theo had openly attacked him. "Do you mean to say you are the Rose?"

"Indeed." Theo added, "Don't worry, the Fair Lands are safe, as Lord Willowvale has already assured you. I love them too."

The ambassador was trembling, caught in a heady mixture of shock and outrage. His fists clenched at his side, as if he wanted to throttle Theo where he stood. But he was bound by the oath he had sworn not to take or harm humans again.

"Are the Fair Lands truly stable?" He looked back at Willowvale.

"They are more solid than I recall ever before," said the other fairy. "I suppose love is as strong as death, and," he glanced at Theo, "death is swallowed up in victory."

Theo said, "I know you are proud, Lord Brookbower, and this is not how you expected your lands to be saved. But can you not rejoice that they *are* saved and your people free from the fear under which they lived?"

The Fair ambassador swallowed bile and hatred, pride and fury. "I can be glad of that, at least," he muttered bitterly.

The meeting with Brookbower was concluded with no more fanfare than this, and Willowvale and Theo met the king again in the corridor.

Willowvale asked, "What of the assassins?"

The Arichtan king pressed his lips together. He studied Willowvale's face without speaking for a moment, and finally said, "I cannot countenance assassination, and certainly not of diplomatic guests." He stopped and swallowed. "But you must understand, Lord Buckley's niece was one of the children stolen by your people. She was captive for just over two weeks, and she has not spoken since she was rescued three months ago. Even my own physician Mr. McCallum examined her, and he cannot find anything wrong with her body. But her mind is… tormented… by the memories of that place, and what she endured there. You say, even the other children say, it was only dancing, but to her, already troubled as she was by childhood illnesses, it must have felt like death."

The king held Willowvale's pale gaze. "Can you fault him for wanting to avenge his beloved niece? Perhaps it might bring her some peace, to know that there were no Fair Folk in Aricht at all."

The Fair lord nodded once. "I understand."

"You will thus understand that I have not yet decided what justice will look like in his case."

Willowvale took a deep, slow breath, marshaling his thoughts. It was true that such an attack on a diplomat was not to be borne, and he would have had Silverthorn's support, however reluctant, if he had declared war in the heat of the attack itself. This admission that the assassins had not been summarily executed was certainly more than enough to overcome any of Silverthorn's objections.

Still, for a moment the Fair lord imagined how he might react, if some human had stolen someone about whom he cared, and tormented that poor innocent until she were unable or unwilling to speak at all. He wasn't sure he loved anyone that much, certainly none of his family. Conceptually, though, he found it difficult to blame Lord Buckley for attempting to kill Brookbower.

For the poison in his own glass… well, he was undoubtedly allied with Brookbower, and while he had not personally stolen the child, he was an integral part of the effort, and was still working on behalf of the Fair king who had ordered the children stolen.

The fact that the poison had nearly killed Miss Berrydell was his own fault, and though he had given it to her innocently, he felt the guilt of this gnawing at him.

It was this guilt that made his voice rough when he said, "I want to see Lord Buckley."

"You want to kill him," Elmerick said flatly. "Aricht will execute its own laws."

Willowvale swallowed. "I will not kill him. I only want to speak with him."

"You swear you won't hurt him?"

"I will not harm him," said the fairy.

The king hesitated. "All right," he said at last.

He led them to the captive himself, and Willowvale assumed, correctly, that this was because he wanted to witness the interaction rather than merely hear about it from his intelligence officers. Guards followed them, alert to Willowvale's every small movement, as if they expected him to attack Elmerick at any moment.

Perhaps they did.

Willowvale considered this thought and shot a glance at the nearest guard, whose sharp eyes met his with hostility and apprehension.

The fairy looked forward again.

Lord Buckley was being held in a guest suite not unlike the one Willowvale had recently occupied, though it was on the opposite side of the palace. Like his own suite, there were guards outside the door, and, being three floors up, it would be difficult for a human to escape out the window. He may have been apprehended, but he was hardly being held in chains.

"Open it," the king said to the guard, who obeyed immediately.

At the sound of the door opening, Lord Buckley stood from his chair near the fire. His face twisted when he saw Willowvale standing behind the king.

"Your Majesty." He bowed to the king. "I see the fairy survived."

"He wants to speak with you."

"I want to kill him, but we don't all get what we want, do we?" The human's clear blue eyes, burning with anger, fixed on Willowvale.

The Fair lord said, "I wanted to ask about your niece. How is she?"

"It is none of your business how she is," Buckley snapped.

Theo stepped forward, drawing the lord's attention. "May I speak with you privately, Lord Buckley?"

"And who are you?" Buckley looked Theo up and down, taking in his immaculate traveling attire and the bloodstains upon his collar.

"Theodore Overton, IV, of Valestria." Theo bowed deeply. "I'm a friend of Lord Willowvale's."

The man's face hardened. "A traitor to all humanity, then?"

"I am the Wraith, my lord, and I am no traitor."

Buckley stared at him. "You're a liar, then?"

Theo opened a door into the veil right there, in front of everyone. Buckley stared at it in shock, then back at Theo, while most of the others peered into the dark tunnel.

"Fine. I'll talk with you. Not with the fairy."

Theo let the door to the veil close. "By your leave, Your Majesty," he said.

Elmerick nodded, and so Theo stepped into Lord Buckley's suite and closed the door quietly behind himself.

"What are you doing with a *fairy*?" Buckley said. "You're really the Wraith?"

"I am, and it's a long story," said Theo. "Might we sit down? I'm rather fatigued." This was not an exaggeration, though Theo would not have admitted to the fatigue if he didn't know it to be a disarmingly vulnerable sort of statement against which Lord Buckley would have little defense.

Buckley nodded. "Sit, then. Have some tea."

"Thank you." Theo sank into the chair with genuine relief. He had slept only a few hours the previous night, and after their long, frigid walk in the veil, he did feel fuzzy with exhaustion.

The nobleman stared at him in impatience. "Well?"

So Theo told him about his gift with the veil, his horror at the plight of the kidnapped children, his many rescues, his Fair allies, the confrontation with the Fair king, and his own unlikely friendship with the irascible Lord Willowvale.

"And here we are," he said at last. "I cannot apologize on behalf of the Fair Folk, and I don't know that Willowvale is ready to humble himself so. I certainly cannot expect you to accept that apology on behalf of your niece. What I would ask, if you would be so gracious to allow it, is to let me speak with your niece, or at least her parents."

"For what purpose?" The man stared at him. "And how can *you*, of all people, call that fairy a friend? Of course your Fair allies were different, but *him*, cold-hearted blackguard that he is? You ought to have higher standards."

Theo said gently, "Have you never done anything you regret, Lord Buckley? There is a great deal of good in him, and I aim to draw it out. I have seen courage and compassion already, and honor, too. He shed blood for me when he believed with all his heart that I had only offered him friendship for a brief time, and I would withdraw it as soon as I had gotten what I wanted from him." He sketched the barest outline of how he and Fenton had wrested Crocus Firethorn's freedom from the Fair king, and how Willowvale had stood up for Theo against Larch's demand for a duel, and how he had provided them a place of rest until they could return home to the human world.

Buckley listened in silence, his arms crossed and eyebrows drawn down.

Theo took a sip of the now-cold tea in his cup, and then looked up the man sitting across from him. "He is a friend, Buckley, and whether you trust him or not, I do. But that is beside the point. I asked to speak to your niece because I know what it feels like to be terrified and alone in an alien world. I can listen, if she wants to weep to someone who understands, and I can tell her what helped me conquer the fear that almost killed me."

Buckley sighed, deep and grief-stricken, and he said, "I would do anything to help her. If you think it might help, even a little, then yes. Her name is Charity. Her father is Sir Briscoe McStretton, and her mother, my sister, is Lady Eliza McStretton. They live in Idosa not far from here."

"Thank you, my lord."

The man shook his head and said in a choked voice, "I cannot describe to you the grief and fear my sister and her husband experienced while their daughter was missing. I would do nearly anything to thank you for returning Charity to us, Mr. Overton."

Theo ducked his head. "You're welcome." He stood. "I will leave you now. May I come visit you again in a few days?"

Buckley gave a soft, mirthless chuckle. "You are welcome to, if I haven't been executed to prevent a war."

"Do you think His Majesty Elmerick will execute you?" Theo asked with a frown.

"Only if he has to." The man gave an elegant shrug. "I would do the same in his place, I imagine. One man's life to save thousands? Of course it must be done."

"Well, if I have anything to do with it, there will be no war and no execution," Theo said firmly.

"I wish you godspeed, then."

"Thank you." Theo bowed again.

CHAPTER TWENTY-EIGHT
Advice and Encouragement

When Theo stepped back out into the hallway, the guard greeted him with a smile. "Mr. Overton, His Majesty and the fairy will discuss matters privately. His Majesty said you are to be given the same suite you were in before."

A servant stepped forward to take Theo's bag from him. "Let me take that for you, sir."

"Thank you. You're Martin, aren't you?"

"Yes, sir."

They walked nearly the entire length of the palace to reach the room Theo remembered. "I take it you weren't in on the plot against Lords Brookbower and Willowvale," said Theo conversationally.

The guard's mouth pinched. "No," he muttered.

"Do you wish you had been?"

The guard shot him a sharp glance. "It isn't for me to execute judgement on behalf of another man, and a lord besides, is it?"

"No," agreed Theo.

"Didn't Willowvale nearly kill you? Don't you want some vengeance?" said the guard.

"Well, I've had the right to it for some time now, I think, but I chose mercy instead. You'd be surprised how much someone can change, if they want to. Or even if they don't at first." Theo laughed to himself, though all the servant saw was a quiet little smile.

"You think the fairy has changed?" the man said doubtfully.

"I hardly know Brookbower, and I wouldn't make such an optimistic assertion yet. But Willowvale? Certainly he has."

The guard frowned. "If you say so," he muttered.

The Arichtan king had taken Willowvale to his private study.

His Majesty Elmerick sat in the velvet-cushioned chair near the desk while Willowvale was left to stand in the center of the room.

The fairy crossed his arms and looked down at the king. A human monarch could not intimidate him by the fact that a king was allowed to sit while everyone else, even a Fair lord, must stand in his presence. Tall and lithe and proud, the Fair lord was as pale and bright as a rapier, and just as sharply dangerous.

Willowvale found himself tired and grumpy. He wanted to go to bed; his side hurt, and although the wound was hardly life-threatening anymore, it was far from entirely healed.

Still, the human king did not seem to realize this; he looked pale and his thick, dark eyebrows were drawn downward in a worried frown.

"I waited so long to execute justice against your ambassador because I hoped to prevent a war. You cannot truly have expected me to execute my own subject more expeditiously," the king said.

Willowvale merely blinked, his expression unreadable.

"You said Miss Berrydell is alive?" asked the king.

"She is."

Willowvale noted with interest that the king seemed to exhibit some muted satisfaction with this.

"Miss Berrydell was not one of the assassins' targets," said the king. "But they did not intend to sacrifice the mission in order to prevent her being collateral damage."

A muscle in the fairy's jaw tightened, but he did not say anything yet. He wished Theo was with him, because Theo seemed to have a preternatural ability to make people talk, to draw out the truth. It had certainly worked on Willowvale.

When the king said nothing else, Willowvale finally said quietly, "If Silverthorn knew of this, he would have declared war already."

Elmerick swallowed, his gaze sharp on Willowvale's face.

"Moreover, I have authority to declare war on behalf of the Fair crown. I am sure you understand how justified I would be in doing so."

"Justified, perhaps, but hardly just or wise. How many innocents would die for your revenge?" Elmerick pressed his lips together.

Suddenly Willowvale was so very tired. He was tired of Elmerick's fear, tired of keeping the pain in his side from affecting his voice, tired of Brookbower's insufferable pride. Tired of his own arrogance and conceit and regrets.

"I don't want revenge," he said wearily.

"What do you want?" Elmerick seemed to think this was some sort of Fair trick, and there was certainly precedent for his caution.

"I want to take Brookbower and the rest of the delegation home to the Fair Lands. I want you to agree to accept a different Fair ambassador, and swear upon your personal honor and the honor of Aricht itself that that ambassador will be safe from assassins and attackers." Willowvale took a deep breath, steadying himself, because he felt his fatigue and despair rising like an ocean wave to crush him. "And… I will tell you what else I want tomorrow."

"Tomorrow."

The fairy said, "Yes, tomorrow. I was *stabbed*, Elmerick, and I'd like to think clearly before I agree to something we both regret." His pale eyes flashed. "I can make you regret it, you know."

"All right. We will continue this tomorrow."

"And my dinner and drinks had better not be poisoned," Willowvale muttered, although he did not actually suspect that Elmerick would be so bold and foolish.

"Of course not," the king snapped, as if stung.

Willowvale managed a thin, mirthless smile.

To the guard at the door, the king said, "Please take him to his suite, and bring him dinner when it is time. His friend can visit. Lord Willowvale, please stay in your suite until we meet tomorrow."

The fairy nodded curtly. "Until tomorrow."

Somewhat to Willowvale's surprise, a servant carried his satchel for him while they walked. They were still surrounded by guards, of course, who kept a sharp eye on the fairy, but this little bit of extra courtesy felt like a gift, for Willowvale felt that he was embarrassingly close to dissolving into an exhausted puddle upon the floor, grumpy and snide and despairing.

When they reached the room, the servant opened the door for him, carried his satchel in, and put it on the settee.

"Someone will bring dinner in about an hour."

"Thank you."

The fairy waited until the door was closed before he sagged.

He unbuttoned his jacket, vest, and shirt, half-expecting the bandage to be soaked through with pale blue blood. Nothing. The pain was internal more than external, and the wound was almost closed. Lord Mosswing's healing magic still swirled in his blood, though not with the heady force of hours before. Tomorrow he would feel a little more coherent, a little more capable of making wise decisions.

For now, he buttoned his shirt back only halfway, leaving it open at the top the way it would be if it were casual Fair attire. He took off his boots, hissing in pain at the movement as he bent to reach them.

He considered growing a patch of moss upon the floor and sleeping on it, and if he'd possessed even a shred of energy, perhaps he might have done it. The moss would smell like magic and comfort.

But he was too tired, so instead he lay atop the bed and fell quickly into a restless sleep.

True to the servant's word, a knock sounded upon the door only an hour later.

Willowvale fought his way up from the darkest, most disorienting depths of slumber and stumbled to his feet. He buttoned his shirt, grimacing, and made his way to the door.

"What is it?" The fairy was thoroughly rumpled, with his shirt buttoned wrong, his snowy curls disheveled, and only socks on his feet. His mouth was grim, and his eyes were shadowed.

"Your dinner and a visitor." Two servants with heavily laden trays waited while Theo greeted Willowvale and swept in, cheerfully confident of his welcome.

When the servants had left the room and the door was closed, Willowvale sank into a chair at the table, still bleary-eyed and wordless. He would have shivered, for the room was quite chilly, but he felt too cold and tired even for this.

"How are you feeling, Ash?" Theo said quietly.

"Like I was stabbed," said Willowvale, "though perhaps like it was a week ago rather than four days ago."

"Well, that's an improvement, I think," said Theo. "I wanted to see if you needed advice or encouragement this evening, and then I will let you rest."

The fairy's pale, silvery eyes followed Theo as the young man poured them both tea. "Thank you," he murmured.

"You look cold," the young man said. He stepped to the fireplace and started the fire.

Finally he sat down on the other side of the table and studied the Fair lord. "Eat a little," he said. "You'll feel better."

Willowvale smiled faintly. "I'm too tired to eat," he said, and he believed it to be true.

"I think you can manage a little. Lord Mosswing's magic will work overnight, and you'll feel better in the morning." Theo smiled kindly. "I've had experience, you know."

The Fair lord huffed softly, something between a chuckle and a grumble. Still, he ate half the rich roast and most of the potatoes on his plate, all of the salad, and even a few bites of the bread pudding, all of which he thought greatly inferior to the hospitality he had been offered at the Overton manor.

Finally he said, "I don't know that I'm fit to accept encouragement or advice at the moment, Theo. Perhaps you might come for breakfast."

"All right. I shall see you in the morning." Theo stood, and, seeing that Willowvale remained slumped in his chair, said, "Would you like me to help you to bed?"

"I'll manage."Willowvale stood belatedly. "Good night."

"Good night."

Normally the Fair lord would have been up for hours after dinner, reading or enjoying a cup of tea or wine at home or with the king or even experimenting with his magic to see what sort of fantastical new plant he might be able to conjure.

Instead, he undressed and went to bed as soon as the servants left the room with the remains of the dinner trays, although it was barely past seven in the evening.

CHAPTER TWENTY-NINE
Overton Hospitality and Lord Willowvale's Letter

At the Overton estate, Lord Cedar Mosswing did as he had said he would and looked in on Miss Astrantia Berrydell.

The Fair maiden was still deathly pale, and she did not wake as he stepped closer. He put his dark hand on her forehead and gave her all the healing magic he could manage without actually collapsing to the floor.

When he turned toward the door, a wave of dizziness overtook him, and Anselm caught him just before he fell flat on his face.

"Let me help you back to bed, my lord," said Anselm.

"Thank you," mumbled Cedar.

In a matter of a few minutes, the young Fair lord was comfortably ensconced in his room. He was deeply asleep before Anselm even turned away.

"You've been up nearly all night again," said Juniper quietly. "Shall I watch for a while so you can rest?"

Anselm smiled at the young fairy. "Lord Mosswing indicated that Miss Berrydell would be nearly recovered when she woke. I think we can both get a little sleep if you would be so kind as to write her a note telling her to ring the bell if she needs anything. I doubt she speaks Valestrian, so it would be best if it were in your language. I'll make her a plate for when she wakes up."

These tasks were complete ten minutes later, and then Juniper and Anselm headed to their respective quarters for a bit of well-deserved rest.

The morning was unusually quiet. Lily, Sir Theodore, and Lady Overton all took themselves to the kitchen at various times, and found that Sophie, Anselm's wife, was already helping the cook prepare breakfast.

Lily and Theo's parents ate a quiet luncheon in one of Lily's favorite spaces in the entire luxurious estate, a room with many windows that looked out upon the garden, now bare and dusted with snow, and painted a lovely rich blue which set off the gold frames of the antique etchings upon the walls.

Snow began falling softly while they ate, and Lily remarked to Sir Theodore and Lady Overton how beautiful the garden was, even in winter.

"I have always loved it," Sir Theodore said.

As the fat flakes of snow drifted gently downward, Astrantia drifted slowly upward from the haze of pain and fever and healing magic.

She turned her head and blinked.

The ceiling was unfamiliar, and the light that filled the room, cool and white, with a softly shifting pattern from falling snowflakes, seemed equally unfamiliar. The walls were papered in a subtle floral pattern she did not remember.

There was a chair near the bed, and she had the vague impression she had seen someone slouching in it, but she could not remember whom it might have been.

A folded piece of paper on the bedside table caught her eye, and she picked it up. Beside the paper was a plate covered by a cloth. She looked under the cloth to see a selection of pastries, some exotic berries which she could not identify, and three different kinds of cheese. A glass of water stood beside it.

She was famished, but before she touched the food, she opened the note.

Dear Miss Berrydell,

The food and water are safe for you. When you would like assistance or more food, please pull the ribbon on the wall.

Lord Mosswing is exhausted, so he is resting, but if you are in distress, I am sure he will offer any magic he can.

This house belongs to Sir Theodore Overton, III, and his wife Lady Helena Overton. Their son, Mr. Theodore Overton, IV, whom you met, is the Rose, more often called the Wraith in the human world. He and Lord Willowvale have already departed for Aricht.

Mr. Overton's wife, Mrs. Lilybeth Overton, is very kind, and she will undoubtedly be glad to assist you when you are ready to leave your room, or if you need help with personal matters, or just to speak with a lady.

Also in the house is Miss Crocus Firethorn, one of the Fair Folk. She is betrothed to Mr. Overton's friend Lord Fenton Selby, who lives nearby. And there is Anselm, Mr. Overton's manservant, and his wife, Sophie; they are my adoptive parents. And there are a few other servants who tend the grounds and do some of the chores.

Please be comfortable here, and know that there is kindness and safety here.

Respectfully,

Juniper Morel

It had been Lord Mosswing in the chair! She lay back and stared at the ceiling. She had known he was reputed to have powerful healing magic, but had not imagined he possessed power great enough to overcome the effects of faebane.

Also, she would not have thought that a great lord like Mosswing would be willing to use his power to save her life. While skilled, she was not valuable enough to the throne to justify extraordinary effort from someone of his status.

She shied away from that thought. Lord Mosswing was the same rank as Lord Willowvale, a marquess, but Lord Willowvale was undoubtedly closer to the king. He had been Silverthorn's trusted confidant for many years. It was ridiculous, even appalling, that Willowvale had somehow brought her here to save her life. She grimaced when she recalled that Willowvale had been wounded, though she did not know how serious the injury. Even if it had been only a scratch, he ought not have spent his time or energy on her.

Lord Brookbower was the priority, regardless of how offensive his views and objectionable his personality.

Lord Mosswing had spoken to her of his friend, the Rose, but she felt so strange and feverish that she could not remember much of what he had said.

She sat up and the room spun sickeningly.

She slid to the floor, half-fainting, and remained there, staring at the rich blue and silver rug, until the roar of blood in her ears receded.

How embarrassing! She was glad no one had been present to see that little display. She leaned on the chair as she rose slowly, using her breathing to push the odd, hollow feeling in her arms and legs to the back of her awareness.

Her stomach twisted itself in a knot of hunger, hard and empty and cold. Her skin felt cold too, as if she had a fever, but perhaps that was merely the hunger and the aftereffects of the faebane.

She studied the pastries and cheese, but did not eat them.

The young fairy, Juniper, would not have lied to her.

But a human could have written the message and signed Juniper's name to it, and she was not yet entirely sure whether she trusted the humans here.

It would be foolish to be saved by Lord Mosswing and Lord Willowvale only to succumb to another poisoned food or drink, if these humans were allied with whomever had planned the assassination in the first place.

She smelled like sweat with a hint of what she had vomited up in the Arichtan palace and again in the veil, though she was not sure if that was merely her clothes or her own breath. Her clothes were sticky with sweat, and she felt chilled and shaky. But upon further attention, she was not wearing her familiar dress, but rather a nightgown of the softest silk. A warm dressing gown was draped over the end of the bed, and she slipped it on. She hoped it had been a woman who had changed her clothes and wondered that she had not woken at this occurrence.

The fire in the grate was low, and she put another log on it and crouched close while she stirred the embers, relishing the warmth on her face.

Her throat burned.

She would need water soon. Even one of the Fair Folk could not survive much longer without water, though nourishment could wait if the humans were not to be trusted.

Astrantia stood again, carefully this time, and waited until the spots in her vision faded before she crossed the room to the ribbon the note had specified.

The room was lovely, with an elegant rug softening the marble floor beneath her feet and antique paintings upon the walls. Out the window, the snowfall had stopped, leaving a white carpet over the manicured garden and the distant hills. Far away behind the hills, low grey mountains loomed. The air was clear, and the late afternoon sunlight glinted upon the snow.

The Fair maiden looked around the room again, noting the differences between the style of the Arichtan court, with which she was now familiar, and this foreign style.

She pulled the ribbon and heard a bell chime somewhere distant.

A few moments later, hurried footsteps sounded in the hallway, and there was a soft knock.

"Come in," she said cautiously.

An unfamiliar man stepped inside. He looked about fifty years old, broad-shouldered, well-dressed, but not exactly like a nobleman. But she did not know the customs of Valestria.

"Miss Berrydell." The man bowed to her. "I am Anselm, and I serve in this house. May I bring you a meal?"

"I would like to speak with Lord Mosswing or Juniper Morel. Or another fairy, if there are others here." A fairy would not lie to her, however disagreeable he might be.

"Miss Firethorn is in the library. Shall I ask her to come to you?"

"Yes, please."

"Shall I draw you a bath?"

"I would like to speak with Miss Firethorn first," Astrantia said. She swallowed, feeling vaguely sick and dizzy.

"As you wish." The man bowed and stepped out into the hall.

Astrantia sat in the chair and looked toward the door. Her mouth was dry and sour, and she wanted the water, but she would not be so foolish as to drink it yet.

Her mind wandered back to Aricht, to the sudden, wrenching agony in her guts of the faebane, of the way it made her magic slippery and difficult to control. She could have ripped everyone in the room to shreds, but that would hardly have done anyone any good at all. Instead, she had kept it contained in a neat little bundle and shoved one of the attackers across the room. But she had not been alert enough, aware enough, to use her magic well.

She had disgraced herself, and the Fair throne, and cost Brookbower and his staff their lives.

Shame and grief doubled her over in the chair, and when the soft knock sounded upon the doorframe, it was all she could do to raise her aching head.

Miss Crocus Firethorn was astonishingly beautiful, and there was absolutely no doubt she was Fair. Her eyes were a bright, clear ice blue, and her hair was the same color. Her lips were the palest rosebud pink, and they made a little moue of distress and compassion when she saw Astrantia.

"Let me help you," she said, and started forward.

Astrantia straightened. "I'm all right." Her voice rasped. "Is this place safe?"

"Yes, of course." Crocus glanced at the tray of pastries and cheese, at the water glass which had not been touched. "You must be thirsty, at least. Here." She handed Astrantia the glass.

"It isn't poisoned?" Astrantia asked.

"No." Crocus knelt on the floor in front of her. "I heard what happened, and I am sorry."

Astrantia took a cautious sip of the water, and, finding that it tasted like any other water she had ever enjoyed, drained the glass.

The water sat cool and heavy in her otherwise empty stomach.

"May I have some more water, please?" she managed.

"Perhaps you ought to let that settle a moment. Anselm said he was going to make you a soothing soup when you woke up. Would you like it now?"

Astrantia looked toward the corridor, but the door was closed. "Is he to be trusted?" she said. "Where is Juniper Morel? He wrote me a note, or someone signed his name to it, telling me about the people of this house."

Crocus's blue eyes softened. "Everyone here is to be trusted, even the Rose."

"What do you mean, *even* the Rose?" A little curl of fear awoke in Astrantia. Brookbower's delegation had received little information about the Rose, so her knowledge was limited, and she was well aware of this fact.

"Let me ask Anselm to bring you tea," said Crocus. "Then we can talk." She did just this, and Anselm hurried away.

Crocus pulled the chair from the corner closer, and then the little table with the plate of pastries.

"If you can stomach it, this might help you feel a little better while you wait for dinner."

With careful fingers Astrantia picked up one of the little pastries which was dusted with a white powder. "What is this?"

"I don't know all the names of all the pastries. The white on top is sugar."

Astrantia bit into it carefully and was surprised to the flaky pastry was filled with fluffy cream. It was as sweet and light as a cloud, and in all her time in Aricht, she had not tasted anything as elegantly indulgent.

She finished the tiny pastry and eyed the others longingly. "So I can trust that the letter Juniper left is accurate?" she said.

"I'm sure it is, but I will look at it if you like." A moment later, Crocus was reading the note. "Yes, this is all true, and it was written by his hand, as far as I can tell." She looked up. "You are safe here."

The pink-haired fairy relaxed. "Thank you. Please do tell me how you came to be here, and about the Rose, and why you said *even he* could be trusted." She started upon the remaining pastries, cheese, and berries with a quiet, steady determination.

A knock upon the door heralded Anselm's return, and Astrantia watched as he entered and put a tray in front of her. The chicken and vegetable soup and buttery roll smelled divine.

"All this is safe for me to eat?" she said, shooting a sharp glance at Anselm.

"Of course it is safe, Miss Berrydell." Anselm's voice had the very faintest edge of affront in it, though he tried to hide it. "Please ring the bell if I can be of service."

"How is Lord Mosswing?" Astrantia asked, suddenly remembering the dark-skinned lord, nearly unconscious, being helped out of the room.

"He is still sleeping."

Astrantia frowned. "Thank you." She looked back at Crocus expectantly.

The two fairies talked for over an hour. Crocus told of her own caution of humans in general and Theo in particular, and of the extravagant generosity and heroism with which Lord Fenton Selby and Mr. Theodore Overton, IV, had set her free.

"The wedding is in only five more weeks," she said with a soft, shy smile. "Lord Selby invited Lord Willowvale. Can you imagine! But Lord Selby thought it only just, after he stood for them both in the duel with Lord Larch." She frowned thoughtfully. "I think Lord Willowvale doesn't know how to be agreeable, but I think he is trying, as well as he can."

Crocus took a sip from her teacup and studied Astrantia's face. "So you see, I am confident that you will be safe here. I have found it to be a place of hospitality and refuge. I found Lord Selby's house similarly gracious, though perhaps quieter, but it would not be accepted for me to stay there before the wedding."

"But you did already, I thought."

"That was merely as a guest, a stranger, and no one really knew it anyway. But now I have been seen in society, and I would not like to besmirch Lord Selby's reputation, or my own, by staying with an unmarried man."

Astrantia pondered this. The social expectations of Aricht were more rigid than those Fair society, and Valestria appeared to be even more strict. Certainly there were expectations, but it seemed that Fair Folk were less inclined than humans to assume the most scandalous thing. Perhaps that was because fairies did not lie, and so any whiff of impropriety was easy to counter with an honest denial. The human world was so fraught with unseen dangers and rules, it was difficult for a fairy to ever feel comfortable. Still, if the Overtons were as kind and generous as Crocus believed, she did not want to tarnish their reputations.

"Will it be a problem that I am here?" she asked.

"Of course not!" Crocus smiled reassuringly and poured Astrantia a little more tea. "First, Mr. Overton is married, and it is expected that married couples may have guests, even unmarried young ladies. It is, of course, presumed that you are Mrs. Lilybeth Overton's guest more than her husband's, and when you meet her, I am sure you will like her as much as I do. Second, Mr. Overton has already departed for Aricht with Lord Willowvale. I am perhaps being more cautious than necessary; both Lord Selby and Mr. Overton have entirely honorable reputations. But I still feel new in Valestria, and I do not want to make mistakes."

Astrantia sipped the tea. The taste was smooth and rich, and it sent little waves of comfort down her aching body.

The other fairy said, "Lord Willowvale left you a note." She pulled it from some hidden pocket and slid it across the little table.

Astrantia pressed her lips together. She was half-inclined to throw it in the fire.

As tempting as the idea was, the note might contain something about his plan to retrieve Brookbower, and so it felt like her duty to open it.

"Excuse me," she murmured. The note was written in a lovely hand, elegant and clear.

Dear Miss Berrydell,

I cannot make any excuse for the actions of which we spoke. I did seek to identify and kill the Wraith, and I did kidnap again two girls the Rose had rescued. My only explanation, and it is not a defense, because what I did was inexcusable, is that I did it out of fear and desperation to save the Fair Lands and our own people.

When I began the mission, I did not truly believe humans equal in worth to Fair Folk, and when I found the Valestrian court so comfortable and blissfully ignorant of our plight, it provoked in me a deep, jealous rage, for I thought, in my arrogance, that such inferior beings had no right to comfort while my own people were in such peril. Then the Rose, Theodore Overton, IV, who had pretended to be an empty-headed social butterfly, saved the Fair Lands with his own blood and a love so pure I was ashamed of everything I was and everything I had ever done. Also, he brought His Majesty Silverthorn an ultimatum that our king had to accept, and Silverthorn agreed never to take or harm humans again, directly or indirectly.

Astrantia took a sip of tea and glanced up at Crocus. The other fairy had withdrawn to sit closer by the fire, giving her the semblance of privacy, while also being available in case she wanted to talk. The tea soothed Astrantia's throat, and she looked down at the paper.

I was forced to admit to myself that humans were far more complex and beautiful and brilliant than I had imagined. Through another series of events which is too long to write now, I found myself receiving unlooked-for kindness from Mr. Overton, again and again, despite my protests, my pride, and the guilt that seemed to grow at every moment.

I was able to render Mr. Overton a small service some months ago, when Lord Larch wanted to kill him. Still, I feel I owe Mr. Overton far more than I shall ever be able to repay, and yet he insists that we are friends, and friends do not keep a tally of favors.

This letter is much longer than I had intended to write. What I meant to say is that I am guilty of what you believe, and I am fully aware of the horror of it. Indeed, I was ashamed at the time, but only out of pride and dismay that we needed, or thought we needed, humans at all.

Now I know that I misjudged humans entirely, and they are just as rich and complex and beautiful as Fair Folk. Not all of them, perhaps, but who am I to judge? I thought them lesser, and instead I find myself in awe.

So when I agreed with you in Aricht that we ought not consider ourselves more valuable than humans, I meant it with every fiber of my being. I admire you for seeing so quickly the beauty that I was blind to for so long.

I do hope you will forgive me for bringing you here, to Mr. Overton's house. I did not want your entirely justified fury at me to cost you the opportunity to receive healing from Lord Mosswing. I intended only to aid you, and I will not trouble you again.

Sincerely,

Ash Willowvale, Marquess of Sparrowdell and the Willow River Valley

Astrantia let out a soft breath.

She could not hate Willowvale after all, as much as she had wanted to.

"When did Lord Willowvale and Mr. Overton leave for Aricht?" she asked.

"Early this morning."

Astrantia closed her eyes and sighed. She felt weary to her bones, aching and faintly sick with the lingering effects of the poison. Or perhaps it was grief and frustration and disappointment. "Can you open a door into the veil? Can you help me get back to Aricht?"

Crocus bit her lip. "I don't know the way to Aricht in the veil. I can open a door into it, and I was fortunate enough to not get lost the few times I traversed it to and from the Fair Lands, but I am not confident in my ability even to get to the Fair Lands safely."

"Would Lord Mosswing take me? Not for myself, you understand, but on behalf of the Fair crown. I'm sworn to protect Lord Brookbower in Aricht."

"I imagine he would be willing to, but…" Crocus stopped and bit her lip. "He expended a great deal of magic to save your life, and that of Lord Willowvale, and I imagine it will be some time before he is fit to walk any distance."

"Was Lord Willowvale seriously wounded?" Astrantia said in surprise. "I had thought…" Well, she had thought that he was perhaps only slightly injured. His voice had been a little strained when they argued, but his arms had been wiry and and strong. Besides, somehow he had made it all the way here.

Crocus's pale blue eyes were grave. "Yes, he was." At Astrantia's expression, Crocus added, "I was not there when he arrived. Mr. Overton and Anselm bandaged him up, and Mr. Overton went to the Fair Lands to fetch Lord Mosswing. He gave you magic first, of course; your situation was more dire. But Lord Willowvale was very near death. That is why they waited another full day before leaving this morning; he wasn't fit to stand up, much less follow Mr. Overton through the veil all the way to Aricht."

Astrantia swallowed and looked down at her tea. Lord Willowvale's letter had not indicated this at all, and it seemed both very brave, and very foolish of him, if he valued her opinion of himself as much as he had indicated that he did.

"Well," she said at last. "I do not want to trouble Lord Mosswing, but I feel it incumbent upon me to return to Aricht as quickly as possible, if he knows the way, and if he cannot take me there, then to the Fair Lands. His Majesty Silverthorn will want a report, and someone there might be able to help me return to Aricht. Even Lord Aspen or Lord Camphor will suffice, if there is no one else. If the king commands them to do no harm to humans, they will obey." She did not say aloud that she was fully capable of killing either one of them if they defied this order to harm humans, and though she would grieve the loss of a Fair life, she was so deeply, righteously angry with both of them that she would consider it entirely justified if they made such an action necessary.

"It will likely be at least tomorrow, if not the following day, before Lord Mosswing is able to travel," Crocus said.

"He is that ill?"

"He is."

Astrantia shoved her chair back and put both hands over her face. She did not want to cry in front of Crocus, however sympathetic and kind the other Fair maiden seemed to be. It was her failure that had required so much from Lord Mosswing, and she felt undeserving of such sacrifice.

Her mind shied away from the thought of irascible, supercilious Lord Willowvale making a similarly painful sacrifice for her. After she had so insulted him in the veil.

Perhaps her insults and outrage at him were justified. They had certainly felt so at the time.

Still, perhaps she had misjudged him, at least a little.

His letter about recognizing the beauty of humans, even after one of them had apparently so grievously wounded him, seemed to indicate that there was depth to him that she had not considered.

"Would you like to talk about it?" Crocus murmured.

"No!" Astrantia exclaimed. "Absolutely not."

Crocus said, even more gently, "Would you like to be alone? Or more tea?"

"I don't know what I want." The world felt that it was closing in on her, with the weight of guilt and inadequacy layered over her current inability to either return to the Fair Lands or to Aricht.

"Miss Berrydell, breathe slowly, please. You're very pale, and you're still weakened by the poison. If you would like to sleep, I will help you to bed."

"I just… I think I want to be alone." Not because she felt ill, or because she did not trust this new friend, but because she wanted to cry, and she didn't want an audience for it.

"Shall I help you to bed first?"

"No, thank you."

Crocus stood reluctantly. "I'll come check on you later, if you don't mind. Perhaps you'll feel better with a little more food in you."

Astrantia nodded without looking up.

How mortifying it was to let her emotions get the better of her! Perhaps she really was still ill after all. She could not control her expression, could not keep the tears from her eyes, so she kept her face hidden until the door closed softly.

Then she sobbed, silent and gasping. At last, exhausted and aching, she fell asleep with her head on the arm of the chair.

Astrantia woke to quiet conversation in the room. "Who is there?"

"It's only Miss Firethorn, my wife Sophie, and me, Anselm," said the servant. "I drew you a bath in the room down the hall. I can help you walk there, if you need help, and Sophie can help you bathe. Miss Firethorn is here to reassure you, if you need reassurance, that we will not harm you."

Astrantia pushed the fuzziness to the back of her mind. "She has assured me of that several times already," she said. "I will choose to believe she is correct. There's no need for you to stay, Miss Firethorn." Then, with a bit of uncharacteristic grumpiness, for she felt quite queasy and sick and disoriented, she added, "I can defend myself if necessary, even now."

"I am sure you can," replied Sophie kindly. "But that will not be necessary."

Astrantia allowed herself to be helped up by the older woman. Sophie was as calm and kind as Anselm seemed to be, and, if Miss Firethorn was right about them, equally trustworthy and reliable.

It was embarrassing to lean on someone else, however kind they might be, so Astrantia walked on her own feet, without assistance, down the hall to the room in which a hot bath awaited. She shook her head when Sophie asked if she wanted help undressing; she was not a noblewoman who required such assistance, and she had carried out these tasks on her own in the Fair Lands even before she had been the only Fair woman in the delegation to Aricht.

She slipped into the water with a sigh of relief and ecstasy. The hot water felt heavenly to her chilled and weary body, and she relished the opportunity to scrub herself clean.

After some ten minutes, a soft knock sounded upon the door. "It's only me, Miss Berrydell," said Sophie's voice. "I have a new clean nightgown, and a dressing gown, and some slippers for you. May I come in?"

"Yes." The tub was hidden from view of the door by a large folding screen made of wood intricately carved in a floral motif.

"Do you need help bathing or getting out?" said Sophie from the other side of the screen.

"No, thank you. May I stay in a little longer?"

"As long as you like. I can heat up more water if you'd like."

"I don't think I'll be that long." Astrantia smiled.

Her body soaked in the warmth as if she had been chilled for days.

By the time she finally washed her hair, rinsed, and rose from the water, the water was nearly cold. Shivering, she dried herself with the thick, fluffy towel that Sophie had put on the nearby stool and then dressed in the clothes neatly folded nearby.

She stepped out into the hallway to see Sophie waiting, even at this very late hour.

"How are you feeling?" the servant asked with a kind smile.

"I'm all right."Astrantia swallowed, feeling fatigued nearly beyond coherent thought. "I'd like to go to bed."

"Of course. Would you like a little food first?"

Her body needed nourishment, but she was so tired she could barely contemplate the idea. "I… I just want to go to bed," she said.

Within minutes, she was curled up in bed asleep.

CHAPTER THIRTY
Reassurance

The following day Astrantia awoke to the sunlight slanting across the bed. She blinked at the ceiling, then turned over and closed her eyes, her mind fuzzy with warmth and a cozy sense of well-being.

She thought drowsily of all that she had heard the previous night, and of the letter from Willowvale, and whether Lord Mosswing might be recovered enough to take her to the Fair Lands.

At this, her sleepy relaxation evaporated, and she dragged herself from the bed. She was only a little dizzy, though she felt oddly trembly and slightly feverish. The gown she was wearing was light and soft, but under the blankets she had been warm. Now she shivered as she pulled the dressing gown over it. She put her feet into the sheepskin slippers that were waiting.

The fire had been stirred not long before, and she wondered that she had not awoken at the sound of it. She ought to be have been more alert.

Still, it was more evidence that the people here could be trusted.

She put another log on the fire and sat close by it, relishing the heat.

It was far too late to be in a panic about getting back to Aricht. Either Brookbower was still alive, or he wasn't, and either way there was nothing she could do about it. She wondered what sort of crisis Mr. Overton and Lord Willowvale would face when they arrived, and whether they had arrived yet. Perhaps they were already back.

It was difficult to keep track of the days. She had been so feverish, and so confused, and then so tired, that everything seemed to blur together. Was the attack two or three days ago? A week ago? Or more?

She glanced over Willowvale's letter again, noting with an odd sense of guilt that he had signed it with his full name and title. Why had he given her that little bit of power over him? Not that she would, or could, use it against him, trapped here as she was. Still, it was a strange gesture from someone so churlish and guarded.

Reluctantly she stood and looked for her clothes, which she found folded neatly on a cedar chest at the end of the bed. She dressed slowly, finding that the movement made her feel vaguely ill.

At last, wearing her own familiar gray dress, she opened the door and looked out into the hallway.

There was no one about, and she debated for a moment before stepping carefully into the corridor.

It was rude to walk around in an unfamiliar house without having been invited to explore. But weighed against her need to assure herself that Lord Mosswing was recovering, and the responsibility she felt to rescue Brookbower if she could, or at least return to the Fair Lands to report to the king, the discourtesy of this exploration seemed minor indeed.

The corridors were spotlessly clean and nearly as luxurious as the Arichtan palace, though far cozier and lovelier in design. The floors were marble, but the inlay was subtle and restrained, and they boasted enchanting designs of intricate knots, leaves, vines, flowers, and ornamented curves rather than the Arichtan tendency toward aggressive angularity. Although she would have preferred some living plants, this Valestrian style seemed much preferable to the Arichtan designs.

She found a sunny sitting room, empty now, and stepped inside. The late afternoon sunlight, for it was now clear that it was afternoon, gave the room a cheerful, cozy air. Perhaps that was part of why she was dizzy; she had missed breakfast and lunch yet again, and she felt hollow and strange, but no longer feverish.

Two velvet chairs and a brocaded chaise lounge clustered near the fireplace, which was laid with wood for its next use. A pair of heavy, elegant bookshelves held books and a collection of porcelain vases. Another glass-fronted shelf on another wall held an odd creature of the human world carved of dark wood polished until it shone and a number of what seemed to be navigation instruments for sailing, though Astrantia was not familiar with all the devices.

Upon the walls were two excellent paintings. One of them depicted a lush bouquet of pink peonies in various states of bloom. From pink buds through the full bloom to one fading blossom, each petal was painting with loving attention to detail, color, and light. Astrantia stepped closer to admire this one, for the artist's passion seemed to have imbued the depiction of lovely flowers with an extra measure of sublime beauty.

She turned to look at the other painting, which was of a town which might be nearby, for the hills in the background looked very much like what she saw out the window. But the vantage point was different, and the light on the distant houses came from a different angle, and she imagined it had been painted on a nearby hilltop.

The sunlight through the window grew more golden as it faded. In the dimming light, the Fair maiden spent quite some time trying to read the titles on the books, with her head turned to one side. The letters were almost the same as those of the Arichtan language, but the words were different, and she could only puzzle out a few of the words for their similarity with their Arichtan cognates.

Soft footsteps sounded in the hall, not sneaky but rather calm and quiet. She turned to look toward the door.

"Good evening, Miss Berrydell."

The face that greeted her was unmistakably Fair, with dark purple hair and bright turquoise eyes, a coloring she had always thought particularly striking.

"Morel?" she asked. She thought that was his name, but her memories of the worst of the poisoning were jumbled and indistinct.

"Yes, miss." He smiled and ducked his head, but she thought it was out of natural politeness and a generally shy personality rather than subservience. "Anselm brought your dinner, and when you weren't there, we went looking for you. We thought, if you were feeling well enough, you might like to have dinner with the family in the larger dining room."

"Who will be there?" asked Astrantia curiously.

"Sir Theodore and Lady Overton, Mrs. Overton, Lord Selby and his mother Lady Selby, Lord Mosswing, and Miss Firethorn."

"What is your position, then? Are you a servant in this house?"

"No, but I like to help. Anselm and his wife Sophie adopted me, and I like to eat with them in their apartment most nights. But I am always invited to eat with the Overtons and their guests, and I often have." The young fairy smiled.

"You seem happy here."

"Very much so." Juniper's smile softened. "I do hope you feel up to it. I think it would be reassuring for you."

"Do I look frightened?" Astrantia eyed him.

"Not at all!" Juniper flushed. "Still, it is pleasant to be surrounded by friends."

"I suppose I ought to meet Sir Theodore and Lady Overton, at least." Lord Mosswing would be there too, and she could ask him to take her back to the Fair Lands.

She followed Juniper through the corridors to a spacious dining room.

It appeared everyone had just been seated, and they stood when entered.

Crocus introduced her to everyone, and everyone to her. Sir Theodore looked much like an older version of his son, with the same sparkling hazel eyes, though there was a weight to his gaze that Astrantia did not recall from the younger Overton. His wife was lovely, with a kindness in her eyes that Astrantia warmed to immediately.

The fairies seemed comfortable at this human table, and Astrantia found this fascinating, for never before had she experienced anything like real friendship with a human. There had been stiffly polite dinners at the Arichtan palace, of course, but not since the children had begun disappearing. Not to mention that she was not expected to speak during these dinners; only Brookbower was expected to interact with the Arichtan king and his staff.

Here at the Overton table, she was startled to find herself addressed directly by her human hostess.

"How are you feeling, Miss Berrydell?" said Lily in her soft, sweet voice.

"Nearly recovered. Thank you." Astrantia smiled. She looked at Lord Mosswing, who sat across from her and one seat to her left. "Lord Mosswing, how are *you* feeling?"

"Quite a bit better. Thank you for asking." He smiled at her, and she flushed. He was strikingly handsome, with his dark skin and his turquoise eyes and his silvery-white curls. Though she was hardly interested in him, and he was certainly not interested in her, it was odd to be addressed with warmth and attentiveness by any Fair lord. It made her feel warm and strange inside, as if he *noticed* her as both a person and a lady.

She felt an unpleasant little twinge inside when she realized Mosswing was not the first Fair lord to speak kindly to her. Willowvale had also shown care and respect for her, in his own awkward way.

Still, Mosswing and Willowvale could hardly be compared. Mosswing was a Fair lord of honor and good family, where Willowvale was merely an unpleasantly biting tool of the Fair throne, albeit of good title and wealth and all those other silly things. The fact that Willowvale had offered her a blanket when she was cold, and had carried out Silverthorn's order to retrieve Brookbower's party, meant only that he was not quite as stone-hearted as she had been told.

She swallowed and tried not to think about how badly Willowvale must have suffered to bring her to this little human enclave of safety.

The conversation that flowed around her was light and apparently designed to reassure her about the friendly intentions of the Overton hosts and all their guests.

A little farther up the table, Lord Fenton Selby smiled shyly at Miss Crocus Firethorn. Lord Cedar Mosswing was still noticeably pale, and he did not eat as much of his dinner as he probably ought to have. Lily smiled at something amusing Sir Theodore said, and then looked up at Anselm to thank him for the little plate of treacle tart which he had put in front of her.

"Lord Mosswing," Astrantia said quietly. He looked up at her, his tired eyes still quick and attentive. Guilt pressed upon her, but she persevered. "I must return to Aricht as soon as possible. Can you take me?"

"I am sorry, Miss Berrydell. I cannot find my way in the veil so easily as to risk your life trying to find Aricht from here."

"Can I… what about the Fair Lands? Can you take me there?" She bit her lower lip, noting the shadows beneath his eyes. "I am sorry to ask it of you," she whispered. "You've already done far more than I deserve. But I *must* return. Lord Camphor or Aspen can take me to Aricht to find Brookbower, if he's still alive. They know the way from the Fair Lands."

Lord Mosswing swallowed. "I can do that."

Sir Theodore interjected from the head of the table, "Miss Berrydell, I know your assignment must weigh upon you, but Lord Mosswing really ought to have a little more rest before he braves the veil."

"I can…" Lord Mosswing said wearily, but Sir Theodore shook his head.

"Please don't," said the human.

Astrantia stared at the human, wondering what sort of claim he had over the younger Fair lord. But then she looked at Mosswing again and sighed. He really did look exhausted.

She looked down. "I am sorry, my lord," she murmured. "When you are ready, I would appreciate your help, but I do not want to endanger you."

The Fair lord said kindly, "If Brookbower was alive when Theo and Willowvale arrived back in Idosa, I am confident they will bring him safely to the Fair Lands."

The young lady bit her lip and nodded. With a little food in her stomach now, she felt heavy and strange, entirely unready to walk for hours in the dark. Still, desperation would have given her the strength, if Mosswing had been game.

Perhaps he would have, if he'd felt as desperate as she did. But he seemed content to trust his friend.

"Do you really think they will be able to help Brookbower?" she said at last. "He is difficult, but he is my responsibility."

Mosswing looked more than half asleep, staring dazedly at his treacle tart without touching it. But he roused enough to say, in his deep, calm voice, "If Brookbower can be helped, Theo can do it. Do not worry, Miss Berrydell."

Miss Firethorn said, "Lord Mosswing, I'd be happy to go with you to the Fair Lands tomorrow, if you'd like another blade."

Astrantia glanced at the other Fair maiden. "Are you trained?" she said in surprise.

"Not nearly as well as you are!" Crocus smiled modestly. "But well enough that I can lend a little aid, and the veil doesn't hate me. I'm sure Lord Selby and Sir Theodore would offer their help, but it would only make the journey more dangerous for you."

The pink-haired fairy looked at the human men, noting their chagrinned expressions. It was fascinating indeed to think of an entire family, and a family friend, who knew so much about the veil.

"I think I'll retire now, if you don't mind," said Cedar almost inaudibly. Sir Theodore and Fenton were at his side in moments. "I'm all right," he breathed. Fenton stood aside while Sir Theodore helped Cedar out of the dining room and down the hall.

Astrantia watched him go, letting the guilt twist deeper into her heart. How could she have pressed him to take her this evening? She had been so selfish.

"I can't… I don't think I can eat any more," she said finally. She stood, and though she still felt strange and weak with the lingering effects of the poison, she could walk on her own. Lord Mosswing had held nothing back when he gave her his magic.

The tears filled her eyes so suddenly, and the grief and guilt flared with such overwhelming force, that she found herself trembling. Her shoulders shook, and she stumbled as she reached the hallway.

"Miss Berrydell!" Crocus's voice called.

Lily and Crocus followed her down the hall, and she wished they wouldn't. But when she sat on the hearth, letting the heat of the fire sink into her back, she found that their soft, kind voices soothed her after all.

She could not remember the last time she had felt a woman's sympathetic kindness, other than the servant who had brought her clean clothes when she bathed. Between the training with weapons, Brookbower's always-biting temper, the perpetual tension between the Arichtan palace staff and nobility and the Fair delegation, she could hardly remember the last time she had spent much time with a woman at all.

Now, with Lily and Crocus quietly conversing, without expecting anything from her, she found that she longed for female friends. In another life, one in which she was not a bodyguard or security, she might have had friends like these.

"Would you like a little tea? It's a soothing blend," said Lily.

Astrantia nodded, and when she accepted the tea cup in trembling hands, she felt a sense of loss and grief. She was nearly asleep before she finished it.

Lily said quietly, "Is this to be expected with faebane? I'm not sure how much more Lord Mosswing can give her."

"She's getting better," said Crocus, with a frown. "I'm not sure anyone has survived faebane in living memory. Lord Mosswing has already done the impossible."

They said a little more, but it came to Astrantia's ears as if through thick cotton, muffled and indistinct, and she could not parse out the meaning. Valestrian took far more focus and concentration than she could muster now.

A few minutes later, Lily said, "Miss Berrydell, may I help you into bed?"

The fairy startled back to wakefulness, her pink eyes were wide and dazed. "What?"

"May I help you into bed?" Lily repeated.

Astrantia stood unsteadily. "I think I can manage," she murmured.

CHAPTER THIRTY-ONE
Meadowhawk's Encouragement

Fourteen hours of sleep did Lord Willowvale a world of good, and he awoke to a knock on his door in late morning with a clear head, significantly less pain to scramble his thoughts, and a sudden, surprising idea which held a great deal of appeal.

Theo had knocked on his door, and, receiving no answer, was just considering stepping through the veil to the other side of the door when the fairy opened it.

"Good morning!" Theo said, delighted. Then, to the servant who had escorted him to the room, he said, "Would you get Lord Willowvale some breakfast, please?"

The fairy stepped aside and let Theo in with a suppressed smile. "I didn't mean to sleep late," he grumbled, but there was no real anger in it. "Did I miss anything important?"

"Not at all. I enjoyed a late morning myself."

Willowvale gestured toward one of the chairs and said, "Sit down, then." He knelt and stirred the coals in the fireplace; the fire was nearly out.

He was still barefoot and wearing only the thin silk trousers in which he had slept. His wound was well-bandaged, but other than that, he was bare above the waist, and the chilly air in the room made his skin prickle.

Theo, on the other hand, was beautifully attired, his elegant silk jacket perfectly neat and his cravat perfectly tied.

"I'm not even dressed yet," muttered the fairy. "Excuse me." He felt that he ought to have been embarrassed, but he could not muster up that emotion. Instead, he merely felt apologetic, for it was rude to receive a visitor, even a friend, in such a state of undress.

Theo waved a graceful hand. "I invited myself in; I could hardly hold it against you that you weren't ready yet."

Willowvale laughed under his breath. "It's all right."

Theo frowned. "You ought to change that bandage."

The Fair lord did not protest when Theo stepped closer and helped him unwrap the cloth. He muttered, "Leave it alone," when Theo bent to examine the wound, but he didn't really mind.

Thanks to Cedar's magic, the wound was sealed with a thin line of tender pink skin, fragile and ready to reopen if Willowvale twisted too quickly. Still, not having another bandage and not inclined to open the door and ask a servant for one, the fairy retreated to the bedroom and dressed.

"How does it feel this morning?" Theo asked when he returned.

"Much better," Willowvale said honestly. "Sore, of course, but I can think straight, at least."

Theo beamed at him. "You sound positively cheerful, my friend! I am delighted to hear it."

At this moment breakfast arrived. Theo poured his friend and himself some tea and sat back while Willowvale ate. At the fairy's frown, Theo said, "I already ate."

The fairy said a few minutes later, "I assume Elmerick will not keep me waiting days for an audience this time. What will you do while I am negotiating with him?"

"I thought I might go see the family of Lord Buckley's niece."

"Why?" Willowvale stared at him.

"She might remember my voice; I changed it while I was in the Fair Lands, but I usually didn't maintain the deception once we were in the veil. I didn't tell them my name, of course, but they found my true voice much more reassuring and comforting than whatever pretense of haughty unkindness I had put on."

Willowvale frowned thoughtfully. "I recall you wore an excellent glamour when I fought you at the children's home, but it was of a human. I assume Mosswing made that for you?"

"Juniper Morel did it, actually. He's gifted with both glamour and binding magic, and he had already been at my estate for over a month by then, while Lord Mosswing had attended the wedding that day but had already departed for the Fair Lands an hour or so earlier."

The fairy nodded. "I did wonder about that. Still, I find it difficult to fathom how so many of the guards were so deceived by you." He studied Theo's friendly face and his warm, kind eyes. "You really don't have the arrogance to pretend to be a Fair lord, and I cannot imagine anyone other than a lord would have been able to extricate the children from the palace itself. Although I suppose you could have taken them directly into the veil. Or did you pretend to be a guard?"

Theo stood and looked down his nose at the fairy. "You find it difficult to believe I can act the part?" His voice was full of snide condescension, and his accent in the Fair language indicated that he had been born and raised in Dewspring-in-the-Wood. "You met me yourself, Willowvale. You really ought not hold against the staff their inability to recognize me, when you had already exchanged insults with me more than once and still did not see through the act."

Then he gave Willowvale a sparkling smile. "Do you remember me?"

The astonished fairy's pale eyes were wide. "I am corrected. You can at least pretend to be as arrogant as any Fair lord. But I cannot think of anyone I might have thought Fair that could have been you in disguise."

"Lord Polyantha Meadowhawk. We met just outside the palace. Lord Mosswing introduced us."

Willowvale's shock was palpable. "I… I cannot… that is incredible!" he breathed.

"Thank you." Theo grinned, his eyes dancing. "I practiced a great deal."

The Fair lord swallowed. "You might have killed me or Silverthorn while we weren't looking. You could have gotten close easily in that guise, or you might have pretended to be a servant. The humility comes more easily to you, I think."

Theo shrugged. "I had no desire to kill either of you, and besides, I wanted to save the Fair Lands, not cause further turmoil."

"You would have saved yourself a great deal of pain." Willowvale let out a soft breath. "I assume you sparred with Mosswing to develop the sword skills that so flummoxed me."

"Yes, both Lord Mosswing and his father. My father is exceptionally skilled as well, and though he does not have Fair training, he did train with the best human tutors both before and after his captivity in the Fair Lands."

Willowvale ran his long, pale fingers through his white curls, leaving them in disarray. "I am in awe," he said honestly. "Lord Meadowhawk! I did think you suspicious at the time, but I only thought you arrogant and untrustworthy, perhaps even one of the Rose's allies, but I never dreamed Meadowhawk himself was human."

Theo beamed. "I hope we're still friends." Then, more soberly, he added, "I did lie to you, after all, and I know that is offensive to the Fair Folk. I lied only when absolutely necessary to save children's lives, you know, not for my own enjoyment."

The fairy shot him a sharp glance. "I have no standing to hold anything against you," he said. Then, half under his breath, he said, "I am grateful for your friendship, and it baffles me that you bothered to save my life once, much less twice over, and without throwing my humiliation in my face even once. I cannot be offended except by the contrast with my own treatment of you. You ought to have stabbed me in the veil and told Silverthorn the creatures of the veil ate me. It would have been true; I'm sure they would have found my corpse soon enough."

Theo sat in the chair across from the fairy and said seriously, "Let's have no more of that sort of talk this morning, my friend. You were in a cheerful mood only moments ago, and I should hate to think I should have ruined such a bright and rare occurrence."

Willowvale smiled and sat back. "All right. I shall endeavor to be less grim than usual. What are you going to say to Buckley's family?"

"I don't know yet." Theo took a sip of tea and thought for a moment. "If they will even let me see the girl, which is not a sure thing, I think I should tell her that I am sorry she had to suffer so long, and be so frightened, and that she is strong enough to heal from it, even if it takes time."

Willowvale's optimistic gleam faded. "That is kind of you," he murmured.

"We will see." Theo finished his tea and stood. "Godspeed, my friend. I should like to have dinner with you, if I may, and hear about your success."

The fairy grimaced. "Godspeed."

CHAPTER THIRTY-TWO
Lord Willowvale's Strategy

While Theo went cheerfully out into Idosa to find Sir Briscoe McStretton and his family, Lord Willowvale steeled himself for his conversation with the Arichtan king.

"When will the king see me?" he asked the guard at his door.

"When you are ready, sir."

Well, *that* was certainly a change from the previous weeks, when Elmerick had kept him waiting simply to exasperate him, as far as Willowvale had been able to tell. The king had wanted to assert his power and remind Willowvale of his apparent powerlessness.

The fact that Willowvale could have used his vines to cause a great deal of damage to the palace, and kill a great number of the inhabitants, had apparently either not occurred to the king, or not troubled him. Even if the king had not known of Willowvale's gift with plants, he knew that every fairy was dangerous in some unpredictable way.

If it had come right down to it, he could have assassinated Elmerick himself, if he were willing to sever all Fair ties with Aricht, and likely Valestria and most other human nations, for a generation or more. It would have been a horrific act, but such measures had been considered in the heat of war more than once.

Still, Willowvale had never desired to stoop to such measures, and he was even less inclined to do so now. He did wish, however, that Elmerick appreciated his restraint and the honor of the Fair Court.

He followed the guard to the royal study that Elmerick had apparently selected for this conversation. The lines of the inlay in the floor seemed just as aggressively angular and ugly as they had a few days earlier. Perhaps the hideously sharp and unlovely style had exacerbated Brookbower's always acerbic mood.

Willowvale snorted softly to himself. Theo must be rubbing off on him more than he'd realized, if he was trying to justify Brookbower's abrasive personality.

"What is so funny?" snapped the guard beside him.

The Fair lord raised his eyebrows and looked down at the guard. "If you must know, I was comparing your floors to the Fair style."

"And you find ours contemptible?" muttered the guard. "Prideful devil, aren't you?"

Willowvale laughed aloud, and the guard blanched.

"Pardon me. You weren't meant to hear that." The guard stopped and bowed low.

"Fair hearing is a fair bit better than you're used to among humans, isn't it?" The fairy gave him sharp, predatory smile. "Do you speak so about all lawfully appointed representatives sent to your king's court?"

The guard said again, "Pardon me, my lord. I spoke out of my place, and not to you at all."

Willowvale let out a *pfft* of mingled annoyance and embarrassment. "Take me to the king and we'll be done with it."

"I won't ask for mercy from a fairy," the guard muttered.

"What mercy do you want?"

"I'm not asking for it!" the man said more loudly.

Willowvale blinked and stared at him. "Do you fear I'll kill you?"

The man's jaw jutted forward, and he set off briskly. Willowvale followed, frowning, his long legs carrying him easily at the guard's quick pace.

One of the other guards said, "I'd be pleased if you didn't tell the king, my lord."

The fairy nodded once and glanced at the offender. "Afraid you'll lose your job, then?"

The guard scowled.

Willowvale laughed under his breath. What an odd feeling it was, to be mocked and feel utterly immune to the insult! His cold, pale face was lit with an odd, subtle smile that gave the guards around him an uneasy fear, as if he would do some unpredictable Fair magic to kill them at any moment.

The Fair lord said nothing else as they walked, though he found with some surprise that the angular patterns in the floor and in the tapestries they passed did not make him quite as tense as they had before. They were intricate and precise, even impressive in their own, unlovely way.

When they reached the door of the study, the guard bowed to him again, though he said nothing.

The Fair lord said, with a feeling of freedom in his heart, "Oh, give it a rest. You can think what you want of me. You're not even wrong. Still, I have no desire to take a man's livelihood for speaking what he believes to be true."

Then he stepped into the king's study.

The king stood at Willowvale's entrance, as if that little bit of courtesy could smooth the way for his arguments.

"Your Majesty," Willowvale said. He bowed, not too low but not shallowly enough to be an insult. His wound ached, but it was a distant and inconsequential sort of pain; it helped focus his mind and reminded him how very grateful he was for his life and the unlikely friends who had saved it.

"Lord Willowvale." The king nodded, as close to a bow as a king would ever offer to anyone.

The fairy stepped forward into the center of the room. It was the same study in which he had met the king that first day, but his feeling as he stood there was entirely different. If anything, he felt an odd sense of pity for the human king, so small and frightened and angry. Elmerick was angry with himself, furious with Brookbower, both furious and sympathetic with the assassins, and terrified of the war he thought nearly inevitable.

The Fair lord said abruptly, "I don't want a war any more than you do, Your Majesty.

"There are few Fair noblemen you will find acceptable as a replacement for Brookbower, and fewer still who would be happy here. I do not want the ambassador His Majesty Silverthorn appoints to be burdened or miserable here, nor do I want the appointee so honored to be endangered by accepting a position of such responsibility.

"The ambassador must have the right to bear arms anywhere in Aricht, but will pledge to use them only to defend himself or herself, or the Fair delegation, or some other innocent in dire need. Weapons and Fair magic will not be used in acts of aggression against your people.

"The ambassador must also have the right to hire human servants and will treat them fairly in accordance with your own laws. You will, of course, provide a complete written outline of those laws for the ambassador's convenience.

"The ambassador will have the right to modify the rented accommodations for the comfort of the Fair delegation, including growing moss, trees, and other standard elements of a Fair abode, and to request and obtain help in doing so from those outside the delegation, both Fair and human. None of the improvements will be designed to be harmful to humans, but if a human manages to injure himself out of foolishness, the delegation will not be considered responsible.

"I also think it entirely justified for you, personally, to pledge on your honor that the delegation will be protected from any and all attacks."

He stopped and studied the king's face.

Elmerick said carefully, "I have no objection to what you have said."

"Then there remains only the selection of the ambassador."

The king let out a soft, relieved breath. "As you say."

"I have a suggestion," said Willowvale. He straightened even more, tall and rapier-thin.

The effect was as intimidating as he might have wished, if he had been thinking about that. He had dressed in the Fair style for this meeting, in a suit that was nearly a copy of the severe silver and white which he had worn when Fenton and Theo had bought Miss Crocus Firethorn's freedom. It suited him particularly well, being cut close to show his willowy figure to perfection; the silver and white fabrics and intricate glittering embroidery accentuated the silver highlights in his hair and the pale intensity of his eyes.

The king swallowed; his heart thudded in his chest, for until the negotiations were concluded, anything that Willowvale said might spell doom for his nation. Moreover, he was acutely aware of the fact that the guards were much too far away to be of any real help if Willowvale decided to kill him personally, and he had seen enough combat to know that the Fair Folk were *always* more dangerous than they appeared.

Lord Ash Willowvale looked as dangerous as any fairy ever had.

"As we discussed, there are a number of Fair lords who would serve honorably here. Most of them do not speak Arichtan well, if at all, and Lord Mosswing, the one you would assuredly prefer if you met them all, is soon to be married and would likely prefer to enjoy his new married life in his own beautiful estate in the Fair Lands.

"Instead, I suggest that you request the appointment of Miss Astrantia Berrydell as ambassador."

The king's mouth dropped open in shock. "A woman?"

Willowvale's lips curled. "A Fair maiden of irrefutable honor. She did not participate in the kidnappings of your children, she did not support it when she learned of it, and her family has suffered in the Fair Lands because of their steadfast opposition to the war.

"Moreover, she was selected as Ambassador Brookbower's security because her magical talents lend themselves to such uses. She also told me she enjoys practicing with bladed weapons, and she moves as someone with a great deal of natural talent. She is a formidable warrior both physically and magically; she would not have been selected for her position here if it were otherwise. Still, when attacked by a hidden adversary by the coward's weapon of poison, she did not retaliate by indiscriminately killing everyone in the room, or even everyone within reach.

"She could have; she could certainly have killed *you*, if she had wanted to. But her honor was far too great to stoop to retaliation against someone even possibly innocent, though she had not been accorded the same respect by the assassins.

"She loved and respected humans before this attack, and her restraint in defending herself indicates she still considers you as individuals who ought not die for another's crimes."

The Fair lord paused and said more quietly, "If you want an ambassador who will be fair and just to your people, I do not think you could ask for better. If you cannot endure respecting a woman as ambassador, I would not have Silverthorn appoint her to be further abused and disrespected by your court, for she deserves far better than she has received."

Then he let the silence draw out, his pale eyes sharp on Elmerick's face. It was an odd gamble, to be sure, for Silverthorn had never before appointed a female ambassador to any nation. To Willowvale's knowledge, no human nation had either. But the Fair lord felt his argument was strong, and Miss Berrydell was a compelling candidate, being both of proven honor and being able to speak Arichtan fluently.

"Will your king appoint a woman?" said Elmerick doubtfully.

"He has not before, but I have a great deal of authority in this matter, and I believe he will take my advice." Willowvale wished this did not sound as speculative as it did.

Elmerick frowned. "What about one of the other lords?"

"What about them?" said Willowvale. "The ones who don't speak Arichtan, or the ones who speak it but fought against Aricht in the war? Come to think of it, Miss Berrydell's magic would have been quite useful on our side during combat, but she did not make it known until after the peace treaty was signed. She has been working for peace longer than most."

"Wasn't there another one? Lord Birchbark?"

"I suppose he is an option," conceded Willowvale reluctantly. "He is honorable, his Arichtan is passable, and he also advocated for peace. Still, you have seen Miss Berrydell's courage and honor with your own eyes."

The king sighed. "Is she even titled?"

"I can have her made so," said the fairy. "But I should think nobility of character ought to be more important to you than a title."

"It is." The king stared at the fairy evaluatingly. "All right. I will release Lord Brookbower and his remaining staff into your recognizance to be taken immediately to the Fair Lands. Lord Brookbower is not to return on pain of death. He understands this. If your king will appoint Miss Berrydell as ambassador, I will accept her as such. She and her staff will swear the oath not to take or harm humans again."

"They will be allowed to defend themselves, even if it results in the deaths of any attackers," said Willowvale coldly.

The king pressed his lips together, then nodded. "If attacked, they may defend themselves, but their actions must be commensurate with the attack."

"Agreed."

Elmerick let out a soft breath. "Then we have an agreement. If your king will not accept these terms, you will return with another proposal."

"I will." Then, with a hint of a smile, the fairy said, "Mr. Overton has his own business in Idosa today, I believe. He has greater talent than I do with the veil, so I will wait for him, and we will depart tomorrow for the Fair Lands. If all goes well, I will likely return before Miss Berrydell, and I will make any arrangements necessary for the delegation's accommodations."

"I want Brookbower out of Aricht as soon as possible."

"I don't know the way to the Fair Lands through the veil," said Willowvale. "I could barely get to Valestria. I believe Mr. Overton could feel his way through the veil directly to the Fair Lands, and if not, he will still be able to take us on a more direct route through the veil than I could manage."

"He's that gifted with the veil?" The edge of concern in the king's voice was unmistakable.

"I was just as horrified as you are," said Willowvale, "when I found that a human could open a door into the Fair throne room." Such relief, triumph, and satisfaction filled the Fair lord that he found himself talking, as if he could not stop his tongue. "Still, it is a rare gift indeed, and if anyone must have it, both your people and mine ought to be grateful it is Mr. Overton."

The king let out a soft breath. "I will give you, Brookbower, and his delegation leave to stay one more night."

Lord Willowvale smiled, his eyes glittering. "Thank you, Your Majesty," he murmured.

When he left the room, he found the same guards waiting to escort him back to his suite. "I'd like to speak with Brookbower," he said.

"Yes, my lord," murmured the guard.

They walked in silence, aside from the echo of their footsteps in the spacious halls.

At last they reached the suites where Fair delegation was staying.

Willowvale knocked upon Brookbower's door.

"What is it?"

"Good news," said Willowvale in the Fair language, and Brookbower stared at him.

"How can it be good news? Have you executed the assassins?" said the ambassador. "Surely the king would not permit that."

Willowvale's snowy eyebrows drew downward. "No. I did not. The assassins will be dealt with, but not today. I had higher priorities in my discussion with the king." Then, with a deeper frown, he said, "Must we discuss this in the doorway?"

The ambassador sneered at the guards and stepped aside. "Come in, then." Then, in Arichtan, he said curtly, "Tea."

The guard shot him a dark look.

Willowvale sighed and ignored the ambassador's ill temper. "We're leaving tomorrow for the Fair Lands," he said. "I'll ask Mr. Overton to escort us to the Fair Lands directly, if he can find the way, or take us by way of Valestria, if it's easier."

"Why Mr. Overton?" Brookbower said, his voice full of pride and fury. "I thought you had talent with the veil!"

Willowvale's temper flared, but he said stiffly, "I don't know the way to the Fair Lands from here, and the magic around the palace is quite strong. I'm sure you know that. Were Lords Camphor or Aspen able to open a door near the palace?"

"No!" Brookbower snarled.

"Then you will understand why I do not want to travel to the other side of the city to be able to enter the veil in order to get lost in it and perish! Mr. Overton will escort us to the Fair Lands with far more kindness than either of us deserves, and you *will* thank him for it." Willowvale felt a hot sense of furious injustice on Theo's behalf.

"I will do no such thing!" Brookbower stared at him. "What has come over you, Willowvale? How can *you*, of all Fair Folk, been twisted into something so unnatural? A *friend* of a *human*! I might have expected it from someone else, but you?"

Willowvale gritted his teeth. "Do you really want to know?"

"I do."

The tea that Brookbower had so rudely demanded arrived just then, and Willowvale stood to receive the tray from the servant.

Then, more to pique Brookbower than out of any real courtesy toward the servant, he said with a smile, "Thank you."

Brookbower's gasp of shock was every bit as satisfying as Willowvale had expected, and he laughed inside as he poured tea for them both.

CHAPTER THIRTY-THREE
Charity

"Charity, this is Mr. Theodore Overton, IV. He says you might know his voice. Mr. Overton, my daughter Miss Charity McStretton."

"Good morning," Theo said gently.

The girl looked at him with cautious curiosity.

"I don't know if you'll recognize my voice, but I remember your feet were so sore that I carried you a very long way through the veil between the Fair Lands and Ardmond, in Valestria."

Sir Briscoe's face tightened, but he said nothing.

The girl gave the smallest possible nod. She looked down at the ground, her golden hair hiding her face.

"How are you doing now?"

The girl shrugged one shoulder, still looking down.

"Are you frightened?"

Another shrug.

"Angry?"

Shrug.

"Do you know how to play chess?"

She shot him a surprised glance, and he smiled sweetly. She shook her head.

"Would you like to learn?"

The girl shrugged again.

After a moment of silence, she glanced at him through her blond eyelashes and then moved to sit at one side of the chess board.

Theo smiled and sat across from her. He explained how each piece moved, and they settled into a quiet game.

Between advice about the pieces and little tidbits of strategy, Theo said, "You know, I was once lost in the Fair Lands."

Her blue eyes fixed on him at once.

"More than once, actually, but the first time I was truly lost was the most terrifying." He moved one of his bishops. "You can take that piece with your rook."

She took it and stared at him, waiting expectantly for the rest of the story.

"I realized, lost in the Fair woods with an ogre hunting me, that my fear could master me, or I could master it."

The little girl swallowed and looked down.

"Miss McStretton, please do not misunderstand me. I do not mean that you ought not feel fear at fearsome things, or that your experience was not terrible. But I believe you are strong enough to rule your fear, rather than letting it consume you."

He looked back at the board. "I am going to take your knight here. But in return you can take my rook."

She did so, her little hand trembling.

"I know what it feels like to be so afraid you can barely breathe or think," he said softly. "I know. I am sorry you had to experience it."

Charity wiped at her eyes and kept her eyes on the board.

After a long silence, Theo asked, "Do you trust me, Miss McStretton?"

She swallowed and looked up at him, looked away, and finally nodded.

"I have a particular friend I would like to have speak with you. He's a fairy."

The girl looked up at him, frightened, and shook her head hurriedly.

"He won't hurt you or take you away. I had several Fair allies and friends in my work, who helped rescue children like you. But this friend was made later. We were enemies, I suppose; he nearly killed me once.

"But he also risked his life to save mine." Theo held her blue gaze with his warm hazel eyes. "I think, if you were willing to listen to him, really listen, what he would say might help you come to terms with what you endured. It might help… well, not lessen the difficulty of it, but realize how strong you are, and how past suffering might affect you, but it does not have to define you."

She chewed her lip and looked away.

"You don't have to decide right now," Theo said. "But when you consider it, know that I will vouch for him."

She nodded at this, but Theo took it to mean only that she understood, not that she was ready to see the fairy.

"May I visit you tomorrow, Miss McStretton?" Theo asked.

Charity looked up at him and smiled. It was a tiny, melancholy smile, but a smile nonetheless.

"Thank you for seeing me. I enjoyed our game. Until tomorrow." Theo bowed to her, and she smiled a little more.

Late that evening, Theo hopped out of a hired carriage in front of the palace gate.

"I'm Theo Overton. I'm a guest here," he said.

The guard let him in, and another guard escorted him up the long road to the palace itself, where he was given into the care of yet a third guard.

"Mr. Overton," the guard said. "Come with me."

"I don't believe we've been introduced," said Theo congenially. "Might I have your name?"

"Patrick," said the guard. "Do you always ask the names of guards and servants and other commoners?"

"I try, yes," said Theo.

The guard eyed him but said nothing else until they reached the guest suite in which Theo was staying. "Here you are, sir."

"Thank you, Patrick." Theo smiled warmly.

"Will you want dinner?"

"Yes, please. I'd like to eat with Lord Willowvale, if he's available."

The guard frowned but said, "I'll ask. Wait here."

This wasn't hard for Theo, who busied himself by stirring his fire. He sank into one of the chairs with a feeling of very justified fatigue.

It was nearly twenty minutes later before he heard a knock on the door. He opened it to see Lord Willowvale, with two guards escorting him, and a servant with a tray full of food.

"Come in!" he said.

The Fair lord nodded to the guards. "Thank you."

Theo thanked the servant and looked at the fairy.

"I already ate," said Willowvale. "You're back late."

Theo waited until the servant left the room and closed the door before he said, "After I left the family I was visiting, I went into the veil and spent several hours feeling out the magic and how it relates to the Fair Lands. I think I could get us directly to the Fair Lands from here now, though with a little more time I could feel out a better route."

Then, with an apologetic smile, he said, "You don't mind if I eat, do you?"

"Of course not." Willowvale watched as Theo carefully disposed of the loose tea leaves in the strainers on the side of the tray and replaced them with his own. "Your tea is much preferable," he said.

Theo chuckled. "It really is, isn't it?" He glanced up at the fairy with a smile. "You seem cheerful," he prompted. "I suppose your conversation with His Majesty went well?"

Willowvale told Theo much of the conversation with the king.

At last, when the fairy had finished both his tea and his account of the agreement with the king, Theo said, "Well done, my friend!"

The Fair lord smiled quietly. "Thank you."

The young man said, "I promised that I would visit the family again tomorrow. If I go there in the morning, we can leave just after lunch. It will make for a long day, since it will easily be twelve hours walking, if not more, but if Elmerick wants Brookbower gone, we can make it happen."

The fairy's snowy eyebrows drew downward, but he said, "I think it best to leave as soon as you return. I will inform Brookbower and his staff of our departure in the morning."

"Thank you."

Willowvale stood then, and Theo did likewise.

"Good night," the fairy said.

"Good night, Ash."

The next morning Theo visited Sir Briscoe and his family again. His visit was earlier than the McStrettons had expected, but they let him in and brushed aside his apologies for visiting before lunch.

"Would you like to play chess?" Theo asked Charity.

The girl bit her lip and studied him. Finally she put out one hand and twisted it.

"What do you mean?"

The girl stood and repeated the gesture, then took a step forward.

"You want me to open a door into the veil?" Theo raised his eyebrows.

She nodded once.

Theo glanced at Sir Briscoe.

"I don't think that's wise," her father said.

She nodded again, more emphatically. She put her hands up to her eyes as if looking through a spyglass.

"You just want to see it?" Theo asked.

Charity nodded again.

"There's no danger in that," Theo said to her father. "I can open a door and let her look in without her entering at all."

"Isn't the veil itself dangerous, though?" the man said doubtfully.

"There are dangerous creatures in it, and the veil itself is changeable and perilous. One could lose one's way, or be eaten by any number of things, or fall in a pit, or drown, or be eaten by the stone floor, or stung by wasps…" Theo smiled. "But in all my years of passing through it, I've never heard of anything coming out of the veil into either our world or the Fair Lands. You can look in all you want in absolute safety."

The little girl swallowed and looked at her father.

"Would it help you to see it?" Theo asked gently.

Charity nodded.

"If that's what you want," said the lord to his daughter. "But I'll have my sword ready."

She gripped his hand for a moment.

Sir Briscoe sent a servant for his sword, for of course he had not been wearing it for Theo's visit. When the servant returned, he drew the blade and readied himself as if he expected some monstrous beast to leap out of the veil at him.

"I'm ready," he said.

Theo opened the door with a twist and a pull of magic.

Sir Briscoe muttered something under his breath and stepped forward.

The door looked like a tunnel burrowed into a hillside, with a rough stone transom and a floor of packed earth littered with tiny pebbles. Still, it was quite obviously magical, because the opening appeared in the very middle of the room, and when Sir Briscoe stepped to the side, the door might have been as thin as a painting, for he could clearly see through the space the tunnel would have occupied, if it were in the world in which they stood.

"Is this Fair magic?" he asked.

"I'm really not sure," Theo said. "Some Fair Folk have the same gift. I don't know if there's really a difference between Fair magic and human magic other than strength."

"Are you one of the Fair Folk?" Sir Briscoe gazed at him in sudden horror. "Is that why you can do this?"

"I am entirely human," said Theo reassuringly. "Though I should remind you that I had a number of Fair allies in my work."

Sir Briscoe looked surprised. "Did you? I had thought they were all our enemies."

"Not at all," said Theo. "Besides my new friend, who was my enemy before, there were others who risked their lives on behalf of the Arichtan children." He met the man's eyes and said, "One of them is a Fair lord, a friend of mine for many years, who risked himself over and over to give me the disguises and information I needed to carry out the rescues. He danced the children off the dance floor with me more than once, and he used his healing magic to save my life. He also recruited a young Fair servant in the palace, who was appalled by what was happening. That young fairy was an orphan, who felt himself hopeless and friendless, and yet he risked his own king's wrath and a terrible death to give human children what he did not think he himself would ever have—home, and family, and safety. There is great moral courage among the Fair Folk, just as there is among humans."

"I had no idea," said the lord.

Theo felt it best to let him come to terms with this revelation in his own time, so he stepped into the veil now. He stood just a few feet inside the tunnel and looked out at the girl and her father.

He flicked a little light to his fingertips and shone it around the tunnel. "There is danger here, Miss McStretton. But just like in the human world, and in the Fair Lands, there is courage and wonder and beauty."

She frowned at him and motioned him out.

"Are you frightened of it?" Theo stepped forward.

Her frown deepened, and she shook her head. She pointed at him.

"You're frightened for me?"

She nodded.

Theo's smile softened even more, from reassurance to sweet gratitude. He stepped out of the veil and let the door close behind him.

"That is very kind of you, Miss McStretton," he said gently.

Over another game of chess, he mentioned his Fair friend again, the one who had been an enemy.

She stared at him cautiously.

"I must go this afternoon," he said. "I promised to help him take the Fair ambassador Brookbower back to the Fair Lands." He glanced the girl's father and said, "He is not to return on pain of death, my lord. If and when another Fair ambassador is detailed here, it will be one who has sworn not to take or harm humans."

"And your friend negotiated this?"

"He did." Theo added, "I will not say that my friend always makes himself charming and delightful. But there is far more honor in him than I saw at first, and I think it would benefit you both to speak to each other."

The girl pressed her lips together in a clear sign that she did not intend to speak to anyone, much less a fairy.

"And I will not press the matter again and become a boor, Miss McStretton," Theo said. "Please know that I will accept your decision with utmost respect."

She swallowed and nodded once.

"If I may, I would like to visit you again in a week or two," Theo said.

The girl nodded.

"Thank you," said Theo sincerely.

CHAPTER THIRTY-FOUR
The Fair Delegation Departs

Theo hired a carriage for the drive back to the palace, having decided that he would save his strength for the long walk that awaited him. In the palace, the servant who met him at the door said, "His Majesty requires your presence."

The young man accepted this with a nod.

The servant escorted him through the palace to a door which he had not seen before. The man knocked on the door, and the king's muffled voice said, "Come in."

The servant opened the door and said, "Mr. Overton, Your Majesty." Then he stepped aside.

"What a lovely room, Your Majesty!" Theo exclaimed.

It was true, though the beauty was of a far different sort than that which had provoked a similar reaction in Lord Willowvale's manor. The walls were a blue like the deepest part of the ocean, and the incredibly detailed tapestries which adorned them were in a style no longer fashionable in Aricht. They still had the angular lines which

Willowvale hated, but being older than much of the palace, the angular style was less pronounced. The fabric glinted with golden threads which outlined scenes of epic battles from Arichtan myths and legends.

The floor was carpeted in blue and white and gold, which set off the rich wood tones in the chair in which the king sat.

"You're taking Brookbower and his staff to the Fair Lands," said the king.

"Yes, Your Majesty."

The king crossed his arms and stared at Theo. Finally he said, "How long will it take to get to the Fair Lands from here?"

"I should think at least twelve hours of walking, likely more, though. I should hope to be there by tomorrow morning."

Elmerick sighed. "I suppose I ought to provision you, then."

"It would be very much appreciated, Your Majesty." Theo knew it was no real hardship for the king to provide food and water for the journey, but the Arichtan monarch no doubt resented any kindness to Brookbower.

His Majesty Elmerick said to the servant standing behind him, "Send to the kitchen for a day's provisions for each of them, then, the five fairies and Mr. Overton."

The servant bowed and hurried out.

The king studied the young man again. "Do you think the Fair Folk will honor the terms of our agreement?" he said.

"The Fair Folk keep their word," said Theo flatly. "If you've worded it wisely, then yes, you can trust the agreement."

"I certainly hope I have," muttered the king. "If Willowvale is negotiating in good faith, perhaps we have a little hope."

Theo said modestly, "I have been working for peace with the Fair Court for some time, Your Majesty, and there are those of similar sentiment in the Fair Court as well. I think there is a great possibility of lasting peace now, however difficult the route there seems to have been." Then he said, "What will you do with the assassins?"

The king pressed his lips together and looked away. "I will likely have to execute them. Silverthorn will insist on it, even if Willowvale hasn't pushed the issue yet."

At this moment, the servant returned and indicated that he had a message for the king. At the king's nod, he said, "Lord Willowvale would like an audience before they depart."

"Send him in." The king indicated that Theo could stay.

The Fair lord strode into the room already dressed for travel, though he did not have his bag. He bowed. "Your Majesty. Mr. Overton."

"Willowvale." The king kept his seat, but this did not convey his power as he might have wished. He was forced to look up at the much taller fairy, for this was not the throne room with an elevated throne.

"I came to ask if you wanted to watch us leave, when Mr. Overton returned, as I see he has."

"Yes, I do. I'll meet you at Brookbower's door in half an hour." Then to the servant, he said, "Pack Mr. Overton's things and the provisions for the party."

"Thank you, Your Majesty." Theo bowed and exited the room, and Willowvale did likewise.

Soon the servants had a generous bag of provisions for each of the fairies, and one for Theo.

Brookbower stood with his arms crossed as he stared daggers at Elmerick. Hawksbane, Tarragon, and Fallingwater stood behind him, their faces cold and beautiful, at least as far as most of the humans could tell. Theo, having more experience reading subtle Fair expressions, interpreted their expressions as boredom and irritation with both the humans and Brookbower.

Theo was the last to arrive, having gone by his own suite at the opposite end of the palace before being escorted to the wing where the Fair Folk had been lodged.

"Your Majesty," he greeted the king first, as was proper.

Willowvale nodded curtly at the Fair servants and said, "Mr. Overton, this is Lord Brookbower's staff, Hawksbane, Fallingwater, and Tarragon. Mr. Theodore Overton, IV."

Theo nodded politely at them.

"Overton," Brookbower sneered.

"Brookbower," said Theo cheerfully. Then with a bow to the king, he said, "Thank you for your hospitality, Your Majesty."

The young man knelt and stuffed the bag of provisions into his traveling satchel, for he wanted only one bag to encumber him if he had to use his sword. With a sidelong look, Willowvale did the same.

Scowling, Brookbower snapped to the servants that they should do likewise. Two of them were carrying both their own bags and Brookbower's two bags, and the additional packages had been unwieldy. At last they were ready.

With a twist and a pull of magic, Theo opened the veil.

Brookbower let out an audible gasp of shock, and one of the servants muttered some Fair oath under his breath.

Theo stepped into the veil and gestured gracefully for the others to join him.

"It is safer to travel without a light, so it would be best to maintain contact," Theo said. "Lord Willowvale, are you armed? Would you take the rear? We'll keep the others between us."

Willowvale gave him a flat look and muttered in the Fair language, "The veil hates me."

"More than it hates Brookbower?"

The ambassador blew out a breath. "I doubt it. Don't fret, Willowvale; if it eats you, I'll tell Silverthorn you died valiantly."

Theo said, "I've never lost a friend in a veil, and I don't intend to start now. Tell me if you get into trouble."

Then, with a last bow to the Arichtan king and his guards and servants, Theo let the door close.

CHAPTER THIRTY-FIVE
An Unexpected Apology

Alone in the dark with a former Fair enemy, a hostile Fair ambassador, and three wordless Fair servants, Theo might have been a little concerned, if not exactly frightened.

Instead, he felt a great sense of elation, for the veil's magic pressed upon his mind, excited and eager to please.

"Give me a moment," he said quietly. He pressed both hands to the wall, noting that it now felt like dry, sandy soil, when it had appeared to be damp earth only a few moments earlier when the light of the Arichtan hall had lit the tunnel.

"Why?" snarled Brookbower.

"To feel the magic."

"Don't you know the way?" Brookbower's voice rose.

"Not yet."

The fairies had arranged themselves with Brookbower nearest Theo, the three servants in a line, and then Willowvale at the end.

Someone shifted uneasily behind Theo, tugging on the strap of his satchel, but he focused on the magic.

"Ah!" he said a moment later.

He set off, and the fairies followed in silence.

The tunnel was as dark as pitch and soundless other than the soft noises of their passage.

"How do you find the way?" said Brookbower after some minutes.

"The magic tells me," said Theo.

"That doesn't make any sense!" snapped Brookbower. "How can it tell you anything?"

Theo laughed lightly. "I certainly don't know much about magic or how it works. You Fair Folk have far more magical gifts than I do! All I can say is that I can generally feel out where I want to go, if I'm patient and persistent."

The ambassador growled something savage under his breath, and from the back of the line, Willowvale chuckled softly.

"What are you laughing at?" snarled Brookbower.

"There's very little point in being annoyed at him," said Willowvale.

"He's human! What right does he have to veil magic?" exclaimed the ambassador. "I will not debase myself by seeming awed by it! It is an affront to all Fair Folk!"

Theo said, "I would have thought that you'd be more ashamed of kidnapping children than by learning a human has a type of magic rare even among Fair Folk. Does it make you feel better to know that it has brought me to grief more than once, or that I've proven my love for the Fair Lands with blood?"

Brookbower growled, "Would that you had bled to death! If Silverthorn did not require my return, and if I hadn't vowed not to harm humans, I'd kill you now."

Theo sighed softly, though this was hardly a surprise.

Willowvale said with quiet precision, "If you harm my friend, I will take great personal and professional pleasure in gutting you, Brookbower."

The ambassador stopped abruptly, jerking the strap on Theo's shoulder. "You cannot be serious!" he said in shock. "You would choose the human over your honor and loyalty to the Fair Lands?"

Willowvale flicked a brilliant light to his fingertips, and it lit his pale face with a cold blue light. His eyes glittered. "I would not tarnish my honor in the slightest. Overton has done more for the Fair Lands than both of us together, and that without any obligation whatsoever. Silverthorn would agree."

Brookbower's green eyes widened, and his jaw tensed. His hands clenched and unclenched at his sides.

Theo said gently, "Come, my lords. There is no need for this. I'm sure you are far too rational to actually kill me here in the veil, my lord Brookbower, because you vowed not to harm humans, and also you know your king requires your return."

The ambassador growled inarticulately, and then turned toward the young man. He grabbed the strap of Theo's satchel.

Willowvale let the light fade.

As they set off again, he said, "If I were Overton, I'd leave you somewhere in the dark to let the veil eat you, but since he didn't do that to me, I doubt he will to you either. You ought to be grateful."

Brookbower muttered, "Don't press me, Willowvale. I didn't vow not to kill *you*."

For the first time, one of the servants spoke. Hawksbane said clearly, "Well, I should be glad to return to the Fair Lands at last, and if it takes a human's aid, I am grateful to the human."

"Traitors, all of you," muttered Brookbower.

"My lord!" said Theo. "You know that is not true, however much you feel it to be so. There is no dishonor or treason in what your assistant said, and Lord Willowvale has always and ever done what he believed best for the Fair Lands, first in nearly killing me, and then in accepting my friendship. It is *wrong* to call him a traitor. Call me whatever names you like, but do not speak slanderous lies about your assistants or my friend, if you please."

The Fair lord was startled by this into a miserable silence. For if there was anything at all that Fair Folk prized above the Fair Lands and honor, it was truth itself. As angry and ashamed and horrified as Brookbower had been by Willowvale's friendship with a human, he was even more horrified to find that he had said something factually untrue.

The veil had been particularly amenable during this conversation, and there were no monsters dangerously close, though Theo did have a sense that one lurked some distance ahead. So they walked without another word for nearly half an hour.

Finally Brookbower said, as if it pained him deep in his soul, "If you wish to assert your honor with a sword, Willowvale, I won't defend myself. You have always been above reproach in your loyalty to the Fair Lands, and I was wrong to say otherwise."

Willowvale blew out an irritated huff. "Apology accepted. I don't require blood." Then, more quietly, he added, "I've received grace enough to extend a little to you."

In the darkness, with the magic of the veil swirling in his mind, Theo smiled to himself.

They stopped for dinner late that evening. Even Theo was tired, though he would not have admitted it, but it had become clear that Brookbower and his delegation were growing fatigued. As fairies they were naturally strong and energetic, but having been captive for months, they had grown unused to walking and other exercise, and they were flagging a little. Certainly they could have persevered, but no one protested when Theo suggested a short stop for their meal.

Willowvale flicked a fairy light to his fingertips and let it spread out along the ceiling, revealing that the tunnel opened up only a short distance ahead. Theo strode on to see what awaited them and found that the tunnel opened into a spacious cavern.

Theo added his own light to Willowvale's and let out an awed breath. Their tunnel ended some fifty feet above the cavern floor, which glittered with crystalline shards as long and sharp as swords.

Above them, the distant ceiling threw back the light in dazzling sparks, as brightly faceted as any jewel.

"How will we cross that?" Willowvale said from Theo's shoulder.

"I don't know yet," Theo admitted. "Let's have dinner and we'll see if the veil will give us a way around it if I ask nicely."

Brookbower said, "Does it often oblige you?" in a strange, tight voice.

"I would not exactly say often," Theo said, "but I believe more often than it obliges others. I very much appreciate its cooperative attitude, even if it has nearly killed me more times than I can count."

Tarragon, who had said nothing until now, said, "I am already shocked by human magic, and I will be more shocked if we make it home alive."

Theo grinned at him. "I fully expect to reach the Fair Lands with everyone safely."

Tarragon gave a soft, doubtful grunt but said nothing else.

They ate in silence, and though the food was not fancy, it was delicious, fresh, and appropriate for traveling. Crusty bread soft and chewy on the inside paired nicely with tangy cheese slices and slices of roast beef. Wedges of red and yellow peppers were packed with hot house tomatoes and cucumbers in olive oil and herbs and sealed in little ceramic canisters. Canteens of fresh water washed everything down nicely.

"That was delicious," said Theo, when he was finished.

"Unless we all die of poison," muttered Brookbower darkly.

When they walked again to the end of the tunnel and looked across the cavern of crystal knives, a narrow path curved down the wall to their left and wove across the cavern floor toward the far side, where it vanished into a dark hole in the floor.

"Ah! Thank you!" Theo said, and he pressed his hands to the wall to better convey his gratitude to the magic. It wriggled and squirmed in his mind, bright and cheerful and delighted by his presence, and glad to be recognized.

They crossed the floor of the room, dazzled by glittering crystals on all sides, for they let the light illuminate their way until they reached the dark hole at the other side. Though from a distance it had appeared to be a bottomless hole, when they approached it, they saw that it was really the entrance to a steeply sloped section of tunnel, which turned and then leveled out again.

In the following hours, they had only one terrifying incident when the ground began to turn to quicksand just as Theo stepped out of it.

Brookbower, just behind Theo, lost his balance and nearly dragged Theo down backwards as he fell to hands and knees, with his feet suddenly stuck fast. He began to sink, and Tarragon behind him was nearly as badly stuck.

Fairy light flared to brilliance, illuminating the little group.

Brookbower's situation was quickly becoming dire as the sand sucked him under as if with malicious hunger. Theo dropped his satchel and flopped to his stomach on the earthen floor, wrapping both arms around Brookbower's under his shoulders.

"You're all right," he said to the sputtering fairy. "Lift your legs out straight behind you, if you can."

As Brookbower did so, Theo pulled him forward with strong, steady pressure.

At first it seemed to be pointless, and Brookbower's great strength made no headway against the suction. Tarragon struggled forward, but as he did so, he sank deeper, until his chest heaved with effort and the sand had risen to his hips.

"Just wait, Tarragon," Theo said breathlessly. "Brookbower will be out in a minute."

Brookbower gave a faint scoff of disbelief. Though he had gotten both hands free of the sand and gripped Theo's upper arms, his body had sunk, and he was now entirely engulfed in sand up to his collar. His breath came in gasps, for the sand pressed against his chest, and it was becoming increasingly difficult to get any air at all. His fingers gripped Theo's biceps with bruising strength.

He was face to face with Theo, but he could scarcely draw breath and the fairy lights above were not enough to keep his vision from dimming. His heartbeat thudded raggedly in his ears, and as he fought against the sand and the growing weakness in his limbs and the agonizing need for air, he could feel it slowing.

"Just go on," he muttered, and he let go of Theo.

With a valiant stretch, Theo managed to grasp Brookbower's waistband, and he curled sideways, heaving the Fair lord mostly out of the quicksand with an effort that left him breathless. Another great heave, and the fairy was free. Theo's heart was beating so loudly that for a moment he almost imagined the veil heard it, for the magic seemed to throb with the same rhythm.

The Fair lord was in no better shape; he rolled over on his back and gasped, his eyes closed.

"Tarragon, can you reach me?"

The servant shook his head, his violet eyes dark and hopeless.

"Oh, come on! You might at least try!" said Theo.

Brookbower, muzzy and weak with the rush of air into his bruised lungs, flopped his head over just in time to see Theo throw his satchel to the fairy servant, keeping hold of the strap.

Then, with strong, steady effort, Theo pulled the fairy through the sand.

By the time Tarragon clambered onto the earth beside him, Theo's arms were shaking with fatigue. "You're all right," the young man gasped. He rolled onto his back and closed his eyes as his chest heaved.

"You went to a great deal of effort for a fairy who hates you and a servant," said Brookbower in an odd voice.

Theo nodded, too tired for the moment to even open his eyes.

For several minutes they recuperated in silence. Theo sat up and leaned against the wall with one long leg bent and his arm resting on it. He drank a little water and closed his eyes again, for he was light-headed, aching, and exhausted after such an effort.

Across the short expanse of quicksand, Willowvale gazed at him steadily. Fallingwater and Hawksbane stood with arms crossed behind Willowvale, looking at the ground. Clearly they expected to be left to die in the veil, but Willowvale merely intended to give Theo time to think.

Finally Theo rose to his feet and offered Brookbower a hand. The Fair lord stared at him. "What is that for?"

"To help you stand," said Theo, and there was no mockery in his voice.

From the other side of the quicksand, Willowvale watched with cool amusement as the other lord snarled his refusal and shoved himself wearily to his feet. Tarragon did accept Theo's proffered hand, and Theo hauled him to his feet with a smile.

By this time it was well past midnight, though it was difficult to have any sense of time in the perpetual darkness of the veil. Theo realized that they had been uncommonly fortunate that no dangerous creatures had been drawn to the fairy lights yet, and he said, "Perhaps you could let the lights fade. I know where you are in the dark."

"You do?" Brookbower said in surprise.

In the resulting darkness, Theo pressed his hands to the wall and asked it for a passage around the quicksand. With a little frisson of delight, it obliged, and the damp, cool clay beneath his palms vanished into a new passage.

"Willowvale, if you would just stay where you are, we'll come to you," Theo said, with a smile in his voice. "Brookbower, Tarragon, please stay with me." At the feel of someone's hand on his sand-covered satchel, Theo started forward.

Ten minutes later, the passage had curved around, up, down, and around again. "And here we are!" Theo said triumphantly.

"I thought you had left us," muttered Fallingwater grumpily.

"I said I would come to you," said Theo. "Let's get on to the Fair Lands then. I'm rather fatigued, and I should hate for it to make me ill-tempered."

"Like others in our party?" said Willowvale blandly.

"I was not going to be pointed," laughed Theo.

So they walked on.

CHAPTER THIRTY-SIX
Lord Willowvale's Generosity

They stepped into Willowvale's front garden at dawn.

"That is uncanny skill," said Willowvale under his breath.

"Do you not fear it?" said Brookbower.

"No." Willowvale turned to look at him. "I admire it, yes, but I do not fear it or begrudge it anymore."

Brookbower sighed and sagged. The quicksand that had gotten in his shirt and trousers had chafed him thoroughly, and weariness tugged at every fiber of his body. The servants were just as fatigued, if not more so, and Willowvale and Theo were hardly in better shape.

Grimly Brookbower started toward the palace, and the little party straggled along in the dim early light.

They were met with astonishment by the Fair palace servants.

Silverthorn himself met them in corridor, having hurried from his bed at the word of their return.

His violet eyes gleamed with fascination and surprise, but he said, "You may refresh yourselves and rest before delivering a full report. Overton, you are welcome as a guest here."

"Thank you, Your Majesty."

Willowvale strode back through the garden, vaguely annoyed without knowing exactly why. Perhaps it was because Brookbower was thoroughly insulting and annoying.

In reality, he had looked forward to having Theo as a guest and reciprocating the hospitality Theo had offered him, but he had not yet realized he looked forward to this. So the fact that Theo was now a guest of the crown felt like a loss he could not identify or describe.

He stepped back into his manor and dropped his bag on the floor for one of the servants. He flicked his fingers to tell the magic of the house to call them, and dragged his tired body upstairs.

He bathed in chilly water, too eager for bed to want to wait for it to finishing heating, and crawled up the hanging ladder to his bed with a feeling of gratitude and fuzzy-headed fatigue.

In the palace, the Fair delegation and Theo were doing much the same in their respective rooms. Theo was offered human food, and he ate a little before clambering into the elevated bed in the room he had been given.

Tomorrow he would return to his beloved Lily. But in the meantime, he would get some well-deserved sleep.

The sun was high in the sky, and the streaks of magenta and cobalt were nearly lost in the brilliance of the cerulean depths above. Theo woke with a start to the odd feeling of swaying, and then realized that he had startled himself awake, for the bed swung gently from the gem-crusted ceiling of his Fair bedroom.

Jasmine crept down the wall, filling the air with its sweet scent and nearly obscuring the steps which Theo had ascended earlier that morning. The window frame appeared to be carved of amethyst, and it sent glittering purple light dancing around the room.

He might have drifted off to sleep again, for it was clear that the king intended to let him rest. But his heart burned with desire for his lovely wife, so he dragged himself from the downy warmth of the bed, refreshed himself in the private bathing room attached to the bedroom, and dressed in the last set of clean clothes from his satchel.

The marble floor of his guest room was inset with a thousand tiny bits of mirror, which reflected the flowers and tapestries upon the walls in a dizzying display. Beneath the elevated bed, there was an enormous mound of moss which Theo discovered to be hollow, and inside there was a little space large enough for several adults to crouch together. The floor of this little cave was also moss, but it was covered in a thick carpet of golden flowers that smelled like honey and sunlight.

The creatures in the tapestries on the walls moved, but mostly when he wasn't looking. A little stream of water burst happily from the wall and fell into a pool in which spiny, star-shaped creatures waved pale yellow tentacles at pink, gold, and green fish. Theo thought that on the whole, the room was a particularly good example of Fair style, astonishing both in its beauty and its strangeness.

Theo opened the door and was greeted by a servant who bowed immediately. "If you are ready, Mr. Overton, His Majesty would like to speak with you."

"I am ready." Theo took up his satchel and followed the servant through the halls to a relatively small study which he had never seen before.

The servant knocked on the door and, at a voice from within, opened the door and bowed. He motioned Theo in.

Theo bowed to the king as he entered.

"It seems I owe you thanks yet again for your aid to the Fair Folk," Silverthorn said from where he sat by the fire.

Willowvale, seated at the king's right hand, had stood at Theo's entrance. A strange, secret sort of smile ghosted over his lips, but he said nothing.

Silverthorn gestured to the seat beside him, across from Willowvale. "You may sit, Overton. Tea?"

"Yes, please. Thank you, Your Majesty." Theo sat, acutely aware of the honor the Fair king was according him.

Willowvale sat too. He poured tea for Theo and handed it to him, and then refreshed his own cup and that of the king.

"Is there anything I ought to know that Willowvale would not have already told me?" Silverthorn said with a raised eyebrow.

The young man tilted his head to the side as he thought over the events of the previous days. "I cannot think of anything," he said at last. "I do think it likely Lord Willowvale did not properly convey the skill with which he conducted negotiations. His Majesty Elmerick did not want war, but he was very close to it. Lord Willowvale exercised exceptionally wise judgment in trying circumstances, and I think he should be commended for it."

Silverthorn stared at him. "Hm," he said at last. "Miss Berrydell arrived only a few hours before you did yesterday."

"Oh!" Theo said in delight. "Then I assume Lord Mosswing is here as well?"

"Indeed. He deserves a commendation too." The Fair king's frown deepened. "Faebane. That is a war crime if I've ever heard of one."

Theo swallowed. "Well, I am sure that resuming hostilities would be to the detriment of both the Fair Lands and Aricht."

Willowvale said, "Perhaps we ought to leave the fate of the assassins with the new ambassador, Your Majesty."

Theo blinked and looked at the Fair lord, startled.

Willowvale added, "Even Elmerick would see the justice in that. Then, when Miss Berrydell extends mercy to them, as she is nearly sure to do, it will reflect well on the Fair Lands and likely eliminate any opposition to her among the Arichtans. Even an assassin who hates all Fair Folk could not fail to see the beauty and grace in such a decision."

The young man smiled, for this seemed like a particularly lovely and generous impulse in Willowvale, both toward Miss Berrydell and the Arichtan assassins. For Willowvale too had been nearly murdered, quite painfully, for crimes he had not committed.

His Majesty Silverthorn looked steadily at the Fair lord for nearly a minute before he said, "I cannot appoint a commoner ambassador."

"So give her a title," said Willowvale without hesitation. "Marchioness, at least, to equal Brookbower."

The Fair king put down his tea cup with slow precision and turned to face the lord squarely. "Is that all?" he said in a low voice. "Give a common maiden a title and appoint her ambassador? Let her pardon the assassins who nearly murdered her *and* you, on whom I rely more than anyone else?"

Willowvale shrugged one shoulder, as if none of these points were significant. "If she is the ambassador Elmerick will accept, I see only positives to it. She has proven herself to be of great honor, both in her service to the Fair Lands and among the humans. They prefer her. She speaks the language. She is more than competent to defend herself if necessary, aside from faebane, which none of us could have predicted or countered. Why should she not serve the Fair Lands as ambassador?"

"A marchioness must have lands," muttered Silverthorn.

Willowvale pressed his lips together, for he knew that several estates had reverted to the Fair throne when the lords holding them died during the war.

But the king said nothing.

Finally Willowvale said, "The Kingfisher Valley estate is unassigned, as is Hart's Peak. There is also the Teal Enclave, Athelas Grove, Piper River Valley, Piper Peak, and Sandwash Lake and its environs."

The silence drew out.

"If you will not relinquish any of the royal lands," said Willowvale at last, "you can give her Sable Hill."

Silverthorn blinked. "Who owns that?"

"I do. It's just not part of my title. It's a prosperous little area, sufficient for a marchioness, if rather small. Just don't tell her it was mine."

"Why not?" The king stared at him.

"She wants nothing to do with me. Whatever lands she receives, they ought to come from the crown." Willowvale's voice was steady.

Theo's perceptive sympathy caught the slightest tightness in the Fair lord's voice, but even the king did not seem to notice it, so subtle was this little hint of emotion.

Silverthorn finished his tea and folded his arms. "Fine. I'll give her the Teal Enclave and Athelas Grove. They're both small, but together they seem fit for a marchioness. You are right—her title ought to equal Brookbower's, since she is replacing him." He pressed his lips together and looked at Theo. "Thank you for your assistance in all this, Overton. I should like your guidance in the following weeks, but Willowvale has informed me that you have already been away from your wife and family for longer than you might wish. Therefore, let me express my gratitude."

The king inclined his head, and Theo stood and bowed in return.

"Thank you, Your Majesty." Then he looked at Willowvale. "Thank you, my lord. You are welcome to visit when you have finished your business here, and please do not forget Lord Selby's invitation."

The Fair lord stood and bowed deeply. "Thank you, Mr. Overton. I look forward to our next meeting." And he smiled with such a light of friendship and gratitude in his eyes that it transformed his hard, narrow face into sudden beauty.

CHAPTER THIRTY-SEVEN
Home

The veil smelled of roses, lavender, and steel, and a metallic scent which seemed darkly forboding. Still, Theo encountered no real dangers on his way home. The veil seemed particularly agreeable and eager to please, and it gave him a short route that required only an hour of walking.

Theo stepped out of the veil at the edge of the garden with a sense of gratitude and relief, buoyed by eagerness to see his beloved wife. He opened the front door and heard laughter from the dining room some way distant.

With a smile on his face, he strode down the hall and stepped into the room.

Lily saw him first, and she jumped to her feet and ran to him. "Theo!"

Heedless of the watching eyes of family and friends, Theo embraced her tightly and bent his head to hers. "I missed you, my love," he murmured in her ear, and his voice was so full of love and tenderness she nearly melted in his arms.

CHAPTER THIRTY-EIGHT
The Sword Maker's Shop

"Where is Miss Berrydell now?" asked Lord Willowvale over lunch with the king.

"She gave me a full report of what she knew of the negotiations, the attack, Brookbower's situation, your escape through the veil with her to Overton's house, and Lord Mosswing's healing magic." Silverthorn eyed him as he took a bite of brilliant yellow plumefish. "She told me of your skill in negotiation and of your sympathies to humans you outlined in your letter to her."

Willowvale's pale cheeks flushed faintly, and he took a sip of the sparkling Fair wine to gather his thoughts.

"It seems you were quite gallant," the king said even more quietly.

The Fair lord swallowed. "I did what I thought right," he muttered. "Where is she?"

"After she gave me her report, I told her she could recuperate with her family. It has been nearly two years since she saw them. She is awaiting her next assignment."

"Did she seem well?" Willowvale couldn't help asking.

The king's violet eyes gleamed. "She was as lovely as ever," he said. "Yes, she seemed healthy. Mosswing looked a little pale, but he said he was merely tired. They left the palace at the same time; I offered her an escort, which she refused. I believe he escorted her home before he went to his own estate."

If Willowvale had not already heard from multiple sources that Lord Mosswing was blissfully in love with, and engaged to marry, Lady Poppy Miscanthus, he might have felt a twinge of jealousy at this news. Instead, he was only deeply relieved that Mosswing was kind enough to ensure that Miss Berrydell was not only well, but safely home after all the danger she had endured.

An hour later, Willowvale mounted his horse, or what passed for a horse in the Fair Lands, and rode out of his garden in search of the sword shop of Sedum and Agaricus Berrydell.

The horse was not exactly a horse like those of the human world; for one thing, its body was a deep indigo, and the feathering of the magenta fur on its legs was much longer than on any horse of the human world. Its mane and tail were also magenta. Its eyes glowed yellow in the night, and it had a particular liking for small furry animals, which it crunched gleefully between its jaws. Still, it looked mostly like a horse, and it ate more blue grass and grain than mice or rabbits, and it consented to be ridden with a saddle and bridle like its equine counterparts in the human world.

Dressed in severe silver and white, Willowvale was both dashing and terrifying on this magnificent steed as he trotted up the wide avenue through Dewspring-in-the-Wood toward the Berrydell sword shop.

He could not remember exactly where it was, and he rode up and down several smaller streets before he found the door. The sign hanging above it was faded, and though the glass in the windows was clean and the counter inside was not dusty, the front room was dark and apparently empty.

Willowvale swung down from his mount and pounded upon the door, loudly so that if Sedum or Agaricus were somewhere in the back, they would be sure to hear. He wondered if they lived above the shop, and if Miss Berrydell were there, and he hoped fervently that they did not, and she was not.

He waited for some minutes, and then pounded again.

A door opened behind him, and he turned to see a fairy looking at him across the street.

"They can't hear you. They're around the back." The fairy pointed to the end of the street. "Go around to the right and then right again, and you'll find the other entrance."

"Thank you." Willowvale jumped back into the saddle and trotted to the end of the lane.

The next street was narrower, and the next so narrow that Willowvale wondered whether the fairy was mistaken. Still, he found the next door and knocked upon it, holding the reins in his other hand.

The door opened almost immediately.

The fairy bowed. "May I help you?" The fairy had bright orange hair, even brighter than Theo's unruly curls, though this fairy's hair stuck up like thistledown above his pale, sharp face.

"Agaricus Berrydell?"

"Yes." The fairy stared at him with a slight frown. "I don't know you, though."

"Lord Ash Willowvale, Marquess." Willowvale watched with a faint sense of satisfaction as the younger fairy bowed again more deeply. "I would like to commission some swords."

The fairy licked his pale lips. "You fought in the war against Aricht, I believe."

"I did."

"Are the swords to be used for a similar purpose?"

"No."

Agaricus chewed his lip for a moment. "Let me get my father, my lord. Will you meet us in the front?"

Willowvale nodded.

A few minutes later, Willowvale stood in front of the shop watching through the glass as Agaricus flipped the locks on the other side of the door. The younger fairy opened it and stood aside to welcome Willowvale in, while his father bowed deeply.

Sedum Berrydell was older, but like most adult fairies, it was difficult to guess his age with any accuracy. His hair was a rich scarlet, and his eyes were a similar hue, which would have been unsettling to human eyes but was merely striking to Willowvale. He had unusually broad shoulders for a fairy; his sleeves were rolled up to his elbows, and his bare forearms were corded with lean muscle.

"I was told you make swords of rare quality, but I have been remiss in not commissioning blades until now. I would like three swords—no, four—the best you can make."

"For yourself?" said Sedum quietly.

"One is for me. The others are gifts."

"My lord, with all due respect, I do not make weapons for use against humans, and I understand you have long been an enemy of humans." Sedum bowed slightly, but there was an edge of defiance in it, as if he fully expected to defend himself against a sudden attack.

"The recipients of the gifts are humans," Willowvale said.

"I will not make weapons to harm the bearers," said Sedum.

"I do not expect you to!" said Willowvale, losing patience. "They are gifts of gratitude and friendship, and I expect them to be exquisite! Don't you want the business?"

"I want to make blades of quality to be used honorably, my lord," said Sedum evenly. "I know who you are, Lord Willowvale; your reputation precedes you."

"Then you must be aware that the Rose now calls me friend, and I am honored to call him a friend as well," Willowvale said. He took a deep breath and willed himself to keep his tone even, though he could not make it warm. "You must know that Lord Bayberry and I shared the honor of killing Lord Larch in defense of Mr. Overton, the Rose."

Sedum's eyes flickered, and he said more carefully, "I heard garbled rumors that Larch was dead by your hand, or Bayberry's, but I thought it was out of obligation. I did not think you bold enough to call the Rose a friend."

"He called me a friend first," said Willowvale, with a despairing thought that he might be forced to explain the whole mortifying series of events to this stranger. "I merely returned, after much effort on his part, what he had already wrought by sheer force of will."

He took a deep breath and steadied himself, for he felt an odd urge to weep. The deep breath did not help, and suddenly his eyes were damp. He brushed at them and said brusquely, "Now, do you see? I want a gift worthy of the Rose, full of honor and protection for him, and as beautiful and full of grace as friendship itself. The other gift is for his friend, and it should be just as magnificent. And one for me, because I implied to your daughter I would look in at your shop. And a fourth, like the others, but for Lord Mosswing, because he saved my life and that of your daughter."

He swallowed an unpleasant lump in his throat and stared at the sword maker.

"Do you see?" he said again. "I want to give gifts worthy of friends more honorable than myself. I don't care how much they cost."

The sword maker gave the faintest smile and bowed more deeply. "My art is always in the service of honor and friendship, my lord," he murmured.

Willowvale composed his face and set a small, heavy bag on the counter. "Is ten thousand an adequate deposit? I want the blade for the Rose's friend by the end of next week, even if the others are not yet ready."

Agaricus twitched but said nothing.

Sedum said, "Let us discuss the specifics of the design and take measurements. How tall is he? How long of arm?"

They spent some time measuring Willowvale and adjusting the measurements as Willowvale described Fenton as nearly the same height as himself and broader of shoulder. They decided upon a hilt with gold inlay and a magnificent ruby fit for a king in the pommel. Sedum sketched the designs for the inlay in the hilt and upon the guard, and Willowvale nodded his approval.

"The Rose is very close in height to his friend, but leaner."

"Emerald for the pommel?" murmured Sedum as he sketched a different design.

"I think so." The designs taking shape were even more beautiful than Willowvale had anticipated.

Sedum said, "This one will be done first, and you can pick it up a week from tomorrow. The others will be done in a month, if not earlier."

The Fair lord rode away with his head high, ignoring the curious looks of the common fairies in the streets. He slept that night with a sense of melancholic satisfaction, for it was good to be in his own bed again, and he had at least begun to fulfill his word to Miss Berrydell, and the gifts he had commissioned were handsome indeed.

But it was impossible not to be a little melancholy, after all.

The next days were filled with preparations for Willowvale's return to Aricht. He and the king spent quite some time talking over the terms of the agreement with Aricht and of the letter of appointment which would be presented to Miss Berrydell.

At last, after countless cups of tea and a not-insignificant amount of Fair wine, they were both satisfied that every detail had been covered. Willowvale, drained and bleary-eyed, was glad to allow a scribe to write the final copies of each document. Besides his fatigue, he did not want Miss Berrydell to see the letter of appointment written in his hand.

That evening he went to the sword-maker's shop, though it was a day earlier than Sedum had promised.

"It isn't ready yet, my lord."

"Do you need another day?"

"We will work through the night to have it ready for you tomorrow, my lord." Sedum bowed.

The Fair lord thought of going to Overton manor, and Fenton's wedding, and the days in between, and the necessity of going to Aricht and how long it would take, and he said at last, "I would rather have it perfect than have it done tomorrow. I will come back in two days."

"Thank you, my lord." Sedum bowed again.

Making such a sword in scarcely a week was already an incredible feat. Willowvale said impulsively, "I am grateful for your attention to detail. Do you need more than two days?"

"No, my lord. It will be ready."

"Thank you." Willowvale nodded and trotted away.

The following morning he racketed around his manor trying to think of things to fill the time. He had Alyssum pack two weeks of meals in his traveling bag, along with his clothes and personal items. In the afternoon he drank far too much tea and sat by the fire and tried to read.

He waited until after lunch before saddling his monster and heading back to the shop of Sedum and Agaricus.

They were waiting for him, and the sword was ready, laid upon a velvet cushion ready for his inspection. The rubies upon the scabbard and the larger ruby in the hilt gleamed.

The Fair lord took it up reverently and stepped closer to the windows, letting the light play upon the razor-sharp blade and the glittering golden inlay.

Of course fairies could not touch steel, so he had caught up the velvet too, but the leather-wrapped hilt and gold-clad pommel and guard were safe. He gripped the hilt and held the sword up, feeling the perfection of the balance and how deliciously fast and light it was, with just the barest possible weight to aid one's strikes.

"It is magnificent," he said at last. "Worth every penny." He turned to Sedum. "Take as long as you like on the others. The one for me may come last." He slid the sword into the scabbard and smiled at the precise, smooth feeling. "How much will they cost?"

Sedum said, "That one is twelve thousand."

Willowvale stared at him. "This is worth at least fifteen. Why do you say twelve?"

The sword maker's scarlet eyes flicked away and then back. "You saved my daughter's life at great personal cost. I ought to give it to you as a gift, but I thought you would not accept it."

"Absolutely not," Willowvale said.

"Moreover, if I think only of business, we have not had work in over a year, and it was scarce for years before that. I would rather give you a low price and get all four commissions than have you walk away now."

Willowvale smiled, and he felt oddly light and free. "I cannot think of a better use of money than to delight my friends, and if I can simultaneously lend a little long-overdue aid those who stood on noble principles to their own detriment, so much the better." He put another heavy bag on the counter and said, "This will finish payment for this sword and serve as a deposit on the others."

He turned to go, and then stopped. "Is she well?"

"Yes," Sedum said simply. "Thank you, Lord Willowvale."

Willowvale nodded once, his throat tight. "Good day."

He showed the king the sword that evening. "Sedum and Agaricus are still around. Did you know?"

"I didn't," said the king darkly.

"It would be a shame to let such a talent fade for lack of use." Willowvale admired how the light caught the fine gold inlay in the scabbard. He pulled the sword out a few inches to show the king the bright polish on the steel.

"It would be no shame to let a traitor's shop perish," growled the king.

"Your Majesty," said Willowvale in a low voice. "They did no harm to the Fair Lands, save in not giving their gifts to the cause of a war which they believed unjust."

The king muttered something under his breath. "Why are you telling me this?" he said more clearly.

Willowvale shrugged one shoulder. "Oh, did you know Sedum and Agaricus are Berrydells? I had forgotten, or I never knew."

His Majesty Silverthorn gave him a sidelong look. "You have a great deal of interest in the Berrydells, do you not?"

The Fair lord said, "I promised Miss Berrydell I would look in on her father's shop. She felt they were frozen out deliberately and unjustly. I find myself in agreement with her, and I aim to raise the status of their shop as their talent and skill deserve."

Silverthorn hissed out a breath through his teeth. "Is this because of your friendship for humans or your affection for Miss Berrydell or both? Or some other reason altogether?"

Willowvale looked at the fire. "Miss Berrydell is not interested in my affections," he said in a low voice. "But that does not mean I intend to break my word to her to right the injustice done to her family. Their exceptional skill has overruled any sense of magnanimity I might have enjoyed, and I feel that I have benefited far more than I ought to from what was intended to be a generous act."

The king put down his glass of wine and leaned forward to meet Willowvale's eyes. "Do you want me to commission a sword from them, then?" he said.

Willowvale blinked and looked at the king more closely. "I would consider it an act of friendship," he said, surprised. "But I do not ask it of you."

The king snorted softly and sat back. "All right. You've asked very little for what you have suffered on behalf of the Fair Lands. I can buy myself an excellent sword, and you can call it an act of friendship if you like."

The Fair lord's pale lips curved in a quiet smile. "Thank you, Your Majesty," he murmured.

CHAPTER THIRTY-NINE
Miss Berrydell at Home

T he Fair woman had, upon arriving home, stayed up far too late telling her father and brother of everything she could think of about the years since she had seen them, from the styles of the Arichtan court and the caution with which she and the other members of the Fair delegation had been viewed to Brookbower's acerbic personality. It was near dawn when she finally pled fatigue and said she would tell them the rest the following day.

Her father fixed her childhood favorite breakfast the next day when she woke, though it was after lunch time. Fried blue eggs, fluffy pink cloud scones made from scratch, baked pears topped with fresh golden cheese, and steaming plum cider. She wrapped herself in her familiar robe and sheepskin slippers, which she had left at home so long ago, and told Sedum and Agaricus how she had found herself recuperating in Valestria from faebane, having been carried through the veil by Lord Ash Willowvale.

"Do you think you misjudged him?" said Sedum gently.

Astrantia's pink eyebrows drew downward. "Perhaps a little. Perhaps he changed, too. Perhaps he does not know who he really is. I certainly can't tell what sort of lord he is!"

The note he had given her before his meeting with the king, in which he explained the disappearance of plants in her room, came to mind. The dispassionate despair in his words, as if his death were inevitable, struck her with a strange poignancy, for in this pessimism he had still taken the time to explain this action to her, as if she had a claim upon his talent, and as if he wanted her to understand that in this, too, he served the Fair Lands.

Only a few hours later, Willowvale visited the shop to begin the commissions. Astrantia was sleeping at the time in her room at the opposite end of the house, so she did not hear Willowvale's arrival or any of his conversation with her father and brother. The faebane had left her a little more tired than usual, and though she did not exactly feel ill, her father had convinced her to rest, and the safety and comfort of her family home made it easier than at any time in the past three years.

That evening they ate a comforting stew that Sedum had started simmering just after lunch, so that Astrantia would feel completely free to rest and recuperate.

The sword maker put a bowl before his daughter and said, "He came by this afternoon."

"Why?" Astrantia stared at him.

"He commissioned four swords. One for himself and three as gifts."

The Fair maiden frowned. "He said he would inquire about the investigations into the vandalism," she said. "He did not indicate any intention to commission blades. For whom are they intended?"

"The Rose, a friend he did not identify, and Lord Mosswing." Sedum studied his daughter's face. "He was adamant that the swords be worthy of the most honorable of friends, and he didn't care how much they cost."

A strange, unpleasant pang of regret made Astrantia let out a sigh. What a difficult, disagreeable fairy! "Was he rude to you?" she asked, half-expecting her father to say that the lord had been rude. Of course he had been rude! Willowvale was always rude, unless he was bestowing unpleasant, unwanted compliments upon innocent, unsuspecting Fair maidens.

Her father frowned. "Not really."

"He must have been," Astrantia muttered.

"He was no more unpleasant than any other lord," said Sedum. "He seemed tired and… raw… and after what you said happened, I can't blame him. He cares very much for the Rose and his friend, and his gratitude and respect for Lord Mosswing were genuine."

Astrantia sighed and put her head in her hands.

CHAPTER FORTY
A Wedding Gift

It was agreed that the Fair king would send the letter of appointment to Miss Berrydell by way of royal messenger to her family home, which was attached to the sword shop Lord Willowvale had visited. Willowvale had been acutely conscious of the fact that Miss Berrydell was likely nearby when he had visited the shop, but he had not realized that the family home was in the same structure.

At Willowvale's request, His Majesty Silverthorn did not send the letter of appointment to Miss Berrydell until Willowvale was ready to depart for Valestria.

The Fair lord woke early, ate a quick breakfast, and set out into the veil.

The veil hardly opposed him at all for the first two hours of his walk though there was an ominous buzzing that followed him for some time. When he lengthened his already hurried strides away from it, the ground disappeared beneath his feet, and he fell for two heart-stopping moments.

Then he splashed into icy water.

The shock of the cold and the sudden immersion, coupled with the unexpected fall itself, were enough to drive the air from his lungs, and he swam upward with a panicked stroke. His satchel dragged him downward.

His head burst from the water, and he gasped for breath, treading water. Thin strands of something wrapped around his legs, and he kicked away, encumbered by the two swords belted at his waist. He conjured a light.

There! There was a rocky outcropping. The frigid water sucked the strength from his muscles, and by the time he reached this relative safety, it was all he could do to heave himself onto the slick stone. His hands slipped and his arms shook, so it took more than one try too, which he would have found embarrassing if anyone had been there to see it, and if he'd had the energy left to be anything other than desperate.

The slick rock sloped down toward the water, so he nearly slid back in as he flopped onto his face and crawled up the incline.

Something caught at his trouser leg, and he jerked away, his brave heart pounding in sudden terror. When he flicked light to his fingertips again and let it spread in a bright mist, he saw only the swirl of something disappearing beneath the black water.

He let the light fade, for he did not want to attract anything else while he caught his breath. His pulse thudded, and he shivered violently, for the stone beneath him was as cold as the water, and his wet clothes were leeching out what little warmth was left in his body.

There was a magical technique to dry clothes, but he was shaking so badly he could hardly gather the magic to do it. Finally he shoved himself upright, shivering uncontrollably. He was no longer dripping, but his clothes were still damp and cold, and they chafed as he set out again.

He walked for nearly an hour, and as he forced himself onward, he warmed a little. He tried again to dry his clothes, but he was too tired to get the fiddly bits of the magic quite right, and it had never been his area of skill anyway. So he pushed on, his mind full of the heavy, dangerous magic of the veil, eager to drop him down a bottomless shaft or let a shadow creature eat him at any moment. The constant wariness wore upon his nerves.

When he finally felt the familiar magic near Ardmond, he opened the door, trembling with relief and fatigue and a chill so deep he felt he would never be warm again. He found himself on an unfamiliar hillside, with the winter wind cutting through his still-damp clothes and sweeping the snow from the top of the hill into a glittering cloud above his head. When he looked around, he could not see the road to Ardmond that he expected. He staggered to the top of the hill and found himself looking down at the road, and to his great relief recognized the turn ahead as relatively close to the Overton manor.

With an exhausted sigh, he dragged himself down the hill and down the road and up the long, curving drive. He knocked on the door and waited, shivering.

The servant opened the door to him with a surprised, "Lord Willowvale!"

Willowvale was so cold he could barely think. "May I…"

"Come in out of the cold, my lord." Anselm opened the door wider and ushered the fairy into the stillness and warmth of the entry hall. The servant's quick eyes took in Willowvale's rumpled clothes and noted the trembling of his hand upon the strap of the satchel over his shoulder. The fabric of his clothes did not show its dampness, but the satchel did.

"Thank you," Willowvale said numbly.

"I'll stir the fire in the blue room, and you can wait there while I fetch Mr. Overton. Would you like some tea, too?" Anselm led the fairy down the hall.

"I would." The fairy felt a sudden rush of gratitude at the servant's simple kindness, and it nearly brought tears to his eyes.

The coals were banked, but Anselm put two more logs on the fire and stirred the coals until they glowed. "There you are," he said. "I'll let Mr. Overton know you're here."

"Thank you." Willowvale's frozen fingers could barely loosen their grip on the strap of his satchel. He let it down to the floor and stood upon the hearth, with the heat of the fire upon his calves and rising to warm his legs and back.

He was still damp, but his shivering faded. He closed his eyes and leaned back against the warmth of the stone.

"Good morning, Ash." Theo's voice startled him out of the hazy fatigue that had begun to envelop him.

"Good morning." Willowvale smiled, without even thinking about it, for it was nice to hear the sound of a friend's voice. "I wonder if I might be able to ask you to help me get to Aricht again."

"Of course you may, and of course I will agree," said Theo good-naturedly. "You look cold. What happened?" He stepped into the room, and Willowvale realized that Mrs. Overton, Lord Selby, and Miss Firethorn had accompanied him. They all greeted him in turn, and, somewhat embarrassed, he stepped off the stone hearth and bowed to them.

"The veil dropped me in frigid water," he said, as if in apology. As soon as he stepped away from the fire to bow to them, he felt cold all over again. A human would have been in worse shape, and he was not yet in grave danger from the cold; still, it was thoroughly exhausting and demoralizing to be so deeply chilled.

To distract himself from his discomfort, he said abruptly, "This is for you, Selby. A wedding gift. Since you're here, I might as well not make you wait for it."

He unbuckled the sword on his right hip, held it horizontally in both hands, and bowed deeply as he stepped forward to present it to Fenton. It was a formal gesture in the Fair Court, though swords this magnificent were hardly a common gift, even between close friends or family.

The ruby in the pommel caught the light from the window and glittered, red as blood. The smaller rubies set around the rim of the scabbard gleamed.

He waited, head bowed and arms extended.

"Willowvale, I…" Fenton seemed unable to speak for a moment. "This is too extravagant! This must have cost a fortune!" He stepped forward and lifted the sword in its scabbard reverently. "I can't accept this."

The Fair lord dug in his jacket pocket and found a coin. "Here." He pressed the coin into Fenton's hand.

The young man looked at him in confusion. "What is that for?"

Theo murmured, "Give it back to him."

Fenton put the coin back in Willowvale's open hand. "I can't accept this, or the sword." His dark eyes were concerned, not even glad of the gift the fairy had given him. "I wasn't angling for an extravagant gift from the Fair Lands when I invited you to the wedding, Willowvale. You must know that. Don't you?"

He offered the sword to the fairy, who raised his hands in protest and stepped back to put his shoulders against the warm stone again.

"Selby, you wouldn't know how to be selfish if your life depended upon it," the Fair lord said. "Of course I know you didn't expect a gift! I wanted to give it to you, and I hope you like it."

The young man swallowed and looked at the weapon in his hands. "It is beautiful," he said softly. "I don't know why you should give me such a gift. If anyone ought to have a gift from you, it should be Theo."

"It is a wedding gift," said the fairy again. "Besides, I have one for Theo commissioned as well. I wanted to have yours finished in time for the wedding."

The two young men looked at him, and Willowvale felt his cheeks heat a little, the only warmth in his thoroughly chilled body. He added, "It is a gift in the human tradition, if you must think of it as a gift at all. As far as I am concerned, you purchased it from me."

"Is that why you gave me the coin?" Fenton laughed softly. "You fairies are tricky creatures. I'm glad you're a friend of mine rather than an adversary."

Startled, Willowvale laughed aloud. "You say that to me? You, who have been friends with Theo for years?" He sagged against the warm stone, tired and suddenly too comfortable to mind the fact that these humans could see that he was shivering and fatigued. Then, more quietly, he said, "I am glad we are friends too."

Anselm stepped in with a tray of teacups and saucers, a steaming pot of tea that smelled of vanilla and butterscotch, and a plate full of petite cream puffs and tiny blackberry scones.

"Come, sit," said Theo.

Willowvale mustered up the effort to try one more time to dry his clothes, but didn't manage much. "I think I'd like to change into some dry clothes," he admitted.

Theo reached out to touch his shoulder and exclaimed, "Of course! You must be half frozen! Come." He led the fairy down the hall to a guest room and said, "I'll ask Anselm to prepare a hot bath to help you warm up. We'll have lunch and you can rest a little. Then we'll decide whether to leave this afternoon or tomorrow."

"As soon as you can, please."

An hour later, Willowvale was enjoying steaming tea in a new dry suit with warm dry socks on his feet. His wet clothes were hung near the fire in his suite, and his boots steamed in the heat. He felt a little silly wearing socks with no boots, but Lily and Crocus had apparently retreated to the library some time earlier, so at least he was not so disrobed in front of the ladies. Anselm had replaced the empty plate of pastries with a full one, for the fairy's benefit, and was nearly finished preparing lunch.

"Why did you want me to purchase the sword from you?" Fenton asked with interest.

The fairy took a sip of tea and said, "Fair Folk can give gifts in the human tradition, and I have done so before. But I did not want you to doubt my intentions. It is customary in the Fair Lands to give the recipient the money to purchase the gift, so as to make it absolutely clear to all concerned that the recipient has not been put in the giver's debt. It is considered courteous, even when unnecessary." He closed his eyes, tired and warm and comfortable, and inhaled the butterscotch and vanilla scent of the tea. "But I do not keep a tally of favors between friends."

So they sipped their tea in a tranquil silence for some time.

Finally Theo said, "How urgent is it that we reach Aricht tonight?"

By now, the Fair lord had become more than a little drowsy, but he took a deep breath and focused his thoughts. "I suppose there will not be a war if I wait until tomorrow, but I must make arrangements for the new ambassador in Aricht, and I do hope to be able to attend Lord Selby's wedding."

At this moment Anselm entered with lunch, and the young men smiled their thanks at him.

"Nearly three weeks remain before the wedding," said Fenton.

The fairy frowned thoughtfully to himself. It would take several days to acquire the property, and several more days to improve it as he intended. Obtaining the Arichtan king's signature on the agreement would not take long.

Still, travel in the veil was never predictable, as that very morning had proven, and he did not want to arrive at the wedding late, soaking wet, exhausted, and foul-tempered. Finally, he said, "I would like to be back in Ardmond by the day before the wedding.

"You will stay here, of course," Theo said.

"I hate to impose upon you further, but the veil has been especially challenging of late, at least for me, and I would like to arrive on time, dry, and clean. I thought I would rent a room in Ardmond."

"Is my hospitality not satisfactory?" Theo raised his eyebrows in mock offense.

Willowvale blinked at him, rather sure he had missed the joke but too fuzzy-headed to figure it out. "It is more generous than I deserve," he said flatly.

Theo chuckled. "You are more than welcome here, my friend. I insist, unless it will cause you actual inconvenience to stay here."

"I do expect to reciprocate the hospitality at your convenience," said Willowvale.

"And I will be honored to accept."

By the time they finished eating, the fairy felt much revived, though the morning's fatigue still lingered at the edges of his awareness.

After a quick conversation with Lily, who had known to expect this trip since Theo's return from his previous trip, a similarly quick conversation with his parents, and a note to be delivered to the palace, Theo slung his pack over his shoulder and returned downstairs to find Willowvale and Fenton enjoying another cup of tea in a companionable quiet.

"Farewell," said Theo with an affectionate smile.

"Farewell, Theo, Willowvale." Fenton bowed.

CHAPTER FORTY-ONE
Beauty and Honor

Half an hour into their otherwise quiet walk, Willowvale said, "Thank you for coming, Theo."

"You're welcome."

Theo found another shortcut, and so they reached Aricht in just under eight hours. It was well after dark, but not yet so late that either of them thought it necessary to find lodging outside the palace.

"Lord Willowvale and Mr. Overton. The king is expecting us," said Willowvale to the guard.

Soon Willowvale was meeting with the king again, for Elmerick did not want to wait until the following day to be assured that Silverthorn was not readying his forces for an invasion. Once the Fair lord had given him the agreement to read at his leisure that night, Willowvale and Theo were escorted to the guest suites they had occupied previously.

They ate dinner in their own rooms, for it seemed pleasant to both of them to climb into bed as quickly as possible.

The following day, Theo visited Sir Briscoe and his family while Willowvale spoke with Elmerick. Over another quiet game of chess under the supervision of Sir Briscoe, Charity smiled a few more times. Not many, but a few.

"Have you ever done anything you regret?" Theo asked.

The little girl stared at him.

"Told a lie, maybe, or said something rude to your mother or father?"

She looked down. A tiny little nod.

"The Fair Folk feel shame just like we do," Theo said. "Oh, look! You can take my rook with your queen." He glanced at her from under his copper lashes, seeing that she was listening cautiously. "Just like humans, they're not always good at understanding their emotions, and certainly not good at admitting them.

"Still, they can grow and change, just like we humans do. I dare say you're braver now than you were last year, aren't you?"

Charity swallowed. She looked down at the board and back up at him. Finally she nodded once, firmly, as if she had come to a decision.

"Do you think you might be willing to receive my friend for a short visit? He won't be in town long; he's preparing the lodging for the new Fair ambassador."

The girl looked at him steadily, and he felt that she wanted more information.

"I can't say much more about that. It isn't my place, of course."

The girl looked down at the chess pieces and put a finger on her remaining rook without moving it.

Theo smiled, and she took the hint, taking his knight. She looked up to meet his eyes and nodded.

"You are willing?" he clarified.

She nodded again.

"I'll bring him tomorrow and introduce him. Thank you." He smiled reassuringly. He asked Sir Briscoe if he would consent to the visit, and the man agreed, albeit reluctantly, on the condition that Theo would swear to run the fairy through if he offered any harm to Charity. Theo vowed this solemnly.

The following morning the Fair lord and his human friend were escorted by the royal guards to the house Brookbower and his staff had occupied during their years in Idosa. The lease was set to expire, and the landowner did not wish to rent to Fair Folk again, given recent events. He did, however, allow them into the house to retrieve any items and personal effects belonging to the Fair delegation.

"You don't have to come in," said Willowvale to Theo as the young man hopped out of the carriage after him.

"Do you not want me to?"

Willowvale shrugged, grimacing faintly. "I suppose there is no harm in it, but I imagine it will be boring." He had a large bag slung over his shoulder, which Theo imagined was likely to have the same delightfully convenient magic which he had previously observed on Willowvale's trunks in Valestria, which would enable nearly anything to fit inside, and reduce the weight to the bearer.

Theo shrugged philosophically. "I came to Ardmond in service of a friend. I would hate to abandon him just because the trip included a task that was less than exhilarating."

So together they explored the house. It was a luxurious three-story row house, at the end of the row, with a large side yard, very near the palace. While the most personal of items had been brought to the palace at Willowvale's earlier demand and thus been taken back to the Fair Lands by Brookbower, Hawksbane, Tarragon, and Fallingwater, the rooms were hardly bare.

All of the rooms had multiple vases of long-dead flowers. All four of the beds in their separate rooms had been lifted on wooden risers so that the fairies must have slept near the plaster ceilings. Perhaps they had glamoured the ceilings to be more pleasing to Fair eyes, to look like glittering crystals or vibrant leaves or flowers.

With some investigation, it became clear that while they had enjoyed the food, flowers, and minor comforts of Idosa, none of the fairies had brought much of personal significance that had not been already returned to them. They identified a few books and trinkets as items that the fairies had likely brought from the Fair Lands, and a few other items purchased in the human world that they might desire to keep.

Still, there was less to carry back to the Fair Lands than Willowvale and Theo had expected. They also gathered all the minor furnishings necessary for a house to function, dishes and cutlery and washbasins, and stuffed them into Willowvale's bag.

They climbed back into the carriage well before noon.

The driver had already been instructed where to go, for the king had required that the new delegation was to lodge closer to the palace in a house of his choosing. He had informed Willowvale of the location that very morning, and Willowvale's grim conclusion was that the king intended to better surveil the new ambassador.

"Can you really blame him?" asked Theo. "Besides, I cannot imagine Miss Berrydell will say or do anything that would reflect badly upon the Fair Lands."

"Of course she will not!" Willowvale muttered. "Still, I cannot be pleased that she will be under such scrutiny. It is uncomfortable to have one's every move watched."

Theo eyed him. "That sounds like the voice of experience," he said mildly.

"My childhood was hardly pleasant," Willowvale said grimly. "I would not wish it upon anyone, much less someone I had hoped to make happier by this assignment."

"Well, I am reasonably sure that no one in Aricht has much facility with the Fair language at all, so her private conversations will likely remain mostly private."

The fairy glared out the window at the passing buildings but refrained from other argument.

"What plans do you have for the building?" asked Theo.

"Flowers."

The young man smiled at the fairy's fierce expression. "I'm sure it will be lovely," he murmured.

Light and shadow flickered over their faces as they passed through the streets. At last they drew up to a row house, just as large as the previous one, though on the east side of the palace rather than the west. Like the other, it was an end unit, with a garden that was quite small compared to either Willowvale's or Theo's estates, but expansive considering the central location of the home within the city.

The Fair lord jumped out of the carriage and surveyed the front of the building with a scowl.

"What's wrong with it?" said Theo in the Fair language, for he did not intend to convey more insult to the Arichtan throne than necessary.

"All the plants are dead," Willowvale muttered. "And it's hideous."

To be fair, Elmerick had not known how very displeasing it would be to Fair senses.

"It's winter!" chuckled Theo. "It will be prettier in a few months."

"It will be lovely by the end of the week," growled Willowvale. He stalked up the brick walk to the wide white-roofed patio and examined the door, which had been freshly painted a cheerful blue overlaid with an intricate, angular design meticulously painted in gold. He curled his lip, but did not voice whatever insulting statement of dissatisfaction he might have been thinking.

He had been given the key that morning, and he dug it out and opened the door.

The rooms were bright and freshly cleaned, and he sighed in relief. He and Theo explored the rooms, noting the beveled glass transoms above the windows that looked out upon the rear garden. The house was sparsely furnished, with beds and armoires but no kitchen cutlery or other small but necessary items. Willowvale was not surprised by this; some of these items were among those that he had taken from the other house.

Together the fairy and his friend wrote a list of everything necessary for the house to be made comfortable that it did not already have. Then Willowvale began to make beauty from the lifeless and frost-covered garden.

There was a sad little excuse for a fish pond near the southern corner, more than half covered by brown vines and dead cannas. The fairy's first attentions were to this area; in an hour or so, Willowvale's fragrant white jasmine and climbing roses had overtaken and consumed the brown creepers, covered the brick wall behind the pond, and begun blooming with joyful abandon. Willowvale threw himself on the ground to sit with legs outstretched, leaning back against a neglected myrtle. He pressed his hands to the ground.

Over the following hour, the tree began to sprout leaves on its previously dry branches, and enormous clusters of buds burst into magenta blooms. In the pond, a little group of lily pads provided shelter for the minnows that had been struggling to survive. The ground grew paths of moss which would lead some fortunate inhabitant from the rear patio of the house in one of several winding routes through the space.

Theo watched in admiration as azaleas, forsythia, and burning bushes grew behind irises, lilies, and dahlias. From dry, brown brush the fairy produced exuberant mounds of oxalis and phlox, rock cress and forget-me-not, as well as more exotic plants even Theo could not identify.

"I confess I cannot help with this," Theo said eventually. "Would you like me to purchase the household items or interview servants or something else?"

The Fair lord looked up at him gratefully. "Thank you, Theo. Whatever you think best would be much appreciated." His mind was full of green beauty, moss and flowers and graceful arches of branches grown to frame artfully cultivated vignettes. His vision of the garden was bright and welcoming, and there was much to do in this winter barrenness.

Theo left quietly, and the fairy focused on the magic. He imagined the view of the garden from the back patio; this little nook between two new burning bushes would be a sheltered little enclave, but it needed color during the spring and summer, so he grew clumps of pink and white daffodils, and yellow daffodils, and purple hyacinths, and then a purple clematis to climb the wall nearby. This area here would be framed by the myrtles, and it would look best with delphiniums and foxgloves.

The magic of the human world did not cooperate with him nearly as effortlessly as the magic of the Fair Lands, and he was hampered by his limited knowledge of the plants of the human world. If he had been doing this task in the Fair Lands, it would have been a matter of hours to bring the garden into full, exuberant life, and the time required would have been just as much dependent upon his ability to imagine what he wanted as the actual magical effort itself.

But here in the human world, he was forced to ask the magic what plants would best serve his vision for color and size and bloom time, for he did not want the garden to be completely locked in the full bloom of summer. Plants and flowers bloomed at different times of year, and the Fair Folk appreciated the beauty of each season. Still, he extended the bloom times of each flower, so that the daffodil blooms overlapped the blooms of the irises for a full two weeks, and the myrtles both bloomed earlier and kept their blooms later into fall. The blooms were larger and brighter, the greens richer, than in any garden devoid of Fair magic.

Theo returned in late afternoon, having arranged to interview several servants the following morning at the house and ordered nearly all the necessary household goods.

He knocked on the door but received no answer. After a second knock, which also produced no answer, he frowned and strode around the house. There was a low fence and a rickety gate, which Willowvale had obviously not yet improved, but beyond this, the garden was a riotous profusion of greenery and blooms emanating from the southeastern corner of the garden, where Theo had last seen Willowvale near the pond. The area nearest the gate was still untouched, all dry, brown grass and weeds, but the green moss of the path extended toward the rear patio in a graceful curve.

Theo fought dried vines and the rusted hinges of the gate to open it wide enough to slip through. He walked through the garden, admiring what the fairy had wrought with his magic. The project may have been unfinished, but what had been done that afternoon was testament to an astonishing talent and an exquisite eye for floral beauty. An elegant weeping willow now stood beside the pond, which boasted white water lilies and fire-colored canna, mosaic plant and water hyacinth. The long, trailing willow limbs moved in the icy breeze, for despite the abundance of blooms, it was still winter in the human world.

"Lord Willowvale?" called Theo.

He came upon the fairy at last, nearly hidden behind the willow branches and the bottom of an exuberant bougainvillea plant which had overtaken the brick wall. The fairy had rested briefly when Theo had left, and then moved to this new location from which he could see the garden from a different perspective. Here he had wrestled with the magic of the human world, testing plants and their light requirements, their willingness to bloom out of season, and their acceptance of Fair magic to sustain them.

At last, exhausted, the Fair lord had sat at the base of the willow, intending to rest a little and then move toward the house, where he would focus on the side yard for the rest of the evening and the following morning. Instead, he fell asleep, his mind full of bright bougainvillea blooms, the same color as Miss Astrantia Berrydell's hair, and plans for astrantia plants near the patio set off by white daffodils and roses.

"Ash, wake up." Theo knelt by the fairy. Willowvale's head had slumped sideways, and his long, white fingers were slack in his lap.

"Wake up, Ash," Theo said again, and the fairy stirred at last with an almost inaudible groan. "You must be half frozen," Theo said. "Let me help you up. I'd like you to meet someone."

This unpleasant prospect jolted Willowvale toward wakefulness. "What?"

Theo gripped his hand and hauled him to his feet. The fairy's hands were so cold that the young man's hand felt like fire upon his skin, and he pulled away as Theo said, "Good heavens, let's get you warmed up so you can be properly civil to the young lady I'd like you to meet."

"I can be civil," muttered Willowvale resentfully.

"I was teasing you," said Theo, with laughter in his voice. "Come on. My father took me to a little inn not far from here when I was young, and the carriage passed it as I was coming back here. We'll get an early dinner and I'll tell you about my friend."

Willowvale found that he was, after all, thoroughly chilled and exhausted, and a little frustrated too, for he had hoped to get more of the garden done that afternoon. "I was going to do a little more," he said, though it was not a real complaint, for he could feel the fatigue in his very soul.

"You've done magnificent work," Theo said, with warmth and admiration in his voice. "The garden is already transformed, although I know you are not finished yet. But we have a little time, and I promised I would introduce you this evening."

The Fair Folk took such promises as seriously as death, so Willowvale protested no more. "Who is this friend?" he said once they were in the carriage Theo had procured. He was too cold to shiver, so he shoved his hands into his jacket pockets with unusual casualness. His fingers tingled and ached with chill.

"Miss Charity McStretton, one of the girls stolen by the Fair Folk." Theo's hazel eyes held Willowvale's pale silvery gaze. "She is Lord Buckley's niece, the daughter of his sister. Miss McStretton has not spoken since she was rescued from the Fair Lands, though she appears otherwise healthy and alert."

Willowvale could scarcely bear to hold Theo's steady gaze, but he felt there was something of penance in forcing himself to. So he said without inflection, "Why should she want to speak with me?"

"Oh, I can't imagine she wants to speak with you at all," Theo said. "I didn't ask her to go that far. I thought, though, that since you have repented of your actions, that it might help her to hear you say it."

The fairy swallowed bile. He could not hold Theo's gaze any longer after all, so he looked out the window. The cold that pervaded his body, the swaying of the carriage, the exhaustion, and the regrets thick and vile enough to choke him, combined to form a sick disgust so deep that for a moment he felt faint. Perhaps if he vomited right there on the carriage floor, he would be able to forget it all.

"I cannot imagine she ever wants to see a fairy again," he murmured. He shivered once, violently, and then again, and closed his eyes. He leaned his head back against the side of the carriage, letting it jolt with every bounce and rock of the vehicle on the road.

"I don't think she wants to either," said Theo quietly. "But I think it would help her to hear that *one* fairy has repented of what was done in desperation. Will you tell her that?"

Willowvale swallowed. "If you think it will help her."

The inn was tiny, elegant little place, and Willowvale wondered later how Sir Theodore had ever discovered it. At Theo's request, they were seated close by one of the fireplaces. Willowvale's belated shivering subsided while they waited for their food. The young man had ordered for them both, for Willowvale had shrugged and looked at the fire morosely when the youth came out of the kitchen to ask what they wanted.

They ate in silence, lost in thought, and, in Willowvale's case, mingled dread and regret.

"One more thing," Theo said at last. "The girl's father, Sir Briscoe, said he would allow you to meet her only on my word that I would personally run you through if you harmed her or kidnapped her."

The fairy raised one eyebrow but said only, "That won't be necessary."

"If I thought the threat necessary, I would never have asked you to meet her, nor would I have called you my friend these last months," Theo said. "But I thought you should know, in case he mentions it. It seems an unpleasant sort of thing to have sprung upon one."

Willowvale managed a wry smile. "I'm not offended, Theo." He took a deep, shuddering breath, as if he meant to say something else, then sighed and frowned at the table.

Soon the carriage drew up in front of the McStretton residence.

The Fair lord's stomach churned, and it was all he could do to climb out of the carriage after Theo into the street. He straightened his jacket and ran both hands through his already-disheveled curls. The icy wind cut through his jacket and prickled on his face. His breath was coming too fast.

Theo looked at him. "I know this is difficult. Thank you."

Willowvale nodded.

The young man bounded up the steps to the door and knocked confidently. "You'll be all right," he murmured almost inaudibly.

The door opened. "Mr. Overton. *Fairy*." The servant glared murderously at Willowvale but stepped aside, letting them step into the spacious vestibule.

"His name is Lord Ash Willowvale, and I would very much appreciate it if you would treat him as the lord he is," Theo said. "Moreover, he is a good friend of mine."

The servant's scowl deepened.

Sir Briscoe McStretton stepped into view from a sitting room to the right.

Theo made the introductions.

"I'm only letting you in on the strength of Mr. Overton's word." Sir Briscoe growled.

Willowvale could not bring himself to thank the man, but he did bow curtly.

"You swear you will not hurt her, or take her, or upset her in any way at all," the man pressed.

"I will not harm her or take her. I cannot promise she will not be upset, but I will swear I will not intentionally cause her any distress." Willowvale felt it was important to be clear on this matter, because it was entirely possible that the girl would be upset at his mere presence.

Sir Briscoe took a deep breath. "You had better not," he muttered.

He had a sword on his hip, and he rested his hand upon it as if eager to use it. But he led them into the elegant sitting room where Theo had visited with the girl before.

The girl was already standing some distance from the door, as if the distance made her safer from the fairy she dreaded. She wore a pink gown with little frills of lace at the collar and down the sleeves; it was cut in the latest Arichtan style, which suited her slim figure well. It was a dress suitable for a cherished daughter of a wealthy family in the lower ranks of nobility.

Still, there was something a little wild in her eyes, the memory of fear and despair that no child should experience.

"Miss McStretton." Lord Ash Willowvale bowed to her. "Mr. Overton said you had agreed to see me."

She merely looked at him, unblinking.

Sir Briscoe said, "I don't know what you think this will accomplish."

"I don't know that it will accomplish anything," Willowvale said with an edge in his voice. "Maybe it isn't about accomplishing anything, as if your daughter is a problem to be fixed. Might I speak with her without you hovering around?"

Sir Briscoe's eyes narrowed. "You may sit there by the fire. My daughter may sit where she wishes, and I will be over here."

Willowvale strode across the room and stood in front of the chair, waiting for the girl to reach the chair across from him. She sat in it, her knees drawn together and her back straight.

The fairy glanced across the room, wishing the girl's father wouldn't watch him. Sir Briscoe and Theo stood by the door. Theo had turned to the side, which didn't exactly give them privacy but at least made it less obvious that they were being closely observed. The girl's father stared at the fairy as if to convey warning, if not outright hatred.

The fairy sat down, and the girl stared at him.

"What did my friend tell you?" Willowvale asked into the silence.

The girl merely looked at him, then out the window, as if she wished to be anywhere else.

The Fair lord waited quietly, in case she wanted to say something.

Finally he said, "I don't suppose he told you I was part of the plan to use human children to save our lands."

To his surprise, the girl gave a cautious nod.

What did Theo expect him to say to help this poor, traumatized child? She was responsive, apparently intelligent and healthy, merely mute. What was Willowvale supposed to do to help her?

He almost gave a bitter little chuckle. Talking kindly had never been his gift, and if anyone could remind the poor girl how to speak, it ought to be Theo.

"I didn't… I didn't think humans were as valuable as we Fair Folk," he admitted, so quietly that Charity scarcely heard him. "I thought a few human children were an acceptable sacrifice to save thousands of lives in my own lands, thousands of Fair women and Fair children. For who would not sacrifice others to save their own?"

The little girl swallowed and looked down at her hands in her lap.

Willowvale rolled his shoulders, feeling tense and unhappy. "I was forced to confront the magnitude of my misjudgment of humans, and the immensity of the horror of what I had done, and it nearly broke me. It would have, except for the friendship of Mr. Overton."

The Fair lord stared at the fire. He felt a strange reluctance to even look at the child, and he was not sure if he were concerned that he would frighten her, or that looking at her wide, clear eyes would shatter him. So he fixed his eyes on the dancing flames and lapsed into silence.

After several long minutes, she shifted, and from the corner of his eye he saw her pull her legs up into the chair beneath her skirt and rest her chin on the palm of her hand. Her eyes were on his face expectantly.

"I don't deserve his friendship and forgiveness," he muttered. "I don't deserve yours either, and I do not even want to ask for it, because I do not want you to feel that you ought to give it to me.

"But," his voice cracked, and he cleared his throat, "I do appreciate the opportunity to tell you that I know now that we were wrong. Even if your dancing had saved the Fair Lands… the cost was too high.

"The whole effort was borne of our desperation and terror, our desire to save our people. But it relied upon our arrogance, our belief that we had the right to sacrifice humans for our own benefit."

The fairy stopped, his throat tight. He felt a strange urge to weep, and he did not want to show this to anyone, much less a human child. So he rubbed his hands over his face and ran his long, white fingers through his snowy curls, hiding his face until he had mastered his expression.

"You don't owe me forgiveness," he said. "But I would like for you to know that I am sorry."

He did not look at her.

The silence felt so fraught with emotion that he felt himself trembling, his breath and his hands and his voice. So he said abruptly, "Do you like flowers?"

He still could not look at her, but he thought that perhaps she nodded.

Humans did not generally prefer living plants to be an integral part of the house structure; they liked their plants and greenery to be neatly contained, especially when indoors. So it took the fairy a moment to find a suitable container for the roses he imagined.

There. The teapot and teacups sitting upon the nearby table.

He stood and stepped closer. He put his hands on the table and glanced at the girl.

She flinched, and he pressed his lips together.

With a wisp and curl of magic, he produced a tiny little rose bush in the teapot. Its roots soaked up the tea and were satisfied, for magically-grown plants required no real sustenance. The branches bore no thorns, and the buds grew and opened in a pale pink that matched the color of the girl's dress. In a matter of a few minutes, the teapot was covered in a glorious profusion of blooms which filled the air with a light, sweet scent.

Willowvale glanced at the girl, noting her wide eyes and a faint look of longing. "You can come see them, if you want." He stepped away, so that she would not have to pass too closely to him.

She edged by him cautiously and bent to sniff the flowers.

"What other flowers do you like?"

She looked up at him with those wide blue eyes and shook her head.

What little girl didn't like flowers? He almost sneered that her answer was ridiculous, but stopped. Perhaps she only meant she did not want to answer.

"Daffodils?"

She shrugged.

With a wave of his hand, he produced a bunch of daffodils in one of the teacups, an unusual variety with wide white petals around a pink trumpet. He glanced at her again. Blue forget-me-nots emerged in a happy little mound from the other teacup, and a little clump of lavender from the third cup.

He swallowed. "May I come to see you tomorrow?"

He waited, his pale blue eyes steady on her face, for a whole minute while she thought about this.

Finally she nodded once.

"Thank you, Miss McStretton," he said. He bowed and fled.

CHAPTER FORTY-TWO
The Grace of a Child

The Fair lord returned to the Arichtan palace and did not even speak with the king before retreating to his suite. Tired and melancholy, he nodded when Theo asked if he'd like company for a cup of tea by the fire. Still, there was an unexpected feeling of satisfaction beneath the guilt and grief.

The flames danced and sputtered, but neither of them said much.

"Do you really think it is possible to change?" asked the fairy at last.

"Certainly it is." Theo looked at him. "You already have."

Willowvale looked down at the delicate porcelain teacup. "Not enough," he murmured.

"Quite a lot, though," said Theo gently. "It was a challenge to be your friend at first, I will admit, but it is not difficult at all now. I cannot take all the credit for that."

The Fair lord chuckled under his breath. "I cannot understand why you bothered," he admitted.

"Sheer orneriness." Theo grinned, then sobered. "You know, it doesn't actually help anything for you to keep torturing yourself. Not even your magic can change the past, but your courage and character can change the future. Just think what change was wrought with a little kindness on my part. You can do the same."

Willowvale sighed. "You do not do yourself justice. It was more than 'a little kindness.'"

Theo only smiled and looked at the fire, a faint flush across his cheeks.

Soon Theo retired to his own suite.

The next day was much the same. The Fair lord spent all morning in the garden, though he retreated inside to collapse by the fire when he grew too fatigued to continue, and he napped briefly on a stiff, uncomfortable couch before continuing the work.

By the time Theo finished interviewing candidates for service in the front sitting room of the house, the fairy had finished the vast majority of the work in the back garden. Theo wandered out to see him sitting on a bench which had been uncovered near one side of the garden with his elbows on his knees and his head hanging down between his bony shoulders.

"Are you all right?" Theo asked.

"Tired," Willowvale grunted and straightened wearily. "The magic here does not like to cooperate with me."

"I wouldn't take it personally if I were you," said Theo, looking across the lush, verdant space. "It has never particularly cooperated with me, either, and most humans can't do much at all." He looked down at Willowvale, who was still sprawled on the bench as if he were too fatigued to even contemplate standing up yet. "You have worked beauty here beyond compare," Theo said honestly. "I would not have imagined such a transformation possible, much less how to make it happen."

"No, you transform fairies and nations," said the Fair lord. "This is trivial in comparison." He swallowed. "I do hope…"

Theo looked down at him, but the fairy did not continue. "That the new ambassador likes it?" Theo said gently.

Willowvale nodded once. He pressed his magic into the air and the ground, and some of the blooms began to fold themselves into buds.

"What are you doing?"

"I wanted to see the effect in spring," Willowvale murmured. "But winter is beautiful too." Many of the flowers retreated into their stems, but others emerged from the ground, where Willowvale had placed them earlier.

With a final effort of magic, the fairy sent the garden through all four seasons in a matter of minutes in a display both riotously colorful and intricately planned, with little vignettes of white and cream hidden beneath boughs of pink cherry blossoms, while irises, lavender, and delphiniums succeeded foxgloves, crocosmia, and asters. At last the garden was still, most of the blooms dormant again. The moss remained vibrant, and snowdrops formed happy little clusters here and there, evidence to any visitor that the garden was not entirely subject to the climate of the human world.

The young man watched in awe, his eyes taking in every shifting color and lovingly crafted nook.

"This is a transcendent work of art, my friend," he said quietly.

"Thank you." The fairy closed his eyes. "I think I am too tired to do anything in the side yard today."

"Didn't you ask if we could visit Miss McStretton this evening?" said Theo.

The fairy let out a sigh like a groan. "I am not brave enough to face her," he muttered without opening his eyes.

Theo looked at him in concern. The fairy did indeed look exhausted, with shadows under his eyes and a pallor even beyond his usual bone-white. "I think you've done more than enough for today. Let me help you up."

Willowvale shoved himself to his feet, dizzy with fatigue and with the magic of the garden still buzzing in his mind. "What can I say to her that will help?"

The wind gusted suddenly, and he nearly fell over; Theo grabbed his shoulder to steady him. "Come on. Let's get a little dinner."

They ate at the same little inn, at a table just to the left of the one they had enjoyed the previous evening. The rich sausage-stuffed chicken, cheesy scalloped potatoes, and roasted peppers and squash were both thoroughly enjoyable and revived the fairy enough for him to ask Theo again, "Is there anything I can say that would help her?"

"You're the one who asked to see her again," said Theo. "Did you have something in mind?"

"No." Willowvale stared at his plate. "No, I... I intended only to give her another opportunity tell me how angry she was, or how badly we had sinned against her and the other children, or... I don't know. Stab me. Whatever would help."

"I don't think she plans to injure you," said Theo solemnly. "Perhaps you might tell her again that you're sorry, if you judge it helpful, and then perhaps you might listen."

The fairy nodded jerkily. "I will rely upon your wisdom, then."

A short time later, they were welcomed, with only slightly more friendliness than last time, into the McStretton house.

Sir Briscoe did not voice the threat that was obvious in every line of his body. "Come in," he growled, and led them into the same sitting room as before.

Charity was dressed in a pale green dress this time, with her hair done up in girlish ringlets. Her grave eyes followed the fairy as he stalked into the room.

She sat in the seat on the far side of the fireplace and gestured wordlessly toward the seat opposite her.

Perhaps this was a kindness. Willowvale chose to believe it was, for he felt near weeping already, and if he must have his eyes fill with tears, he would much rather have it occur with his back to the girl's glowering father.

"Thank you, Miss McStretton," he murmured. He sat stiffly, his long, lean body as taut as the string of a bow.

His pale eyes studied her face, and she looked toward the fire, her cheeks flushing.

He looked down. "I'm sorry," he said. "I did not intend to make you uncomfortable."

She shrugged one shoulder and looked back at him with an intensity that surprised him. He endured the scrutiny without a word, trying to keep his expression as calm and reassuring as possible.

He fought the urge to look away, to look anywhere but at her steady gaze. It was easier to endure Elmerick's fury than her well-hidden distaste and grief.

"Is there anything I might say or do to… to… help you recover from your ordeal?" he said at last.

She shook her head at once. She looked him up and down, and then stood. He stood too, tall and lean and hard, with his shoulders tense and his pale hands clenched at his sides.

The girl swallowed and surveyed him again. She glanced toward the flowers still blooming in the teapot on the nearby table.

"Would you like some more flowers?" he said, as if flowers could help a child put the past behind her.

Charity smiled, just a little, and the fairy took an unsteady breath.

There wasn't another teapot or teacup near at hand for more flowers, and she hadn't exactly indicated she wanted them anyway. Still, he wanted to do something. His fingernails dug into his palms.

The girl opened her mouth and said, "I am not afraid of you."

Lord Willowvale let out a breath like a sob, and for a moment he could not speak. When he found his voice, he said, "Thank you, Miss McStretton."

The silence in the room felt suddenly richer and brighter.

"Charity, you spoke!" Sir Briscoe said, in a soft, surprised voice.

What a ridiculous statement, thought the fairy through his shock and relief and elation. "Of course she did," he muttered. Then, to the girl, he said, "Still, you didn't have to tell me that. Thank you."

"You're welcome." She swallowed and gave a sudden little curtsey, then smiled as if she were embarrassed by the impulsive gesture.

Willowvale smiled back, awkward and surprised and sweet, and the girl's smile widened.

He bowed to her, and unlike when he had bowed to her father, it was not merely a motion required by custom and courtesy, but an expression of respect from the deepest part of his heart.

"Thank you, Miss McStretton," he said again, for it seemed the only appropriate response to grace.

CHAPTER FORTY-THREE
Perseverance in Generosity

The following four days were filled with more work in the garden and the ambassador's residence. They did not visit the McStrettons again, though Theo imagined that if they had, they would have been welcomed with more friendliness.

"I hate to ask you to stay longer, when your wife is waiting for you and your life in Valestria is so comfortable," Willowvale said over dinner a few days later. He had put the finishing touches on the rear garden that day, planning the extended bloom times of each flowering plant to provide maximum beauty and color while still honoring the seasons and their changes. No fairy, as much as they delighted in the fullness of spring and summer, would actually wish to eliminate winter altogether; the barren, frozen beauty of a garden was a delight all its own, however briefly they might wish to enjoy it.

Theo took a sip of his tea and studied the fairy across from him. The perpetual line of frustration and annoyance between his snowy brows was much faded, and though he was even paler than usual with the fatigue of his magical exertions, he looked almost happy, in a melancholy sort of way.

"I told my wife that I might be gone until Lord Selby's wedding," he said at last. "I cannot deny that I would dearly love to return this very night; your company is enjoyable, but I'm sure you understand I prefer Lily's company over all others." The fairy gave a quiet, amused huff, as Theo had intended, and the young man continued. "However, I thought I might explore the veil here over the next day or two. It seems you're making incredible progress, and I would like to see if we can find a shorter path from here to the Fair Lands. If so, perhaps I can convince the path to stay in place for you."

"I cannot imagine Elmerick would consent to that."

"I cannot either, but he can hardly do anything about it. I think I can convince it to only be a path if you are the one walking it, so it would not be a wholesale invitation for fairies to come through whenever they want."

The Fair lord sighed softly. "I wonder that you would trust me so."

"Have you not proven yourself trustworthy?" Theo took a sip of tea. "You might have had a war several times over if you wanted one. Besides, someone must facilitate communication between the new ambassador and His Majesty Silverthorn, and I see no reason why it ought not be you, at least occasionally. It certainly can't be Camphor or Aspen, and there are very few others for whom it would even be possible."

Willowvale swallowed and looked down.

At last the house was ready. A chef had been engaged, as well as a general servant for more menial tasks like laundry and and general chores, who would come once a week. The garden had been transformed into an oasis of peace, comfort, and beauty in the center of the human city. The kitchen was stocked with dishes, silver, and nonperishables, and furniture, fresh linens, and other necessities had been purchased. Willowvale had even selected several excellent paintings of flower arrangements which he had hung upon the walls. The windows had been cleaned, so that the light came through the beveled glass transoms in gleaming rainbows across the floor and walls.

Upon discussion, Willowvale and Theo decided they would go to the Fair Lands to report that the house was ready and then would return to Valestria, where Willowvale would have a night, a full day of rest, and another night before Lord Selby's wedding.

Accordingly, they departed for the Fair Lands early the next morning.

Only four hours later, they stepped into Lord Willowvale's garden.

"Your skill grows by the day," said the fairy in astonishment.

"Thank you!" Theo said. In short order, they were welcomed into the palace and invited to enjoy lunch with Silverthorn.

The dining hall of the Fair king was a magnificent experience of a thousand astonishing sensations, from the river which flowed down one wall to the cut crystal roof overhead which made one feel as if one were sitting down in the middle of a gemstone. Moss crept across the floor and birds sang joyously from their perches atop tapestries woven of silk, gold, and light itself. The scents of Fair foods mingled with petrichor and jasmine, roses and salt breezes in a heady mixture.

Despite the grandeur of the room, only the king, Willowvale, and Theo were to eat there, and Theo's plate was full of human food rather than the Fair equivalents which looked so odd to human eyes.

"Be welcome here, Mr. Overton," said Silverthorn, his violet eyes glinting. "This is human food, procured for you in hopes that you would give me your advice on our new peace with Aricht."

Theo understood this as the reassurance it was, for it would have been easy for the king to merely say that human food had been procured without specifying that that human food was being served to him at this moment. "Thank you, Your Majesty."

Willowvale reported to the king what he had done in Aricht, though he did not describe the extravagant generosity and beauty of his work in the garden and upon the house in any real detail. "The house has been made ready for Miss Berrydell. Did she accept the appointment as ambassador?"

There was an odd, expectant stillness in him after this question, for it would be strange indeed, and disappointing, to have gone to such exhausting trouble only to learn that some other lord would accept the position rather than Miss Berrydell.

"She did," said the king, with his eyes sharp upon Willowvale's face. "She did wonder that she had been selected."

"You did not tell her of my part in it, I hope." Willowvale's voice was tight.

"I did not. Elmerick's letter requested her by name, and that is what I told her." The king took a sip of his wine and said quietly, "I am not so cruel as to thwart you in this, Willowvale, though I do not understand your motive. Why should you not want her to know of your regard for her?"

"She is aware of my regard," said Willowvale shortly. "I do not wish her to feel that she owes me anything. Not even gratitude. She earned Elmerick's respect on her own; all I did was inform him that she could be appointed ambassador, if he requested it and you consented."

"She ought to at least thank you for saving her life," said the king. "She conveyed her thanks to Mosswing most sincerely. I had no idea Mosswing's magic was that strong, and to use it on behalf of a commoner is remarkable." Silverthorn turned a sudden, sharp eye upon Theo, who had been listening quietly. "I assume that was not only at your request but also your direct influence upon his character."

Theo frowned. "Lord Mosswing has been a good friend for many years, and I have always known him to be generous, honorable, and kind. My only part in it was to ask him for his help, for he was not aware Miss Berrydell was in distress until I pounded upon his door."

Willowvale said, "I have thanked Mosswing already, but I will more properly convey my gratitude when next I see him."

Soon they were off again to Valestria. The veil seemed quiet and melancholy, which fit Willowvale's mood, and it had an odd, fresh scent like the wind over high cliffs near the sea, which Theo felt was appropriate.

They stepped into the Overton garden at the most beautiful moment of sunset, while the sky glowed pink and orange in the west. Willowvale stopped in wonder. "I've never seen colors like this in the human world!" he breathed.

Theo looked up and smiled. "Did you ever look?"

"I don't think I did." The fairy was transfixed, his lips lifted in a childlike smile.

When the colors faded into indigo and then into blues so deep neither of them knew their names, they sighed and walked across the lawn toward home and hospitality.

The day of rest between their late return and the wedding of Lord Fenton Selby and Miss Crocus Firethorn was entirely appreciated by both Willowvale and Theo. Willowvale spent much of the day drinking endless cups of tea by a fire in one of the Overton sitting rooms, alternating between reading and staring at the flames or out the window at the frost-covered garden. Theo checked on him at intervals, but spent sweet hours with his lovely wife, reminding her in all possible ways that she was cherished, body and soul.

"Dinner is an hour, my lord," said a voice, and Willowvale looked up to see the young fairy Juniper standing by the door.

"Thank you."

Lord Cedar Mosswing and his betrothed, Lady Poppy Miscanthus, arrived some time later, for they too, were to be guests at Overton manor before attending the Selby wedding the following day. They were ushered in to the dining room, where Theo, Lily, and Willowvale waited.

"Willowvale." Cedar bowed politely to him. "I trust you are fully recovered."

"I am. Thank you." Willowvale bowed in turn to both Cedar and Poppy. "I am in your debt, Mosswing. Not for my life, for I do not count it so dear, but for that of Miss Berrydell." A debt between Fair Folk was a grave thing, and Willowvale had considered this statement and its possible repercussions for much of the day.

The dark fairy blinked, and then smiled, his white teeth bright against his skin. "There is no need for that," he said. "Consider the debt absolved. I did it for the sake of compassion and for Miss Berrydell herself, not for you."

"Still, I should like to repay you in some small way, for it grieved me deeply to know that she suffered, and you relieved that suffering with your talent." Willowvale cleared his throat, for he felt it tightening with emotion. "What shall I do to express my gratitude?"

"I will think on it," said Cedar gravely.

Though Willowvale scarcely spoke at all throughout dinner, he felt an odd sense of comfort. He and Mosswing had never been friendly, though they had hardly been open enemies; of course he hadn't known that the other fairy supported the Rose until Theo confronted Silverthorn, and he had scarcely known Lady Miscanthus at all. She was a striking beauty, and she looked both happy and a very good match for Mosswing, with her quiet elegance and soft, lovely smiles.

Such a kind-hearted lord as Mosswing, gifted in every way, deserved every happiness.

CHAPTER FORTY-FOUR
The Selby Wedding

The wedding the next day surpassed every other event of the last decade, save the Overton wedding last autumn. All the most fashionable nobility were there, along with some unexpected guests: Theo's manservant Anselm and his wife Sophie, their adopted Fair son Juniper Morel, Lord Cedar Mosswing and Lady Poppy Miscanthus, neither of whom had never before been seen in Valestrian society, and Lord Ash Willowvale, who had made himself thoroughly detestable for many months and now dared attend this lovely event as if he were welcome.

No one said anything during the ceremony, of course. Lord Selby's customary quiet reserve was overcome by his rapturous joy, and his eyes filled with happy tears when he saw his lovely Fair bride stride toward him down the aisle of the church. Her strides were long and stately, and not as slow as they might have been, for she was too delighted by the sight of him to slow her steps to match the music.

The reception in the Selby dining hall and great room were intimate and warm, full of laughter and compliments and a sense of surprised enchantment. There were baked apples and mulled cider, puffed cream pastries and candied oranges, gingerbread, bacon and cheese tartlets, and a hundred other delicacies Willowvale could not even name.

Theo introduced Lord Mosswing, Lady Miscanthus, Anselm, and Juniper to several of the noblemen as Fair allies of the Wraith and his personal friends. This was not exactly an admission of his identity as the Wraith, but it was certainly enough to hint at it. He introduced Lord Willowvale as a new, quite unexpected friend, and the fairy bowed coldly in response to the glares he received. The inclusion of Willowvale in their party was nearly enough to extinguish any possibility of Theo being the Wraith in the minds of the noblemen.

The young man danced with his beloved wife, smiling down at her through three songs in a row before reluctantly saying, "We ought to dance with other people, my love."

When Lily stretched to whisper into his ear, he bent closer.

"Must we?" she asked, with laughter in her voice.

Theo pressed a scandalous kiss to her cheek. "Unfortunately we must, if we do not wish to insult everyone."

"Oh, I suppose we don't wish to do that." Lily's eyes sparkled with joy and love. "But will you promise to dance with me tonight, when we're alone?"

"As long as you wish."

So Theo danced with Lady Miscanthus, Lady Overton, Lady Crocus Selby, Lady Araminta Poole, Lady Hathaway, and with a dozen other ladies of his acquaintance, while Lily danced with her brother, her father, Theo's father, Lord Selby, Lord Mosswing, and others. When the dance with Sir Michael Radclyffe ended, she found herself on the edge of the dance floor near Lord Willowvale.

"Would you like a drink?" the fairy asked in his cool, elegant voice.

"Yes, please." She watched him accept two glasses of sparkling wine from the nearest servant and hand her one. "Thank you."

"You and Mr. Overton look very happy together." The fairy's pale eyes flicked over her face. "I am glad of it."

"Thank you," she said again. This attempt at pleasantness, which clearly felt awkward to the fairy, warmed her to him. She had not felt sure that she trusted him, even after his expressions of gratitude to Theo. But now, she saw the tension in his shoulders as the dancers whirled by, the way his hard expression softened as he caught sight of Theo and Fenton as they laughed together across the room.

"Would you honor me with this dance?" he said abruptly.

She put her hand in his and looked up at him. "I will."

He said nothing else throughout the dance, but he thanked her politely when the dance finished. His pale cheeks were slightly flushed with the heat of the dance floor and the quick steps, and he almost smiled as he bowed over her hand again. "Thank you, Mrs. Overton."

"I wonder that you dare show your face here," Lord Radclyffe growled at the fairy when they happened to meet at the edge of the dance floor.

"I was invited," said Willowvale, trying in vain to keep his voice even.

Radclyffe blinked and looked him up and down, noting the exquisite cut of Willowvale's human clothes. "Are you lying, fairy?" he asked dubiously. "Who would have invited *you*?"

"Selby invited me," Willowvale said, his voice clipped. "I am just as astonished as you are, I am sure."

Lily was about to say that Lord Willowvale was part of their party, but before she could open her mouth, Theo appeared, beaming in delight. "Oh, Lord Radclyffe! It is a pleasure to see you tonight! You met my friend Lord Ash Willowvale months ago, I believe."

"Your friend?" Radclyffe's voice lowered ominously. "I heard he nearly killed the Wraith."

"The Wraith is fully recovered," Theo said with a twinkle in his eye. "Let us put the past behind us, my lord, and be delighted together for Lord Selby and his lovely bride."

Radclyffe eyed the fairy dubiously. He leaned forward and murmured a question in Theo's ear, and the young man's smile widened even more. "I'm quite sure, Lord Radclyffe. I would be best pleased if you would treat him as the friend he is."

Lord Radclyffe had long suspected that young Overton was the Wraith, but he had never before attempted to confirm this hunch. He was aware that his son Sir Michael knew the Wraith's identity, and had noted with interest that Sir Michael, as well as a number of other young noblemen, seemed to orbit Theo, their attention always subtly inclined toward him. Still, Theo was engaging, even magnetic, and this attention was not conclusive proof. Seeing Theo introduce the arrogant Fair lord as his friend, Radclyffe's curiosity finally had finally gotten the better of him, and he had murmured in Theo's ear, "If you are quite sure you're recovered, I will believe you, but if you would like me to stab him on your behalf, I am more than ready."

Willowvale retreated to a corner not long afterward, for it was easier to look on than to listen to Theo try to defend him to the other guests. A melancholy sort of satisfaction settled over him.

It was good to watch Theo and his wife dancing. Their smiles were so sweet and genuine, so sparkling with love and delight in each other. The music was not the equal of Fair music, but it was exceptionally good for the human world, and the food had been delicious. The laughter of the human guests was not as musical as that of Fair Folk, but it was good and honest, and it made him smile a little.

Anyway, Selby deserved every bit of this happiness. A steadier, honest, honorable man could hardly be imagined, and Willowvale felt a pang of mingled pain and pleasure when he thought of the small part he had played in encouraging Selby and his bride to express their affection for each other aloud.

He had scorned the very idea of marriage, knowing himself to be cold and bitter, and not wanting to inflict the misery of his company on some Fair maiden, much less suffering the company of someone else. But it was impossible to remain so against marriage as a concept when Theo and Mrs. Overton so obviously delighted in each other, and Selby and his wife were so likewise so happy. Marriage might be pleasant indeed.

The wedding was beautiful, and he was almost entirely happy.

CHAPTER FORTY-FIVE
The Wraith's Magic

After a delicious breakfast the following morning with Theo, Lily, Lord Mosswing, and Lady Miscanthus, Lord Willowvale departed for the Fair Lands carrying in his bag a generous supply of tea from Theo, as well as his own clothes and personal items.

He was able to open a door to the veil directly from the far edge of the Overton garden.

"Why is there so much magic in your garden, Theo?" he asked. "I've wondered for months."

Theo frowned thoughtfully. "I suppose I can tell you, if you promise to not to tell or use it against humanity."

The fairy vowed solemnly that he would never use it against humanity, against which he had no animosity, and that he would not to tell anyone, ever, for any reason other than to save a life. Theo accepted this caveat.

"When my parents escaped from their captivity in the Fair Lands, they could not at first fully free themselves, for they had eaten

Fair food many times. My father had been captive for years, and my mother for many months.

"My mother in particular was transported through the veil many times by her captor, and after the first few times, she used a gossamer-thin thread of binding magic to loop into the veil, over and over, so that there was a strong, steady pull to help her into the veil when she was ready to use it.

"When my father was ready, together they drew on this binding magic to enter the veil, as if they were squeezing themselves through a crack scarcely wide enough for a thread. My mother has only a very weak gift with the veil, but the veil liked them both immediately, and it helped them escape to the human world. They stumbled out of the veil near the border with Aricht after nearly two days in the dark, hungry and exhausted and covered in orange slime from some incident in the darkness. But they were unhurt.

"They called upon some friends of my mother's parents in the nearest town and were received with joy and astonishment.

"When they returned here, to my father's family home, my mother and her parents stayed as guests of the family for several months; my mother could not be parted from my father, and her parents did not want to leave them."

"That's not much of an answer," said Willowvale. In this sheltered corner of the garden, the wind was blocked by hills and hedges and the winter sun warmed their shoulders.

His human friend's hazel eyes glittered with pride.

"It was all I knew for some years, and I didn't figure it out on my own either," said Theo with a smile. "It turned out that my father had filled his shoes and pockets with the soil of the Fair Lands, so even as he left it behind, it came with him. He had no time to explain this plan to my mother until they were in the veil, and he had no assurance that it would work.

"This soil was incorporated into the garden in our estate, and by some chance or providence, the area where it was most concentrated happened to be my favorite in which to play as a child. For a time, there was a crabapple tree there, and when I was very young and running over the estate escaping my lessons, I ate crabapples from it, sharp and bright and sour, until my parents learned of this and cut it down immediately. It was replaced with a rose bush, which is quite lovely but less likely to infuse one's blood with the memory of Fair magic."

Lord Willowvale stared at him in astonishment. "So there is Fair magic in your blood after all!"

Theo shrugged. "My mother does have a natural talent with the veil, however slight; I suspect that the Fair magic in the soil and the apples merely accentuated and strengthened what natural talent I was born with. Do not forget I have practiced a great deal, and I have carefully cultivated my relationship with the veil itself, so that it aids me because it chooses to, not because I force it to."

"But your parents are no longer bound to the land with Fair soil in it," said Willowvale. "Nor did you use such Fair soil when extracting the children from the Fair Lands, at least to my knowledge."

"I did not. However, most of the children were not fed enough for the Fair Lands to have a strong hold on them." Theo's breath hitched, for he was still affected by the unthinking cruelty of this. "Moreover, the land's magic itself was tremendously weakened, and one of the first aspects where that became clear was the hold of the magic upon human children. Had an adult human been captured, we would have had considerably more trouble freeing him, but the magic of the Fair Lands has never gripped children as tightly as adults. I assume this is because children are judged less responsible for their actions; they are presumed to have less agency over what and when they eat, in particular. The Lands themselves are quite just in this matter, I think; the magic holds children less strongly than adults, and prisoners less strongly than free people, and captive children more loosely than any others, as far as I can tell. Still, I'm sure the magic in my veins must have helped a great deal. Once they were in the human world, their frightening memories and hatred of their experiences in the Fair Lands helped the magic slough off them more easily than it might have otherwise."

The Fair lord let out a soft breath. "You're half Fair yourself, I think; with magic in your veins and knowledge and intuition like that. Did you know it would work, when you found the first prisoner and pulled them into the veil?"

Theo smiled to himself. "I carried them into the veil for months, and once I shoved a boy through the door when I was in a very great hurry and my arms were full with his little sister. They could hardly be said to be walking out of the Fair Lands if I were carrying them. I think it helped, especially for those who had been there a little longer and those who were older."

"But you knew it would work." Willowvale's voice was wondering.

"I knew I would find a way, because I could not bear to abandon them."

The fairy studied him again, and then bowed deeply. "I am honored, Theo, that you told me," he said. "And I am more honored still that after all you and your parents endured at the hands of Fair Folk, and at my hands, that you saw fit to extend compassion and friendship to me, most undeserving of all. I should like very much to reciprocate the hospitality you so generously offered here, when you next visit the Fair Lands."

Theo smiled, warm and kind and sweet. "I will be honored to accept, Ash."

And Willowvale felt a strange little flutter of joy that this courageous, ridiculous, compassionate hero would address him as a friend. "Thank you," he said in a choked voice.

Then he stepped into the veil and started toward home.

CHAPTER FORTY-SIX
A Surprising Encounter

T he veil smelled odd, and it took Willowvale quite some time to identify the scents. There was a hint of sage blossom, a stronger scent of dandelion, a sweet sort of incense and soot, and the very slightest hint of apple blossoms. The effect was oddly comforting, as if the veil meant to convey the reassuring thought of healing and peace. It was decidedly less threatening than the scent of blood and iron he'd smelled on several other occasions.

Still, there was an ominous thudding like the distant steps of some giant, and he slipped through a narrow gap in the stone only to find that it began to close upon him, and he barely escaped with his ribs intact.

Nevertheless he reached the Fair Lands by late afternoon, and he stepped into the gloriously bright sunlight and a chilly breeze that whispered through the bare branches above his head.

He sighed wearily and headed toward the house.

Several minutes later, he turned the corner of the hedge and nearly ran headlong into someone.

"I'm so sorry!" She turned and hurried away.

"Miss Berrydell!" he said in shock. "Wait!"

She turned to face him, her cheeks flushed. "I didn't mean to… why are you here?"

He took a step forward, for she seemed poised to run like a frightened wolpertinger, and she stepped back away from him. Not that she couldn't defend herself; she was not *afraid* of him, certainly.

"This is my garden," he said gently. "I didn't mean to startle you."

"I didn't know. I am so sorry," she whispered. "I didn't mean to intrude."

"You are not intruding. You are welcome here." He swallowed, wishing he could step forward again, but he imagined she would flee if he did so.

"I thought you were in the human world." She stopped, her lips trembling. "I thought this was part of the palace grounds, and His Majesty gave me leave to admire the garden on my way back home."

"You are welcome here," said Willowvale again, as if by saying it he could make her more comfortable. She looked anything but comfortable. "The palace grounds end just there. What brought you to the palace today?"

Astrantia's cheeks flushed even more deeply. "His Majesty sent for me. Perhaps you heard that I was offered the appointment of ambassador to Idosa."

"I had been informed of that, yes."

She was so beautiful that the Fair lord could barely speak, for he was too occupied with drinking in her face, the liveliness of her magenta eyes and the depth and brightness of the magenta hues of her hair. The curve of her cheek as she smiled was sheer perfection, though he wished that it were a genuine expression of delight rather than an awkward, uncomfortable expression that was nearly a grimace. If he were someone else, perhaps she would smile more joyfully.

"Congratulations," he said, after a slight pause. "I believe Elmerick requested you by name."

She raised her chin a little in modest, entirely justifiable pride. "He did. I hope that I can improve relations between our two nations, in a way that was more challenging for Brookbower to effect."

Willowvale smiled. "That is an exceptionally kind way of putting it. I am confident in your abilities and inevitable success."

The Fair maiden let out a soft, agonized breath. "I ought to thank you," she said. "You saved my life at great personal expense, and I am grateful for it after all."

She bowed low before him, every line of her slim body graceful and perfect. But her extended fingers were trembling, as if the awkward moment were too much to bear.

"And are you well now?" Willowvale said, with a hitch in his voice.

"Quite well. Thank you." She bowed again hurriedly. "My father is waiting for me. Please accept my apology for detaining you, my lord."

"I am delighted to have been detained, Lady Berrydell," he said, belatedly remembering her new title.

She blinked. "I… I just learned of my new title an hour ago. How did you know I am now a lady?"

"His Majesty informed me when he decided it was appropriate for you to have a title the equal of Brookbower's."

Astrantia looked at him for a moment longer, as if she wanted to question him more thoroughly, but then decided against it.

"Good day, my lord," she murmured and turned away.

"May I escort you home?" he asked, with the eagerness obvious in his voice.

"No! No, please. I don't want to put you out of your way."

"I don't mind at all."

"It isn't necessary!"

"I would count it an honor," he said.

"Please don't put yourself to any trouble," she said again. "Thank you, my lord, for the generous offer." Then she hurried away.

As he watched her go, he realized distantly that he was trembling. When she was out of sight behind a hedge, he sighed. The beauty of his garden seemed pale and melancholy now in comparison with the bright joy that had just hurried away with such determination.

CHAPTER FORTY-SEVEN
A Reflection

The steady, rhythmic rasp of a whetstone told her Agaricus was working, so Astrantia continued on through the shop toward the back room.

"How was your meeting?" Her father looked up from the sword on the workbench, where he was preparing the settings for a series of opals. The stones themselves had been cut and polished already and were laid out in a neat line at the back edge of the bench in the order in which they would be set into the guard.

Astrantia sighed and threw herself in the worn, overstuffed chair, which had been in the same corner for decades for that purpose. "I suppose it went well," she said thoughtfully. "Though I am thoroughly bewildered."

Her brother studied her face. "What happened?"

"The meeting with His Majesty was quite simple. He merely told me that in order for me to be accepted by the Arichtan court, he judged it necessary for me to have a title that equaled Brookbower's. If

I had no title at all, it could be perceived as an insult to the Arichtan court, and if we did not intend to make war upon them again, we should facilitate good relations as much as possible. So I have been titled a Marchioness, as of an hour and a half ago."

Sedum put down the burnisher with a precise click. "Did he ask some great price for this honor?" he said tightly.

"He required that I agree to uphold the honor of the Fair Lands in the human world, and I agreed to this. He did not require me to swear to his interpretation of what that would entail; I had the feeling he expected and hoped I would interpret it as I saw fit."

The older fairy took a deep breath and let it out slowly, pondering this. "What else happened?"

"Along with my new title, I was given ownership of two small pieces of land, the Teal Enclave and Athelas Grove. I am assured in no uncertain terms that although they are small, they are rich in magic and resources, and the Teal Enclave also boasts a small but exquisitely crafted home carved directly from the cliffside, which gleams with sapphire and topaz deposits."

"Why do you not look more delighted, then?" said Sedum. "This is a great honor."

"I nearly walked into Lord Willowvale in the garden." Astrantia groaned and covered her eyes.

"And?" said Agaricus. "Was he rude?" There was a teasing tone in his voice, and Astrantia groaned again.

"No, he was entirely polite, and it was *excruciating*, Agaricus! He knew about my title before I did, unless he had met with the king in the twenty-some minutes since I had left the palace, and I doubt that. I was intruding upon his lands, too! I thought he was in the human world; the king implied as much, although perhaps I misunderstood. I thought he was… I don't know. In Valestria, I suppose."

"How did you end up in his lands?" Sedum frowned.

"His Majesty gave me leave to enjoy his garden on my way back home, so I was just following a path. The royal grounds are extensive and lovely, even in winter, and the path was curving, with bare branches making patterns on the blue moss. I felt like I could breathe, and I almost stopped just to sit somewhere and think a while. But I knew you wanted to hear what the king had said, so I hurried along without paying as much attention as I should have. I turned the corner around the hedge, and I suppose he must have been turning toward me as well."

Her cheeks flushed.

"What did he say?" probed her brother. "I don't see why a lord being polite to you should be excruciating."

"He congratulated me on the appointment and my title, and he complimented me. He asked if I was well, and I said I was. I thanked him for saving my life." She had to swallow, for her throat felt tight with some emotion she could not name. "I was so cruel to him in the veil. He might have saved my life out of duty; it would be beyond reasonable to do so, but I would not rely upon him to be reasonable in regards to duty. But I would not have expected him to speak so kindly to me." She stopped and buried her face in her hands. "And his letter! I cannot put it out of my mind. What if I judged him according to who he *was* and not who he *is* now?"

Astrantia had not let either her father or brother read Willowvale's letter of explanation to her, but she had told them the general outlines of it.

"And," she said despairingly, "I apologized for detaining him, and he said he was delighted to have been detained! What sort of nonsense is that?"

Agaricus huffed softly. "It sounds like he was pleased to see you."

"He asked if he could escort me home, and I said no, and he said he would count it an honor, and I asked him not to put himself to any trouble. And then I ran away like a coward."

Her brother chuckled. "Is he so terrible, then?"

"Well, he *was*," she said. "He complimented me in Idosa too, but I thought I'd ended that in the veil!"

"Would it be so horrible to let him walk you home?" said her father with a frown.

"I don't know! I thought he was awkward, then I thought he was an arrogant villain, and now I think he's just... prickly and difficult, and he makes me uncomfortable with that vulnerable look in his eyes. Why should he be kind to me? I haven't been kind to him! He shouldn't want to spend another minute in my presence!"

Sedum laughed. "Astrantia, now you are being ridiculous. You are beautiful and accomplished, and he respects your character. Why should he *not* want to spend time with you? It would be strange if he didn't."

"What exactly did he promise you with regards to our shop when you were in Idosa?" said Agaricus.

"He promised he would ask the king whether there had been any progress on the investigation into the vandalism. I can't imagine there would be, and I would not expect any real update after all this time." She frowned. "Why?"

"So his decision to spend a remarkable sum on gifts for humans, and Lord Mosswing, with whom he was never before friendly, was likely made after you insulted him in the veil."

"Do you think he is attempting to purchase my affection?" Astrantia frowned. "I find that difficult to believe, both that he would want to and that he would think it available for purchase."

"Not at all. No fairy could fake the emotion he showed me when he spoke of the recipients of his gifts. I am convinced he intended to be extravagant in his gifts to his friends regardless of who made the weapons. However, I believe he was immensely pleased that his lavish spending would benefit your family."

"He promised only to ask the king, not to do anything to benefit my family at all. There is no reason why he should want to." But there was an uncomfortable twinge in her breast as she realized that there was indeed a reason. "He cannot bear me any affection now. It makes no sense."

Sedum said, "Astrantia, my dear, when has love ever made perfect sense? We always love despite our own flaws and despite the flaws of our beloved, because love is a reflection of the divine, not a reflection of our own selfish nature."

Astrantia buried her face in her hands again. "I find it difficult to believe Willowvale, of all people, would reflect the divine," she muttered.

"Is it not even more difficult to believe that we could ever fully comprehend the plans and ways of the divine?" said Sedum.

The Fair maiden shook her head. "Of course it is *possible* that grace can change someone. I just find it difficult to believe it changed *him*."

Agaricus laughed aloud. "It sounds like you dislike the fact that he's being pleasant more than you disliked his unpleasantness."

Astrantia scowled at him. "Of course I don't dislike the fact that he's being pleasant! What a nonsensical thing to say."

Her brother laughed again, soft and low and amused. "Why are you trying to convince yourself you hate him?"

"I'm not!" she snapped.

Then she put her hands over her face and wept.

CHAPTER FORTY-EIGHT
Too Kind

His Majesty Silverthorn had directed Lady Astrantia Berrydell to select her own staff for the new delegation. Though she was less angry with Hawksbane, Fallingwater, and Tarragon than she had been with Brookbower himself, she still had no intention of bringing them back to Aricht. Instead, she interviewed five servants that His Majesty offered as possibilities, as well as three other fairies with whom she and her father were acquainted.

In the end, she selected three of the king's personnel and one of her childhood friends. Iris Gentian would serve as her personal servant, while the others would manage the house, grounds, and other minor tasks. In truth, the delegation would have been entirely adequate with only the ambassador herself and a personal servant as befitted her status. The others were sent to reinforce the importance of the delegation rather than actual need. None of them other than Astrantia spoke a word of Arichtan, so they would need to have at least one human servant, especially at first. She would arrange for them all to have lessons in Arichtan as well.

The swords for Lord Cedar Mosswing and Mr. Theodore Overton were finished the day before Astrantia was to depart for Idosa with her new delegation. The one for Lord Willowvale himself was not finished yet, but Sedum decided there was no reason to make the Fair lord wait unnecessarily for the other two.

"Would you like to come with me to deliver them to Lord Willowvale?" Sedum asked that morning.

"No!"

"I really don't see why you hate him so much," Sedum said abruptly. "I would not have expected to like him, but I very nearly do. Besides saving your life, it seems he has entirely changed his attitude toward humans which you so despised."

"I know," Astrantia said miserably. "How can I face him when I judged him so harshly, when he had already begun to change?" She remembered the fury in her voice when she told him she despised him, and the wretched despair in his voice when he agreed with her.

"What would make you feel better, Astrantia?" Sedum asked. "To avoid him? To apologize? To tell him you are angry that he is not as horrible as he was before?"

"I don't want to see him at all!" she exclaimed. "He's… troubling, that's what he is. He was too kind to me after what I said to him, and I don't like to think of him loving me enough to brave the veil, wounded as he was, for me, knowing that I despised him. It is almost too much to bear when I think him a villain. I couldn't bear it at all if I knew for a fact he had truly repented of his actions."

"Don't you *want* him to have repented of them?" asked Agaricus, frowning.

"I… I don't know!" she said. "I want him to have repented, so that he is a better lord and advisor to the king, a better person, but I don't like how it makes me feel about my own guilt. Don't ask me such questions, Agaricus! I don't appreciate having to voice my own selfishness and cowardice so clearly."

Agaricus carefully, kindly, enfolded her in his strong arms. "Oh, little sister," he murmured. "You do love him, I think. A girl likes to be crossed a little in love now and then."

"What strange creatures brothers are!" she exclaimed. "That is not at all what I said!"

"It is obviously what you meant," said Sedum. "Are you coming or not?"

"Absolutely not."

CHAPTER FORTY-NINE
To Influence a King

When the sword maker delivered the swords to Willowvale, the lord was receiving the Fair king in his largest and most luxurious sitting room. The fire blazed in the grate, and Willowvale was sharing some of the tea Theo had given him, to the king's great delight.

The Fair monarch and the lord examined the swords.

"These are beyond compare," said Willowvale at last. "They are even more beautiful than I had hoped."

"I cannot gainsay that," murmured the king. "I believe I want one for myself, too."

A giddy sense of vindication and excitement made Sedum take a deep breath. He chose his words carefully. "I will endeavor to please you, Your Majesty, but I must tell you the same conditions under which I took Lord Willowvale's commissions."

"And what are those conditions?" growled the king.

"I do not make weapons for use against humans, and my art is always in the service of honor and friendship." Sedum bowed, as if this would somehow make these conditions more palatable to a king who had warred against humans.

"And beauty," added Willowvale, with another glance at the swords.

With a dismissive little huff, the king sat back in his chair. "The sword I want is in the service of friendship. I will not use it against humans, if that is your condition."

The sword maker blinked, for he really had not expected the king to agree at all, much less with so little argument.

"How much is Willowvale paying for these?"

Willowvale said, "Fifteen thousand each."

"Make me one worth twenty thousand," said the king. "Amethyst, opal, whatever you think best."

"Yes, Your Majesty. Shall I draw some designs and bring them to the palace for your approval?"

Silverthorn waved a hand carelessly. "I am sure it will be superlative."

"And the measurements?" Sedum asked. "I will need to know your arm length."

"Close enough to Willowvale's that the difference will not matter," said the king. "I do not intend to fight with it anyway."

"Yes, Your Majesty." The sword maker bowed. "I will bring you the finished sword, then."

They made other minor arrangements, and then Willowvale directed Alyssum to pay Sedum for the swords.

When the sword maker was gone, Willowvale said, "Thank you, Your Majesty."

The king gave him a sidelong look. "Don't thank me. You're not in my debt, Willowvale, and I did you no favor. I made a small start toward repaying what the Fair Lands owe you."

The Fair lord laughed softly. "I think we ought to acknowledge it as friendship, Your Majesty."

"If you want to think of it that way, I will not attempt to dissuade you." The king's lips curled in a grimace. "I've never had a friend."

Willowvale's smile widened.

CHAPTER FIFTY
Heartache

T he new Fair delegation met at dawn at the palace gate, as instructed by the king. Lady Astrantia Berrydell had been allowed to select the fairy who would lead them through the veil. Lord Mosswing did not know the way and she could not face Lord Willowvale yet, which left only Lords Camphor and Aspen as options.

She had reluctantly selected Aspen as the more taciturn of the brothers, and had made him swear that he would do no harm to any humans, nor would he step foot into Aricht at all, before she consented to accept his guidance. The king also required him to swear that he would bring the delegation safely to Aricht or back to the Fair Lands, or die trying, out of concern that Aspen would somehow attempt to sabotage the delegation.

Lord Aspen managed to get them to the edge of Idosa in about sixteen terrifying hours, in which they narrowly avoided being eaten by something that squelched in the dark. It retreated when Astrantia thrust a hint of power at it and sent it tumbling; they never saw the creature, and Lord Aspen declared that was far preferable to letting it get close enough to give them nightmares.

"I may not approve of your appointment, Berrydell, or your title, but you are handy to have in the tunnels," he said.

"Thank you," she said stiffly, for this seemed an uncommonly generous thing for Aspen to say.

Aspen huffed in the dark, as if annoyed to be thanked for anything resembling friendliness.

Still, he said it was one of his better routes and was pleased to have encountered so little difficulty.

"Here you are," he said at last. He opened the veil to reveal the street dark and empty. He craned his neck and looked around without stepping into the street. "No idea where you are. Good luck." He gave her a sharp, not altogether friendly, grin as the fairies of the delegation stepped past him into the human world.

Then he let the door close, to walk alone back to the Fair Lands, while Astrantia and her staff were left to figure out what to do next.

In the shadows, it was challenging to figure out where they were, but since the palace was upon a hill in the middle of the city, they were eventually able to find their way by walking uphill. This simple method of navigating was not without its challenges, for the incline was not remotely uniform and it was easy to lose one's bearings in the circuitous streets, especially on such a cloudy and moonless night. Still, Astrantia had an excellent sense of direction, and once they had been able to get a sense of the general slope and a glimpse of the top of the palace through a break in the roofs, they made good time.

All in their party were tired, and Astrantia nourished an uncomfortable sense of guilt about the fact that the three servants were carrying more weight than she was. She offered again to carry a trunk, now that she didn't feel the need to keep one hand upon her sword.

"I would hate to have to tell His Majesty Silverthorn that I let you carry your own trunk into the Arichtan palace," said Mardara gravely.

"I cannot imagine he would ask," said Astrantia.

The Fair servant shook his head. "Please do not order me to give it to you," he said. "My shoulders are not so weak as to require that the honored ambassador of our people carry her own trunk."

There was not even a hint of teasing mirth in his voice, only a dogged determination, so Astrantia sighed and dropped the matter.

Although she had been given the address of the house which had reportedly been prepared for them, it was on a street the name of which Astrantia did not recognize. Besides, it seemed advisable to present themselves at the palace before attempting to find the house.

"I am Lady Astrantia Berrydell, ambassador from the Fair Lands, and these are my assistants," said Astrantia at the gate.

"Come with me." The guard let her in immediately.

They were conducted with little fanfare to a sitting room, where they waited for some time. The fairies put the various trunks on the floor and stretched their shoulders and backs, but did not otherwise relax.

The servant returned and led them to the throne room, where the Arichtan king sat upon the throne.

Astrantia had only seen him actually sit upon his throne once before, when Brookbower's delegation had been formally received into the human nation. She raised her chin. His Majesty Silverthorn had conveyed to her that Elmerick was furious with the would-be assassin and his accomplices, but this did not mean that he was not still equally furious with the Fair Folk who had so terribly used the human children. The Fair Folk she now represented.

"Miss Berrydell," the king said.

"Your Majesty." She bowed deeply, letting every graceful line of her body convey both respect and pride. "May I approach the throne?" She pulled the letter from her jacket and held it out, letting him see that she had no weapon.

Not that she needed one, but if he wasn't already aware that she didn't need one, she certainly wasn't going to tell him.

"You may."

She presented the letter to him and stepped back.

Oak Silverthorn, King of All Seelie, to Valor Elmerick, King of Aricht, of the human lands,

Lady Astrantia Berrydell, Marchioness of the Fair Lands, has been appointed ambassador from the Fair Lands to Aricht at your request. She now bears the title Marchioness, the equal of that of that former ambassador Lord Linden Brookbower, who will never again step foot in Aricht on pain of death from your people or mine.

Please accord her every honor and respect due to her appointment and title, as well as the personal honor she has demonstrated toward your people. Note too that I will hold you personally responsible for her safety, as well as that of her delegation. Any harm that comes to them will be held against Aricht itself.

Sincerely,

HRH Oak Silverthorn

The Arichtan king pressed his lips together as he read this.

"Welcome back to Aricht, Lady Berrydell," he said. He folded up the letter and put it aside. "I am glad to see that you are recovered."

"I am, thanks to the healing magic of a Fair lord," she said.

"It is late. Let me offer you the hospitality of the palace, and you will be escorted to your house in the city tomorrow." The king nodded to a servant by the door. "I have pledged my honor for your safety, Lady Berrydell."

"What of the assassins?" said Astrantia. "Where are they?"

The king sighed. "Lord Buckley and his co-conspirator are still detained here. We will talk about them tomorrow."

Astrantia agreed, and shortly afterward she and her staff were in guest suites, with fires started for them by the palace staff and a late dinner being prepared.

Soon the servants arrived with a dinner tray for each of the fairies and bowed themselves out.

She had thought that she had put the horrible experience behind her, that the memories were only memories. In the safety and gracious hospitality of the Overton estate, and then the longed-for comfort and familiarity of home, it was easy to put those thoughts from her mind. Now, looking at the pork roast and scalloped potatoes, herbed peppers, and wine, her stomach churned with fear and loathing. The agony of faebane, the helpless retching and nausea that made the world swim, the feverish crawling that felt like worms beneath her skin, they were all so very fresh and raw, as real and present as the fire crackling only a few feet away.

If she had been at home, she would have buried her face in her father's chest for a moment, breathing his scent of gold and fire and smoke, and reminding herself that she was the daughter of the greatest sword maker ever to put hammer to blade. She would have thought of her mother's courage and fierce love in the last moments of her life, a bright light that had guided Astrantia's actions for many years.

If she had been at home, she would have known the food placed before her would not bring inevitable, agonizing death.

For there was no Lord Cedar Mosswing with his extraordinary healing magic here in Aricht, no Lord Ash Willowvale to brave the veil, ignoring his own wound, to bring her to a foreign land and safety. No ability to even open the veil and flee into it herself, to die in the veil rather than on the rug here in this guest room.

If she ate this food and drank this wine, she was choosing perhaps to die here. She was choosing to trust this human king, who had pledged his honor for her safety, but had already failed once in this basic responsibility of a host.

The Fair maiden took a deep breath and let it out as slowly as she could, using the control to slow her racing heart.

She took a sip of the wine, noting how it was inferior to the wine of the Fair Lands. She could detect no hint of poison, but she had not exactly tasted the poison the first time, either; she had merely been able to taste the bitterness of the human wine at first. Only once the pangs had started twisting in her belly had she realized the danger.

A bite of bread, then another cautious sip. Then, with resignation, a good swallow of wine. Either she would die, and Silverthorn would find out eventually and there was nothing she could do to preserve the peace, or she would live for now.

When she finished the meal, her stomach felt twisted in knots, but it was only the nerves she would not acknowledge rather than poison that wracked her.

At last, the tray having been returned to the servants outside, she slipped into her night clothes and then into bed. She had underestimated how much courage this assignment required. Lord Willowvale must be bold indeed to have returned so quickly after being so grievously wounded on a mission of peace.

She had underestimated him. She had judged him prickly and prideful, when he was wounded and awkward and proud.

Tomorrow, she would have to face the assassin and his co-conspirator.

The Arichtans did not disturb the Fair delegation the following morning, so the fairies would have slept late, tired as they were after a long and arduous trip through the veil, except that Astrantia's sense of dread about the meeting with the assassin woke her much earlier than she wished. She dressed in the Fair style, for it seemed reasonable to her to represent her people in her attire for these first few days in Aricht, even if she would dress in human attire for future visits. The cut was not so very different than what was in fashion in the human world, though the Fair fabric stretched in ways that silk and satin could not. The confining styles of the human world, made in human fabrics, constricted her movement too much to allow good use of her arms if she needed to defend herself.

To be sure, she was not afraid the human assassin would be able to harm her physically; the poison he had used was the next thing to an admission that he was no match for a fairy in single combat, if the fairy had any warning at all. But she did not look forward to facing the hatred of someone so bitterly opposed to her species or to peace with her people.

First, however, she met with His Majesty Valor Elmerick.

"You understand the political issues with an execution, I am sure," said the king. "Not to mention that I am personally sympathetic to the man's grievance against the Fair Folk. Of course I did not sanction the attack; I was not aware of it, and I would have prevented it, had I known of it. But the man's niece was one of the children kidnapped by your people, and she was so traumatized by the experience that has not spoken in the months since she was returned to the human world."

The Fair ambassador frowned. "That is tragic indeed. Has she recovered now?"

"Not to my knowledge."

"I would like to speak with her before I see the assassin." Perhaps, if she could reassure the child, she could make some sort of headway with the angry nobleman. It seemed a tenuous hope, but whether this effort made a difference with the man or not, it seemed like the right thing to do. The child deserved an apology from someone on behalf of the Fair Folk, and as ambassador, it was her responsibility.

His Majesty Elmerick had been informed by his intelligence personnel that Theo had visited the McStrettons several times, and that later he had been accompanied by Willowvale. The officers surveilling the young Valestrian and his Fair friend had not been able to ascertain exactly what had transpired within the McStretton house, and the king had not wanted to further disturb the McStrettons by asking them directly.

The king studied the Fair maiden before him. Her magenta eyes, dark with subdued emotion, were steady upon his. She was not afraid, or if she was, he could not tell. "What would you tell her?" he asked.

"I will apologize on behalf of the Fair throne for what she suffered," said Astrantia.

"Did your king give you leave to do that?" asked Elmerick in surprise.

The ambassador smiled, her pink lips curving softly. "His Majesty gave me authority to represent the Fair Lands, and this is how I choose to carry out my mission here."

"I will require them to attend a meeting here this afternoon," said the king. "In the meantime, I will have my staff escort you to the house Willowvale prepared for you."

Astrantia nearly flinched. "Willowvale prepared the house?" she asked.

"Of course he did," said the king. "It wasn't Overton's place to do it, and no other fairies were permitted here until your king accepted our terms."

The fairy swallowed and nodded. "Of course." She ought to have known. She *had* known; she just had not wanted to think about it.

What was she afraid of? That the house would be horrible? Irascible he might be, but Willowvale hardly seemed petty enough to tarnish the honor of the Fair Court to enact some trifling retaliation for her unkind words in the veil. Besides, his letter was not remotely petty, and if it was not warm, it was certainly not cold or angry either. Angry at himself, perhaps, but not her.

When she had met him in that mortifying intrusion into his garden, he had been almost friendly, if such a thing could be imagined. He had been as warm and kind as he knew how to be, asking after her health and congratulating her on her new position. *Delighted to be detained*, indeed. Not to mention that he knew of her new title.

Silverthorn had never been particularly forthcoming about anything, at least to her knowledge, so not only were Willowvale and Silverthorn even closer friends than she had guessed, but Willowvale had likely asked him directly about her in order to obtain this tidbit of information. How uncomfortable it was to imagine herself being spoken about, as if she were an object of interest!

Other questions lurked at the back of her mind, but she did not want to ask them yet. She did not want to know the answers yet.

So she said only, "I look forward to seeing our new home, Your Majesty."

Soon the Fair delegation was packed and loaded into two carriages which departed the palace while the sun was still low in the sky. The wind was not exactly warm, but it was less icy than when she had last felt it several weeks earlier.

The carriage drew up in front of a house, and the driver jumped down to open the door and help the Fair ambassador out. She let him take her hand and let her down, as if she had been a lady all her life, though it seemed both silly and presumptuous to assume this dignity.

Then she looked up.

The house was stunning. Willowvale had commissioned an artist to modify the angular golden design upon the blue door with little vines, leaves, and golden blooms in the shape of astrantia blossoms which wove between and through the sharp lines, softening and beautifying the design in a way that was infinitely more pleasing to Fair senses while avoiding actual insult to the Arichtan artist who had likely believed his work excellent. The wide flagstone path to the white-roofed patio on the front of the house was lined with pink astrantia blooms, which could only be blooming at this time of year by Fair magic, and cheerful white mounds of snowdrops, white and purple crocuses, and white trilliums. Moss paths wove through the front garden, edged with pale blue blooms and petite lilies of the valley.

Even Astrantia, not gifted with the magic of plants, could feel the power thrumming through the garden. The very soil sang in welcome when she stepped onto the path.

Silverthorn had given her the key when she had last seen him, and she pulled it from her jacket now. It was bronze; of course Willowvale would not have brought an iron key to the Fair Lands, much less given to Silverthorn or to her.

The rest of the delegation followed her, depositing the luggage in the front room while they explored the house. The front sitting room was bright and fresh, with moss upon the floor and white trumpet vines climbing two walls. Two large oil paintings, one of white peonies and the other of pink and white roses, in ornate gold frames adorned the other walls, vying for space with a delicate tracery of white lichen.

From the windows she could see the front garden and the myrtles, azaleas, and roses which would bloom in the spring, and the narrow side garden with variegated ivy climbing the brick wall between the yard and the street and pink dianthus sheltering beneath redbuds and more azaleas.

Every room was a new work of art, with paintings that depicted the most beautiful flowers and landscapes of Aricht between vibrant blooms and leaves of a thousand shades of green.

By the time Astrantia reached the third floor, where the bedrooms were, she could not speak for the emotion that filled her. It should not have surprised her that the beds swung, suspended by vines, near the ceiling, nor that the largest room was obviously intended to be hers. Bright pink and white astrantia blooms clustered in each corner. The elegant wooden desk sat upon a bed of moss with pale blue flowers across from the fireplace, and the chair behind it was upholstered in silk that matched the pink of the astrantia blooms. The chairs and settee by the fire were upholstered in white silk brocade, which contrasted beautifully with the dark wood.

The beauty of it all was so carefully considered, so extravagant an expenditure of Fair magic in this human land, that she half-expected a note from Willowvale. What it would say, she could not guess, but it seemed that he wanted her attention.

He had gotten it, too.

But there was no note, in this room or any other. She explored the garden, which brought tears to her eyes with its beauty. Every little nook, every thoughtful combination of bloom color, petal shape, leaf form, and plant habit, felt like a gift.

It was a gift, but there was no response required or even expected. He had created this splendor without being sure she would even see it.

"Lady Berrydell," said Iris behind her. "The driver said His Majesty asked you to return for lunch at the palace, and the family you were to speak with would arrive in the early afternoon."

"I will be there in a moment." When the servant retreated, Astrantia sat upon the bench beside the little pond. Even now, in the barren winter, the sheltered garden promised exuberant life and verdant beauty in the warmer months.

Of all gifts she could have imagined, this seemed most personal and most thoughtful, for it was conceived to make her stay in Aricht as delightful and pleasing as the human world could be. It had cost

Willowvale, too, for the magic was his personal magic, given freely and generously, in the service of beauty which he had likely believed he would only rarely, if ever, see himself.

It was all for her.

Her heart ached. As the carriage rolled to a stop in front of the Arichtan palace, she took a deep breath and pressed the pain down until it was only a melancholy longing laced through with guilt, so quiet and indistinct that she would not have been able to identify it even if she had wanted to.

The rest of the Fair delegation had been left at the house to unpack and begin to interact with the human chef and domestic servant who had apparently been hired. This was yet another oddity, for Astrantia had been informed that Mr. Theodore Overton, IV, had been the one to interview and hire these two people. It was strange indeed to have a Valestrian nobleman, however low in status, involved in these decisions, and the fact that he was the Rose only made it stranger.

Still, when she had met these two servants briefly, she had liked them, and there was every reason to be grateful that she did not have to manage this task herself.

Soon she was seated in a small dining room in the palace, where she ate alone under the close scrutiny of the single palace servant attending her. Putting each bite in her mouth was not quite as uncomfortable an experience as it had been the previous evening, but her stomach still churned with nerves, not to mention how awkward it was to eat alone while being so closely watched.

When she finished, she was escorted to a sitting room, small and intimate compared to others in the palace, but still far grander than any in most noble houses.

The McStrettons had already arrived, and they stood near the fireplace. His Majesty Elmerick stood near them with his arms crossed, frowning thoughtfully.

At her entrance, the king nodded to the servant at the door, who performed the introductions.

The man bowed to her and the lady and girl curtseyed politely, eyeing her in obvious curiosity.

Astrantia bowed in the Fair tradition, with her right arm gracefully outstretched, every line of her body conveying elegance and easy power. Though her Fair dress was relatively subdued compared to current fashions in the Fair Lands, it was far brighter and more lovely than anything in the human world. The bodice was a bright white fabric very much like silk, but it was of the Fair lands, so the texture was different. It was both sturdier and softer, and it had a faint stretch to it that human weaves could not achieve. A narrow line of magenta floral embroidery edged the neckline and the short sleeves; the color of this set off her magenta hair and eyes to perfection. The skirt was full with layers of frothy white silk edged in more embroidered flowers of magenta, pale pink, sky blue, and indigo, as if a vibrant garden grew from the bottom hem of each layer of fabric. As it was winter, she wore a matching jacket over the short-sleeved dress; this jacket was a deep sapphire blue with pink and white embroidery upon the cuffs and a brilliant pink lining. Altogether, she looked stunning, in the Fair fashion, and dazzling in comparison to the pastel greens and blues which the McStrettons wore.

The girl let out a soft breath. "You are *so* beautiful, lady," she breathed.

The ambassador blinked. "You are quite lovely yourself," she said kindly. "Would you converse with me?"

Charity nodded. "What would you have me say?"

"Well, anything at all, I suppose. I was told you had not spoken since you were rescued from the Fair Lands by the Rose, whom your people call the Wraith." Astrantia smiled. "I am glad to hear you speaking now."

The child opened her mouth, hesitated, and said in a rush, "It's still hard sometimes. But I think the other fairy helped."

"The other fairy?"

"Lord Willowvale," Sir Briscoe interjected. "He visited twice."

Astrantia asked, "And what did he say to you that helped?"

Charity's soft blue eyes filled with tears. "He said… he said that he and the Fair king had thought humans less than fairies, and that they were desperate to save their own people, and he had realized how wrong he was about us. He said he didn't expect forgiveness, and he didn't exactly ask for it, but I should have told him I forgave him. He said he was sorry."

The Fair ambassador's heart twisted so tightly that she could barely speak for a moment. "He said he was sorry?"

The girl nodded. "I told him I wasn't afraid of him, and that was true. But I should have told him I forgave him. I have now, but I couldn't bring myself to say it at the time. I don't like to think of someone's guilt weighing upon them forever."

"What a kind-hearted thing to say," said Astrantia. "That is good of you."

"He didn't have to apologize to me," said Charity. "He didn't even kidnap me himself."

"I assume Mr. Overton made him apologize," said Sir Briscoe grimly. "Still, it helped, and I am glad of that."

Charity shook her head. "Mr. Overton might have made him come, but no one made him say what he said to me."

"Well," said Astrantia. Her mind whirled. "That is… I am glad it helped. I was going to apologize to you on behalf of the Fair throne for what you suffered at the hands of my people."

"You were not part of the plan, though, were you?" said the nobleman.

"No, nor did I know of it until after Lord Brookbower and his delegation were arrested." Astrantia sighed and met Charity's eyes. "Still, I now represent the Fair throne here in Aricht, and thus it is my place to express my personal regret and the guilt of the Fair crown for what was done to you, Miss McStretton, and to other children. His Majesty Silverthorn has sworn to never take or harm humans again, and we Fair Folk honor our vows. I am proud to have met you, Miss McStretton."

She bowed again deeply, first to the child who had suffered and then to the parents who had grieved for her.

"Thank you, Lady Berrydell," said Charity. The little girl took a deep, tremulous breath, and said, "My uncle… will he be executed?"

Astrantia licked her lips and glanced at the king, whose troubled look deepened. "What do you think should happen to him?" the fairy asked gently.

The girl brushed tears from her cheeks and looked at her mother. Lady McStretton raised her chin and said, "My brother is impetuous, and I know you have reason to hate him, Lady Berrydell, but…" She stopped and sucked in a breath, trying to compose herself. "He is not a violent man. Can you find it in your heart to pardon him?"

Astrantia felt the weight of the woman's grief and fear. "His crime was not only against me, but against the lawfully appointed representatives of the Fair Court. Such a pardon would hardly be justice, would it?"

Trembling, the woman pressed a hand to her mouth but said nothing else, though her eyes filled with tears.

The king nodded to one of his advisors, who ushered the McStretton family out of the room.

"Does the assassin know that Miss McStretton is speaking again, and that it was Lord Willowvale's kindness that encouraged her to do so?" Astrantia said to the king. If the words sounded a little accusatory, perhaps it was not entirely by accident, because it seemed to the Fair ambassador that this could be a grave oversight on behalf of the king toward his own subject.

"He was informed of Miss McStretton's improved condition this afternoon." The king studied her. "I am sure you understand how reluctant I am to actually execute Lord Buckley and his co-conspirators. Of course the assassination attempt cannot be countenanced, and of course there must be some sort of trial and sentencing. But execution? When I was so merciful with Lord Brookbower? You cannot truly expect it."

Astrantia sighed. "No, I do not. I want to speak with him, though."

She and the king strode through the palace in a tense silence, aside from the sound of the boots of the guards and the click-click of the king's elegant shoes. Her own shoes were silent, as she preferred them to be, but her skirts made a swishing sound that softened the echoes.

At Lord Buckley's door, the group stopped.

"Open it," said the king.

One of the guards complied.

The man was standing when the door swung open, and he bowed to the king. "Your Majesty."

The king nodded.

"Lord Buckley," said Astrantia, with a slight, elegant bow.

"Miss Berrydell." He bowed to her, which she had not expected.

"I am honored to now serve my people as ambassador on behalf of all Seelie Fair Folk, and I have been given the title Marchioness, the equal of Lord Brookbower's title." Astrantia smiled a little, though it was more a feeling of satisfaction than mirth or humor.

"I see. Lady Berrydell, then." Lord Buckley bowed again. "I was informed that you had returned to Aricht. Is there to be war, then, or will my death prevent further bloodshed?"

The Fair ambassador studied his face, so grave and proud, so unwilling to grieve his own expected death. She sighed softly. "I do not want war."

The man's gray eyes were steady on her face, and he pressed his lips together in a pale line, but he said nothing.

"Just like humans, we Fair Folk are individuals, not a monolithic species opposed to your kind," Astrantia said. "There have been changes in the Fair Court I never imagined possible, and in certain fairies I would never have imagined possible.

"Lord Brookbower is banished from your lands on pain of death, as are the Fair lords who stole the children. I was unaware of the plan until we were detained, and my staff is entirely new and was opposed to using children from the beginning.

"Can we not live in peace?"

He said, "I have no quarrel with you personally, Lady Berrydell, but I hardly think you're asking for my forgiveness. My anger burns against Brookbower and whoever else was involved in tormenting my niece and the other children."

"I was told you were informed that your niece spoke this afternoon."

"I was." His voice cracked. "I am glad of it."

"I understand that this step in her healing was largely due to Lord Willowvale."

Lord Buckley straightened even more. "I find it difficult to believe that arrogant wretch ever did anything kind in his life, and I certainly will not credit any progress in Miss McStretton's healing to him."

Astrantia stared at him in consternation. "She told me he apologized to her, though he did not kidnap her himself; he apologized for what she suffered, and she forgave him."

The man swallowed. "What do you want from me?" he said at last. "If you want a war, there's nothing I can do to stop it. If you want me dead, legally, I imagine a sincere threat to His Majesty will accomplish that. Or you could simply kill me yourself."

"I want peace between our peoples, Lord Buckley," Astrantia said. "Lord Willowvale apologized to a child; he didn't have to do that! I don't require an apology from you, but I do require a solemn vow, upon your honor, that you will not harm or threaten me or my staff, or any other fairy legally in Aricht."

"And if I so swear?" Buckley raised his eyebrows. "Then what? You'll pardon me?" He gave a low, bitter laugh. "That is the most ridiculous thing I've heard yet. You were the only innocent member of the Fair delegation, and the one who suffered most; why should *you* pardon me?"

"Because I choose to." Astrantia took a deep breath. "Because I can. Because I'm stronger than my pain, and I want peace more than war between our peoples. Can you accept peace rather than vengeance? Your niece can, Lord Buckley. Do you really think you have more reason to be bitter and angry than she does?"

The man let out a soft breath. "I will swear to take no further vengeance upon Fair Folk for what has past, but I will not swear not to oppose a fairy if I see one harming children in the future."

Astrantia smiled. "I will accept that."

All this time, the Arichtan king had stood in silence, letting the human lord and Fair ambassador find their own tense peace. Now Astrantia looked at him and said, "Your Majesty, I will accept a similar vow from the other conspirators, and I, and the Fair throne, will require no further punishment, provided you and your subjects uphold the peace we have forged."

His Majesty Elmerick smiled as he said, "You have my word, Lady Berrydell."

CHAPTER FIFTY-ONE
A New Friend

That very week, Lord Ash Willowvale presented the sword he had commissioned for Lord Cedar Mosswing to the recipient. He rode out early in the morning to the Mosswing estate some distance east of Dewspring-in-the-Wood.

Willowvale had never before set foot on the Mosswing estate, though he had ridden past it. It was an expansive property, far larger than his own, though more remote and with less access to the king. Since it was so large, it contained both gardens almost as carefully manicured as his own, since Mosswing employed a gardener with plant magic, and miles of surrounding forested hills.

His monster tossed its mane and screamed when one of the servants attempted to take its reins, and Willowvale hushed it. It consented to be led away to the stable, though it muttered and growled its displeasure all the while.

When he strode up to the door, the doorman allowed him in and took him to a sitting room. Cedar appeared in the door a moment later.

"Willowvale." The dark lord eyed him curiously.

Willowvale had dressed in what he felt to be a particularly cheerful suit; not only was the cut the height of fashion, but he had selected a pale blue jacket and trousers edged in sapphire blue embroidery, and a deep magenta silk shirt that made his pale skin nearly gleam in the cool winter sunlight. The similarity of the magenta to Astrantia's hair color was not exactly intentional, but when the fairy had realized it, the thought of her had provoked a quiet, melancholy pleasure.

"Mosswing." Willowvale bowed. "Forgive me for intruding. I wanted to give you this as a token of my appreciation for the generosity of your actions toward Lady Berrydell." He held the cloth-wrapped sword out in both hands and bowed deeply.

"What is it?" Cedar approached and took the bundle, though he did not unwrap it.

"A gift in the human tradition, if you will accept it." Willowvale's hands trembled at his sides, and he clenched them, not wanting this motion to betray him. He kept his voice steady. "I have already said I am in your debt. This is not enough to repay you for what you did for Lady Berrydell, but it pleases me to offer it as an inadequate expression of my gratitude."

Cedar sighed. "Willowvale, I have already said I do not consider you to be in my debt, and certainly not for her life. You don't have to do this."

Willowvale smiled, sharp and bright. "I choose to. And so that there is no doubt of my motives…" He dug in a pocket and pulled out a coin, which he handed to Cedar.

The other fairy accepted it gravely, folded his fingers around it to assert full ownership, and then handed it back.

When Cedar folded the velvet back to reveal the bejeweled scabbard, he let out a soft breath. "This is beyond reasonable, Willowvale," he said.

"What is a reasonable expression of gratitude for a life?"

Cedar stepped back and drew the sword, his turquoise eyes taking in every intricate curve of the filigree, every sparkle of the priceless gems upon the guard. "This is Sedum Berrydell's work, isn't it?" he said at last.

"It is."

"I haven't heard of Sedum and Agaricus in years. I didn't know they were still in business."

"Lady Berrydell believed they were intentionally frozen out when they refused to support the war. She felt it unjust." Willowvale swallowed, feeling unexpectedly vulnerable. He cleared his throat. "I thought it both fitting and gratifying to purchase gifts for those I respect and value from such an artist, who put principle above expediency or popularity."

"As you did," Cedar said flatly. "You never once considered your popularity when you sought to kill the Wraith."

Willowvale's breath hitched, and he turned away, unwilling to look at the sword, much less Cedar. "I was wrong," he muttered.

Cedar shrugged a shoulder. "I was not intending to throw your sins in your face, Willowvale. I was merely noting that you, too, have sacrificed for your principles. It is a painful thing to acknowledge when one has staked one's life upon the wrong ideas, and it takes uncommon courage to change course."

Willowvale felt his heart thudding in his chest. "I don't expect kind words from you, Mosswing. Don't feel obligated to give them." He bowed sharply and turned away.

"Willowvale!" Cedar said.

"What?" The pale fairy's long strides had already taken him halfway to the door, but he paused.

"Will you come to my wedding next week?"

Willowvale turned and stared at the other Fair lord. "Why would you want me there?"

"Why would I not?" Cedar's white teeth contrasted sharply with his dark skin as he smiled. "I think I would like to be able to call you a friend, and my other friends will be there to see my joy in Lady Miscanthus made complete."

"If you wish me to attend, I will be honored to do so."

"Thank you." The dark fairy's smile seemed warm and sincere, and he added, "A week from tomorrow, here, at ten."

"I will be here." Willowvale bowed again.

The veil was less obstreperous than usual the following Friday, and Willowvale stepped into the human world well before noon. He climbed to the top of the nearest hill to get his bearings and found the road between Ardmond and the Overton estate visible between two hilltops not too far away.

His strides were long and easy as he walked down the hillside. The wind gusted, catching at his long coat and tangling his white curls, but the scent of the air was more like that of the very beginning of spring than the dead of winter. The Fair lord had dressed in the human style that morning; it seemed fitting, given that he was visiting human friends. Besides, he wasn't sure whether dressing in the Fair style would appear insulting in the human world. It was one thing to be called upon unexpectedly and be found dressed in the style of his own land, but to call upon a friend in the human world wearing Fair clothing might be viewed differently.

He reached the road only a mile and a half from the turn to the Overton manor and turned toward his destination. The brilliant sun made the winter-drab landscape seem bright and hopeful, and he smiled to himself.

His pale cheeks were flushed with the wind and the pleasant heat of exercise by the time he strode up the steps of the Overton manor and knocked briskly upon the door.

"Lord Willowvale. Come in." Anselm welcomed him in with a little more friendliness than before.

"Thank you," said the Fair lord. He followed the servant to what had become his favorite sitting room in the human world. A fire already burned, and soon he was joined by Theo and Lily, who greeted him with warmth and kindness.

"This is for you," the fairy said. He bowed deeply and presented the cloth-wrapped sword to Theo with no more fanfare than this.

Theo had known this was coming; Willowvale had said as much weeks earlier. Still, the sword was beautiful enough to take his breath away.

"It is beautiful," he said softly. "Thank you." He accepted the coin from the fairy and gave it back with a deep bow of his own.

Willowvale found himself smiling as Theo admired the artistry of the weapon. "I am glad you like it."

"You didn't have to, you know." Theo looked up from the sword to the Fair lord.

"I owe you far more than a sword, Theo. I would be deeply grieved if you would not accept it."

"I would not want to grieve a friend," said Theo. "Still, I do not like to think of you feeling indebted to me."

Willowvale swallowed. "The debt I feel is of gratitude, and it is not a weight that burdens me, but a lightness that strengthens me. Still, it is a debt, and I do not think I shall ever be able to repay it." He cleared his throat from the uncomfortable tightness and smiled. "I do hope to enjoy tea with you for many years to come, and while I cannot hope to adequately convey the depth of my gratitude, I shall be delighted to commission you as many swords as you like."

Theo laughed. "That won't be necessary." He bowed and said, "I hope you will stay for dinner."

The fairy smiled again, feeling that the expression was not as strange upon his lips as it had been in previous years. "Lord Mosswing invited me to his wedding tomorrow, and though I hope the veil would not detain me all night, I should like to arrive in time to get properly dressed and travel to his estate."

"Stay the night, if you like. We'll leave first thing the morning and go directly to your home, so you can freshen up, and we can step through the veil if time is tight."

"When will I have the opportunity to reciprocate this hospitality?" said the fairy despairingly. "You heap generosity upon my head like coals!"

Theo laughed, for he could tell this protest was at least partly in jest, if not entirely. "Shall we invite ourselves to stay with you tomorrow night, then?"

The Fair lord's expression brightened. "Yes! I would like that very much."

CHAPTER FIFTY-TWO
The Mosswing Wedding

T he following morning Lord Fenton Selby and his new wife Lady
Crocus Selby arrived in time for an early breakfast. Anselm
packed Theo, Lily, and Anselm several days' worth of food, and
Willowvale laid magic upon it so that it would be hot and fresh
whenever they unwrapped it, so they were not limited to what could be
eaten cold.

Theo led the way through the veil, of course, and he did not want
Lily at the rear, so she found herself with one hand in the warm, strong
hand of her husband, so familiar and reassuring, and her other hand in
Juniper's hand. Juniper walked between Lily and Crocus, Crocus held
Fenton's hand, and Willowvale held the tail of Fenton's jacket.

Lily thought how strange it was to be traveling through the veil
with Willowvale. He had so deeply terrified and disgusted her with his
arrogant disregard of humanity, had nearly murdered her beloved
husband in cold blood. Yet Theo had undone him, and this strange,
new Willowvale, with his odd, awkward smiles and a shy sort of hope

in his eyes brought pity and compassion to her heart. He wanted to be different than he was, and though she did not feel the warmth Theo seemed to feel toward this erstwhile enemy, she could not hate him, either.

They stepped into Willowvale's garden less than an hour later, having encountered no difficulties or dangers in the veil at all.

"Mrs. Overton, I cannot express how remarkable your husband's skill in the veil is," said Willowvale. "Every time I am amazed anew."

Lily couldn't help smiling. "I am quite impressed with him myself," she said, with an impish gleam in her eye.

She was delighted to find that Theo's cheeks flushed, and he said, "Well, my love, I am always delighted to please you, but I cannot help but think we ought rather to admire Lord Willowvale's garden, don't you think?"

The Fair lord laughed aloud, and the sound was as bright as the early sunshine glittering on the dew adorning the fantastically colored leaves around them. "I didn't realize that you were so easily flustered by an honest compliment, Theo. I shall endeavor to do so at every opportunity."

Theo's flush deepened, and he said emphatically, "I would much rather you not! Please, Ash."

Still smiling, Willowvale began to lead them toward the house. "I should like credit for restraining my compliments, then, for I am sincerely in awe of your skill and find it quite difficult to limit myself to one expression of admiration each time I see it demonstrated."

"I appreciate your restraint from the bottom of my heart," said Theo, and Lily laughed at them both. Fenton smiled quietly, and even Crocus and Juniper, cautious as they were of Willowvale, found themselves amused.

When they reached the Fair lord's house, Lily stared about in amazement and complimented the fairy on the beauty and elegance of the house, though it was all strange to her. The juxtaposition of moss and marble, stained glass and jasmine, carved wood and rough lichen, all served to heighten the beauty of each contrasting element, so that one's attention was drawn from one gorgeous vignette to the next. Theo realized that Willowvale preferred a quieter, more steady sort of beauty than Silverthorn did, for though he obviously had the ability to modify the plants as he chose, there was little change between each of Theo's visits. A bank of foxgloves in one corner might have shifted to make way for a bunch of crocosmia, tulips, and scabiosa, but for the most part, the manor and its verdant decor were unchanged from one visit to the next.

Willowvale's guests were offered tea and rooms in which to change clothes and refresh themselves, while the Fair lord changed into a suit appropriate for a wedding. Though Theo's skill with the veil was unmatched, it was never safe to assume one would arrive with one's clothes pristine, so everyone had brought their attire for the wedding.

When they were alone in a guest room, Theo helped Lily lace up the back of her dress, which was a lovely deep green velvet with extravagant jewels around the neckline and down the sleeves. It was both elegant and warm, for the weather was still quite chilly.

Lily, in turn, admired Theo as he dressed in a fashionable suit with a deep green waistcoat that coordinated perfectly with her dress.

"You are stunning, my love," Theo said, his eyes alight with passion.

"And you are irresistible." Her smile deepened as he ran his hands over her shoulders and pulled her close.

Within only a few minutes, their Fair host was also ready, and they walked together toward the front of the house, where a carriage was waiting.

At the sight of the matched pair of monsters harnessed to the carriage, Lily stopped in her tracks. "What are those?"

The two creatures Willowvale used to draw his carriage were high-stepping and proud, with golden-green eyes and cobalt blue hides with an iridescent sheen, like an oil slick on water. Their hooves, half-hidden beneath long fringes of navy hair, were a bright pale gold, while their tails and manes were a bright turquoise. The creatures were well-matched in size and temperament, too, for they tossed their heads and hissed, showing their sharp teeth.

"Horses," said Willowvale. "Different than yours, but similar enough."

"Those are *not* horses," Lily said firmly. "They're like nightmares of horses."

Still, she allowed Theo to help her into the carriage, and Crocus followed her.

Theo, Fenton, Juniper, and Willowvale climbed in after them, for the carriage was quite spacious. Theo privately suspected it employed a little of the space-shifting magic used in the traveling chests, for it seemed improbable that six people could so easily find room in a carriage which had appeared so close to the usual size from the outside. Willowvale thumped the roof of the carriage and it set off toward the Mosswing estate.

The drive was quiet but pleasant. As they turned up the long drive to Lord Mosswing's house, Willowvale said, "Mrs. Overton, I am sure my warning is unnecessary, but let me echo whatever warning your husband has already given you about making promises, however innocent, to any of Lord Mosswing's Fair guests. I would recommend never being alone with anyone, male or female, aside from your husband, of course. Selby, I am confident you will be equally cautious."

"Thank you for your warning, my lord," said Lily gravely. "I will be cautious, and my husband has already warned me of the dangers."

"I will, of course, endeavor to protect you from any danger," added Willowvale, with a glance at Fenton to include him in this offer without being so insulting as to voice it aloud. He did not directly address Crocus, for he presumed her to be aware of the dangers of any gathering of Fair Folk.

"Thank you," Lily said. Theo, Fenton, and Crocus echoed her, and Willowvale's pale cheeks flushed a little.

"I'm sure it will be unnecessary," the fairy muttered.

The carriage pulled up at the front door of the Mosswing estate and the driver opened the carriage door. Willowvale hopped out, then Theo and Fenton, and they helped Lily and Crocus out with utmost courtesy.

Lily's hand trembled on Theo's arm as he escorted her up the stairs, and he pressed a hand over hers. "Courage, my love," he murmured into her ear. Then he said to the others, "I believe this is the first time you have visited Lord Mosswing as well. It will be a delight to introduce you to a home I have loved for many years. Lord Mosswing and I met in the garden just over there." He pointed to the left.

Then they strode up the steps and were welcomed into the manor.

Lily and Fenton stared about in wonder, for Lord Cedar Mosswing's manor was just as alien and marvelous as Lord Willowvale's was to their human senses. They had arrived a little early, for Theo had wanted to congratulate his friend before everyone arrived. Cedar received them at the doorway to the great hall in which the wedding was to be held.

The floor of this enormous room was an intricate mosaic of low-growing lichen and moss that formed an immense image of the Mosswing family crest. The walls were composed of vast slabs of amethyst lit from within by fairy lights which danced jubilantly, throwing purple light across the floor. There were cascades of white fairy roses in the corners and something that smelled like gardenias, though it trailed like jasmine and the blooms were enormous white trumpets that glittered silver upon the edges.

The crystalline ceiling refracted light in thousands of rainbows that rippled across the floor. Birds and butterflies pirouetted through the air above them, singing in tones more musical than any heard in the human world.

"Thank you for coming." Cedar bowed to each of them in turn, and they greeted him with varying degrees of formality. After congratulations and pleasantries, Cedar explained that two particular servants, Basil and Phlox, a couple with whom Theo was already friendly, had been specifically assigned to ensure that only human food and drink was to be offered to Cedar's human guests, and that they were to be surveilled and protected at all times by these and three other fairies to whom they were introduced.

"I did make it clear to all my guests that any harm or entrapment attempted against you would incur my utmost fury and result in the villain's quick and painful death, so I cannot imagine anyone will attempt anything." Cedar smiled reassuringly. "Still, I would not want to take chances with such cherished friends."

Theo thanked him solemnly for taking such care with their safety. If he thought such measures unnecessary for himself, he appreciated every measure taken for the safety of his wife and friends.

Soon the musicians in the corner began to play quietly, and the cheerful melody twined about the room like golden light, energizing the conversations and prompting Lily to whisper to Theo, "Is the music magical?"

"*Everything* is magical here, to some degree or another," said Theo. "It isn't particularly dangerous, though. Your shoes are comfortable?"

Lily nodded, and Theo said, "Good."

The ceremony itself was conducted on a platform that appeared without warning at the eastern end of the room. Cedar and Poppy stood before the assembled guests and sang so beautifully that Lily found tears streaming down her face. Even without understanding the Fair language, the magnificence of their love and the tender desire evident in their expressions was enough to bring anyone to tears, and the purity of their voices together was like the music of starlight.

His Majesty Silverthorn sang over them in a voice like thunder and the crashing of ocean waves, and the birds sang louder in a melody that twisted and danced over the king's deep tones. Then the king dropped a glittering net over their heads and said a few solemn words of congratulations.

The musicians continued to play softly. Beneath their intricately woven net of jewels and golden threads, Cedar and Poppy strode out upon the air above them, held aloft by magic, and the long train of Poppy's brilliant cobalt dress spread out behind her as if in a soft wind. Her skirts were so voluminous that there was no immodesty in this unexpected feat, though Lily blinked in surprise and concern at first. Lord and Lady Mosswing bowed gracefully to the king, and then drifted to the floor with dignity and delight.

When they reached their guests, the entire congregation bowed to them, and the music swelled until their heartbeats matched the driving rhythm, and their feet could not stay still any longer, and the rest of the night was a glorious confusion of music, dancing, laughter, and joy. The whole floor became a marvelous kaleidoscope of whirling colors and music.

Lord Mosswing and Juniper had, unknown to Willowvale, attended Theo and Lily's ceremony in the church; Willowvale had not seen the ceremony and had arrived at Overton manor only to surveil the guests. Willowvale had seen Fenton and Crocus's ceremony in the great reception hall at the Selby manor, and the humanity of it seemed uniquely beautiful to him.

Still, this Fair ceremony struck Lord Ash Willowvale in the heart in a different way than the human ceremony had. This joy might have been his, if he were different than he was. Kinder. Brighter. Warmer.

He could not remember why he had once been so opposed to marriage; it now seemed to him entirely desirable to spend life with a magenta-haired beauty, full of fiery strength and honor. What a joy it would be to face trouble and triumph with such a companion, and what a painful realization it was to acknowledge that he would never experience that blessed union of souls.

The sky overhead changed from brilliant blue to a dazzling array of pink, orange, vermillion, gold, and indigo, and the colors were broken up and thrown around by the cut crystal ceiling like the dancing leaves of a tree, so that every moment was a new marvel of color. As the sunset faded and the sky turned to navy and then to a star-strewn inky black, the cerulean and magenta streaks of the Fair sky were easier to see, and the fairy lights above them spun with as much energy as the guests did.

Lord Laurel Bayberry appeared at Willowvale's shoulder as he watched Lily dancing with an unfamiliar fairy with blue skin and pale pink hair. "I am as surprised to see you here as I was to be invited," the wolf lord said.

"I could say the same," Willowvale said. "I trust you are well. I have never seen you without your wolves."

"They are in the gardens." Bayberry lifted his lips in a faintly menacing smile and looked toward Theo, who was dancing with Crocus, and Fenton, who was taking a brief break from dancing to stand with Juniper, unwilling to leave him alone. Still, the young nobleman kept a protective eye on Lily. "I don't suppose you know how to induce Overton to release his hold over me, do you?" Bayberry said at last.

Willowvale huffed softly. "I do not. I somehow gained his friendship long before I wanted or valued it. My advice, if you will accept it, is to suffer his friendship as well as you can."

Bayberry snarled under his breath. "I was afraid of that," he muttered. "I have no desire to be made kind-hearted, as you have been."

Willowvale blinked and turned to the other Fair lord. "Is that what you think of me?" he said, astonished.

The wolf lord laughed. "Are you not watching over these humans, as if their safety matters to you more than enjoying the excellent refreshments and entertainment Mosswing has provided? Yes, you have grown tender; even I can see how your eyes light up with friendship and warmth when you look at them."

Willowvale let out a short, hard laugh and turned back to the dance floor. "I am not ashamed to have changed, Bayberry," he said. "I am ashamed of what I was, but I will not walk in that shame as if it is all I am. I will value the grace by which I have been changed."

Bayberry let out a sigh that sounded like a growl, but said nothing else.

The Fair guests were still dancing when the sun rose again, their boundless energy buoyed by joy for the happy couple and endless supplies of Fair wine and gourmet treats. The human guests were starting to slow. Lily's feet ached and though the music was beautiful, her head felt fuzzy with fatigue.

"Are you tired, my love?" said Theo in her ear.

"I hate to admit it, but I am," she replied. "Though it does seem discourteous to be the first guests to leave."

It was true; Fair weddings were a multi-day extravaganza of music, dancing, wine, and edible delights, with displays of magic at intervals. The first display was always conducted by the newly married couple and symbolized the joy of their new life together. Since Fair magic came in so many varieties, it was always fascinating even to the Fair guests to see how the two newlyweds would combine their magic into one display.

At this moment, Poppy caught sight of Lily's face, and, perhaps perceiving that the humans were growing fatigued, spoke briefly into Cedar's ear. Then they approached Theo and Lily.

"Forgive me, Mrs. Overton. You must be fatigued; I understand human weddings do not last as long as Fair celebrations do. Thank you for coming." Cedar bowed deeply to them, and then to Fenton, Crocus, and Juniper, who approached just then. "Willowvale, thank you for coming too, and for your care of our friends."

Willowvale bowed with a smile. "Thank you for inviting me. I am honored to count you as a friend."

Though Cedar had offered to let them stay the night, or rather the morning, Theo said they had promised to stay with Willowvale, so in the brilliant late morning they clambered back in Willowvale's carriage and headed toward his estate for some well-deserved rest.

Lord Ash Willowvale, so ill-tempered and solitary, was quietly delighted to offer these guests the very best of his hospitality, from the loveliest of his guest rooms festooned with fragrant jasmine and golden trumpet vines, to the softest hanging beds with silken sheets, to aquamarine bathing tubs filled by waterfalls. Each room had been readied with a selection of tea and human refreshments and laid with logs for a fire.

"Please, ask for anything that will make your stay more comfortable," he said as he bid them farewell for mid-morning naps.

"Thank you, my friend," said Theo with an appreciative smile.

CHAPTER FIFTY-THREE
Continued Success

Spring came upon Aricht in a rush of fresh green and warm breezes.

Most mornings Astrantia would rise before the sun or the servants, prepare herself some tea, and sit on either the front or back patio to watch the sun rise. The front of the house faced south, so from both the front and rear she could see the sunrise, although the first moments were obscured in the front by the new leaves on the myrtles and in the rear by the wall separating the garden from the street. As it was winter, the view was better at first from the rear patio, but as spring drew onward and the angle of the sun shifted, she enjoyed the sunrise from the front patio more often.

The garden became more beautiful by the day, and every morning as the first pink rays of light touched the leaves, she felt a new rush of gratitude toward the disagreeable fairy who had conceived of such loveliness, and who had spent his magic to give it to her.

To be sure, she had not forgotten his sins against the humans. But as the time passed, and the peace of each little nook in the garden ministered to her wounded heart, she thought of the words in his letter differently. He had not apologized to her because his crimes were not primarily against her; she had no claim to expect or demand an apology. He had not lied to her.

He had accepted her judgment and admitted his crimes with unflinching honesty, though he had repented of them. His explanation was not to absolve himself or gain her approval; the purpose was merely to explain how and why he had agreed with her about the value of humans, and to ask her forgiveness for saving her life.

With the distance of time, and the comfort of the garden, and the respect and success in her new position, she felt more keenly the unkindness in her words to him. She had been angry, and justifiably so, when she believed he had lied to her, but when she had met him in his garden, she might have been kinder or warmer.

She had not wanted to encourage him in his foolish affection for her. How ridiculous it was for him to look at her that way!

The work helped take her mind off him, at least sometimes.

His Majesty Elmerick had been as accommodating and respectful as a king ever was to any ambassador, which she considered quite remarkable given that she was both Fair and a woman. She spent her time visiting the children the Wraith had rescued from the Fair Lands, and she apologized to them, one by one, for the trauma and terror they had endured. She showed them small glamours, little kittens and flowers made of light and butterflies with jewel-bright wings; partly this was to make them smile, and partly it was intended to show them that not all magic was terrifying.

Not all fairies were terrifying.

Never once did she have occasion to use her defensive magic, and she was glad of it.

One evening, after meeting with the last stolen child and returning to the palace for a scheduled dinner, she said to the king, "Thank you for allowing me to speak with the children, Your Majesty.

It is not easy for them to see a fairy, but I hope I have been able to reassure them about the peace between our peoples."

His Majesty Elmerick said, "I am most pleased with your work here, Lady Berrydell. I will commend your king for the wisdom of suggesting your appointment."

Astrantia hesitated, and then said, "Your Majesty, I was told *you* asked for me by name. Was that not true?"

"I did." The king smiled. "But *your* king's envoy suggested it. Lord Willowvale made a most compelling argument."

"Excuse me?" Astrantia's voice rose. "*Lord Willowvale* suggested my appointment?"

The king raised his eyebrows. "Did you not know already? Of course he did, and he was right."

"What argument did he make?"

"He pointed out your proven honor as the only member of Brookbower's delegation to be kept utterly in the dark about the kidnappings of children, and your outrage when you found out about it. You speak the language well, and though you could have killed a great many Arichtans when you were attacked, you did not want to murder innocents who had not been involved in the plot. You did not serve in the war against our people, nor did you ever support it.

"The only real impediment to your being appointed was that you were a woman, and Willowvale said that your king would not argue if I requested you by name. He was right." He met her gaze steadily. "I am pleased with what you have done, and my only complaint that you weren't appointed originally instead of Brookbower."

Willowvale *again*.

"Thank you for your honesty, Your Majesty. I am glad to have been able to start repairing relations between our people." The words stuck in her throat. "I did not realize Willowvale had so much influence here," she muttered.

The king said stiffly, "I hated him when he arrived. But I know a good suggestion when I hear it, even if it comes from an arrogant Fair lord. Not to mention that he used considerable restraint when he was attacked, as well. I know what fairies can do with plant magic on the battlefield."

"That is true," Astrantia conceded. "Thank you, Your Majesty, for your candor and your assessment of my accomplishments. I am pleased to serve my people here."

"When you next send a letter to your king, I would ask that your messenger carry a letter from me as well. I will commend you in it."

He was as good as his word. The messenger arrived only two days later, a teenage boy who ran all the way from the south side of the city to the palace.

"A fairy is waiting in the veil at the corner of Dunsany and Bridgeway. He said to come here and tell you and the Fair ambassador," he told the guard at the gate. Within a few minutes, a messenger and a carriage, along with the boy, had been dispatched to the Fair ambassador's house, with a letter from the king. When they arrived at the verdant oasis, the messenger jogged up the path and informed Astrantia of the waiting fairy.

The Arichtan servant given the honor of carrying the royal message vacated the carriage for Astrantia to ride inside alone, a courtesy which Astrantia felt rather strange, but apparently it was necessary in Aricht. The servant, the boy who had brought the message, and the driver all rode on the outside benches.

When they arrived, there was a small crowd of people gathered a safe distance from Lord Aspen, who leaned elegantly against the wall of the veil, with his arms crossed over his chest in a pose of utter boredom. The door looked like a passage cut into the bricks of a milliner's shop, though what could be seen through the opening was clearly not the interior of the shop. A mossy passageway curved away behind the fairy into darkness.

He uncrossed his arms and bowed, though it was not as deep as it probably should have been, given her title. "Lady Berrydell." He continued to ignore the onlookers, who watched him with a mixture of curiosity, fear, and hatred. His Fair attire was casual, for he had not expected to see any human dignitaries. The soft, fawn-colored trousers, loose, sky-blue shirt that gleamed with gold embroidery, violet boots, and brilliant pink gem upon his right thumb seemed weirdly ostentatious to the Arichtans, but to Astrantia, he looked tired and annoyed both by the veil and by the fact that he had been required to make this inconvenient journey.

"His Majesty Silverthorn commanded me to come and get your report, as well as to ascertain when you would like to return home for your allowed time of refreshment and visitation with your family." He handed over a letter from his jacket. Forbidden from stepping foot in Aricht, he crossed his arms again and leaned against the edge of the veil after a glance over his shoulder.

"Thank you. Please stay while I read this." Astrantia glanced at the seal only long enough to note that it was, indeed, that of the Fair king.

"I told the boy you would pay him for the message," said Aspen.

Astrantia dutifully paid the youth, who flushed and bowed. He had nearly forgotten that he wanted to be paid, so distracted was he by the Fair beauty before him.

The letter was merely a statement that upon Lord Willowvale's request, Silverthorn had inquired about the investigation of the vandalism of her father's sword shop and had found nothing. Folded into it was a short note from her father, stating that Willowvale had been greatly pleased with the swords he had commissioned, which did not surprise her at all, that the king himself had commissioned an even more extravagantly ornamented weapon, and that Lord Mosswing had commissioned a sword for his new wife, as well as one for a young friend. The patronage of the king and these two lords had apparently entirely reversed the earlier social ban on their work, and they were now so busy that lords were now gladly reserving their time for commissions over a year in the future.

Astrantia had a written report of her actions ready for the king, as well as a letter for her father and brother, but Aspen waited without comment or complaint while she hurriedly wrote out an addendum to each missive. To the king, she expressed her gratitude and the hope of visiting her family in another two months. To her father, she gave the date of her intended return, contingent upon the king's approval, and said that she was delighted by their well-deserved popularity and the reversal of their fortunes. She brought a little flame of magic to her fingertips, melted the wax, and pressed the seal into each letter in turn.

"Thank you, Lord Aspen," she said.

"It is always my honor to serve the Fair Lands," he muttered.

When the door to the veil closed, the onlookers turned their attention to Astrantia. She smiled at the nearest woman, who flushed.

"It's a bold thing for you to be in Idosa, after what your people did," the woman said.

"I never supported the kidnappings, and my king has repented of the plan. Can we work together for a better future?" Astrantia said.

The woman shrugged, and Astrantia nearly turned away. Then, realizing that this was another opportunity to build rapport with Arichtans, she added, "I do hope we can."

CHAPTER FIFTY-FOUR
Spring Blooms

Spring came just as suddenly to Valestria as it had to Aricht, with a burst of fresh green and cool fog in the mornings that gave way to golden sunlight and a thousand early blooms.

Every week when Lord Ash Willowvale came to Valestria, he marveled anew at the beauty of the human world, and at how he had so little appreciated it the previous summer. Perhaps it was the light of friendship in his life that made everything seem so lovely and new.

Still, he was not without his private, hidden sorrow, and he held it close, letting the grief and regret prick his conscience, and if he did not relish the pain, neither did he shrink from it. For he had finally admitted to himself how deeply he had loved and how dearly he had hoped to better know Lady Astrantia Berrydell.

The memory of how he had disappointed her, and the knowledge of how he deserved her approbation, made every moment of friendship with Theo and his family and friends sweeter, for they knew how undeserving he was. He did not hope to change Lady

Berrydell's mind, of course, but as the spring grew brighter and warmer, the pain of his many regrets began to fade, leaving gratitude for these humans, especially Theo, with his extravagant grace and relentless love.

One week, after enjoying a ride over the verdant, windswept hills north of the Selby estate with Theo and Fenton, he said, "Spring in the Fair Lands is also quite lovely. I would very much like to share it with you, if you would accept my hospitality for a few days. With your wives, of course."

Theo gave him a sparkling smile. "We will be delighted to." Fenton echoed this sentiment.

The following week they enjoyed a remarkably pleasant three days in the Fair Lands, where they admired Willowvale's extensive gardens at the very height of their late spring beauty and went on an excursion to a nearby lake, where they picnicked on the rocky outcroppings overlooking the crystalline water. They were joined here by Cedar and Poppy, who were delighted by the opportunity to share the beauty of their world with Theo, Lily, Fenton, and Crocus.

Their Fair host had, over the course of his many conversations with these human friends, proven himself to be well-read in all the Fair classics, as well as a few of the better-known authors of Valestria, which he had read while studying the language. Thus he had at least one topic of conversation with which to engage in pleasant discourse, which did not come without effort to him on most topics. Still, it had become easier to speak with warmth, to smile, and to see the humor and beauty both in his world and the human world, and if he was still a quiet, grave personality, his reticence was more by habit and inclination than bitterness or ill-temper.

On the last morning he hosted the young Overtons and Selbys, the whole group enjoyed breakfast and morning tea on a high balcony from which they could see much of the garden and the surrounding Fair city. The sun glittered on the amethyst-crusted roofs and gilded spires nestled between roof-top gardens filled with a thousand varieties of blooming trees and plants.

Willowvale glanced at his guests and back out at the gorgeous view. "Thank you for coming," he said quietly. "It is a rare joy to share the beauty of a Fair morning with anyone, and more rare still with those I esteem so highly."

Theo said, "Thank you for your hospitality, my friend. I have enjoyed every moment of our stay, and I do hope we can exchange visits for many years to come."

Then, after a moment of silence, the young man said more quietly, for the Fair lord's ears alone, "Ash, for someone so happy, you seem a little troubled."

The fairy's pale cheeks flushed a little, and he looked down at his tea. He sighed. "I suppose I am mourning what I realized too late would complete my happiness." He smiled and met Theo's hazel gaze. "I am far happier than I deserve, Theo. Please don't make too much of my melancholy. There is nothing to be done about it, and I do not mind it so much. It reminds me of what I was, and how very much I owe you for forcing your friendship upon me so that I had to change."

Theo smiled quickly, appreciating the words, but he did not entirely accept this. "Is there really nothing to be done?" he asked gently. "Will you not confide in me? I can keep a secret, you know."

Willowvale chuckled softly and looked away. "Oh, you know already, I'm sure. I think, if there were anything to complete my joy here, it would be a certain magenta-haired Fair lady who has made her home in Aricht, who cannot possibly be made happier by the sight of my face."

The young man reached across the intervening space to put a hand on the fairy's hard shoulder for a moment in sympathy. "Do you really think she still despises you?" he said.

Willowvale nodded, his eyes fixed on the gilded spires in the distance. "I see no reason for her opinion of me to have changed," he said.

Theo said, "You don't think her heart might have been softened by your heroic trek through the veil to save her life and the beauty of that garden you made for her?"

The fairy blinked and glanced at him. "Why should that change her opinion of my character?" he asked.

Theo laughed softly. "Well, maybe it didn't much at first, but I doubt that after months of enjoying that magnificent garden she is entirely unsoftened toward you."

Willowvale sighed and looked out at the view again, which glittered with a thousand colors of crystal amid all the gardens. He smiled just a little. "It's all right, Theo. You don't have to encourage me in hope in this matter. I am content to think of her enjoying it, alive and whole and happy, and if I long to see her beauty with my own eyes, that is my own selfish desire and does not serve her at all."

Theo said, "I don't see selfishness in you, Ash."

The fairy caught a breath like a sob. "Thank you, Theo."

"I would encourage you, when you're feeling particularly bold, to go visit her," said Theo. "I don't think she will see it as troubling her."

"She despises me, Theo." Willowvale swallowed. "The memory of her saying those words with such hatred is exquisitely painful, and I don't know how I would bear it if I heard her say them again in a new, fresh way."

Theo put his hand on the fairy's shoulder again in quiet sympathy. "I cannot imagine she would be so cruel," he said. "Now that she has had a chance to appreciate your courage and generosity, I imagine she might appreciate a chance to tell you so."

Willowvale's shoulder twitched, and he said, "Your optimism far surpasses mine. I would be grateful merely to see her face and to know that she is happy."

"Then tell her so," said Theo.

They sat in silence for some time, and Theo refreshed his own tea and that of their Fair host. They spoke no more of the matter, but Theo's words lingered in Willowvale's mind.

CHAPTER FIFTY-FIVE
A Humble Question

Clear, bright moonlight streamed in the window, silvering the coverlet upon the bed. Astrantia got up and closed the curtains, but then she merely lay there in the dark, every bit as awake as before.

She dozed briefly in the early hours of the morning, but woke before dawn.

With her dressing gown around her shoulders and tied about her waist, she slipped out the bedroom door and down the hall.

The city was quiet at this hour.

She slipped outside and sat on the front step of the wide patio. A few stars still glinted, but in the east, the sky had begun to turn a soft, clear pink. The garden was still misty and cool, and the enormous myrtles with their pink blooms loomed over the garden path.

After six months as ambassador, she felt a little more comfortable in the role than she had at first.

The garden was singularly beautiful, and on mornings like this, she could often be found sitting on the steps or on the wicker sofa on the patio. The mist seemed like a blanket cast over the city, full of promise and possibility. As the sun rose, it would slowly vanish, until you could see halfway across the city from the rooftop terrace. Situated as it was on the hill near the palace, the rooftop sitting area had a rare view, and would have been a coveted location for any Arichtan nobleman. Even from the front patio, she could see some distance once the cool morning mist dissipated.

The house had likely cost more than Silverthorn had expected to spend, but she had seen no resentment in his responses to her reports.

The house itself was perfectly lovely by Arichtan standards. The floors had marble inlay in the geometric style so favored by the Arichtan court, but which had grated upon all the Fair Folk. When he had arranged for the house and its furnishings, Willowvale had ordered rugs which covered many of the most objectionably angular elements.

Jasmine and climbing roses crept up the walls, and bougainvillea and fuchsia fought for space in other rooms. Pink, purple, and white azaleas softened the corners of the sitting rooms and dining room. Caladiums sprouted in the shade near the tiny pond in the garden in the rear of the house, and bold orange canna had bloomed exuberantly beside fragrant white gardenias.

Moss, adorned with tiny pink, white, and yellow blooms, crept over the floors in the bedrooms. Tulips, bleeding hearts, and crocuses had sprouted in the spring in any number of unexpected places.

The house and its environs had been transformed from a stiff, unpleasant example of Arichtan luxury into a vibrant, living paradise to Fair sensibilities. It has become an oasis for the birds and insects of the Arichtan capital, too. Hummingbirds screamed insults at each other as they flew about, tasting the abundance of a thousand types of flowers, and the constant buzz of the wings of dragonflies and bees was almost as soothing to Fair hearts as magic itself.

On this morning, with the city still quiet and an oriole just beginning to sing from somewhere in the trees, she felt almost delighted with the world.

Almost.

The steady, quiet little thread of guilt in her heart tugged at her, and she sighed. If that disagreeable Lord Willowvale were here, she would… well, she would have to acknowledge that his repentance had affected her. Was it not courageous indeed to admit one's deepest shame, without flinching or prevaricating, to someone whose good opinion one desired? He had apologized to Miss McStretton, and apparently in a way that didn't terrify the child, but instead gave her some measure of peace.

Not to mention the generosity of his actions toward her brother and father.

Or the magic, time, and consideration he had spent to transform this Arichtan house from angular unfriendliness and discomfort to beauty and serenity, with a thousand thoughtful details and myriad lush, colorful nooks.

The humility and grace of his actions, after her harsh judgment of him, felt like a weight of conviction, for just as he had thought too little of humans and repented of it, she had thought too little of him and repented of it.

But he had demonstrated the courage and compassion to apologize to a child, and she had fled at the earliest opportunity the last time she had seen him. She owed him an apology and gratitude, if she were brave enough to face him.

The mist over the city was lit with the pink of sunrise, casting everything in a bright, hopeful glow. Some way down the street to her left, a tall figure strode toward the house.

His strides were long and quick, and she thought suddenly that he looked very like Lord Ash Willowvale, though she could not see his face in the shadow of the building. His shoulders were set just so, and though she thought it highly improbable that the Fair lord who so unsettled her would be walking through the streets of Aricht, she felt a little frisson of nervous hope.

When he drew closer, she realized with a start that it *was* Willowvale, and she stood. At her movement, he looked up and, if she didn't imagine it, slowed just a little, as if he were cautious of her. Still, he drew up to the end of the walk just outside the garden.

She took a step toward him.

He stood there a moment, his pale, silvery eyes drinking her in. His clothing was Fair, and she thought suddenly that he was terrible and beautiful, with his silver curls all ruffled and his narrow lips lifted in a strange, shy, hopeful sort of smile. He could smile after all.

"May I enter?" he said, without taking his eyes off her.

Astrantia nodded, her heart thudding. "The garden is beautiful," she managed.

He slipped in the gate, leaving it open, and walked to her. "Are you happy here, Lady Berrydell?" His voice shook, just a little, and she thought there was no reason for *him* to be nervous.

Why did he have to be so uncommonly handsome? And how had she not noticed until now?

"I am, save for the apology I owe you," she said. "I judged you too harshly, and you showed me such grace and generosity in return."

He let out a soft, surprised breath and looked at the ground for a moment before meeting her gaze, his eyes warm and bright. "You are too kind. What did you say of me, that I did not deserve? You spoke the truth to me, and I consider it a gift, however painful it was at the time." He added even more softly, "I wanted only to see you, to assure myself that you were happy here. I did not mean to trouble you."

"You came all the way here through the veil just to ask if I was happy?" She swallowed.

The Fair lord nodded once, not looking away from her face.

"I can thank you for most of my happiness here. For the beauty you created here, for your apology to Miss McStretton, for what you did for my family… for saving my life." She could barely whisper for the emotion that choked her.

Willowvale's eyes did not leave hers. "I delighted in imagining that it would make your time here more pleasant," he said. "I would say it was all for you, and most of it was, but my apology to Miss McStretton was for her sake, though I found healing in it as well. Everything else was for you."

"But why?" Astrantia breathed. "Surely you did not fall in love with my unkindness or impertinence."

"No, with your lively mind and your upright character and your strength of will. With your compassion upon the assassins, refusing to injure innocents even in distress."

The Fair maiden caught her breath on a sob, and Lord Willowvale sucked in a quick breath.

"I am sorry, Lady Berrydell," he said, and then, with infinite tenderness, he said, "You are too generous to trifle with me. If your feelings are still what they were when we spoke in the veil, tell me so at once. *My* feelings and hopes are unchanged, but one word from you will silence me on this subject forever."

The sweet expectation in his voice unravelled what little control she had held over her feelings, and she said, "How can you imagine my feelings unchanged? *You* are changed, and my understanding of you has changed, and altogether you are as honorable and kind and generous as any lord I have ever met, and more."

He took her hands in his and bowed over them. "Am I to understand that if I dared court you, you would not be utterly repulsed? For my heart is already yours, and I would like the chance to show you how ardently I admire and adore you."

"You have shown me who you are, and I am yours."

Forever after Astrantia was grateful that she had been looking at him when she said this, rather than looking down at their entwined hands in shyness, for the expression of heartfelt delight, diffused over his face, became him so well that it brought tears to her eyes, and the sweet words with which he told her of her importance to him made his affection every moment more valuable.

CHAPTER FIFTY-SIX
Absolute Joy

The summer that followed was wholly unique in Lord Ash Willowvale's experience, for every moment increasing joy and lightness pervaded his very soul.

He spent the rest of that beautiful day in the company of Lady Berrydell, enjoying her delight in the garden he had made for her. Their conversation over dinner was warm and kind, and Willowvale was so elated, so full of unexpected happiness, that he had no trouble at all asking all the right questions of his beloved, so that she grew more comfortable and more delighted by his company every moment.

He stayed that night in a sitting room on the ground floor of the ambassador's residence; it was short work to grow himself a thick, soft carpet of moss, and only a few more minutes to elevate it with a network of vines from the ceiling.

The following day, they departed together for the Fair Lands, Lady Berrydell having explained to the Arichtan king that she wanted to speak with her father about a personal matter of some urgency.

The veil made itself exceptionally agreeable, and they arrived in Willowvale's garden only a few hours later, neither bruised nor dirtied by their passage. They went directly to the sword shop of Sedum and Agaricus Berrydell, where Astrantia spoke to her father and brother privately while Willowvale stood in the front room, his hands clasped behind his back and his heart thundering so that he thought he might faint.

"I thought you hated him," said Sedum.

"So did I," said Astrantia, her cheeks flushing pink. "But as it happens, he had already begun to change when I misjudged him so harshly, and though he had no reason to think he would ever see me again, he persisted in such generosity toward not only me, but also a child in Aricht, that it could not be understood as anything other than true nobility of character. He *is* good and kind, Father, even if he was not always so."

"You really love him?" said Sedum, laughing under his breath with joy at the light of love in his beloved daughter's eyes.

"I do, Father. I do very much, and I think you will too, when you get to know him." She looked up at him expectantly. "Shall I tell him you are ready for him?"

"Yes." But before she was allowed to leave the room, he wrapped his strong arms around her, and she returned the embrace, pressing her facing into his neck.

Lord Ash Willowvale remained closeted with Sedum Berrydell for some time, and when he emerged from the room, he bowed low over Astrantia's hand.

"If you do mean to accept my proposal," he said softly, "I would like it very much if you would call me Ash. My friends do, and I see no reason for unnecessary distance or formality between us."

"Ash." She found to her surprise that the name suited him. "It is a lovely name," she said, and to her delight, he blushed.

"I am glad it pleases you," he said.

Much of the rest of the summer was spent in Aricht, for Astrantia was still the Fair ambassador to that human nation. Ash visited every week, for several days at a time, and if the ambassador's neighbors questioned the propriety of these visits, the human servants in the house squashed the rumors with the unexpected news that the pale Fair lord was both respectful of his intended and unexpectedly kind to the human and Fair staff.

The question of where they might live after their marriage was not resolved in one conversation or even two, but there was no animosity or conflict, for both assured the other repeatedly that they wanted their beloved to be happy.

In the end, they were married in the late summer, and all Ash's human friends were invited to the ceremony, which rivaled the Mosswing wedding in extravagance and loveliness. After their wedding, they spent time in both Aricht and the Fair Lands, for Ash maintained his beautiful estate beside the palace. They visited Valestria often, for Ash was quietly determined that Astrantia love Theo and his other Valestrian friends.

Thus there was a great deal of travel through the veil from that summer on, and the veil proved agreeable more often than not.

"What changed you, Ash?" Astrantia asked one evening shortly before the wedding, as they sat together on a balcony overlooking Dewspring-in-the-Wood under a sunset like paint streaks across the sky. "For I know I misjudged you, but you did change, too, didn't you?"

"Love," said Ash, with a catch in his voice. "The lack of it was like asphyxia of the soul. I loved the Fair Lands, or thought I did; I gave my life for them without hesitation. But I gave without love, and when I saw love, it shamed me. *Theo* shamed me, and I was made better by it. The relentless love of that human, whom I had thought so foolish, proved to be more profound, more sublime, more formidable than any selfish pride or anger I might have held close. I was dazzled and awed, and I could not help but be changed. I understood that he loved the Fair Lands, because I knew them to be lovely; I did not understand at first that he loved *me*, and I still don't understand why. His friendship is a gift I can never earn."

Astrantia had watched his face as he spoke, so she saw the warmth in his pale eyes, the soft curve of his lips as he smiled. "What a grand thing it is to be loved!" she said. "But what a far grander thing it is to love! The heart becomes heroic, by dint of passion."

"Yes, he is heroic," said Ash, his faint smile deepening. "Love must be, I think, if it is to be genuine."

"I meant you," said Astrantia.

Ash looked at her, startled, and her sweet smile of admiration was warm and bright as the Fair summer night.

ABOUT THE AUTHOR

Thank you for purchasing this book. If you enjoyed it, please leave a review at your favorite online retailer!

C. J. Brightley lives in Northern Virginia with her husband and young children. She holds degrees from Clemson University and Texas A&M. You can find more of C. J. Brightley's books at www.CJBrightley.com, including the epic fantasy series Erdemen Honor, which begins with *The King's Sword*, and the Christian fantasy series A Long-Forgotten Song, which begins with *Things Unseen*.

SNEAK PEAK:

THE
LORD
OF
DREAMS

PROLOGUE

W hen Claire was seven, she had a very strange dream.

Impossibly tall trees towered above her, the sound of their distant rustling like whispers. The air in the dappled shadows was cool and still, broken only by a murmuring of unseen water. Claire looked down at her bare feet, skin pale against the deep green moss covering the earth. Static made her pink nightgown cling to her slim legs.

Where was she?

A fluttering overhead caught her ear, and she looked up, her eyes searching the shadowed branches. Nothing was visible, but the whispering of the leaves seemed to increase ominously. She began walking carefully toward the sound of water, chewing her lip.

What was this place?

Her feet padded on the moss as if it were thick green carpet, soft and cool against her skin. She made her way through sparse brush, the leaves parting before her invitingly.

Screech!

The sudden cry behind her made her start in fear, and she froze, looking back into the shadows. It was darker, as if the sun had not only disappeared behind a cloud, but descended to the horizon in a matter of moments.

Her heart thudded, and she whimpered a little. Another angry cry gave wings to her feet.

She flew through the brush, tiny twigs and leaves slapping her in the face and across the arms. She glanced behind her once, not sure what she expected to see.

Green eyes glinted in the twilight.

Claire cried out and stumbled when her foot hit a nearly buried rock. She fell headlong, her hands splashing into a pool of water.

"You aren't right. You're not what you're supposed to be!"

Claire looked up to see a boy of about her own age glaring down at her.

"There's a… a…" She pointed helplessly behind her, too terrified to look for the eyes of the creature that had pursued her.

"Yes. A cockatrice." The boy's blue glare intensified. His eyes were rimmed in red, and she had a fleeting thought that perhaps he had been weeping. "You should know better than to wake a sleeping cockatrice." His eyes flicked behind her with a frisson of fear, and he grabbed her shoulder. "Back you go, then." He pushed her into the pool of water, hurrying her deeper while glancing over his shoulder. A final shove sent her flailing, the water closing over her head. Her last glimpse of him was of his silver-white hair plastered down by water, one arm flung up against a beaked maw that struck with cobra-like speed. Claire screamed, water filling her mouth.

She woke, trembling and sweaty, tangled in her blankets.

About the Author

Dan is an author and educator who has lived in Connecticut for their entire life. They received a degree in education and later wrote their Master's thesis on representation of women in same-sex relationships in contemporary Spanish literature and cinema.

What Everyone Deserves
2017 Rainbow Awards Honorable Mention
"Although the story deal with some real 1950s issues – discrimination, homophobia, interracial couples and hate crimes – it did it in a way that perfectly suited the characters and the story." - Divine Magazine
In this 1950s period drama, Junius is a New York City fertility demon with a crush. Ever since falling from heaven he's been alone. Except for the mothers and children he watches over.

James Kelly Rosenburg, a black soldier with snowflakes in his hair, walks right into his life with a big problem. James Kelly, turned vampire during the war, is new to New York and its prohibition against vampire killing in city limits.

Junius offers to teach him to overcome his bloodthirsty instincts and live a proper Manhattan life. Their growing friendship leaves them both conflicted as they explore a city both welcoming and alienated by their kind.

That Doesn't Belong Here
2018-2019 Rainbow Awards Honorable Mention
"I liked the ... atmosphere that he created, alongside the paranormal creatures that roam the street. I liked that he wrote characters I could emotionally care for. If Ackerman writes another LGBT fiction, I will give it a try for sure." - Ami, The Blogger Girls
That Doesn't Belong Here begins when Levi and his friend Emily discover an impossible creature in an abandoned pick up. The thing is wounded, frightened and the two friends cannot leave him to the mercy of rubberneckers and tourists. This novel explores what it means to be a person, as the creature, Kato, begins to display not mere intelligence or friendliness but what can only be explained as humanity. The question of who we are allowed to love arises for Levi and Kato, as they are not just crossing the boundaries of gender or sexuality, but of species.